Dominic's Quest

F J Atkinson

ISBN-10:1492730181
ISBN-13:9781492730187

To my wife, Yvonne. Thanking her for
her patience and support.

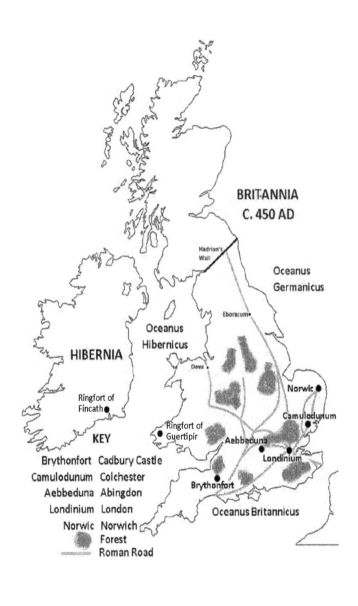

BRITANNIA
C. 450 AD

Hadrian's
Wall

Oceanus
Germanicus

Eboracum•

Oceanus
Hibernicus

HIBERNIA

Deva •

Norwic ●

Ringfort of
Fincath ●

Camulodunum
●

Ringfort of
Guertipir
●

Aebbeduna
●

Londinium
●

KEY

Brythonfort   Cadbury Castle
Camulodunum   Colchester
Aebbeduna   Abingdon
Londinium   London
Norwic   Norwich
Forest
Roman Road

Brythonfort
●

Oceanus Britannicus

PROLOGUE

The two mastiffs flanked Griff and stood at almost half his height. Griff, indulgent as ever, scratched at the smooth fur beneath the dog's collars, prompting them to crane their bull-like necks in pleasure. Craving his attention, both dogs now raised their broad, wrinkled heads towards him.

Griff's attire was British high status. An intricately embroidered tunic lay over a silk undershirt. Tucked into leather knee boots, his saffron-dyed woollen trousers were of a fine weave. A russet, overlaying cloak of wool, clasped by an elaborate, golden serpent brooch, kept out the worst of the searching easterly wind that blew between the thatched, boarded houses in the town of Norwic.

He watched as the Saxon, Ranulf, rode into the town followed by his band of gnarled raiders. Walking behind the group; secured together by neck halters; their hands bound with hemp; trudged a group of trail-haggard captives.

'Not as many this time,' said Griff, as he met Ranulf and cast his eyes over the bedraggled group.

'No, the bastards keep dying on me,' said Ranulf as he dismounted and faced Griff. 'I thought you lot were a hardy race, but it seems that a gentle stroll through field and forest in the rain is enough to make a slave want to lie down and die.'

Griff again looked the slaves over. 'At least the ones who make it to Norwic have stamina. I'll sell them on with that in mind ... who knows, maybe I'll get more gold for them if I point out their robust constitutions.' He squinted in the watery autumnal sunshine as he peered closely at them. 'I see some here who may go to Hibernia. My buyer is specific in his requirements.'

'Talking of gold,' said Ranulf, 'my price will reflect the danger I endure every time I have to travel further afield to seek untouched villages. These slaves came from the west, not far from the protected land. It's only our speed on the raids that prevents our engagement with well-armed Britons.'

Griff smiled resignedly, as he anticipated the robust haggling that would occur later with Ranulf. He knew he commanded a grudging respect from the man, because he possessed the thing that all Angles and Saxons coveted: gold. As a highborn Briton, he had been able to use the wealth of his family to buy off the raiders when they had first threatened his estate.

Known only to him since his father had died, his family's gold now lay in a place secure and hidden. Griff, for his part, still lived the Roman life. The imperialists had built his villa many decades before, and he still enjoyed the comforts of bath and spa. In contrast to the comparative squalor of those who lived around him, his life was a paragon of opulence.

Griff *himself* loved gold, and his personal wealth had grown as he realised he could profit from the captives the Anglo-Saxon raiders brought back to Norwic. These, he 'sold on' for a high return. They were destined for Hibernia where British slaves were highly coveted.

'Step to the front!' barked Ranulf, as he turned to the captives. 'Let yourselves be seen by your betters.'

The dogs gave low, menacing growls as the line of Britons moved closer to Griff. He took his time as he appraised them and considered their potential for profit. He fondled the blond hair of a slender girl who stood shivering and terrified in the line. She was eleven or thereabouts and would be pretty when cleaned up. She was his first choice. A cattle chief in Laighin, Hibernia, who had requested such a girl, would further trade her on for many cows—the mark of wealth in Hibernia. She must be pure though. He had instructed Ranulf that such a child must remained unsullied, otherwise she would be worth nothing.

Next, he approached a huge youth. He stood a nose away, as he peered into the lad's simple, trusting eyes. A dullard by the look of him. Twenty years old or so, and big with it. An uncomplaining workhorse if ever he saw one. *No harm in testing him then.* Without warning, he punched the youth hard in his stomach, causing him to double up and retch.

Another lad, younger, went for Griff. Griff quickly grabbed the collars of his hounds as they made to savage the boy. Amidst much snarling and barking, Ranulf intervened, quickly knocking the adolescent to the ground.

Griff allowed Ranulf to land two hefty kicks before stopping him.

'No! ... no more; he's just what I'm looking for. It'll affect the price I get for him, and the price I'll pay you, if you damage him further. Now I have the three I want: the girl, the workhorse, and a fiery young warrior who will make an excellent guard for the cows in Hibernia. Do what you will with the rest. We can agree a price for these three later.'

Ranulf nodded and beckoned for one of his men to herd the three into a wicker-enclosed wagon that waited nearby.

Griff was about to walk away when Ranulf stopped him and pointed to two older Britons in the line of captives. 'Ah yes,' said Griff. 'Usual price for old meat I take it.'

CHAPTER ONE

Weeks earlier, Maewyn had helped his brother, Aiden, out of a scrape yet again. As a slow, clumsy fellow, Mule, as everybody knew Aiden, had predictably upended a flagon of water in the hut where he lived, drenching the fresh floor rushes laid down by his mother only days before.

'You sluggard!' shouted Maewyn. 'Mother'll thrash your arse when she returns from her trip. Come on. We need to get more rushes from the marsh. We can undo your clumsiness and save you a scolding from da at the very least.'

Mule looked despairingly at the floor and then at his younger brother. 'S-s-sorry Pat … it's my big feet again. Da says that I'm even clumsier now I've grown so big.'

Maewyn merely sighed, then left the hut with Mule following dejectedly in his wake.

Scudding clouds, pushed along by a sharp breeze, cast fleeting shadows over the settlement. The harvest had been a good one, and Govan shoveled the last of the surplus grain into the bell shaped storage pit at the edge of the village. He looked to his young daughter, Elowen, who knelt beside a pile of wet clay. 'Now for the part you like,' he smiled, '… the bit where you get mucky.'

Elowen pushed her hands into the clay and slopped it on top of the pit opening. 'You know I make a good seal for the grain, da,' she said, as a twinkle of mischief came into her eye, 'and besides, you make a fierce warrior when daubed with the clay.' With this, she grasped Govan's cheeks with her muddy palms. After leaving a respectable smear across his face, she ran off squealing with Govan in pursuit.

Govan quickly captured her and lifted her aloft, and returned with her, laughing and wriggling, to the pile of glutinous clay. 'Not such a clever lady now, are we?' he said with mock sternness, as he dangled her over the clay and allowed her long blonde locks to touch the glop.

Elowen was upside down and helpless with laughter. 'No da, NO!' she screamed as Govan continued to dangle her over the pile. A further scream prompted him to set her back down on the ground, where he gave her a smeared face to match his own.

They sat beside the pile, laughing as they took in each other's grimy features. Govan looked fondly at Elowen. 'If mother still lived she would call us a couple of cuckoos,' he said.

Elowen smiled, a hint of sadness in her eyes, as she recalled mother who had died of fever two years ago, but before nostalgia could take root, Govan nudged her.

'Look out ... here comes cousin Mule ... Maewyn too,' he chuckled. 'Looks like Mule's been a daft lad again, by the look on Maewyn's face. Hey Maewyn! What's he been up to this time?'

'Clumsy bugger again,' said Maewyn sulkily, as Mule looked on sheepishly. 'Knocked a full jar of water over. Can't afford to make mother angry, or she'll stop our trip to see Flint at Brythonfort.'

'Better get it sorted out then,' said Govan. 'If you want to train alongside brother Flint, you need to keep out of scrapes. Elowen will help you, won't you lass?'

'Of course,' said Elowen, as she stood on tiptoe and ruffled Mule's hair. 'You great ox,' she laughed. 'I'll go and fill the flagon with fresh water.

They left, leaving Govan to cover the clay-plugged storage pit with turf. When he had finished, he walked across to the ditch and palisade that encircled the village. Here, a man stood knee-deep in green water, whistling as he pulled out great clumps of accumulated vegetation.

'Get your back in it,' laughed Govan, as he jumped with a great splash into the ditch beside his brother. 'Robert and old Simon from Brythonfort will be less than pleased if they find out we've let their defensive ditch get clogged up again.'

Bran stretched, taking the kink out of his back. 'Yes that's for sure, but finding time to do all the jobs around here isn't easy.' He pointed towards the tall wooden palisade that encircled the ditch. 'At least that's in good order. It should keep anything out. Man or bear.'

'It's men *I* worry about,' said Govan, grunting as he pulled a great clump of wet greenery from the ditch. 'We've been lucky up to now; lucky that we lie in the west of our isle; lucky that we're protected somewhat by Brythonfort and its knights, although I wish they had the men to patrol here a bit more often.' He straightened, frowning, as he looked past the ditch and towards the linear fields that lay beyond the village boundary. 'Still, I worry, though,' he continued, as he turned his gaze back towards the village, '… about our folk; our children; our future.'

'Mmm,' pondered Bran. 'God knows what would happen if my boys, especially Mule, were left abandoned and alone.' He smiled, as his thoughts fell on his much-loved, lumbering son. 'Which brings me neatly to him. I saw him heading to the reed beds with a cross-looking Maewyn after they'd been talking to you. Always looking after him is Maewyn; you wouldn't think him five years younger. So what's he been up to this time?'

'Nothing which can't be fixed,' said Govan. 'I believe it was a bit of an accident involving reed flooring and water. I sent Elowen to fill the—'

He stopped mid-sentence as Bran, who had been looking towards the fields, gripped his arm. 'Get your family together,' he murmured. 'I'll get mine. We're being watched.'

Two fields distance away, Irvin, a British tracker and fighting man hired by Ranulf, wheeled his pony to canter the five miles back to the main body of men.

Ranulf looked enquiringly at his scout as he approached—Irvin's demeanor indicative of fresh news.

'Well?' he asked.

'A village, still untouched ahead on the trail,' said Irvin, as he hastily dismounted. 'Looks like a sizeable settlement, so it should provide rich pickings. Two men were clearing a ditch when I got there. They saw me unfortunately.'

Ranulf frowned as he looked up the trail. 'Pity they saw you,' he grumbled, 'now they'll be ready for us. Was the village fortified?'

'Ditch and palisade.'

Not good, thought Ranulf. Not good at all. Especially now they were vulnerable to attack from the nearby British garrison. They were too close to Brythonfort for comfort; too far west for his liking. But what could he do. The market for slaves was stronger than ever. The opportunity for profit greater than ever; the danger was also getting greater since the easier work in the east had

8

dried up. But there was absolutely no way around it; accumulating gold meant taking risks these days.

He turned to his men. 'Archers, prepare for flame arrows, we have a fence to burn down again. Plunder lies up the track, so we need to collect any saleable folk who dwell outside the protection of the stockade. That'll give us an easy start.'

Maewyn and Mule stood in the water at the edge of the wetlands. They had already gathered an impressive pile of rushes, but had become distracted, in the way that boys do, when a water vole had glided close to them. Mule had procured a large branch from the foreshore and had parted the reeds with it. Maewyn peered through the resultant breach, looking for the vole.

They turned on hearing the wild splashing from behind. As they watched, a group of riders passed by, thirty strides away, riding through the shallows toward the settlement. Without thinking, Mule waved his branch in the air in greeting. 'No!' said Maewyn as he pulled Mule towards him and knocked the branch out of his hand. 'They're not Arthur's men you jester, look how they're dressed. They're Saxons.'

'Sorry, I didn't know,' apologized Mule, 'I thought—'

''You *never* think, you just act like a fool!' said Maewyn, immediately regretting his words when seeing the hurt on Mule's face. 'They've seen us now. We need to get into the reeds and hide.' He grabbed Mule shirt and ran with him into the reed beds.

Irvin, who was ever vigilant and riding at the front with Ranulf, caught the movement in the corner of his eye. 'Over there in the marsh … two of them … boys, I think!'

Without checking the stride of his pony, Ranulf shouted behind him. 'Alfwald! Sigward! Two in the reeds! Go and bind them, then get back to me!'

Two raiders peeled away and rode towards the main body of water. Standing in their saddles, they soon spotted the two boys who had begun to run deeper into the reed beds.

Alfwald took the lead—his pony creating a great splashing as he goaded it through the knee-deep water. It did not take long to reach the boys. Mule had fallen on his face in his haste to get away. Sigward quickly dismounted and grabbed him. Alfwald approached Maewyn, who stood with his fists raised and bunched in defiance.

The boss on Alfwald's buckler crashed against Maewyn's head, knocking him in the water beside Mule. Dazed by the blow, he entered a swirling, bubbling, muffled underworld, but before he could take a watery breath, a huge fist darted into the water grabbing the fabric of his tunic around his chest. He emerged with a great whooshing gasp, all his fight gone.

Sigward panted as he pulled Mule's hefty bulk to the banking. Maewyn too was marched to the water's edge by Alfwald. The discarded Saxon ponies, meanwhile, stood nonchalantly drinking from the marsh.

Alfwald dealt with Maewyn's resurging feistiness by again knocking him to the ground.

'Lively sod this,'he grunted to Sigward, as he bound Maewyn's hands together behind his back. 'Better drag him away from the water's edge or he'll wriggle into it and drown. Ranulf will have my bollocks on a platter if that happens.'

'Glad this big un's not as lively,' said Seward. 'I'm fucking drained just draggin' him from the reeds.'

Next, Alfwald tied Maewyn's feet. Then he rolled him onto his belly and secured his hands and feet together by a short rope, so that they almost touched. Seward repeated the procedure with Mule. The men stood and briefly admired their handiwork as they observed the trussed and immobile boys.

Maewyn shimmied himself next to Mule as the Saxons rode away to rejoin Ranulf. His hair was drenched and his face smeared. He spat out mud, fighting the impulse to gag. 'A *right* fix we're in,' he said, trying not to cry. 'They must have found our settlement. Da will be forced to fight now.'

Mule had none of his brother's resolve and readily bawled. 'It's my fault again,' he sobbed. 'If I hadn't waved the branch, we wouldn't have been spotted … wouldn't be in this mess.'

Maewyn's heart went out to Mule as he sniveled beside him; his mucus running down and forming globs which sat proud of the dusty floor. 'No, we wouldn't,' he said quietly, 'but they were coming anyway, and we would've met them eventually. We can only hope that da gets the chance to come and look for us.' Groaning, he attempted to move his arms. 'Bugger! These ropes are tight. Please let him come soon.'

Hoping to catch sight of his sons, Bran ran around the edge of the stockade in a frenzied dilemma. He knew the boys had gone to the reed beds, and would be targets for the approaching war band. Govan had pleaded with him to withdraw behind the protection of the palisade, reasoning there was nothing he could do for them now.

Bran's thoughts whirled. What was he supposed to do? Abandon them? What would he tell his wife? Sorry but I had to save my own skin so I hid behind the palisade.

He ran to the gate where Govan counted in the last of the ploughmen and herdsmen as they returned from the fields. Now, he had made up his mind. 'Shut the gate Govan, I can't leave them out there, I won't be coming in.'

Govan nodded resignedly, knowing he would do the same if Elowen had ventured beyond the protection of the stockade. Thank God *she* was inside the fence. He threw Bran a well-used, cast-off sword donated to the village by Flint. Although shabby looking, the sword had been honed to lethal sharpness, thanks to the attention given to it by the village smith.

Bran tested the balance of the sword as he ran down the track away from the village. It felt right in his grasp, even though he had received only rudimentary training in its use. Arthur had insisted that all the men in the villages in his protectorate would receive basic weapons instruction.

This would give the villages a level of autonomy and enable them to offer some resistance to raiding war bands. Erec, a weapons instructor from Brythonfort, alongside Withred, the Angle and ally, had visited most of the villages and given instruction on the use of ax, spear and sword. The villages possessed some donated hardware, but local smiths had forged most of the weaponry now owned by the communities. Withred had also given a tactical insight in what to expect when faced with the brutality of a Saxon attack.

Bran loosened his shoulder by swinging the sword around his head as he ran. His intention was to find his boys and protect them as best he could. He knew he could not fight a huge force alone, but still intended to protect his sons. To the death if it came to that.

He had not long to wait before he heard the sound of riders. A nearby drainage ditch was his only cover, and he had barely enough time to fling himself into it and lie low as the riders hastily approached then passed him. He could not see his boys and this set him in a panic. Had the bastards killed them? Maybe drowned them in the marshes? As soon as the riders were a safe distance from him, he left the ditch and ran to the reed beds.

Maewyn, who had managed after much wriggling to roll onto his back, shouted with joy as he saw his father approach. Mule, who was still floundering on his belly, stopped his own wriggling upon hearing Maewyn's cry. Then he felt his binding being severed, and was able to roll over unfettered onto his elbow and look at his father.

'I couldn't help it father, I only meant to wave—'

'We haven't time for that now, lad,' said Bran, immensely relieved, as he proceeded to release Maewyn. 'They've gone to attack the village, and I need to decide what to do next. You and Maewyn's life is the important thing now.'

Govan stood behind the stockade with a group of twelve men. All of them were armed, the most common weapon of choice being the ax. The women and younger children had withdrawn to the huts. The raiders had just arrived and it soon became clear that one was a fellow Briton.

'You may as well let us in!' shouted Irvin, from beyond the palisade. 'We'll get in anyway, so why make it hard for yourselves?'

Some of the men were about to shout back, but Govan gestured them to be silent.

'If you let us in and open the gates, it will be better for you!' continued Irvin. 'We will take what we've come for and leave your structures intact! Most of you shall remain and will not be harmed!'

Again, his offer met with silence.

Eventually Govan replied. 'Why is a Briton riding with murderers of his own people? Why have you abandoned your own folk? Doesn't the fact that your masters speak not our tongue tell you they shouldn't be on our isle?'

Irvin was unperturbed. 'That is not for discussion. What matters now is you let us in without bloodshed! Resist and we will burn your settlement to the ground, starting with this fence! Believe me when I say this—we will spare no one if you defy us this day! The only survivors will be those we take back to Norwic to sell!'

Again, there was a pause as Govan looked to his men. Fearful but resolute stares met his gaze. Some shook their heads, dismissing Irvin's offer. Others merely looked impassively at the floor, their breath sharp and rapid, as they hefted their axes and spears, readying themselves for battle.

'Your fire does not frighten us!' shouted Govan. 'Rather, it should give *you* nightmares, for you are all destined for the flames of the burning pit! All of you will go to hell! So in answer to your proposal, I say this: turn around and go back to your festering rat hole of a town! All of you go back, for no man here is willing to kneel to you!'

Ranulf had understood enough of the conversation to make his decision. Turning to his men, he gave the order. 'Archers, prepare your arrows and encircle the palisade.

Let loose your arrows when in position. I want a good even burn, all around the fence. I also want arrows released into the compound.'

One of the men held a pot filled with mutton fat. The archer's dipped their hemp-wrapped arrow tips into the fat, then ran into position at intervals around the palisade. Lit at intervals all around the compound, small ground fires provided the required flame.

Ranulf walked around as his men ignited their arrows and sent them into the tinder-dry palisade. Some arrows soared skyward to drop into the compound, describing white, incandescent arcs as they shrieked eerily through the air.

Govan had no choice but to order his men to shelter from the airborne attack as best they could. Soon the village was in turmoil as the thatched roofs of the huts began to burn.

The panic grew, as villagers, unsure of what to do to escape the flames, ran around in confusion. Two men, pierced with flame arrows, emitted awful screams as they rolled about on the ground, thrashing wildly.

Govan's thoughts now centered upon Elowen. He ran to their hut, which had started to steam as its roof succumbed to the searing heat. He panicked when finding it empty. Trying to think straight, he looked around … and then it hit him. *Water! She went for water!*

He ran through the mêlée—through the thick smoke that swirled everywhere. A shift in the breeze allowed the smoke to part a little, and he saw the outline of the well. *Please let her be there,* he thought, *please God, let be there.*

A burning figure passed him by. Govan looked on aghast as a woman, clothes and hair aflame, hurtled towards the well. Upon reaching it, she toppled over the low wall and fell shrieking into the water below.

A flaming arrow fell from the air and narrowly missed Govan as he stood by the well. He saw two of his fighting men a distance away. 'I can't believe this is happening,' whispered Govan, horror-struck, as the scorching air caused their clothing to combust.

Worryingly, his own jerkin was now starting to smolder. Frantically, he tugged on the well rope next to him, but the bucket met resistance from the dead woman below. Another tug released it. He pulled up a bucketful of cool water, and dumped it over his head and body, causing a swirl of steam to hiss from him.

He lowered the bucket back into the well and dragged it back up. With the brimming bucket in his grasp, he again thought of Elowen. She was not in their hut ... not at the well, so where could she be?

Then it dawned on him. *Maewyn and Mule!* She had gone for water for *them*! Mule had spilled water on the floor of his hut!

He ran with the bucket to Bran's hut. It smoldered but was still intact. Coughing, he entered the hut.

'Elowen! Elowen!' He began to panic. His cry was unanswered.

The hut had no windows—the only light coming from the open doorway. In the gloom, Govan overturned a table, then a straw pallet.

And there was Elowen, cowering and terrified, having gone to ground when the arrows had started to fly. Her clothes, too, had started to smoke. Govan remembered the bucket he still carried. He threw its cool contents over her.

Gasping, Elowen came to life. Govan pulled her to her feet. 'We have to get out,' he said. 'This hut will be in flames soon.'

They ran outside, hand in hand, to witness hell itself. Arrows still hurtled into the compound. Many villagers now lay dead, from smoke, flame or arrow. Govan pulled Elowen towards the well. When reaching it, he drew yet more water and dumped it over their heads. Repeatedly, he drenched them both until they were dripping. Fearfully, he looked around; looked for a way out, but could see none—could see no possible way they could survive.

Ranulf stood with Irvin watching the inferno. A frown creased his face. 'It burns well ... too fucking well! All our profit is being roasted inside.' He glanced towards the fifty-odd men who stood behind him, all waiting for the fire to breach the palisade. 'They'll have nothing to do,' he stated. 'No man in there will be capable of fighting.'

Irvine pointed at a section of palisade that glowed red. It sent off a myriad of sparks and grey ash into the air. 'That looks ready to come down. No doubt any survivors will pour through it when it does.'

Ranulf studied the fence then turned to his men. 'Be ready for whatever comes through the gap. Anyone sale-worthy is to be spared. Kill the old, if any managed to survive; and kill all who resist.'

As they watched, the section of burning fence crumbled and drifted to the ground. Ranulf and Irvin peered hard into the smoky, shadowy interior, and soon, human forms began to emerge.

Bran crouched by a holly bush. Numbed to silence, he held his boys close as he watched the blaze. Mule's brown eyes were open wide in shock, the fire reflecting in his pupils as he grasped his father's hand. Maewyn wept as he observed his life burning to oblivion before his eyes.

They had managed to keep hidden when the raiders had ignited their village. The bowmen had then departed to answer Ranulf's summons, leaving them alone.

Another section of the palisade burnt through and collapsed in a shower of sparks before them. Glowing, pink-grey embers scattered to strew across the ground. A bare-foot old man stumbled through the gap amidst a swirling of smoke. The wind caused the smoke to billow and shift so that Bran lost sight of him.

'It's uncle Eoghan!' shouted Mule, as the smoke again shifted. 'Look, he's jumped into the ditch, we must help him. He's drowning!'

Eoghan had flung himself into the ditch; the mad rage to feel cool again, overriding his fear of water. Furthermore, he had plunged into a deep, recently cleared, section of the ditch.

Bran was in a quandary. His wife's brother had suddenly appeared, and then just as quickly, disappeared. Could he risk leaving Bran and Maewyn while he helped Eoghan? What if the Saxons returned— they could be back in a flash on their ponies.

The emergence of Govan and Elowen ended his dilemma.

He looked Mule in the eyes, 'None of them can swim,' he said. 'I have to help them. Stay here and do not move. Stay with Maewyn until I return.'

He looked to Maewyn, who wiped his arm across his streaming eyes, creating a grimy streak across his face.

Attempting to be brave, the boy said, 'I'll make sure he stays here with me.'

Bran gave Maewyn's arm a comforting squeeze, then ran across to the ditch.

Eoghan had not surfaced. Unthinkingly, Govan had also jumped into the ditch still holding Elowen's hand. Bran plunged into the water and managed to grab Elowen as she returned gasping to the surface. Able to stand in the water on his side of the ditch, his mouth barely clear, he dragged her across and pushed her out. 'Run to Maewyn and Mule by the holly bush,' he said. 'Wait there until I return with your da.' Elowen scrambled up the side of the ditch and looked helplessly back to her father. 'Go now run to them!' shouted Bran. Elowen turned and stumbled across to Maewyn and Mule.

Govan floundered and attempted to connect to Bran, who waited with hand outstretched, but before they could make contact they heard shouting. It was what Bran had dreaded. The riders had returned and had seen them. His thoughts went to the children. He shot a desperate look of apology to Govan, then turned away and climbed out of the ditch.

CHAPTER TWO

Everything was a blur as Govan's lucidity returned. He felt the surface beneath him and was surprised at its warmth. A woolen blanket covered him. He heard the voices

'He's awake. Quickly Murdoc, here. He's awake!'

Govan blinked and tried to make sense of things as the images became clearer. Above him, with blond hair braided and clean, stood an attractive woman. An angel maybe. This was heaven then—the place all the Christians talked about. Peace, warmth, beauty.

The angel spoke again. 'Govan can you hear me? You're safe now. You're in Brythonfort.'

Govan's discordant thoughts suddenly became clear. 'My daughter, Elowen,' he looked around him, close to panic. 'Where's my daughter Elowen?'

Martha sat beside him and stroked his brow, her face troubled. She looked to Murdoc, who held his own daughter, Ceola. Martha's heart went out to Govan as she looked to him again. 'We didn't find her. She wasn't amongst the dead. Neither were her cousins. We think they were taken by the raiders.'

Govan, frenzied now, made to leave the bed. 'I must go then, I can't just—'

Dizziness hit him, and he fell back into the bedding. After a moment, Murdoc helped him to sit up and rest against the bolster. 'I know how it feels to have a child stolen,' said Murdoc gently, as he glanced towards Ceola. 'We are meeting this day to decide what to do. Rest now Govan. Save your strength for the days ahead of us.'

Govan looked to Murdoc, then to Martha. 'The boys, Maewyn and Mule … you say they have gone too? What of their father: my brother, Bran?'

Martha was barely able to answer and looked down at her feet, unable to meet Govan's desperate, questioning eyes. 'They killed him,' she said in a hollow voice. 'Beside the ditch … that's where his body was found.'

Govan squeezed his eyes shut as his body shook with sobs. Martha held him, whilst Murdoc looked on grimly.

After what seemed an age, Govan's grief was exhausted, and he was able to speak. With swollen and pained eyes, he looked at Martha. 'Why did they not kill me? Why am *I* left in this awful world?'

'They struck you with something blunt, the side of an ax maybe, and left you for dead as you clambered out of the ditch,' said Murdoc. Luckily, for you, they were in a hurry. They usually ensure no one survives. Too close to Brythonfort for their comfort, you see … they had to be away.'

Govan regarded Murdoc. The man was dark, his eyes green and penetrating; eyes that reflected an inner goodness; eyes that were also tinged with their own loss. He, too, had experienced tragedy, Govan could tell that.

An awful truth then dawned on Govan. 'My brother's wife, Nila, she's here, visiting Flint.' He looked desperately at Murdoc and Martha. 'A husband and two sons … she's lost a husband and two sons … how ever will she cope?'' His hand went to his head and he felt a bandage. He closed his eyes as his tears came again.

Brythonfort stood on a huge, multi bank earthwork, made by the Brython people a millennium earlier. A thick dry-stone wall ran in a great, lofty, unbroken loop around the stronghold, and was enhanced every two hundred paces by high wooden watchtowers. A great timber hall stood at the highest point of the earthworks. Between the hall and the curtain wall was an assortment of domestic huts, stables, armories and workshops—these dotted at intervals over the wide grassy slopes.

Most of the peasant inhabitants of Brythonfort had arrived seeking sanctuary from invasion, and some were permanent residents within the protection of the walls. Others farmed land around the fort, providing some food for its population. In exchange, they received a good level of protection from the garrison. A weekly market held outside the gates ensured a steady flow of people and goods to the fort.

The great hall contained a number of round tables, and it was at one of these that a huge, raw-boned man sat. His tousled, auburn hair fell to his jaw line, and his brown eyes had a hard cast to them as he, Arthur, spoke quietly to Flint (son of Bran), who sat by him. The knight Gherwan sat at his right hand.

Commissioned by Arthur, the table had been fashioned by the artisan, Robert, and his team of workers. It was round because Arthur believed that all men were equal, and thus no one could sit at the head, or the foot, of any table in the hall.

The son of a wealthy landowner, Arthur had had the leisure as a youth to become skilled in the use of the sword and saddle. It had been the steady flow of the raiders from across the Mare Germanicus, which had finally led Arthur to offer his services to Rome, so before taking the stewardship of Brythonfort, he had ridden for twenty years with the Romans, first as a tracker and scout, then as a knight, as his formidable performance in battle was recognised. He had come to accept the stability and protection that Rome had given to Britannia, having seen how his folk had lived in peace under their later rule. He had fought many battles beside them, and always his opponents had been the Anglo Saxon and Jute invaders. In gratitude to his deeds, Rome had bequeathed the mound of Brythonfort and the surrounding lands to him on his discharge from the legions. Along with many of the discharged knights who had rode alongside him, he had immediately set to work to fortify the bastion, further strengthening the imposing buttress. The recent departure of the Romans from Britannia had further increased the importance of the safe haven of Brythonfort.

A force of over two hundred well-armed men now kept the surrounding lands empty of invaders, allowing the farmers to produce grain and meat for themselves and for the tables of Brythonfort.

Arthur nodded his greetings as a small assembly of worthy people made their way to him. 'Gentlemen … *and* ladies,' began Arthur, as he smiled at Martha and Nila who were late arrivals to the assembly. 'As you know, grave events have befallen the lands around us: a village laid to ruin, and its inhabitants either callously slaughtered, or taken captive. There's little we can do for now to stop our land in the east being stolen by the Saxon hordes, but I feel duty bound to protect the people within the shadow of Brythonfort.

'In this, I have recently failed, and feel that redress is due to the survivors of the village. Flint has implored me to get his brothers back, along with Elowen his cousin. None of the other children survived the raid. The only two adult survivors sit at this table; Nila who was fortunate to be here visiting her son when the attack occurred, and Govan, her brother in law, who survived injury and will now tell his tale to us.'

Govan looked around the table; looked at the hard looking men who sat, pensively, awaiting his account. Nervously, he began. He told his harrowing tale, much of it only recently remembered after his concussion. His discourse with Irvin, the Briton working for the Saxons, evoked much interest and caused a stirring in the room.

Dominic, the tracker and fearsome combatant, held up his hand to speak. 'By your leave Govan, but I feel that if we are to find the children, the only clue to their whereabouts will come from what the Briton said from behind the palisade. Think carefully. Did he mention the place they had come from?'

Govan ran his hand through his hair as he looked at the tabletop and tried to remember what had passed between himself and Irvin. Frowning, he strained to recall the finer details of the conversation.

Eventually he looked up as his recollection improved. 'Yes, some of it's come back to me,' said Govan, now nodding his enthusiasm. 'The man who shouted over the fence, said something like, *"Unless you let us in, we will spare no one, apart from those we take back to the North,"* … or was it Northwin … I'm not sure exactly what he—'

'Norwic,' interposed Withred. 'He must have meant Norwic.'

Govan looked at the gaunt, longhaired man who spoke with a strange accent. Yet another man who looked as if he could smash the table to firewood with his fists. Where *had* Arthur got these people from? He shrugged. 'Yes … that may well be what he said, but I couldn't swear to it.'

'I suspected Norwic before you began to speak,' said Withred. 'What you have just said confirms it as far as I'm concerned.'

Gherwan had been listening intently to the conversation, his hands together as if in prayer, his forefingers touching his pursed lips. 'Why Norwic, Withred?' he asked. 'What made you think of that place? Indeed, where is it?'

'It's on the eastern seaboard, north of Camulodunum, near the old Roman town of Venta. I went there once in my old life. The settlement is recent. Several villages, now grown into one larger community. The land thereabouts has fresh water, plenty of timber and good soil. Furthermore, a deep river gives access to the sea. The wharfs were awash with herring when I visited. It's an ideal place to live. I billeted there for a while. We fought the local tribe who were resistant to foreign presence at the time. A truce prevails now with this tribe … the Iceni if I remember correctly. I'm afraid some of them are now in cahoots with the raiders. Hungry for gold, no doubt.'

Arthur assessed the information. 'It seems that the Briton on the raid who spoke to Govan was one of them. Access to the sea, you say? Easy to ship slaves out then?'

Withred nodded. 'Yes, it had already started when I was there; on a small scale then. But as the market for slaves grew the trade increased. Many were shipped to Hibernia, where British slaves are highly prized. As soon as Govan mentioned the word *north*, it confirmed what I already felt. Norwic is the place to look.'

'And *look* we will,' said Arthur. 'I have a plan which I've already discussed with Flint and Gherwan in anticipation of the news we've just received. We feel there can be only one way to go about this.'

He paused as he considered the roles of the people he had invited to the assembly. All of them were recent arrivals at Brythonfort. A year gone, they had ridden into his bastion with some of his scouts. Apart from Withred, all of them were survivors from Saxon incursions. They had fought valiantly and completely wiped out a force of fifty invaders while protecting a village deep in the eastern forest. The battle had been the talking point at Brythonfort for months afterwards. Known as the *battle at the ox carts,* the conflict had also cost the lives of almost every man of fighting age in the village. Faced with further invasion, the survivors then had no option but to leave and seek the sanctuary of Brythonfort. The men who now sat at the table had come through the battle, and although the resources at Brythonfort were not limitless, Arthur had been more than willing to accept men of their caliber.

However, Arthur had struggled at first to accept Withred. As a member of the Angle tribe, Withred had once ridden with the invaders, but had grown increasingly disturbed at the conduct he witnessed on the raids. Captured by Dominic's group and spared after offering to help them, he had not let them down.

The man was proven and reliable. Arthur now knew this and accepted him. Above all, he was formidable. Arthur had to suppress a chuckle as he recalled Dominic's eloquence on the matter of Withred's capabilities. Dominic had said, 'I would rather have Withred stood *inside* my cave pissing out, than stood *outside* my cave pissing in.'

His eyes briefly rested on Dominic now. The bald, craggy woodsman had removed his wolf head hat—a trophy from a long ago wolf attack. Dominic was a gem, pure and simple. An iron-hard Briton who had trained and tracked with the Romans, then chosen to live a solitary life in the forest. Ten years later, he had met up with a desperate group of British fugitives who had entered the forest as they attempted to hide and survive. Dominic had saved them all.

Murdoc was one of the fugitives. He had lost everything, apart from his infant daughter, Ceola. Arthur now considered Murdoc's inclusion in the proposed plan. His friendship with Dominic went a long way back, way before their chance encounter in the forest, and together they were an effective force. It would be foolish to split them up, so Murdoc would go to Norwic as well.

Arthur again smiled as his eyes fell on Augustus. Not counting his two brothers, he was the only village fighting man to survive the battle at the ox carts. A burly, bearded butcher, he possessed eyes that always seemed to sparkle with an inner amusement. Bushy, curly hair encircled the sides of his bald head, and he was stout in both disposition and build. Better not to underestimate him though, thought Arthur. The man was powerful, and word had it that he was fierce and uncompromising when faced with adversity.

Arthur addressed the group again. 'Now that we know the likely whereabouts of the slave market we can discuss what to do next.' He turned to Flint. 'Maybe you would like to talk a little about this.'

Chosen to train in Arthur's military because of his physical prowess, Flint was a young man of twenty-three. This day, his eyes were red rimmed, his face stark, as he looked at the assembly. He began. 'All of you have been chosen because of your capabilities which will be put to use on the forthcoming journey. We have the means here at Brythonfort to defend ourselves, and those around us …usually.' He paused and looked to Govan and Nila. 'Although my mother and uncle may now have good reason to argue with me on that point.'

Nila spoke for the first time. 'I have lost a husband, and *you* a father, as well as having two sons taken. Your uncle Govan has had his dear Elowen taken as well, so maybe we *should* doubt the effectiveness of the protection of Brythonfort.' There was silence in the room for a short while before Nila continued. 'Yes, it would be easy to feel let down, but for those outside the walls, your patrols cannot be everywhere at all times. No doubt, the raiders watched the area and struck when they knew it was safe.'

'They probably did,' said Flint. 'So all we can do now is to strive and get our loved ones back, and that must be done with a small party of men. No job this for a large group.'

'Indeed no. An army would find plenty to fight in the east, but would have little chance of finding the children,' added Gherwan. 'Beside, it would weaken our garrison here if we left with a huge force for a journey that could take God-knows how long.'

'This is where we hope *you* can help us Dominic,' said Flint looking at him. 'Your skill at reading the ground, as well as your local knowledge made you an easy choice when we were working out how to go about this.'

Dominic, who had been listening intently to the discussion, looked up from the ebony inlay he had been studying on the table. 'I'll do it for you with pleasure; it will be good to travel again.' He looked to Arthur. 'I take it that when you say *covert* you mean we'll be travelling anonymously?'

'Yes, we thought you might pose as a group slave traders. Our intention *was* to send you to Camulodunum where we suspected the slaves might have been taken. Now we know it's Norwic, that will be your goal. There, you can infiltrate and find out who has passed through the town.

'But what about Withred?' asked Dominic. 'He is well known amongst them—a man of great deeds.'

'Ah, we come to Withred,' said Arthur, exchanging a knowing glance with Flint. 'His inclusion is important because he is the only one at Brythonfort who speaks the Germanic tongue; my grasp of Latin would be of no use on the eastern shore.' He studied Withred, seemingly embarrassed at what he was about to say next. 'Er, yes … the problem of his renown has occurred to us.' Arthur hesitated again, and Withred barely suppressed a smile at the display. Arthur cleared his throat. 'Therefore we hope it would not be too big an assault on his vanity if we asked him to cut his hair, and *maybe* grow a beard.'

Augustus exploded with laughter, unable to contain himself. 'At last I will have a twin,' he chortled, '…a bald headed, bearded, heathen, twin. What chance will they have against two of us!'

Withred's hand shot to his long dark hair. He smiled, and then laughed, as he noticed that his show of vanity had not been lost on the others. As Augustus' infectious laughter infused the room, causing much amusement, Withred smiled wryly.

'By *cut my hair* I take it you mean I join Dominic and get a sharp knife close to my scalp.' He raised his voice so it was audible above Augustus' outburst of baritone mirth. 'Yes … of course I'll change my look … and no doubt some of you will be happy about it.'

'A small sacrifice, I think,' said Flint, 'if we can get the captives back.' He looked towards Murdoc as the laughter abated, then at Augustus. 'I would be glad to have you two as well.'

Murdoc frowned, seemingly confused. 'I for one will be glad to help. But will it not look odd—four Britons and an Angle travelling together?'

Flint started to answer, but Withred got in first. 'Not in Norwic. It's quite common there for Britons to mix with folk from the continent. As I mentioned before, some *Britons* are now actively involved in trading people.'

Arthurs face flickered with disdain. 'What have we come to? That makes them worse than the foreigners. Learning to live with them is one thing, but selling our own people into bondage? No … they will pay for their involvement in such a trade, but that will come later.'

'There's no place for me then?' asked Govan, his disappointment plain for all to see. 'To sit here and do nothing will send me mad.'

'Two days ago you were close to death, uncle,' said Flint. 'You are much improved but still not strong enough for the rigours of the journey. It would be no use to Elowen if you died on the trail and left her orphaned.'

Nila took Govan's hand and stroked it in consolation. 'We will wait for them together Govan. You for your daughter, and me for my sons. It will help if we keep each other strong.'

A respectful moment passed before Augustus spoke. 'Slave buyers we are then. I take it we are to set out as soon as possible?'

'Yes, you've no time to lose,' said Arthur. 'You need to get going tomorrow. Dominic knows the country beyond here better than anyone, and I'm sure he'll know the best roads to take.'

Tomas walked in the garden copse with Simon and Rozen. 'There,' said Tomas as he pointed to a low-lying herb on the ground. 'The blue flowers gave it away … Thyme, if I'm not mistaken.' Rozen nodded; her smile giving encouragement but asking for more. 'Its oil can be used on bandages to stop wounds going bad,' added Tomas, frowning now as he tried to remember. 'Introduced by the Romans along with many other herbs … its leaves can also be boiled in water to treat belly ache.'

'Very good,' said Rozen, 'and well-remembered. Another one you can tick off your list. Don't forget that it is also useful for killing parasites—crabs and lice, in particular, do not like it.'

Tomas scratched his neck at the mention of parasites, then surreptitiously checked the inside of his britches to be sure that nothing sinister dwelt down there.

Now fifteen, Tomas had been under the yoke of the malevolent Saxon, Egbert, when enslaved after the sacking of his village. The man had brutalized him, but Tomas had managed to escape and meet up with Dominic.

Since arriving at Brythonfort a year earlier, he had worked with both Dominic and Rozen and gradually he was gathering an all-round capability as a woodsman and healer. When he was not ambling in the nearby woods, tracking and learning the signs with Dominic, he was studying herb lore with Rozen.

Rozen, a widow, had a great knowledge of the subject, handed down to her by her own mother. She enjoyed teaching Tomas the arts of healing and loved to spoil him, having no children herself. And so, she treated Tomas as a son, calling him *Merlin*—a nickname given to him by Arthur's scout, Will, who had compared his guile at the *battle at the ox carts* with that of the small hunting hawk.

Simon for his part, enjoyed the company of Rozen very much, and the two of them had grown close … *very close*. Of a similar age—Simon was sixty-nine—Rozen had soon grown fond of him, attracted by his gentle humour and easy disposition. As another of the forest fugitives, Simon, along with Martha (a young woman from his own destroyed village), had been rescued from Saxon capture by Dominic and Murdoc.

A gregarious man, Simon now filled his days ambling around Brythonfort, teasing the children and conversing with his friends. He also lent his practical skills to Robert and his team of artisans who were responsible for the maintenance and building work at Brythonfort.

His latest job had been the refurbishment of a shrine which stood in a corner of the great hall. Many of Arthur's men had ridden for Rome as auxiliaries, and had adopted many of their ways, including the worship of their Gods. As soldiers, they paid homage to the war deity, Mars, and made offerings to him before leaving Brythonfort. Arthur was relaxed in the matter of religion, and Brythonfort was a great melting pot of beliefs. Apart from Roman deities, Christianity, although now in decline, still had its adherents, as did many of the Celtic Gods. Indeed, the worship often became intertwined and inseparable, creating an ever-changing diversity.

Simon now walked with his arms around the shoulders of Tomas and Rozen as they left the herb plantation. They walked by the moat that ran alongside the drystone curtain wall of the bastion. When reaching its one gate, they nodded to the guards and entered. Dominic walked towards them on his way to the nearby woods to check on his many animal traps.

'How went the meeting?' asked Simon.

Dominic told them of Arthur and Flint's plan.

'So no room for me on this trip?' asked Tomas.

'No we travel as slave buyers, and your age doesn't fit the ruse,' Dominic said. 'We leave tomorrow, so I have no time to lose. Come on lad you can help me check the traps. Looks like you and Will will be taking over from me for a while.'

CHAPTER THREE

Swathed by crumpled, rose-coloured sheets that framed him like a silken fan, Griff woke to find he was in bed alone. He rose to one elbow, squinting as he looked towards the marble archway that led from his bedchamber.

'Titon! Chronos!' he shouted. Immediately, two large black dogs padded through the arch and jumped onto his bed.

He laughed as the dogs licked his face with slobbering tongues. Griff chided them half-heartedly. 'Silly darlings. Away with you, you poppets … at this rate I'll not need to bathe.' He playfully pushed them away, but the dog and bitch licked even harder, happy to ignore Griff when his tone suggested their play could continue.

After another bout of giggling and licking, Griff rose to his knees and pushed the dogs away again. 'I mean it. Down now! Off the bed!' he ordered. This time, the dogs jumped down and sat to attention by the bed, still yearning his attention.

He looked again at the marble archway, frowning. 'Ciaran, my love, come back to bed, it's too big in here alone.'

Carrying a bowl of fruit, a youth of seventeen, dressed in a white linen bed gown, walked through the doorway. With a flick of his head, he tossed his copper coloured curls back away from his face. His carriage was graceful … almost feminine; his hands slender; his fingers ringed with gold. He placed one hand on top of the head of the nearest dog, giving its skull an indulgent scratch. As he chewed a grape, he looked at Griff and sat delicately on the edge of the bed. 'I was hungry and you were snoring like a swine,' he said. 'Besides, it's time you were up; the servants await your instructions.'

Griff lay back, his hands laced together behind his head. He smiled and frowned at the same time as he studied Ciaran. 'Only two years since I rescued you from the dung heaps of Hibernia and you're already telling me how to run my household. Ten cows you cost me. I think I would've been better buying a herd of asses, they'd be less stubborn, that's for sure.'

'Maybe … but would they bring fruit to your bed in the morning?' said Ciaran as he shoved the bowl over to Griff. 'Would they keep you warm at night?'

Griff took a grape from the bowl and tossed it to the nearest dog. The animal caught it with a hollow snap. He fed the other dog in the same manner, and then turned his attention back to Ciaran.

'Possibly not,' he mused, as he ran his gaze over the youth's slender body, '… possibly not.' His eyes hardened and his smile barely turned up the corners of his mouth as he suddenly sat up and grabbed Ciaran by the arm. 'Now get your ginger cock back under these sheets,' he ordered, 'before I set the dogs on you.'

Later that morning, Griff took the air in the spacious, enclosed courtyard of his Roman villa. His family had procured the place after growing fat and rich on the proceeds of slavery. They had acted as agents; first for the Romans, then for the Saxons, when they had become the dominant occupiers. He had been alone since his father death—his mother and only sister murdered years earlier after a failed kidnap attempt. Served by a small household of slaves, he now lived a life that most Britons could only dream about, as he enjoyed the luxury of bathing, heating and sanitation

As he proudly appraised his opulent surroundings, a stocky Negro man approached him. 'When do they arrive?' asked Griff.

'It should be soon, my lord,' said Ambrosius, the head of Griff's household and occasional envoy to Hibernia. 'They left yesterday, so by my reckoning they will reach the ruins soon.'

'Ready my chariot then,' said Griff. 'I've no wish to miss their arrival.'

Daveth and Marya bumped around in the dank enclosed wagon. A brief tangle of wickerwork set in the twine-secured door afforded them their only light, and provided a restricted view of the track behind them. Strangers before their capture by Ranulf, they had formed a bond on the long trek from the west after being dragged from the fields by Ranulf's outriders, seemingly earmarked for some purpose. What their role would be, they did not know—gardeners or cooks for wealthy owners, Daveth had speculated.

Of advanced years—Daveth was sixty-two, Marya fifty-nine—they had been surprised at their inclusion in the group of slaves—most of whom were young or adolescent Britons. They had seen many of the younger children die on the trek eastwards; their young bodies unable to recover from shivering, gnawing cold brought on by heavy rain and bitter winds.

After arriving exhausted at Norwic, Daveth and Marya had been the last two to leave the slave line. Standing hunched and cold, they had watched as the other captives were taken away in secured wagons. They had been surprised to see that a Briton—a man of means by the look of him—had been the main buyer at the market. This same Briton had looked them over, his chin cradled in his hand as he frowningly appraised them. He had mockingly raised Marya's dress with the ebony baton he carried, sharing a joke with the brutal slave raider who stood beside him. They had then endured the close proximity of the Briton's two stocky, savage-looking dogs, which had sniffed them all over. The slave raider had then pushed Marya and Daveth into the wagon.

'Maybe we're to work as a pair,' said Marya, as the wagon bumped and shuddered, seemingly finding every rut in the track below them. 'They've kept us together so why not?' Her tone was desperate, as she again succumbed to the fear that had ebbed and flowed since her capture.

'Maybe so,' comforted Daveth. 'Best not to think too much about it, though … best not to raise our hopes. Our journey will end soon, you'll see. Then we'll know.'

Another hour passed before the wagon reached its destination. The driver, a stout, surly Saxon, untied the twine securing the door, and impatiently beckoned them to climb out.

At first, they struggled to see anything after leaving the gloom of the wagon. Squinting, Daveth raised his flat hand to his forehead, and soon the white light subdued into clarity. 'Where in the name of Christ are we?' he said in awe, as he looked at the terraced stone steps that surrounded them.

The grey oval of the small, provincial amphitheater was unkempt, and had long ago fallen into disrepair. Weeds, such as dock and dandelion, had colonised the many cracks and fissures in the stone. Decades earlier, theatre productions and occasional gladiatorial bouts had graced the enclosure, but the only patrons since the Romans had left had been foxes and rabbits. Dry, crispy leaves, stirred by a light breeze, skittered across the chalky floor and whispered around their feet. They turned, alerted by a movement from behind. The Saxon driver had climbed into the enclosed cart and shut the door. He peered at them from behind the wicker mesh — his eyes a combination of fear and expectation.

Marya's voice was small and panicky as she looked back at Daveth. 'Whatever has he done that for? Why has he shut himself into the cart?'

Daveth gave Marya's hand a reassuring squeeze as he looked around the deserted amphitheater. Puzzled and hesitant, he replied. 'I don't know … maybe we're to be collected here by someone … maybe this is the place we'll be handed over. I think we—'

Marya flinched, interrupting Daveth. She pointed to the rim of the terracing where a lone man stood at its highest point. Stirred by the gusting breeze, his sand-coloured cloak and long dark hair swirled in harmony around him as he impassively watched them.

'See … he may be our new master,' said Marya, as she strained her eyes to get a better look. 'I think it's the man who selected us at the town. He must have bought us for himself. Soon we'll be …'

A sense of dread replaced her resurging hope, and she became silent, as two huge, familiar dogs appeared from behind the man and stood by him — the three figures framed by a churning backdrop of grey sky.

'I don't like those dogs,' stammered Marya. 'He let them too close to us before. They have black souls. They're demons.'

Daveth said nothing, his eyes locked on the dogs, scared now and fearing the worst.

From above, Griff had watched as the cart had entered the amphitheater and stopped. The driver unharnessed the horse and led it outside the arena through its one gate. When returning, he had exchanged places with the prisoners and climbed into the safety of the enclosed wagon to watch the show. Griff smiled when seeing this. He knew the man would enjoy what was to come next. They still loved an event these people. Still loved the smell of blood. Still craved for it even now. Just a one-man audience, but he would give him his entertainment all right.

Emitting low menacing growls, the dogs pulled against Griff's restraint. He looked at the dogs, then at the two slaves who now huddled together in mutual protection. A lizard smile flickered across his face as he considered the futility of their position.

'Feed!' he snapped suddenly, causing the dogs, which were still restrained, to rear upon their back legs with their forepaws clear of the ground. He pulled back with all his might as the dogs gave out rapid barks, then let go suddenly when his shaking arms could no longer cope.

As if released from a catapult, the dogs shot down the stone terracing, growling threateningly as they hurtled towards Daveth and Marya.

Marya screamed as Daveth took her hand and started to run to the exit of the arena some eighty paces away, but they had gained little ground before the dogs were upon them. The leading dog jumped into Daveth's back, knocking him to the ground. Instinctively he turned and met its snapping jaws with his forearm. Grimacing, he tried to rise to his knees as he pushed against it. The dog shook its head to aid the grinding effect of its bite, ripping away shards of flesh as it did so. After shaking the meat from its maw, it turned its attention back to Daveth, who lay now on his back, shocked and disorientated, his maimed arm held aloft.

Marya fared even worse. Knocked to the ground by the other dog, she fell onto her belly and, at once, placed her hands over her head as a shield. Her screams, dreadful and heart-rending, filled the arena as the dog shredded through her hands and into scalp.

After its relentless bites had laid bare the back of her skull, the enraged dog looked for softer flesh to gorge upon, and by shoving with its head, was able to turn Marya over onto her back. Immediately it went for her neck, tearing repeatedly at her exposed throat, ripping out her larynx and trachea in a frenzy of uncontrolled savagery.

As Marya's struggle ended, the dog, eager to fight live prey, joined its sibling, which was going to work with gusto upon Daveth. Both dogs now began to inflict terrible damage upon him as he rolled over on the chalky soil of the killing pit in a desperate attempt to protect himself from their meat-rending bites. His resistance only made things worse, leaving him wishing for death as the dogs bit into anything that came before them. Prolonged and dreadful, he was to witness much of his own dismemberment during his ordeal, until his body finally succumbed … firstly to shock, then mercifully to death.

Throughout the attack, the Saxon driver whooped and banged on the inside of the cart door as his bloodlust whisked him into a high frenzy. Griff walked slowly down the steps as the carnage unfolded before him.

Unmoved by the display, having witnessed it many times, he was nevertheless satisfied the dogs would have a good feed.

He considered their need to feed on live prey. That way, they would protect him at his command. The old bastards would have died soon anyway, and he had done them a service taking them from their grinding existence in the fields. He knew there would be many more. Indeed, he would continue to provide his dogs with a ready supply of fresh meat. Ranulf would always sell the old ones for a low price; it was part of the deal.

'Titon! Chronos! To me!' he shouted as he reached the flat floor of the arena. The dogs raised their bloody muzzles from Daveth's entrails and trotted obediently over to him. Griff looked to the wagon. 'Come out now, he ordered. 'The show's over. Time to tidy up.' The door opened a hands width as the Saxon looked nervously through the crack. 'Out man,' repeated Griff, impatiently. 'They won't touch you unless I tell them to, so get this offal into sacks and take it to my villa. I've no desire to waste good dog meat.'

CHAPTER FOUR

Six riders left Brythonfort headed for the eastern shore. Withred rode at the front of the group alongside Dominic. Both men had changed their appearance. Gone was Dominic's wolf's head hat—an adornment of renown that would be too easily noticed—replaced now with a cloth band which encircled his head.

Withred, for his part, had shaved his head entirely, revealing several white battle scars across his scalp. One day's growth of dark whiskers covered his angular features—the density of the shadow hinting that his face would soon be covered with thick beard. The result was astounding. When first revealing the change to the others, they had gasped at the transformation.

Augustus had looked to his companions in disbelief, and exclaimed, 'God's he was frightening before, but now he'd make Grendel shit his pants.'

Later that day, as the group rode over a demanding, broken, track, Dominic seemed frustrated. 'It'll be good to get on the Roman roads,' he said, as he goaded his horse through an outcrop of broom that colonised and sprouted across the entire width of the track. 'Once on the good roads the miles will fly by.'

'You reckon they'll still be in good repair then?' asked Withred.

'Not perfect after all these years, but far better and quicker than riding through land like this. I know the roads here like the back of my hand … I should do, I've ridden on most of them scores of times when scouting for Rome.'

Withred looked up the track, as if hopeful to spot the Saxons they pursued. 'I've ridden many of the roads myself and they *are* quicker, but we're six days behind the raiding party. How long did you say this journey will take?'

'We should reach the road tomorrow, and I reckon four days will bring us to the ruins at Calleva. After that, possibly another three days to Londinium.'

'Not much left of that place now,' remarked Withred. 'Last time I was there it was mostly a ruin. A few homesteads here and there and not a lot going on since the Romans left, but we need to be careful when we get beyond Londinium. The land thereafter, north and east, is peopled with Saxons, Angles, Jutes. Most are merely peasants and farmers, but there'll be roaming bands of warriors as well.'

'We shouldn't be troubled if we stick to our story,' Dominic said. 'As Arthur said, some Britons live alongside them now. But you're right; we do need to be careful the further east we travel. The road northeast from Londinium should bring us to Camulodunum, and by travelling the Roman road we should be there in two days.

'Now that *is* a viper's nest we need to avoid,' warned Withred. 'If I'm going to be recognised it'll be in Camulodunum. The place is crawling with raiders.'

'Avoid it we will, then,' concurred Dominic. 'We've no need to pass through the place anyway. We can easily skirt round it. Three days past Camulodunum should see us in Norwic.'

Flint, who had ridden to the front and listened to the latter part of the conversation, was concerned. 'That's twelve days or thereabouts,' he frowned. 'By my count the raiders will be half way there by now.'

'I think maybe not,' reassured Dominic. 'If they're force-marching captives they'll be moving much slower than us. What takes us twelve days will take them sixteen, I guess.'

Flint rapidly did a count in his head. The result promoted a tone of panic in his voice. 'If that's right we'll still arrive two days after them. Elowen and my brothers could be anywhere by then. Can't we move faster? Get there before them?'

Withred shook his head. 'We don't have the luxury of fresh horses every day, so we have to pace ourselves … find the right balance. Otherwise we'll exhaust the horses and end up walking.'

'Then let's hope the journey goes smoothly,' said Flint. 'I fear for the children, the longer this goes on.'

Five days later they approached Londinium. The first thing they saw from distance was the town's most impressive feature: its wall. Tall and thick, the structure was still complete, having been the last great construction project completed by the Romans. The rest of the town, though, was in the process of slow decay. Most of the population, British and Roman, were long gone, and only a few Saxon families now lived in the town. Many of these had erected rough shacks against the wall, and most survived by scavenging for loot, or combing the river mud for lost or discarded artifacts. Some fished the river—the catch supplementing their findings from the river mud. Their findings, they bartered for provisions.

As he rode over the timber pile bridge into the town, Murdoc observed the river. The Romans had named it Tamesa (the flowing one) according to Dominic. He noticed three figures on the shore. Two of them, a man and a woman, carried stout sticks, which they jabbed into the mud. Occasionally they would bend down to examine a find, and either toss it to one side, or place in the wicker basket at their feet.

A bare-foot, girl child, no older than six years; her blond hair, long and unkempt; her smock dress, dirty and tattered, walked behind the woman, copying her in her child's way as she scraped ineffectually at the mud with a thinner stick. She reminded Murdoc of his own daughter, Ceola, and his heart immediately went out to her.

Flint rode beside Murdoc and could not help noticing his focus of attention. 'Sweet little thing,' he said. 'She's probably a Saxon child. It seems they don't have it all their own way. The poor mite seems half starved.'

Murdoc looked towards the pony tethered to Augustus' horse. 'No harm in giving them some oats and dried meat, then. They seem harmless enough.'

Withred, who was riding behind, had heard the exchange between Flint and Murdoc. He opened the pannier attached to Augustus' pack pony, and removed a hunk of dried mutton and a small sack of oats.

'Come,' he said, as he slung the provisions over his horse's withers. 'We'll give them something to cheer their day, and perhaps find out a bit of news about the land hereabouts.'

The woman picked up her child as the six riders approached. They seemed friendly enough to her, but their austere appearance still gave her cause for concern. A bearded man with a shaven head coaxed his horse down the muddy banking as he approached them. She could tell he was not a man to cross, not a man to get on the wrong side of. She glanced to her man who stood beside her and placed her hand on his arm. She was relieved when the bearded man smiled and dismounted before them—relieved further, when he spoke their tongue.

'We wish you no harm,' said Withred. He offered her the meat and oats. 'Please take these, we have ample.'

The woman paused a while, unsure of what to do. Her man nodded to her and she took the bundle. 'Thank you,' she said, 'the food will fill our bellies tonight.'

The others arrived and dismounted. Augustus waved and smiled at the child. 'Beautiful she is,' he said to the woman. Withred translated and the woman beamed.

The man was spare of build and dressed only in a thin linen tunic, which was beltless and reached to his knees. His feet were bare, and his legs coated with orange mud up to mid-shin. 'Thank you for the food,' he said. He looked up the slope, towards the nearby wall. 'The day draws on, and though we haven't much to offer, you're welcome to stay with us tonight.' He offered his hand to Withred. 'My name is Godwine. Hild is my wife, and Udela our daughter.'

Withred took his hand, followed by the rest of the group as the tension relaxed. Godwine led them from the river and into the town. Augustus sat Udela on his horse, and chattered to her in Celtic as he led it up the slope. Hild walked beside them, her hand on Udela's back in support.

When they entered Londinium, the Roman layout of streets was plain for them to see, but due to years of looting and reclamation, most structures had lost their walls and roofs. The result was a town that looked victim to an earthquake. Goats bleated, and hardy little pigs grubbed amongst the rubble, feeding on scraps and plant growth that had colonized the streets. All the animals wore the mark of their owners and were a vital source of milk and meat.

Godwine led them through a maze of streets, defined by low-lying, broken walls, lichen-grey and stained with red. Soon, they came to the town's high defensive wall and so to Godwine's dwelling.

Two vertical, timber piles, ten paces apart, and attached at their top with a beam, stood ten paces from the wall. Two more hoisted, horizontal posts attached the frame to the wall, forming a cube—the roof and two sides of which, Godwine had covered with stitched goat's skin, leaving the front open. A circular stone fire ring sat at the entrance to their simple dwelling. A huge bundle of firewood was stacked beside the hut, some claimed as flotsam from the river, some bartered from a woodsman who came to the town twice weekly with a cart piled high with kindling.

As he had walked into the town, Flint's feelings had been ambivalent towards the family, as he wrestled with their reason for being on his isle. Were they not invaders? Just as much to blame for his father's death and his brothers' abduction as the men who had attacked their village?

Yet, as he looked at Godwine and his family, witnessed their hardship, observed their poverty, he could not help but feel for them. Maybe they had no choice. Perhaps Godwine had come to Britannia to give his family a better life, although how anything could be worse than scavenging for treasure on the muddy banks of the river, he could not imagine. Perhaps even the little girl was British. She may have been born in Britannia.

Whatever … it did not take long in the company of Godwine and his brave little family, before he saw them merely as people—no different from his own family … just people trying to survive in a savage and uncertain world.

The design of Godwine's hovel seemed to be popular amongst the inhabitants of Londinium. Built against the city walls, and sitting at intervals as far as the eye could see, were many similar structures.

Some were mere dwellings, some used for butchery, some used as smokehouses. In these, strips of pork and salmon hung from elevated racks with fires set below them; the fish having been netted from the river; the pork having been butchered from the domestic stock. Moreover, it was possible to barter goods and finds for the meat and fish.

Murdoc saw a few strips of dried salmon resting on a rough table within Godwine's dwelling. 'We exchange food for our findings,' said Godwine as he noticed Murdoc's interest in the salmon. 'Also, a man comes every week and takes some more of our loot away. We get useful items from him: pots, flints and irons.'

Why not catch the fish yourself?' asked Murdoc. 'That way it would cost you nothing.'

'We have no nets,' explained Godwine. 'It would cost us a year's findings to obtain one.'

With Udela on his knee, Augustus sat beside Hild, who sorted through the day's finds from the basket. Much of it appeared worthless to him; a strip of curled dry sandal leather; rusted pieces of iron, probably from a sunken merchant boat, and other indistinguishable items, made up the bulk of the contents of the basket. What a difference a simple fishing net would make to their lives, mused Augustus, yet it seemed so unobtainable to them.

Hild smiled when she saw the dismay on Augustus' face as he appraised the pile of seemingly worthless debris. She reached into the goatskin pouch that attached to a cord at her waist. With Withred translating, she said, 'Everything's got a value here, even old bits of leather.' She took a silver coin from her purse. 'But this, I found this morning, and was too valuable to throw into the basket. This will ensure we eat for many days.'

Augustus' bearded face split into a grin and he held Udela in the air, tickling her tummy with his bald head. 'This skinny little rabbit's going to turn into a fat little piglet,' he laughed, as Udela emitted a helpless belly chuckle above him.

Dominic, who stood by his pack pony nearby, could not help but smile. 'No need to barter your coin while we are here Hild,' he said, as he fished through the pony's pannier. 'Tonight we all eat from *our* provisions. You will eat like a wildman from the forest, cooked by me … *the* wildman from the forest.'

'Hild is most grateful, but says we've done more than enough to help them already,' translated Withred. 'I've told her nonsense. *We* provide the fare tonight.'

As dusk came, they ate a hearty supper and chattered long after dark, aided by Withred's translation. Later they took their places around the fire and slept well.

When morning came, they bade their farewell to Godwine, Hild and Udela. Although with them for less than a day, they felt a great fondness towards them— admiring their indomitable spirits; their incessant cheerfulness and strong unity. All shook Godwine's hand, all hugged Hild and Udela before leaving. Then they continued on their quest, their hearts lifted by their chance meeting with good people.

'We need to be ever more cautious from here on,' warned Withred, as he rode through Londinium's eastern gate with Dominic. 'I used this route many times when riding with Osric. It's the main way from Londinium to Camulodunum. We'll see Saxon war bands soon, and we need to have our story ready when we do.'

Withred's worries proved groundless that day. The people they encountered were mainly merchants and stockmen. The road was in good repair by the standards of other less used routes, their passage often being blocked by herds of tough little sheep, driven always by Saxon folk.

The second day out from Londinium dawned cool and grey and the group was on the road at first light. The land now seemed completely devoid of Britons, a fact not lost on Dominic.

'The last time I passed here, it was as a scout for Rome,' he informed Augustus who rode beside him. 'I was a boy of seventeen then and learning my trade with an old Roman named Livius.' He smiled fondly when remembering the old scout. 'What he didn't know about wood lore and tracking was not worth knowing. All over this isle, as far north as the great dividing wall, some say even beyond that, he had tracked. All over the empire as well. I learned some Latin from him, he learned some British from me. But one language we rarely heard in those days was Saxon. Every one of these farms and homesteads were owned by Britons.'

Dominic fell into contemplative silence, while Augustus, as ever captivated by Dominic's reminiscences, waited patiently for him to continue. 'Rome protected us you see,' resumed Dominic. 'As long as we accepted their rule, they protected us. Five years later, they were gone, and twenty-five years later we've come to this: the entire south-east invaded and settled; Britons either slaughtered or driven westwards.'

Flint had joined them at the front. 'Then thank God you met us in the forest when you did,' he said grimly. 'Your fight at the ox carts was a great feat, but was but one battle. Now we have the power of Arthur behind us, and we won't be trodden on like the poor souls who once farmed these lands.'

'That's for sure,' contemplated Augustus, 'yet it worries me that they raid so close to Brythonfort. A huge clash will come soon I fear. One way or the other, this must be sorted out.' He tensed as he noticed a movement up the track. The others had seen it too. A group of riders moved down the road towards them—their bearing in the saddle and the tack of their ponies suggestive of having spent many weeks in the field.

Withred readied himself for their encounter as the war band came to a halt before them. 'Hope you've captured plenty of pretty slave wenches for us,' laughed Withred as their leader, a grizzled, middle-aged man, appraised them.

The man, a Jute named Wigstan, was hung over having spent his night drinking twelve flagons of ale and whoring in Camulodunum. He was eager to continue his journey back to his settlement in Cantiaci.

Through red-rimmed, rheumy eyes, he studied the traveller before him. The man's accent told Wigstan he was native to the Baltic—an Angle, and fearsome looking to boot, with his dark beard and shaven head. He looked at the rest of the company. Again, hard looking men. All had seen action. Of that, there was no doubt.

'What's your business on the road Angle?' demanded Wigstan.

'Didn't you just hear me,' said Withred. 'Slaves are my business. We travel to Norwic to buy them. It's men like us who make it worth your while suffering the hardship of campaigning.'

'You need to hurry then,' said Wigstan. 'We left Norwic four days ago, but our slaves were already spoken for. They get harder to find, and the gold they fetch reflects their scarcity. So you'll have to dig deep into your purse … not an activity popular with Angles I hear.' Wigstan waited until the ripple of laughter died down from his men. 'The easy pickings have gone, you see. The further west we go, the more likely we are to meet resistance.' He looked at Dominic who stood beside Withred. 'What say you craggy one? Is it a girl or a boy that you desire?'

Some of the men near to Wigstan sniggered at this. Withred replied for Dominic. 'Your wit is lost on him, I'm afraid. He's British you see. One of the growing numbers of high born natives who seek slaves for themselves.'

'And your role in this?' asked Wigstan, a hint of suspicion now in his eyes. 'I've never seen you in Norwic before. Where've you been hiding?'

'On the continent, my friend,' said Withred immediately. 'My trade has always been there. Then I heard that money could be made here; buying and selling slaves.' He nodded back towards Dominic. 'Money to be made also by acting as a go-between for rich Britons.'

Wigstan looked the group over again, his mouth a thin line as he considered Withred's explanation. 'They don't spend money on clothes, do they, these rich Britons of yours. They look a bit raggedy-arsed to me.'

'They're dressed for the trail,' explained Withred, casting a look at his companions. 'Their finery would not last a day on these roads or in this awful fucking weather.'

Wigstan's look hinted that he was not entirely convinced. He looked over the Britons again, his head now banging from his excesses of the previous night. Finally, tired of the encounter and eager to be on his way, he guided his pony to one side to let them through. His followers did the same. 'Why the bald head?' he asked, as Withred passed.

Withred stroked the top of his head. His expression was one of mock pain as he looked at Wigstan. 'Too many nights spent in flop houses. The nits were driving me mad, so it had to come off.'

'I'd avoid Camulodunum then,' warned Wigstan, as he shifted in his saddle and scratched at his crotch. 'You'll be shaving the hair from you cock and balls as well if you sleep with the whores in that town.' Again, there was laughter from his men as Withred and his group rode through and reached the empty road beyond.

The Jutes turned in their saddles, unmoving as they watched the Britons depart. Withred cast a glance back at them. *Ride away you bastards,* he thought as he set his horse to a trot. *Lose interest in us and ride away.*

He allowed his breath to leave him in a slow, quiet sigh as he heard the Jutes turn and move on. Murdoc joined him. 'Well done,' he said. 'You were cool back there. They seemed satisfied by what you said, but Christ Jesus! the tension. What's the plan now?'

'Not to enter Camulodunum, that's for sure,' said Withred. 'Dusk will see us at the gates of the town, but tonight we camp away from the place. It's far too dangerous to go in there.'

They continued their journey and the day passed without further peril. As darkness came, the travellers camped a mile distant from Camulodunum.

The town was a nucleus for many returning and out-setting war parties, and had been Rome's most important town after Londinium for much of their reign. Preferring to stay away from the ruinous towns, the first Saxons had avoided Camulodunum, but its strategic importance and convenient location near to the eastern shore, had led eventually to its occupation.

The town, though very old, now had a frontier feel about it, and many different garbs were evident in the streets. Warriors, fresh from plunder and pillage, strutted round in gaudy ostentation, in contrast to Saxon farmers and traders dressed in rough woven clothing. The good housekeeping and sanitation that was typical of Roman occupation had broken down completely, and now dogs and pigs scavenged throughout the filthy streets. In places where the ground was clear of buildings, landless families had established impromptu smallholdings.

Many establishments now did a brisk trade in whores and ale throughout the night, and the town's dull, red radiance was visible from several miles away.

Murdoc lay propped on one elbow beside a low fire as he observed the distant glow. 'Seems like a vipers nest that place,' he remarked. 'No doubt Egbert dipped his snout in the trough when he was there.'

Dominic shoved a stick in the fire, using it as a poker as he pushed the settled layer of smoldering branches upwards, thus creating a tunnel that allowed a fresh combustion of flames. He frowned when hearing the name of their former tormentor—a truly evil man who had finally been disposed of when captured by Flint and Gherwan after trying to flee with Murdoc's daughter, Ceola.

'No doubt he did,' mused Dominic, 'and there're many more where he came from.' He looked at Murdoc, who seemed troubled by his recollection of Egbert. 'But none to hurt Ceola or Martha; not now they're in Brythonfort.'

Flint sat beside them. 'But still, as you say, many more where Egbert came from. My brothers and niece are proof of that.'

'I would've lost everything, and ended my own life if you hadn't found and rescued Ceola that day.' said Murdoc. 'I'll repay you for that; believe it Flint, even if it means travelling until I drop.'

Flint stared into the fire, his youthful features dancing in shadow. For the first time since starting the journey, he felt deflated and unsure. 'Thanks Mur, but we've still three days travel before we get to Norwic, and we still don't know if that's where they were taken.' He attempted a brave smile as he looked to Dominic and Murdoc who regarded him now with mild concern. 'But Withred seems convinced they'll be there,' he continued with more hope in his voice now, 'and that's good enough for me. Tomorrow may bring news and hope.'

The next day their progress was steady along the much-used road between Camulodunum and Norwic. Even with heavy use, the eastern road was still in good condition. Originally built wide enough by the Romans to accommodate two horse-drawn wagons passing on both sides, the road was easily wide enough to take the sporadic traffic that used it now. They came upon more groups of armed riders, but on these occasions, the riders, in their haste to reach their destinations, were to ignore them. Yet whenever they approached, ever aware that someone could recognise him—even with his changed appearance—Withred would raise the cowl on his tunic and cast his face in shadow.

Two more days passed uneventfully, until on the third afternoon after leaving Camulodunum, Norwic came into view.

Withred looked concerned as he scrutinized the town. 'We need to be careful now,' he warned the others. 'There must be people here who know me.' He stroked the twelve-day growth of dark beard that thickly covered his face, then ran his hand over a head that had been frequently and fastidiously shaven. 'I just hope the transformation works,' he added.

'You'd fool me, you ugly bastard,' grinned Augustus, as he stood in his saddle, trying to get a better look as they approached the town, 'and I've known you *too* long.' He sat down again. 'Not as big as Camulodunum this place … looks much newer though.'

'It's grown since I was last here,' said Withred. 'It was more a collection of small settlements then. All of them built beside the river. The Wensum we called it, meaning *the winding*. Not much space between the settlements now by the look of it, though. The place must be doing good trade for it to have grown to this.'

'Not all of it *good* trade,' commented Flint.

'Indeed no,' agreed Withred. 'That's why we've travelled twelve days to get here.'

Dominic and Murdoc, who had been riding behind, now joined the others at the front. 'We need to remember that we are rich Britons from here onwards,' Dominic said. 'That means we sleep in the town tonight. Well-to-do Britons do *not* sleep on the ground on the outskirts of town.'

Augustus pulled his horse to a halt and dismounted. He pointed to a small copse of trees nearby. 'We need to dress like rich Britons then. Time to get into our finery … over there.' He rummaged through his pack and removed a richly embroidered tunic. 'The last person to see me dressed like a jack-a-dandy was the wife when we were wed. A nice tunic I had on that day as well. Didn't keep it on for long, though.'

Murdoc gave a shudder of mock revulsion. 'No Gus, please,' he pleaded. 'You've just planted a scary image of your big, fat, hairy arse into my mind.'

He rode his horse into the copse as Augustus hooted his appreciation. After dismounting, Murdoc removed his own lavish tunic from his pack. He held the garment before him and admired it. 'Never expected Brythonfort to have attire like this,' he commented. 'Thought it would be all weapons and armour.'

'The sooner we're into it, and into the town, the better,' said Flint, as he pulled his own tunic over his head. He threw an opulent, striped, woolen cloak across his shoulders, securing it with a gilt bronze brooch. Frowning, he looked towards the town. 'Let's hope we're not too late for them,' he said.

As wealthy traders, they approached the town; the plain leather tack of their horses now adorned with gilt bronze ornamentation that rivaled that upon their own clothing.

A busy market was in sway—the streets thronged with townsfolk, warriors and merchants. Everywhere, children weaved and ran between the milling adults. Small boys, lost in their games, bumped against the legs of the crowd, rattling against the stalls as they chased each other around the square.

Some stalls groaned with herring; the strong smell suffusing the air with its sharp tang. Bundles of fleeces, towering twice the height of a man, occupied one corner of the cleared space. Upon these a man stood, taking bids from the merchants who bustled and shouted below him.

Nearby, a pig rotated on a spit. A rough table before it, held large pewter platters stacked with pork. The seller, noticing Dominic's group approaching, pitched for a sale. 'Good sirs, come and try my tasty swine. The finest in Norwic. A piece of silver will feed you all.'

Dominic cast a half glance to Murdoc, who stood beside him. 'A Briton, by the sound of it,' he muttered. 'Let's see what we can find out from him.' They dismounted and secured their horses to a nearby hitching rail.

Dominic removed a coin from the purse at his belt. Arthur had supplied each of the men with a full purse— the coins useful as bartering items rather than currency since the Romans had departed.

He held up a silver coin to the man. 'Will this do, fellow?' he asked, as he displayed the coin.

The pork seller took the coin, and after biting it gave Dominic a crooked grin. 'By your leave, I needed to check that it's genuine,' he explained. He held the coin between his thumb and forefinger, displaying it back to them. 'I know a man who makes these into ornaments. They're much coveted. I'll give him half a pig to craft a pendant from it, and then I'll exchange the pendant for a whole pig.'

'Good business all round then,' said Dominic, as he passed haunches of loin back to Murdoc and the others. You're Iceni I take it?'

'Yes … and you?'

'Trinovante. We live near the great forest, west of Camulodunum. The Saxons leave you alone then?'

The man nodded. 'As long as you provide a service you're all right here.' The seller looked around ensuring he was not overheard. Satisfied, he continued—his voice just above a whisper. 'Their warriors are arrogant fuckers, though. Think they can take what they want, when they want. We can do nothing but try to get on with them. We haven't the means to resist them, anyway.'

'I hear they still raid and sell our people as slaves,' Dominic said.

'The bastards would sell their own grandmothers if there was a market for crones,' sneered the pork seller. 'And talking of markets … yes, they sell slaves all right. Bring them here in droves. Nobody's supposed to know, but word gets around. They try to keep us calm, though God knows why. They could get rid of us if they felt like it.'

Flint now stood beside Dominic—his quick glance warning, *Don't say too much.*

'They keep the trade in slaves quiet then?' asked Dominic.

The pork seller gave an anxious glance around him again. 'Like I said … word gets around.' He gave his head a slight nod backwards, telling them to look, behind and beyond him. 'See that stockade, back there, with the guard posted at the gate ... that's where they take them. Word has it that the captives are criminals who've done bad things like murder and rape, but that doesn't wash with me. I've seen children taken in there as well.'

Flint tensed when hearing this. 'Children you say? Have you noticed any children taken in there lately?'

'Yes, two days ago. Two boys and a girl,' replied the pork seller, without hesitation. 'I remember it well, because I've two sons and a daughter myself, and I thought how awful it would be to have them taken from me.'

Flint's look at Dominic pressed for urgency. 'Thank you for the meat,' Dominic said, reading the look. 'Most tasty it is, but we must be to our business now. Maybe we'll see you again before we resume our journey.'

They bade their leave and walked a distance away before conferring. Flint was desperate to act. 'We need to find out how to get into that compound,' he insisted. 'It seems it nestles beside the river. No doubt that's where the boats dock.' He looked to Withred. 'When at Brythonfort, you said many slaves go to Hibernia, so we have no time. We need to do something *now*.'

'Yes, but nothing that will make things worse,' advised Withred. 'The first thing we can do is talk to the guard at the compound. See what we can find out.'

There was agreement and the group walked towards the compound leaving Augustus to watch the horses. As they approached, the guard became alert, his tone brusque. 'What's your business here?'

'Gold is our business,' said Withred amiably. 'Gold we can spend on slaves.'

'I'm not the man to do business with,' said the guard. 'I make sure nobody gets in or out of here; that's my job, not selling slaves, so you'd all be better fucking off.'

'I thought not,' laughed Withred, ignoring the man's rudeness. 'Neither is it your want to possess a fair tongue, but that wouldn't be your job either.' Withred pulled a silver coin from his purse and held it for the guard to see. 'No, fellow, it is information we seek from you, not slaves.'

The guard hesitated, eyeing the men with suspicion before taking the coin. He assessed them. Prosperous they were judging by their clothing. These were not the usual flabby specimens. These were *hard-looking* men— hard looking men dressed in finery. Maybe wealthy warriors grown rich from plunder; men who had decided to exchange the rigours of the trail for the easier life of commerce. He frowned as he studied Withred. There was something familiar about the man. Perhaps he had ridden with him once. Maybe he was right in thinking these men had once raided as warriors.

He turned his attention to the coin in his hand before closing it within his fist. 'What do you want to know,' he asked.

'Just who deals with the sale of slaves?' said Withred.

'The best man for that is a Briton named Griff. Most sales go through him.'

'And where would we find this Griff?'

They turned to look as the guard pointed to a huge, plank-walled, thatched building beyond the market. It reared higher than any other structure in town.

'That's where he spends his time when he's here,' informed the guard. 'The place is also an alehouse and brothel. It's also the only place that offers overnight lodgings.' The guard gave them a little sneer. 'Looks like you'll have to stick your snouts in the trough tonight if you're staying.'

'What does this Griff look like? How will we recognise him?' asked Withred.

The guard gave a snorting laugh. 'No need for me to tell you what *he* looks like. Just look out for a fop flanked by two hellhounds. They never leave his side. Believe me; you'll know it's him when you see the dogs. Don't upset him though, or his dogs'll chew your cocks off.'

'Nice to know,' commented Withred, 'but they won't have to be tall dogs to reach mine. Many thanks, we'll take our leave.'

A worried frown creased Withred's forehead as they walked back to Augustus and the horses. 'I know that man,' he said to Murdoc. 'When I first came to Britannia I fought alongside Hengist and Hosta, and that guard was just a youth then. Bloodthirsty fucker he was. He's aged since, but it's definitely the same man.'

'Looks like your changed appearance worked then,' said Murdoc. 'He didn't seem to recognise you.'

'I'm not sure about that,' said Withred. '*Something* seemed to stir him.'

When they reached Augustus, they told him their news. He looked up to the sky, and then to the huge thatched building. 'It's starting to get dark,' he observed. 'We may as well go and take up our lodgings and hope the Briton shows up.'

After riding their horses across the market square, they came to the building. A high thatched roof swept down to plank-built walls that stood barely higher than a man. No windows pierced the walls, and the building's only source of natural light and ingress was its wide doorway.

Inside was a large open space lit by a central fire. Clay oil lamps set around the walls provided further illumination. Day or night, the inside of the building remained gloomy yet atmospheric. No rooms existed within, but privacy was provided by the provision of many curtained stalls that stood against the inner walls and ran around three quarters of the structure.

A huge, open central space was evident. Here, sporadic bursts of laughter erupted from small clusters of men who stood conversing in the dimness, supping ale and regaling each other with tales.

Across the bottom wall ran a stout table that held several barrels of ale. Stood by the table was the proprietor, who talked to another man. Both were Saxons by the look them, so it was decided that Withred would do the talking again.

The man, Godric, watched him approach. 'Lodgings, Women, or both?' he asked in anticipation.

'Just lodgings and ale for now,' said Withred. 'Too tired for women … been on the trail all day. We'll pay with coin if that's acceptable.'

'As long as it's gold or silver,' said Godric.

'We seek a man named Griff,' said Withred, getting straight to the point. 'We were told he comes in here.'

Godric looked past Withred and nodded towards the distant door. 'You won't have long to wait then.'

They turned to observe Griff swagger across the floor towards them, a lively mastiff on either side of him.

'*Fop*'s not the fucking word for him,' said Augustus as Griff approached them.

Encircled with a band of twisted gold, Griff's long, dark hair bounced around his head as he walked. His silk tunic was purple in colour, richly embroidered, and tied at the waist by a white calfskin belt that matched the calfskin of his boots.

Godric reached behind the table for a jug of wine and poured it into a silver goblet. 'He'd love to be a Roman would Griff,' he muttered to no one in particular. 'Too good to drink God's ale, he is. Gets me to import this piss instead. He's even assumed the purple tonight. Thinks he's a fucking emperor. What a cunt!'

They moved aside as Griff reached the table. He took the proffered chalice from Godric, his jewel encrusted fingers twinkling and reflecting the lamplight. The dogs circled him, barely suppressing their yelps and looking at him in expectation. Griff clicked his fingers at the man who stood beside Godric.

A plate of chopped, raw mutton lay on the table. One by one, the man threw pieces of meat to the dogs. These they expertly snapped from midair, their excitement rising to a near frenzy as they gave out sporadic barks of impatience.

Withred glanced at Dominic, his eyes darting to Griff. Dominic took the hint. 'Nice dogs,' he said. 'The Molossus breed are they?'

Griff's studied Dominic from over the rim of his goblet as he took a sip of his wine. He saw a rough man in fine clothes who had seen action by the look of him. His companions too seemed wise of the world and solid.

He placed his goblet back on the table and paused deliberately before answering. 'They're not Molossus, they're bigger and better than those whelps,' he said loftily, as he wiped his mouth with the fine cloth provided by Godric. 'These are bred for export by a man in Aebbeduna, and each would cost a peasant a year's harvest.'

'And I can see why,' flattered Dominic. 'Never have I seen finer beasts.' He made to stroke the dog nearest to him, but gingerly withdrew his hand when his action met with a throaty growl. He turned his attention back to Griff. 'Talking of peasants, we're here to buy some. We were told that you're the man to do business with.'

Griff's eyes narrowed slightly. 'Slaves you want, eh?' He brazenly studied Dominic, looking him up and down, wondering what a man as craggy as he could possibly want with slaves.

Nevertheless, he would give him his answer. 'Yes … you heard right, I'm the man to see for slaves in Norwic. All of them criminals who would suffer a far worse fate than bondage if not sold on by me, I might add. All trade goes through me. I'm the main buyer. No barter though. I take gold. Nothing other than gold.'

Dominic patted the purse at his belt. 'We have gold in abundance *and* specific needs.'

'And what would those *needs* be?' said Griff, eyebrows raised.

'I'm looking for a young wench for my son, and some stout lads to work the fields on my estate.'

'Then, I'm afraid I can't help you. I do have two older ones I could possibly let go, but no others.'

'You're sure you have no younger ones?' persisted Dominic. 'I heard from a man on the market that some children were taken into the stockade a couple of days ago.'

'You heard right then,' confirmed Griff. 'And the children you speak of would fit your needs perfectly. A young girl of eleven or so, and two youths. But they are already sold. Destined for Hibernia. The boat docked this evening and leaves tomorrow … with them on board.'

Dominic glanced towards Flint, who looked troubled and intense. 'We are rich,' stated Dominic, 'and would hate to miss out on this. Whatever you've been offered for the youths we will double the price.'

Griff immediately shook his head in dismissal. 'Like I say, they're already sold. My customer is long standing and I already possess his gold for the sale. Selling them to you would risk my business with him. The youths will ship out tomorrow, and in ten days' time stand on the boggy peatland of Hibernia.'

'Would it not be good business to sell them to us for a good price, and then send your client the next group that meets his needs?' reasoned Dominic.

'No … it can't be done,' dismissed Griff. 'One boat sailed two days ago for Hibernia, and the one that now sits in the dock will be the last one to sail this year. I'll lose my client if I don't send him the slaves, and that would cost me a fortune in the long run. The answer is no, my friend, and that is the end of it.'

Flint's agitation turned to near panic when hearing the final refusal. He was about to interject when Augustus placed a hand on his arm. 'Not now,' he said discreetly. 'It's no use; the man will not move on this.'

Ever the businessman, Griff gripped Dominic's arms and gave him a winning smile. 'But don't fret my friend,' he consoled, 'slaves are coming in every week. Why not wait a day or two. I'm sure I can supply what you want if you hang around for a few days.'

Just then, a drunken Harlot stumbled towards the beer table and started to pester Godric for wine.

Giving Dominic a knowing leer, Griff nodded towards her. 'You may as well try out the women why you wait.' He swept his arm around him, inviting them to study the

66

interior of the building. 'I own this and the women,' he boasted. 'Why not try out the women. There'll be a generous discount if you buy slaves off me later'

Dominic had already decided what had to be done, and was eager now to speak with the others away from Griff. 'Maybe we'll do just that,' he said. 'Thanks for your time. I hope we can do business soon.'

Griff nodded and returned to his wine as Dominic led the others from earshot. Flint was frantic. 'We have to get them out,' he hissed, close to frenzy. 'We have to get them out tonight or they'll be lost forever.'

Withred's eyes flickered as he rapidly considered the options. 'Yes, we have to get them out of the compound,' he agreed, 'but it won't be easy. There's only one man guarding the gate, but we don't know what awaits us on the other side. As soon as it gets dark we need to get moving.'

One hour after dark, they left the lodging house. Godric had left the beer table and gone behind a curtained stall with one of Griff's whores. A mixture of snores and carnal grunting came from the other stalls as they passed them by. Of Griff, there was no sign.

A soft rain met them outside as they walked towards the stockade. Withred had formulated a plan with the others. They knew what to do. He approached the guard—the same man he had spoken to earlier.

The man was immediately alert to them. Straight away, he looked towards Withred. 'I've been thinking, and I know who you are—' he began, but his revelation was cut short by Withred dagger, which was quickly and skillfully thrust under the guard's breast bone and into his heart.

Augustus grabbed the guard as he slumped forward. He dragged the body into deeper shadow. 'Hope he deserved it,' grunted Augustus, as he lowered the dead guard out of sight.

'Definitely did … was a horrible, murdering bastard as I remember,' said Withred as he crouched and wiped his hand and dagger clean on the guard's tunic.

Dominic wasted no time sliding back the iron bolt on the door of the compound. He opened the door a hand's width and peered through the crack. 'Can't see anything,' he said to Murdoc who stood behind him. 'Looks quiet though. Follow me.'

He entered followed by the others just as the clouds shifted, allowing the moon to illuminate a series of bulky shadows within the compound. Two hundred paces along, they could see the outline of a single-masted boat bobbing gently at its mooring. Dominic peered into the gloom. His eyes again fell upon the bulky shadows. 'They look like enclosed wagons,' he said. 'Can't see any more guards, though.'

Murdoc and Flint joined him, as Withred and Augustus stayed back to watch the gate. 'The prisoners are probably left in the wagons overnight,' said Flint, his voice urgent and low. 'That's why there are so few guards. Even if they manage to get out of the wagons, they still have to get past the stockade.'

'Let's get to it then,' said Murdoc. He paused a moment, his eyes straining to penetrate the gloom. 'We've not seen the last of the guards though, you can be sure of that.'

While Withred and Augustus stayed by the gate ready to deal with anyone who might decide to check on the compound, Dominic approached the first wagon.

Secured from the outside, Dominic teased the stiff bolt free from the wagon door and entered. He heard the women's terrified intakes of breath before he saw them. Their dark shadows became clearer to him as his eyes adjusted to the dim light. One of the women looked ready to scream as Flint entered the wagon behind him. Murdoc, meanwhile, looked on from outside.

'Don't let the dogs in please,' pleaded the calmer of the two old women as Dominic crouched before them, his hands to his lips in a shushing gesture.

'We are friends', assured Dominic. 'You are free to go now if you wish.'

'You're … you're letting us go?' asked the woman nervously, as she looked beyond Dominic towards Flint and Murdoc. 'You've not brought the dogs?'

'No … you can go,' Dominic said in puzzlement. 'Why do you keep mentioning dogs?'

The old woman hugged her shaking friend who had begun to weep fitfully. 'Shh, shh, my love,' she said, as she rocked her in her arms. She looked to Dominic. 'A guard has been taunting us all day. Told us that the fine looking Briton had bought us for his dogs … said that we were to be fed to them alive. Said, "*What possible use would anyone have for old cunts like us?*"'

Murdoc, who stood crouched at the back of the wagon with Flint, gaped incredulously. 'Jesus,' he muttered, as the gravity of the woman's disclosure sank in. 'She must mean Griff. Sweet Jesus Saviour; he feeds the old ones to his dogs.'

Flint pushed to the front of the wagon—urgent now. 'We look for three children, two boys and a girl. Have you seen them?'

'Yes, they put them in the wagon next to the boat,' confirmed the woman without hesitation. 'We thought they might be headed overseas.'

'Thank you,' said Flint, as he breathed his relief at the news. 'The gate is open, and the men who stand there are friends. You are free to go.'

Augustus stood just outside the stockade with Withred. Both were alert to any noise or movement that could come their way from the town. With everything quiet, Augustus turned to look through the opening, hoping to reassure himself that Dominic and the others were making progress. He saw shadows approaching. Without turning around—his eyes still locked on the shadows—he felt for and grabbed Withred's shoulder. 'Two figures approach and I don't recognise them,' he warned.

Withred was alert and beside Augustus at once, his knife drawn and ready.

The scurrying figures halted ten paces away. 'We were released by the men,' said the woman nervously. 'They said you were friends and would let us through.'

'They're old women,' said Withred to Augustus. 'They must have been in one of the wagons.' He studied the two dark figures a while longer. The woman who had spoken seemed the braver of the two and huddled her cowering companion close. 'Step closer so we may see you,' instructed Withred, his voice low. 'We will not harm you.'

The women were hesitant and nervous, but did as Withred bade.

August was immediately troubled as he looked—first at the women, then at Withred. Withred reciprocated the look as he assessed their chances of survival. They had little chance, he concluded inwardly, because they would have to fend for themselves. They could not travel with them back to Brythonfort, because, quite simply, they would not survive the journey.

He beckoned to the women. 'Come through,' he said. 'Skirt the edge of the town and take the road from it towards the forest. Try to find someone to take you in, then lie low until the chase ends. Go now while it's still dark. May Nerthus protect you both.'

The women passed them by, their eyes brimming with fear and thanks. They stumbled across the grassy knoll before them, heading for the edge of town.

Dominic, Murdoc and Flint trod slowly past the other wagons. A quick look beyond the wagon's open doors confirmed they were empty. Only one wagon now remained unsearched as they approached the boat.

'The door's locked this time,' Dominic said, as they neared the wagon. 'That means it contains something of value … probably children.'

He made to approach the door when a shadow fell upon him. Backlit by an oil lamp that shone on the boat, a figure stood on the vessel's prow, casting a long shadow towards them. Dominic crouched. The others immediately did the same.

A sailor urinated in the water; his tunic hitched up and held under his chin. Oblivious to the three crouching Britons, he farted loudly as his trickle abated.

A cry came from the bow of the boat. 'Eth, you pissing pony! Put your dick away and check the prisoners!'

The sailor, Ethelmar, retorted with a laugh. 'I might as well leave it out; it'll be used on the next batch of slaves as ever.'

Upon hearing this, Dominic and the others quietly moved towards the deep shade behind the wagon.

Augustus whispered to Dominic. 'Another who deserves death by the sound of it,' he opined.

The cracking of Dominic's knuckles served as a reply for Augustus.

As they crouched, they heard the rattle of keys as Ethelmar lurched towards the wagon door. Dominic glanced at his companions as the significance of the noise dawned upon him. He considered the options. They needed the key and now was the only chance they had of getting it. It was no use waiting for the guard to leave. They would find a locked door if they did that.

Ethelmar cursed as he struggled to guide his key in the lock—the gallon of ale that sloshed in his belly impeding his coordination. 'Bastard ... get in you bastard ...you—'

His impatient mutterings stopped as Dominic slid his arm around his throat, cutting off his air supply. He pulled him around the back of the wagon and out of sight of the boat. Dominic allowed himself to fall into a sitting position, dragging the struggling, choking sailor to the ground. Placing his free hand on Ethelmar's forehead, he twisted his skull violently, whilst pulling counter wise with his other arm. Murdoc flinched at the sharp crack, which signalled the breaking of Ethelmar's neck.

Dominic pushed Ethelmar's body away and stood up. The sailor still grasped the keys to the wagon. Dominic stooped to retrieve them.

Panting from his struggle, he took Flint by the arm. 'Come with me,' he said to Flint. 'Murdoc ... you stay hidden and watch the boat in case they send others to check the wagon. We need to get this done quickly and get them out.'

72

Dominic easily engaged the key and released the lock. Flint followed him, eager to get his brothers and niece away from the boat and out of town. He was quickly through the door and into the gloom of the wagon. Like the old women earlier, the children shrank instinctively away from the door as Flint and Dominic entered.

'Quickly, Elowen, Maewyn, Aiden; it's me Flint. Get yourselves —'

He stopped abruptly. *Something was not quite right*. Unable to see their features in the dark, he could nevertheless see their shadowy forms. All the children were roughly the same height. Flint guessed that all three were probably of a similar age.

He approached the middle child—a girl—and gently pulled her towards the faint light near to the doorway. His heart sank as he observed a pale and terrified dark-haired child who averted her eyes away from him. He turned to Dominic, his face ashen and sick looking. His tone was desperate. 'It's not her, Dom. This child is not my niece.' He looked towards the other two figures at the back of the wagon. 'And those boys are not my brothers.'

CHAPTER FIVE

The boat's rectangular sail billowed and snapped in the stiff breeze. The vessel was clinker built with overlapping planks held with rivets. Its midsection was wide to accommodate its cargo. Double ended, with symmetrical bow and stern, it was able to reverse at speed without the need to turn around, making it maneuverable in tricky seaports. Five banks of oars, fore and aft, were unoccupied; their use unnecessary in the fresh conditions.

Tubs of butter, bundles of fur, sacks of wheat, and ingots of iron, nestled in the boat's midsection. A tent-shaped, goatskin cover, raised by a wooden beam high above the deck, protected the cargo from the elements. Under the cover, three young people sat with their backs against the side of the boat as it tossed and fell in the swell.

Elowen had her arm around Mule as he retched once again, unable now to bring up anything other than bile.

'Throwing his guts up again is he?' laughed Osgar the Saxon in his broken British, as he walked under the canopy on his way to the prow. 'He'd better toughen up, before he gets to his new master or he'll feel the lash against his cheek. They take no shit over there, believe me.'

Maewyn's eyes flashed. 'It's not his fault, he's being sick,' he defended. 'It can happen to anyone. Even men on this boat—men who are used to the sea—have been sick. I've heard them throwing up over the side.'

Osgar stopped abruptly in his tracks to study the group in more detail. The dimwit could puke till his belly burst as far as he was concerned; he wouldn't last more than a few days in Hibernia anyway. Big he may be, but

74

weak and stupid with it. The girl was young and pretty though, and he still intended to find out what she was like under her grubby dress, even though the captain had insisted that nobody could try her out.

Who would know, and what did he care if the cattle lord in Hibernia had already paid gold for her, thinking she was pure. He'd be well on his way back to Norwic before the Hibernian cunt would find out she wasn't. No. Fuck the captain; he, Osgar, would have the girl when the opportunity arose. As for the youth, he had too much to say. Was far too ready to give him lip. But he could sort that particular problem out now.

He shot over to Maewyn and grabbed him by his ragged shirt. 'Now then you little fuck, giving me slaver again eh,' he said, as he lifted him to the edge of the gunwale. 'Maybe a dip in the cold water will teach you to keep your slit shut.'

Maewyn kicked out, his foot landing solidly between Osgar's legs. Osgar immediately doubled over and grasped his groin.

'What's going on in there?' The booming cry came from Cenna, the boat's stout captain. His expression was at first stern when he ducked under the awning to investigate the ruckus, but a huge smile creased his broad, ruddy face when he took in the scene. 'By Frio's tits, look at you Osgar, beaten by a lad. *What* a woman you are!' he laughed.

Osgar straightened as the stabbing pain in his loins and abdomen abated. He drew his fish-gutting knife, furious now at his belittlement by Maewyn and Cenna. He made to lunge for Maewyn.

'No you don't!' roared Cenna, as he strode over to Osgar and knocked him to the ground with a beefy swipe of his hand. 'The cargo's not to be touched. How many times must I tell you? It's alright for you; you can skulk off and sign for another boat when we get back from this trip, but I'll have to answer to Griff if there's any complaint from Hibernia.'

Osgar got back to his feet, still furious, but, for now, compliant. 'The shit needs to be taught a lesson at any rate,' he fumed. 'There's no harm in taming him a little for his new masters.'

'Get back to work,' snapped Cenna. 'Taming this lad isn't your concern. His new masters are more than capable of doing that from what I hear. Get now to your job. We approach the Britannia Gaul strait and need to keep our eyes peeled for sand banks.'

Osgar reluctantly complied, giving Maewyn a withering glare as he walked away.

Cenna turned his attention to Mule. 'You need some food inside you boy. Something to bring up.' He placed his hand inside a nearby barrel and took out an apple. He tossed it to Mule, who caught it, before handing it quickly to Elowen. Rapidly he brought his hands back to his mouth as he again dry-retched.

Cenna looked at him pityingly 'You think these seas are bad. Wait till we turn into the strait. And after that the Hibernia sea.' He stooped to place his hand on Mule's brow, and looked at him closely, as if examining faulty cargo. 'You may get some relief tonight boy, when we anchor near the shore. Perhaps the winds will be lighter there.'

As the boat tacked shoreward later that day, Maewyn held Elowen's hand and considered their predicament. From Norwic, the other captives had gone inland to destinations unknown, but he, Mule, and Elowen had been lucky enough to stay together. Just the three of them all from the same village. Two brothers and a cousin now on this boat in this great sea, and never had he seen such a sight.

He remembered how they had gasped in awe, despite their fear, when seeing the sea. The marsh near his village was the biggest expanse of water he had seen until then, but it was nothing compared to this. It was almost too much for him to take in— a great expanse of water stretching on forever by the look of it. Where they headed for now, he had no idea. Hibernia was a name he had heard mentioned repeatedly, and he guessed it was their destination, but where it was he didn't know. Over the sea, for sure, but how far was anybody's guess.

The sound of labouring men, as they shouted and cursed their way through their tasks, filtered through to them under the shelter of the canopy. It made Maewyn think about the *bad* man on the boat. Most of the sailors treated them with indifference, and the captain seemed merely industrious and stern, but Maewyn was seriously troubled about the man they called Osgar. He had not seen the last of him; that he knew. The other crewmembers left them alone, but not him; the man always had something to say to them; bad things; mocking things—to Mule in particular. And the way he sometimes looked at Elowen—the way he licked his salty lips as he ogled her—worried Maewyn. She was only a girl, and he knew h would do all he could to protect her from Osgar.

The boat suddenly pitched and swayed as it changed course, causing Mule to retch again.

'I think we may be heading inland to stop for the night,' said Maewyn, as he knelt beside the gunwale and peered at the choppy seascape from under the canopy. He squinted at the horizon as the boat tossed and rolled, and thought he saw a distant blur of green just as the boat crested a big wave. He sat down again beside Elowen, his hair wet from the spindrift. 'It'll be our second night by the shore since we boarded,' he said. 'Looks like they don't sail through the night.'

Elowen nodded and took hold of Mule's hand as he retched again. 'Pity none of us can swim,' she said. 'If we were close enough, maybe we could get to the shore and escape.'

'That's why they leave us untied,' said Maewyn. 'Where can we go? We can't walk on water.'

'The Christians say Jesus could.' said Elowen, her child's mind going off at a tangent. 'Said he could do all sorts of things. Make the dead breath again. Make water into wine.'

'They're all fools,' said Maewyn dismissively. 'That's why everyone laughs at them …why everyone throws pig shit at them.'

Mule shifted not knowing where to put himself, such was his discomfort. 'I want da,' he sobbed. 'They shouldn't have killed him. He was only trying to help us. He'd know how to stop me puking.'

Elowen put her arm around him. 'Uncle Bran was a brave man,' she comforted. 'They'll make up songs about him and he'll be remembered forever. Brave Bran, the father of Maewyn and Aiden, they'll sing.'

Maewyn shut his eyes and leaned his head back against the gunwale, his face close to a grimace as he thought of his father. He had tried not to think of him. He had enough to put up with. Enough responsibility on his shoulders now his da was gone. He had to look after his brother and cousin. If *he* didn't, who would? The men, especially the nasty one, would hurt them.

Try now as he may, he couldn't push away the image of his da—of his heroic death. How, when the riders had come upon them, his da had been labouring to save Elowen and uncle Govan from drowning in the ditch. He had barely enough time to scramble out of the water before the riders attacked him. He'd been so fearless to face them alone. Maewyn remembered how his sword had been a fiery blur around his head as he wielded it— its burnished blade reflecting the fire from the burning village.

He had cut down two of the approaching riders, and these had fallen in the ditch, staining its churned waters red. But there had been too many of them. Even his da, who he believed could do anything; who he believed could face any foe, had not been able to stand long against them.

Maewyn squeezed his eyes shut and softly banged the back of his head against the gunwale as he revisited the image of his da's death. Brave to the end, his da had soon been overwhelmed—knocked to the ground by a spear thrown by a dismounted man. Other riders had then fallen upon him and finished him with many more spear thrusts. Maewyn had run at them then, growling like an animal, but they had laughed at him and quickly dropped him to the ground and bound him. His brother and cousin had suffered the same treatment, and so their fate was set and here they were—sitting on a boat with strange people, heading for a strange land.

Much shouting shook Maewyn from his thoughts. At the prow, looking for sandbanks, Osgar stood on the gunwale to give himself a loftier view of the water below him. He barked instructions to the steersman, who used a single oar to maneuver the boat.

Maewyn again looked over the side of the boat towards a distant landmass. 'We're closer to shore now,' he said to Elowen. 'A huge forest seems to cover the land from what I can see.'

Two hours later, the boat dropped anchor in a sheltered bay, close to a shingle beach. Oil lamps, placed at intervals around the boat, provided light as darkness came. Later, the crew took their sleeping positions, some preferring to sleep on the open deck under the stars, some opting to join the captives under the canopy.

Much to Maewyn's consternation, Osgar had chosen to settle under the canopy, and after picking up a small iron ingot from a cargo barrel, he settled down with his back against the gunwale across from Maewyn, Elowen and Mule. He had watched as Cenna, a traditionalist who always slept in the open air, had taken his sleeping bundle to the aft deck and quickly fallen to sleep.

Osgar stole a furtive look around and turned his attention to Maewyn. At first he said nothing, merely glared at him, his features cast in to devilish shadow by the flickering oil lamp. He spat on the deck, to emphasise his intent. He tossed the iron ingot from hand to hand in a gesture of threat.

'Kick me in the balls would you, you little cunt,' he hissed, unable to contain himself any longer.' Have you any idea what I'm going to do to you?' he nodded towards Mule whose stomach had settled since the boat had taken shelter. '...do to him as well?'

Maewyn shifted uncomfortably, but said nothing. He looked down the deck towards where he guessed the captain had taken his bed for the night.

'Don't worry,' sneered Osgar, 'I won't do anything now. I'll wait till the time's right, then I'll see to you all.' Now he looked at Elowen and a crooked-toothed leer cracked his pocked face. 'Her … I'll fuck till her eyes pop out. She'll be broken in good by the time she gets to her new master.'

'Why would you do that?' asked Maewyn, unable to hold his tongue any longer. She's just a girl. Can't you manage a full-grown woman? Is your cock too small?'

Osgar was across the deck in a flash, and grabbed Maewyn—clamping a grubby hand over his mouth, while Elowen and Mule looked on, dumbfounded.

'Smart tongue haven't you; you British cunt,' he hissed. Well listen good. I've a sharp fish knife on my belt, and I'll use it to cut that wriggling, shitty, worm from your mouth before you're handed over. I'll be doing 'em a service, I will. They'll probably give me gold when I tell them what a mouth you have on you; what a—'

'Will you shut up down there!' the cry came from the prow. 'Let a man get to sleep will you!'

Osgar froze, his hand still clamped over Maewyn's mouth, as Maewyn gave him a wide-eyed stare. Finally, he pushed Maewyn away. 'Remember what I just said.' He held up his finger in warning. 'I'll take care of the lot of yer before this voyage's over.' He nodded in emphasis, his face ugly and threatening as he took his place beside the gunwale and continued to stare at Maewyn.

CHAPTER SIX

The Hibernian ringfort resembled an emergent ripple on a vast green pond. Two huge earthen banks—the inner one topped with a high wooden palisade—encircled an inner compound. A huge roundhouse sat in the centre of the compound. Two lesser but still impressive roundhouses flanked the larger structure, and these stood nearer to the high wooden fence.

The country beyond the ringfort was undulating and green. Many homesteads lay within sight of the giant ringfort, all of them tiny versions of it. Between the forts, huge herds of cattle grazed on common land. Dotted liberally around the landscape were arable fields—fallow now, a month after the September harvest

Fróech mac Findchado felt deeply satisfied as the massive ringfort slowly grew on the horizon. Elaborately painted, his two-wheel chariot shouted to the surrounding world that he was the king's son and next in line. Behind him, seventy similar but less garish chariots, each piloted by a recently blooded warrior, sliced through the wet Hibernian fields as they approached King mac Garrchu's bastion. Further back still, a herd of seventy cows followed the chariots, driven by a group of twenty well-armed and mounted men.

Fróech skillfully played his pony's rein to slow it to a trot, thus allowing his brother, Colman, to ride alongside him. Like Fróech, Colman wore the symbol of the snake upon his forehead. Fróech glanced at the sack that lay between his shins in the chariot. 'Do you think father will be content with our harvest?' he asked Colman, as if unsure.

Colman affected a look of bewilderment, his eyes feigning deep consideration as he cogitated over Fróech's question. He reached between his feet, and lifted and raised a similar sack. 'Content he will be, I think,' said Colman, as if unsure himself. 'Maybe two sacks of produce will win his favour.'

'And if not two, then maybe the other thirty sacks that lie in the other chariots behind us!' erupted Fróech with wild fervour, unable to play the naïveté any longer.

Colman reached into his sack and took out a severed head, grasping it by its braided red hair. 'A harvest of heads for father!' he yelled, triumphant now. 'And recognition of our prowess on the battlefield.'

Behind them, a great cry went up as other heads were held aloft.

Encircled by a deep ditch, the first embankment of the ringfort loomed above them now—its great height and width signifying the importance of the people who dwelt within its confines. Beyond it was yet another embankment—a sign of even greater prestige—and through its high, wooden gate, Fróech rode with his warriors in a frenzied and victorious return; the macabre spoils of their victory displayed for all to see.

Fincath mac Garrchu grinned and placed his hands on the table as he heard the cheer from outside. He sat at his place of prominence in the great roundhouse, where long tables formed a huge square with enough seating to accommodate two hundred feasters. A great weight of food, ale, and wine filled the tables. Women and children sat at the tables, along with men who were too old for conflict. Many gaps remained, ready for the victors when they arrived. Adolescent boys and girls—all of them slaves—carried huge chargers of meat to the tables.

One of Fróech's scouts had arrived the day before and informed Fincath of his sons' forthcoming arrival. Everything was now ready for them. A hum of expectant conversation infused the room as slave boys brought in spears. Shaft first, they shoved them into the earthen floor at the centre of the square. Here they wavered, spear-tips uppermost.

A huge man carried a large, heavy-looking wicker basket towards the spears. After placing it on the ground next to the spears, he looked to Fincath, who nodded. He stooped and opened the basket, then lifted out the snake.

Grunting with the effort of lifting the heavy animal, the handler placed it around his neck. Placid and albino, it curled loosely around his neck and shoulders. Turning on the spot, the man displayed it to the crowd. All were silent and hushed.

Ten years had passed since Griff, eager to cement a good trade relationship with Fincath, had travelled to Hibernia and presented the snake to him. Griff's trade links to Numidia had enabled him to contact a man he knew there and barter five slaves for the animal. Griff frequently boasted to anyone who cared to listen, that it was the best business he had ever done. Astounded at the visage of the python, Fincath had soon adopted it as the emblem of his clan. Deification had followed, and they had named it Glycon, after Griff had told him of the snake God of the early Greeks, which bore the same name.

Fincath, who also wore the indelible mark of the snake on his forehead, walked over to the handler and reptile. Taking hold of the snake's neck, he drew its head towards his. The snake rapidly flicked its tongue as it observed Fincath; its pink eyes impassive and inscrutable.

Fincath brought the snake's head towards his mouth, making sure his hands clamped shut its jaws. Bringing his lips to the scaly rim of the snake's mouth, he kissed it long and hard. As he did, the crowd began to clap rhythmically, whilst chanting Fincath's name.

The roundhouse stood as a dark hulk silhouetted against the star-speckled night. Yellow fanlight spilled out from rents in its thatched roof and rustic door. Outside, as they approached, Fróech and Colman smiled to hear the throb of the chanting.

Fróech pointed to his own forehead and the snake that adorned it. 'Sounds like father is showing Glycon to the masses again,' he said.

Years ago, like his father and brother, he had endured much discomfort, when a man skilled in the craft, had drawn an intricate charcoal drawing of the snake upon his forehead, then pressed sharp, bone needles into his skin. The result was an eternal image for all to see; an image that only the highborn—Fincath, Colman and Fróech—could display.

'A lively night awaits us, I'll swear,' said Colman, as he lifted and snapped the reigns of his pony, sending it into a canter.

The conversation turned from a chant to a wild cheer as Fróech and Colman walked in, each carrying a maimed head. These they rammed onto the spears, before turning with arms outstretched to take the adulation of the people surrounding them.

Fincath proudly embraced his sons, as the handler put the serpent back in its basket. Both brothers had inherited his stocky, strong build, and shock of blazing red hair. Their woolen tunics and breeches bore the grime and blood of the campaign, and these stark reminders of their slaughter they wore now with pride.

The cheers gained a new intensity as other warriors entered the roundhouse, each carrying a head. Like Fróech and Colman before them, they shoved the heads onto the spears, and soon all spears displayed a head. In total thirty-three heads were produced.

Fincath took to his feet and held his arms aloft as a new wave of wild cheering erupted. He gloried in the noise with eyes shut and his face held to the roof of the roundhouse. After several minutes, he lowered his head and looked to the warriors, then to the cheering mass, his eyes moist.

He signalled for silence and pointed to the heads. His voice became a menacing growl that grew in intensity. 'This is what happens when thieves ride into our tuath and take what is ours. This is what happens when stinking Uí Dúnlainge rats tread the lands of the Ui Garchon. All of us Laigin people, but unable to live peacefully together it seems.'

A murmuring of assent and shouts of 'yes!' rumbled around the room as Fincath ramped up the intensity of his address. 'Next time it will be their women's heads that adorn the spears! Next time, their children will be taken to task, so that the Uí Dúnlainge seed is cut off forever!'

He walked his sons to the table as the cheering renewed to a new passion. Placing his arms around them, he proudly faced the room and shouted joyfully: 'Never has this dynasty had two more formidable warriors to protect it. But that cannot be said of Quinn the thief.' He pointed to the spears. 'To see *his* sons you need look no further than the centre of this room.'

The room hushed as Colman walked to the spears. Two of them, he pulled from the ground and held aloft. 'These are two of Quinn's sons!' he shouted, 'and if any of his other spawn try to avenge him, they too will end up with bloody heads upon spear shaft bodies!'

Wild laughter boomed around the room as a smiling Colman disdainfully threw the head-topped spears to the ground. He walked back to his place at the table beside his father.

'Feast now and rejoice,' commanded Fincath to the room. He pointed to a door set into the floor near to the spears. 'I can promise you that even more entertainment awaits us after we have stuffed our bellies with beef and ale.'

A ripple of knowing laughter went round the room. Fincath embraced Colman and Fróech, as the other warriors took their places at the table. A buzz of excited conversation broke out anew as other families greeted their warrior sons.

Fincath poured his sons a goblet of wine each. 'Only the best wine from Gaul for you two fine lads,' he praised. 'Griff sent it to keep me on his side. Sent it with the last batch of slaves. Throws the wine in as a gift to strengthen my trading bond with him.'

'And good wine it is,' said Fróech, after taking a thirsty gulp from the goblet. 'And speaking of slaves, when can we expect the next shipment?'

'Ah, the British wench,' smiled Fincath knowingly. 'I wondered how long it would be before you mentioned our latest treasure.' He looked at Colman and winked. 'The red haired Laighin girls don't stir your brother's loins it seems. Sees himself with a straw head does Fróech.'

Colman smiled ruefully. 'Don't I know it, father. He never shut up about it when we were in the field.'

Fróech shook his head as if to say his brother was exaggerating. 'Don't believe him, father. I told him she would be worth forty cows and you might decide to trade her on to Quinn Uí Dúnlainge.'

'That was before the thieving bastard decided to steal our cattle,' said Fincath. 'Forty cows is her worth, that you've guessed right, but I'm told that you brought *seventy* cows back from your raid—thirty that were stolen from us plus another forty in recompense.' He patted Fróech arm and smiled. 'So you see, I already have my forty cows, and will still have the British girl when she arrives. Besides, I have no wish to trade with Uí Dúnlainge any time soon. Indeed, it looks like a prolonged war is about to start between us. So the girl will be kept.'

Fróech nodded, satisfied with his father's words, but before he could respond to them, a mountainous platter of beef was placed before him.

Fincath, who had expected the delivery, immediately jumped to his feet and banged his richly embellished silver tankard upon the tabletop. 'The time has arrived, good friends,' he shouted. 'The sons of this tuath have attained a great triumph and now the *hero's portion* will be consumed by the man who led the victory.' He paused as a slave refilled his tankard with wine.

He gulped it down in one draught, some of it spilling onto his graying, ginger beard as he did so. With an 'ahh' of appreciation, he held up his empty tankard and shouted to the assembly. 'Empty your goblets! We drink to the feasting hero!'

A roar resounded as Fróech plunged his hand towards the platter and removed a fistful of beef. This he stuffed into his mouth. Grinning as he chewed through it, he took the applause and cheers of the room.

He sat down next to his father after he had completed the act. The feast got into full swing, then, and the room droned with conversation and merriment. Fróech slowly picked his way through the meat platter until only half of its bulk remained. Then, as an act of grace, he walked around the hall, offering the meat to everyone at the feast.

Three hours of raucous revelry passed, as poets put Fróech's victory deeds to verse. A druid also walked the hall. Dressed only in woolen trousers, the druid, Conchad, had stilts strapped to his legs, so that he walked twice the height of a man and was visible throughout the room.

His torso was naked and his head was beardless and completely shaven. This great expanse of skin was Conchad's canvas. Painted in great, intricate swirls, his body, head and neck were a riot of crimson and blue design.   Hidden completely under a covering of ochre and woad pigmentation, none of his natural skin colour was visible, and throughout the feast, Conchad indulged in soothsaying and predicted great future victories for Fincath mac Garrchu.

Fróech, after a time spent circulating the room, reminiscing and laughing with his fellow warriors, took his place again by his father's side. He took a great quaff of wine and asked, 'What of other slaves? Do you have a replacement for the lad who was murdered?'

'As always, I was specific in informing Griff of my needs,' said Fincath. 'A fair British wench; a stout lad for the fields, and a feisty youth to guard the cattle, were my instructions to him. However, until the boat arrives, we don't know if he found the people I asked for. He already has my gold though. He always insists on prior payment, and has never let me down before, so I've no reason to doubt that he'll not deliver as usual.'

'*About* the lad, Lorcan, who was killed before the raid,' said Colman. 'I'm told we hold his murderer in the cellar?'

'Indeed, we do,' confirmed Fincath. He pointed to the cellar doors set in the earthen floor in the centre of the room. 'In there skulks Kael—the rat who killed young Lorcan. Found after the raid when his pony trod a hole in the peat fields as he attempted to flee. Found knocked senseless … Lorcan dead nearby. Time now I think to exact the justice that his parents desire.' Fincath looked tellingly to Fróech and Colman, 'Usual justice … you know the routine.'

They nodded and left the table, then walked to the doors set into the floor. The conversation in the room faltered, then died.

At a signal from Fincath, a white, long horn cow entered the roundhouse, led by a herdsman. Fróech and Colman awaited it at the centre of the room.

Colman walked over to the tables, where a coil of rope had been set aside. Fróech removed an iron bar that secured the heavy, wooden cellar doors. After opening the doors, he walked down the steps into the cellar. Moments later, he reappeared, dragging a blinking, disoriented man into the dim room. His appearance met with catcalls and hostile shouts from the drunken crowd.

Colman and Fróech were forced to duck to avoid the shower of meat bones and other debris that many of the crowd threw at the prisoner.

'Your name is Kael and you murdered a boy!' shouted Fincath. His proclamation brought silence to the room. 'Because of your actions, you must endure the *trial of neck*.'

As if stirred by Fincath's words, the cow gave out a great lowing, promoting a new wave of jeering and throwing. Kael the murderer stood hunched and naked, his hands bound behind him as Colman tied the rope around his neck. Kael dropped to his knees, his head bowed in fear and shame. A sturdy, square frame, supported by wooden trestles, towered twice the height of a man next to him. Colman threw the end of the rope over the cross member of the frame, then tied its loose end around the neck of the cow.

The cow's handler led it away from the frame, taking the slack from the rope. The rope screeched against the wood, as it became taut, forcing Kael to take to his feet. Fróech held up his hand, instructing the handler to halt the cow.

A middle-aged man and woman, who glared at Kael, had joined Fincath at the table. Fincath addressed Kael, his tone judicial. 'I've no need to tell you what happens next. You have witnessed the trial of neck many times in this hall. You can still live, however. Indeed, you have two chances to live. Your family can pay the fine of three cows, or you can force the cow to step backwards. Either way you will walk from this hall tonight.' He held Kael in his stare a while, then nodded towards the man and woman who stood beside him. 'Murderer … what have you to say to Lorcan's parents?'

Kael tensed as the cow moved its head, causing the rope to tighten further around his throat. 'I regret what I did,' he gasped hoarsely. 'My family owns no cows ... so they have nothing to offer you in recompense. The act I did was unforgivable, but resulted from an argument ... that went too far. I beg for forgiveness ... and give you my pledge that I will ... one day acquire the three cows needed to settle my score.'

The room was hushed and tense after Kael delivered his plea for clemency. Kael looked on, hardly daring to hope, as Lorcan's parents had a hurried, whispered discussion with Fincath. His hopes crashed when he saw them shake their heads.

Fincath nodded to the cow's handler as he again addressed Kael. 'Your terms are not acceptable, and your trial with the cow will now commence,' he said with finality.

The cow stepped forward, raising Kael to his toes as the noose tightened further, causing his carotid artery to stand out like a thick rope for all to see. The cow's next step hoisted him from the ground, promoting a choking cackle from Kael, as his bladder released a spray of yellow urine into the deadly silence of the hall.

An air change forced Fróech, who stood beside the wooden frame, to look towards the door. Latchna, a scout, bloodied and panting from the effort of a long forced ride, stumbled into the hall. The scout's intensity was such that the cow shied away from him and took two steps backwards. Kael crashed to the ground, causing the silence in the room to end.

Amidst the cheering and jeering Fincath looked towards his druid. Conchad came to him after looking down upon Kael. 'He has to live,' insisted the druid. 'A sickness will befall all the cattle of this tuath if you do not uphold the rules of the trial of neck. That is my forewarning. Your son's will also die of pestilence, along with many who sit in this hall if you put the murderer through the trial again.'

Fincath absorbed Conchad's words. He turned to Lorcan's parents, a grim cast to his eyes, and told them of Conchad's prophesy.

Lorcan's father looked to Kael, who seemed barely alive, his tone incredulous. 'He killed my son and now he is to *walk free*?' Looking to Conchad, he asked, 'Is there no other way?' Conchad shook his head. The man slumped back into his seat, feeling thwarted of justice, and intent now on consoling his distraught wife.

Fincath looked towards Kael who still choked and spat blood onto the dusty floor of the hall, mixing it with his urine. 'Take the rope from his neck and throw him out,' he shouted. Responding to the command, two men grabbed Kael and dragged him past the jeering crowd. 'Throw him through the gate, he is never to return to this ringfort,' continued Fincath as the guards took Kael beyond the doors of the great hall.

Fincath turned now to Latchna. 'You certainly seemed to be sent by fate. What causes such haste in you this night … and whose blood do you wear?'

Latchna, exhausted, gripped Fincath by the arm. 'The slave boat you await entered the estuary and sailed up the river, and all is not well,' he gasped. '… and this blood you see upon me is the blood of thieves.'

CHAPTER SEVEN

Ten days had passed since the boat had embarked from Norwic. Mule's stomach had taken five days to settle; from then on, he had been able to consume the meagre offerings of gruel and water supplied by the captain, Cenna.

Maewyn and Elowen now sat beside him, under the protection of the boat's awning as they had done for most of the sailing. The rigging above them creaked as the stiff breeze had the boat skipping over the waves. Now well into the Oceanus Hibernicus, the captain had instructed his men to stand on the prow looking for landfall.

Since threatening Maewyn on the first night, Osgar had restricted his aggression to glowering stares whenever Maewyn looked his way. However, this day—as he looked at the children who sat against the bulwark—he realised things were different. Today they would reach Hibernia and he intended to fix the mouthy whelp. He would also *see to* the girl. He had spent most of his time on the trip forming a plan; working out how he could gain satisfaction and revenge.

He had persuaded the captain to allow him to escort the slaves from the boat to the settlement, two miles inland, where agents of the cattle lord awaited their delivery. That's when he would kill the whelp; kill his big, stupid brother as well. The girl he would relish—take his time with. The captain didn't fully trust him, though, and had insisted that three other men would accompany him. But Osgar knew he was too clever for the fat oaf. The three men the captain had picked all owed him favours … they would turn a blind eye … even have a go at the girl themselves … even have a go at the boys—after him of course.

He'd tell Cenna the delivery had gone well, and then they'd be away at once. He knew the captain was eager to catch the favourable breeze that had started to blow. Once back at Norwic, it would take weeks for the news to reach Griff, and by then, he'd be well away.

He rolled a barrel of cheese towards the side of the boat, passing close to Mule as he did so.

'Belly's all right now is it, limp-brain?' he mocked in a childish voice. 'Maybe you're ready to add some salt to your diet—try this.' He placed his forefinger against his right nostril and hawked out a great, green globule of snot. It landed, elastic and vile, upon Mules foot, causing the boy to bring his hands to his mouth as he heaved up a flood of vomit.

Anticipating Maewyn's reaction, Osgar did not wait, but fell upon him at once—his fish knife held inches from his eye. 'Oh no you don't.' he snarled. 'You don't kick me in the balls this time, you little swine … but why are you so angry again? I just gave your brother his salt ration, that's all.'

Maewyn spluttered with rage, unable to free himself from Osgar's sinewy grasp. Elowen intervened. 'Don't give him cause to hurt you, Maewyn,' she urged, close to tears. 'He wants you to fight with him. It'll be over soon, and we'll be off the boat and away from him, and never have to see him again.'

Maewyn's eyes rolled madly towards Elowen as he continued to struggle. He returned his glare to Osgar. 'Let me go,' he snorted. 'Get off me, you bully.'

The shout *'Land in sight!'* came from the prow, but Osgar continued to grip Maewyn. 'It would be better if you listened to the pretty girl, it would. Like her says,' said Osric now dramatically affecting Elowen's distressed voice, *"It'll be over soon."* You can be sure of that. When we reach shore it *will* be over for you.'

Maewyn stopped struggling. Osgar shoved him away and stood up. He pointed a threatening finger at him. 'Now keep sat, till you're shouted for, and no cheek or I'll have your tongue with this knife.'

As Osgar smirked and walked away, Maewyn grabbed his goblet, leant over the side of the boat, and filled it with water. He sloshed the brine over Mules foot, sending Osgar's snot slithering away across the plank decking.

Elowen took Mules head in her arms and held him close. Both of them sniveled and wept whilst Maewyn, ignoring the instruction from Osgar who had gone to the stern, stood to observe the seascape. He was surprised to see that Hibernia was nearer than expected; green and flat it occupied the entire horizon.

'We'll be off this boat before nightfall,' he said, as he knelt before Elowen and Mule. 'Then we'll never see that bad egg again.'

'Maybe other bad eggs await us,' said Mule, as he wiped the sleeve of his tunic across his eyes. 'What if our new master is as bad as him?'

'No point in worrying about that until it happens,' said Maewyn. 'As long as we're together we stand a chance.'

Two hours later, their passage became calmer as the boat entered an inlet and sailed in the freshwaters of a wide river. On either side, the green land encroached ever nearer as the boat zigzagged upstream trying to catch the breeze. Cenna, the captain, stood on the prow, barking

96

instructions. All the crewmembers knew their task, and they furled the huge, square sail as soon as a great wooden quay came into sight. Then rowers took over, fore and aft, for the tricky maneuvering required to dock the boat.

Maewyn, Elowen and Mule knelt against the bulwark, arms folded across its top, as they watched the boat move slowly sideways towards the quay.

The dockworkers did not strike Maewyn as being particularly unusual. He hadn't known what to expect—had thought that maybe the people of Hibernia would be different, but the men who caught the ropes thrown to them by Cenna seemed ordinary to him. Their language, too, was similar to his own, although sounding strange and slightly muddled to his ears.

Great coils of rope hung over the stout wooden jetty and served to cushion the bump as the boat was finally steered adjacent to the dock. After further shouting and instruction from Cenna, the crew threw coils of thick rope to the men standing on the jetty, and these they tied to stubby capstans, thus docking the boat securely.

Ignored for the time being, the children leaned against the gunwale, fascinated as they watched the men at their work. First, the wooden gangplank was lowered down to span the narrow gap between dockside and boat. Then, the process of unloading commenced. Manhandled from the boat, the barrels and sacks of produce all bore their own individual mark, daubed at Norwic to match the mark of their purchaser. Men now approached Cenna, each carrying the mark of their masters. Once matched with the mark on the sacks or barrels, Cenna allowed the produce to be loaded onto open wagons. The unloading continued until midafternoon until the piles of cargo were gone. As the last of the wagons trundled away, the dockside stood empty and bare.

The boat, by now, was riding higher in the water, causing the gangplank to slope down to the jetty. Cenna, who stood on the dock below, now beckoned Maewyn, Elowen and Mule to leave boat.

Cenna looked to Osgar. 'Tie them by their hands,' he instructed. 'They are worth more than all the iron, cheese and grain we've just unloaded, and they go to the King of this province, so *do not* lose them. Do you think you can manage that?'

Osgar nodded, and Cenna pointed towards a track that wound up a small hill beside the dock. 'Just follow the track, do not leave it, and you will soon come to a small settlement. That's where you'll hand them over.'

He handed an intricately daubed parchment to Osgar. 'Give this to the buyer and he will give you an identical one in return. It's a sign known only to Griff and the King of this province.' Cenna took hold of Osgar's shoulders and looked him directly in the eyes, so near that their noses almost touched. 'Listen to me, Osgar,' he emphasized. *'Do not* hand over the slaves unless you receive an identical parchment in return from the King's buyer. I have to take the parchment back to Griff to show proof of sale or he'll have my balls for sweetbread.'

Osgar considered this. He would keep the original parchment, maybe roughen it up a little, and give it to Cenna when he returned. How would Cenna know it was not the Hibernian parchment? He was about to offer his assurance to Cenna, but the captain had not finished.

He still held Osgar in his grip as his tone took on an even greater intensity. 'Listen to me carefully now, man. *Do not* touch the goods. I know you have issues with the boy, but he must not arrive harmed. Moreover, the girl *must not be violated*. As I told you before her worth will be nothing if she is not a virgin. They *will* know, believe me. The first thing they'll do is check her purity.'

Cenna let go of Osgar and pointed to three other crewmembers who stood nearby. He prepared to dismiss Osgar. 'They will go with you,' he instructed. 'Now get on your way; I expect to see you back here well before nightfall.'

Osgar rubbed Cenna's grip out of the top of his arms and turned to his three companions. Exchanging a furtive, knowing look between themselves, they proceeded to bind the hands of Maewyn, Elowen, and Mule.

The Hibernian dock master owned a cart and heavy horse. A gift of grain and butter had secured the loan of it to Cenna for the day. Osgar took the reins, and sat in the cart's high wooden seat with two of the men. The children sat in the back of the cart alongside the remaining man.

Concerned, Maewyn looked at Elowen and Mule. Their condition had worsened after enduring ten, water-soaked, wind-tossed days. Mules ruddy chubbiness had gone. Now he sat gaunt and spare, his eyes dull and detached. Elowen's blond hair was lank and filthy, her dress torn and grubby. Her once-twinkling, mischievous eyes now held no hope. Like Mule, she had drawn into herself.

As for Maewyn; his feisty and defiant spark had been quelled to an ember, yet it still smoldered. A spark of such intensity would defy twenty sea journeys—twenty Osgars. As he considered their predicament, he realised their business with Osgar was not over. Why else would the man be so keen to take them to their new masters. He had seen the glance Osgar had given to the other three. He now feared the worst.

As he sat in the wagon with his arms around his brother and cousin, he watched the back of Osgar as he goaded the horse up the hill's winding track. Mentally, Maewyn cleaved the skull of the man; imagined he threw him off the cart and kicked the other men onto the ground.

Osgar felt pleased with himself. He had fooled Cenna and was now in control. As he crested the hill leading from the dock, the land unfurled and fell away before him. A mixture of heath, woods, and agriculture blanketed the landscape in an intricate collage of browns and greens.

A curling of smoke beyond the furthest wood, three miles away, indicated the location of the settlement where the exchange would happen. Except that it would not happen. Osgar did not intend to give up the children.

His first glance at the landscape showed it to be mostly empty land where he had already spotted a small wood, a mile distant, where he would have his fun with the slaves.

Although rutted and uneven, the road allowed for a steady passage, and soon they reached the wood. Here, Osgar guided the horse and cart into the tree cover away from the road.

Maewyn gripped Elowen's hand as the cart abruptly stopped.

Osgar turned to look at them. 'All this way and all that hardship,' he mocked, as his twisted smile fell short of his cold eyes. He turned to Mule. '… and all that puking,' he added with a cruel chuckle. He continued his taunt, now directing it towards Elowen 'Suffered much, haven't you, girl … and for what? For it all to end here—lying dead and defiled in a ditch.'

Maewyn tensed against his bindings and made to gain his feet, but the man in the cart had been expecting it and grabbed him around the shoulders. Elowen and Mule shrank against the wooden picket sides of the cart, their eyes wide with terror.

'Throw the cunt out, onto the ground,' barked Osgar to the man. 'I'll deal with him at once, and don't any of you get any ideas with the girl until I've done her first.' He jumped off the cart and took out his knife just as Maewyn hit the floor. Dazed, Maewyn viewed Osgar as a malevolent blur standing above him.

Unable to resist taunting him, Osgar displayed his knife to Maewyn. 'See this,' he promised. 'This is going to pluck out both your eyes, then your clever little tongue. Oh, that I could leave you like that to wander this land as a freak. But I can't risk you living to tell, or should I say *gabble*, your tale.'

Maewyn's awareness slowly returned, but he was too weak to resist now. He heard screams coming from the cart as the other men slapped Elowen and Mule into silence.

Ready to die now, Maewyn thought of his da, and compared him to the evil man who now knelt before him. His father was everything this man was not. His father was sweet natured … funny … caring. He held on to the thought of Bran—his beloved father—and the thought gave him comfort and peace as Osgar's knife approached his eyes.

Saeran Uí Dúnlainge had trouble sticking in his own skin, such was his anger and hatred towards Fincath mac Garrchu and his sons. They had defeated his army and killed two of his brothers. They had weakened his clan, almost to the point of total dismemberment. His frustrations boiled within him, born from the knowledge that he could not wreak immediate retribution upon them. He had to wait and allow his people to lick their wounds and this did not lie easily with him.

He rode with six of his men towards the docks, hoping he could negotiate a good price for the grain and other foodstuffs that were stored there. For the fiftieth time, Saeran cursed the sons of mac Garrchu for burning many of their storage huts to the ground.

To save time they had ridden through rough country that offered them a more direct route to the docks. Through field and forest, they had threaded their way, and before him now he could see the track that led to the sea.

His brother, Beccan, rode on ahead, having already reached the track, and Saeran became concerned when Beccan suddenly halted his pony's progress and deftly and quietly turned and returned to him.

'There are people in the grove—Saxon folk by the sound of them,' said Beccan. 'They ride in the cart from the dock. Taking slaves to Fincath's trading post up the track, I'll guess.'

Saeran quickly assessed the situation. An opportunity this, he thought, to get back somewhat at Fincath and his clan. The slaves would be valuable and desired by Fincath. If he could steal them, it would give him leverage with the man; allow him to negotiate for the return of the stolen cattle. He glanced at the four well-armed men behind him—all well proven and formidable.

'How many are they?' he asked Beccan.

'Four, I think. Though it was hard to tell, as I only glimpsed them briefly.'

Saeran set his pony to a trot. 'Follow me,' he said decisively. 'Kill all but the slaves.'

As Osgar knelt on top of Maewyn, he relished the pop that would come when his knife entered the eyeball of the all-too-clever British shit. Strangely, the boy had become calm … seemed to be at peace. Rather that the lad had mouthed at him, so he could hear his fancy words replaced with screams of mercy. That would be so good to hear—would almost be as fulfilling to him (give him almost as big a bulge in his pants) as the business with the girl which would follow.

Maewyn, who was ready for his life to end, arched his eyebrows in utter surprise when Osgars malevolent, ugly head flew from his shoulders, as Saeran's sword, wielded with all the hate and power of a frustrated man who had lived for days under the shadow of humiliating defeat, ended Osgar's vicious ponderings and his life.

Warm blood squirted from the neck as his body fell upon Maewyn. Repulsed, he pushed the body away, as the cadaver's heart continued to briefly pump, causing a slowly abating flow of blood to escape from the stump of his neck.

He wiped the greasy blood off his hands and onto the ground, its metallic stink causing him to retch. Frantic activity was happening around him as Saeran and his men quickly dispatched the other Saxons.

Utterly surprised, they put up little resistance. Two men fell to spears hurled with savage force from close range. Dragged from the cart, the remaining man met Beccan's sword thrust with his open, gasping mouth — the sword, slick with gore, pushing an amalgam of skull and scalp from the back of his head as it emerged.

Beccan now dragged Maewyn from the floor and threw him into the cart where he landed in a heap. Still bound by their hands, Mule and Elowen were astonished to the point of silence as Maewyn joined them.

Saeran lifted Osgar's head by its hair and looked with disdain at its twisted features before throwing it into the trees. 'Drag their bodies into the shrub cover,' he ordered. 'And good work, all of you.'

Saeran assessed the situation. Things had changed. They still needed grain from the docks, but also needed to get back safely to his tuath with the captives. He was aware that travelling back through the rough country would be hard work with two wagons, but it was the only way. Without doubt, Fincath would be livid and send riders to look for the slaves, but he would search the roads first and that would give them time, because Fincath had no way of knowing who had stolen them. That he'd find out later, when they offered him a deal.

Elowen looked with alarm at Maewyn. A great smear of blood covered him from neck to waist. 'Don't worry,' he reassured her when seeing her concern. 'It's not my blood, it's Osgar's.'

Relieved, Elowen sighed. 'We have new masters it seems,' she whispered, still unsure if she should be talking. 'They must want us alive or we'd be in the bushes now with the others.'

'Shh!' said Maewyn, as Saeran came to them.

Saeran rested his arms on top of the picket walls of the cart as he looked at them. Maewyn saw a man who was not easy to read; large in frame with an almost feminine face. He seemed, nevertheless, stern and uncompromising.

'You will stay in the cart unless I tell you to get down,' he said with quiet authority. 'Do you understand me?'

The three of them nodded, unsure of how to take this man with the strange accent.

Satisfied, Saeran turned to his brother. 'Beccan, take two others to the docks and get the grain. I'll await you here and make sure we're not disturbed or found until you get back.'

Three hours passed, during which Saeran and his other two men took turns watching the nearby track for sign of other travellers. None came until Beccan trundled over the rise of the hill driving another cart—this one filled with grain.

After instructions from Saeran, a man took the reins of the cart containing the children, and steered it through the trees and onto rough ground away from the track. Beccan followed with his cart. Saeran and the remaining men followed behind—two ponies now spare and secured to the other mounts.

Mule looked at Elowen as the cart bounced and swayed over ruts and tussocks. 'It's almost as bad as the boat,' he moaned. 'I'd give anything to just be allowed to walk on my own two feet again.'

'At least we don't have to put up with Osgar,' said Elowen, her voice soft with affection for Mule. 'And you now have a strong stomach after your time on the boat.'

Two hours of bumpy passage passed before the sun began to dip below the tree line. Weary from a heavy day of travel and conflict, Saeran decided it was time to strike camp. He allowed a low fire to comfort them and the six Hibernian warriors sat around it talking quietly as Maewyn, Elowen and Mule sat within the darkness of the cart. Given hard strips of dried meat to chew on by one of the men, they still had their hands bound before them as they fed.

The men ate beside the fire, and when the hour grew late settled down beside it. Soon the discordant sound of varied snoring was audible to the children in the cart. Bound now by their ankles as well as their arms, they prepared to spend an uncomfortable night on the wooden floor of the wagon. Saeran had gone quickly to sleep; confident the children were going nowhere. One man took watch at the edge of the encampment.

Mule shifted uncomfortably in the back of the wagon as Maewyn got to his knees to look over the edge of its boarded sides. 'The guard walks to the woods two hundred paces away, then walks back here to check on us,' he said to Mule, who had decided to sit against the side of the wagon in an effort to ease his discomfort.

'So what?' said Mule. 'He's hardly likely to find us gone is he?'

Maewyn looked to the five men lying around the fire. Convinced they were asleep, he turned to Mule. 'Look at my feet,' he said.

Mule's eyes grew big, his mouth taking on an astonished O shape, as he saw that Maewyn's feet were free of the binding that had secured them earlier. He looked to Maewyn's bound hands and saw that he held a knife.

Elowen had been lying quietly, listening to the exchange between Maewyn and Mule. She noticed the knife at the same time as Mule. She raised herself up on one elbow—her whisper loaded with alarm. 'What are you doing with that? If the men catch you with it, they'll skin us with it. Put it—'

'Quiet' hissed Maewyn. 'The man comes towards us again. Lie down and pretend to sleep.'

Upon reaching the wagon, the guard looked over the side. Satisfied the children slept, he turned to walk back to the edge of the clearing.

Maewyn opened one eye, confident the guard had left them. A minute passed before he again knelt in the wagon and satisfied himself the guard was a safe distance away. Elowen and Mule were immediately alert, waiting for Maewyn to enlighten them further.

He still held the knife as he turned to them. 'It was Osgar's' he explained. 'When he dropped on me after he lost his head, his knife fell to the ground beside me so I shoved it down my britches. The others were too busy with the fight to notice it.'

'What are you going to do now then?' asked Mule. '*Kill* them all like da would have done?'

Elowen's face took on a look of alarm as she looked to Maewyn, hoping he was not about to try anything that would leave them all dead.

'No silly!' said Maewyn as he moved to Elowen and started to slice through the bindings on her hands. 'We're not going to fight them. We're going to escape!' he handed the knife to Elowen. 'Now me,' he said.

Elowen shakily complied, leaving Maewyn completely unbound. He cut free Mule and Elowen. 'Lie down, as if you're still tied up,' he said, as the guard approached.

Again, the Hibernian looked into the wagon. Again, he was satisfied the children slept. He walked back to the trees.

'It won't work,' whispered Elowen as soon as the guard was out of earshot. 'We only have the time it takes for the man to come back to the wagon to get away. They'll catch us before we've gone a hundred paces.'

'Not even that long,' said Mule. 'He's coming back again already. He must know something.'

The guard, Cronan, lost in his thoughts as he patrolled the space between the cart and the woodland edge, had suddenly realised that his time for sleep had come. He walked to the snoring men by the fire, knelt beside Beccan, and shook him by the shoulder. 'Your turn, Bec,' he said. 'Thanks for keeping my place warm.'

Beccan blinked as his sleep-befuddled brain attempted to gain its bearings. After wiping the dribble from his mouth, he wearily gained his feet.

'How are the captives?' he yawned, as he rubbed the sleep from his eyes

'Sleeping as deeply as *you* were a moment ago,' said Cronan as he lowered himself into Beccan's vacated, warm place by the fire. 'And trussed up like chickens for the roast.'

Beccan scratched his crotch, then stretched his arms— elbows uppermost, fists on chest. He went to check the children for himself. Peering into the darkness inside the cart, he heard rhythmic, heavy breathing. He thought about testing the twine he had secured the children with earlier, but a noise, a distance away near to the trees, commanded his attention.

When reaching the trees, he peered into the darkness, alert for further sounds. The silence failed to allay his unease. He decided to settle against a tree, satisfied he could view the distant cart from there as well as guarding against any possible ingress into the camp.

Maewyn had rolled onto his belly to peer through the slats in the cart. 'This one's not walking around,' he said. 'Settled against a tree he has, and the other one's snoring like a pig already.' He looked at Elowen and Mule. 'If we're going to get away, now's the time.'

'But even if we manage to get away, where will we go and how will we live?' asked Elowen, anxiously.

Now infused with urgency, Maewyn had raised himself onto his elbows. 'I don't know, but anything would be better than what could happen to us as slaves. We don't know if these people are any better than Osgar, and look what *he* tried to do to us.'

Elowen still wavered, but Mule broke in. 'I want to go back home,' he stammered, close now to tears. 'If staying in the cart means we can't go back home, then I think we should get out of it.'

Maewyn sat up now and looked towards Beccan, then returned his gaze to Elowen His voice betrayed a quiver of emotion as his desperation grew. 'Please girl, it's our only chance. The guard seems settled over there. Come on now. Follow me over the back of the cart. Please … do it for me.'

A tear painted a white tracery down Elowen's grubby cheek as she witnessed Maewyn fighting to keep it together. After a further pause, she relented as she realised he was their only hope—if *he* broke there would be no hope.

'Yes, we'll go, then. But do it now before I have time to think about it,' she said, as her heart hammered, and she realised they were approaching the point of no return.

After checking they were unobserved, Maewyn slipped quietly over the back of the cart, followed by Mule. Elowen was the last to leave, and there they stood: frozen.

Maewyn was the first to act. 'Grab my shirt and don't let go,' he said to Mule. 'And you, Elowen, grab Mules shirt. We can't allow ourselves to wander in this darkness. That would be the end of it.'

He led them away from the camp keeping the cart between them and the men. Every crack and rustle in the woods caused them to tense with fear, but no chase followed. Two hours, then three passed. They saw no one.

'The sky lightens,' said Elowen as they took their first rest against a bank of crispy, dead bracken. 'They must know we've gone by now.'

'The woods are still quiet though', reassured Maewyn. 'The land here's tricky and confusing. We can only hope they've gone off on the wrong trail. Now we must—'

'Smoke! Beyond the trees over there!' interrupted Mule with his boyish fervor. His good eyes had spotted a curl of grey in the distance. 'Let's go and see where it comes from. Maybe there're good folk there. Folk who will help us for a change.'

Maewyn pondered their options. He hadn't thought much about what they would actually do after getting away from the men. He knew it would be daylight soon. Then they must hide. They had to find food and water, or whoever found them would discover only bones and shreds of clothing. They needed help, he knew that now, but how was he supposed to know if people were good or bad? Maybe if they got close to the source of the fire they could watch from a distance and decide what to do.

He stood up. Then Mule took his offered hand and Maewyn pulled him to his feet. 'Come on then, we'll move as close as possible, and spy on whoever burns the fire. As long as we're quiet we should be safe.'

The monastery sat in a secluded peaceful valley a day's ride away from the main track to the coast. Several huts provided accommodation for the Monks. Beside the huts, a guesthouse loomed large and welcoming—its thatched roof allowing an outpouring of smoke from the warming fire that burned within.

Surrounding the guesthouse, and similar in construction to it, were other buildings of varied size and function: a scriptorium for copying, a refectory and kitchen, a library, a smithy, a kiln, a church, and two barns. The barns held a goodly quantity of grain; the stubbled, fallow fields nearby having provided a fine harvest. Huge ponds, used for breeding fish, covered the rest of the Monastery grounds.

The first monks had arrived in Hibernia decades earlier from mainland Europe. As Christians, they had fled when the heathen hordes (Vandals, Sueves, and Alans) had raided Gaul and other areas. Since then, native Hibernians had swelled the ranks of the clergy, until a peaceful religious community had grown to thrive in the quiet valley.

Able to manufacture ironwork and pottery, the monks were useful suppliers of high status goods. This usefulness was not lost upon the heathen cattle lords who knew them to be no threat and left them alone to live their lives in the valley.

Just like every day since he had come to Hibernia from Gaul (now fifteen years gone), Rodric had risen at first light—his job to milk the small herd of cows. The cattle were kept for the sole purposes of providing milk—the eating of four legged creatures being strictly forbidden. Ten of them now ruminated in a building next to the barn where they awaited his attendance. As ever, though, he intended to take his walk around the monastery's extensive grounds before he saw to the cows. But first things first, and the first thing he had to do was pray. Matins was the first of seven pray session during the day. As Rodric walked towards the small church, he met a freckled, ginger-haired youth. 'Is it to be Latin or Celtic this morning, Ingomer?' asked Rodric, as a twinkle glittered in his laughter-creased eyes.

Recently ordained, Ingomer still struggled with his pronouncement of Latin words, much to the amusement of Rodric and the other monks. He grinned mischievously. 'Merda, caco, pissio,' he said. 'How's that for Latin this fine morning?'

'I'd stick to Celtic if I were you,' said Rodric, trying not to laugh. 'If the Bishop hears you speaking such words he'll have you flogged.'

Their talk continued in the same vein, with much laughter and teasing, until reaching the church.

Ingomer ran his flat hand down his face, as if wiping away his smile, just as they entered the church. The result was a suitably pious expression, which made Rodric want to laugh again. With his own smile suppressed but still playing at the corners of his mouth, he entered the church with Ingomer. Twenty minutes of sombre chanting later, Rodric emerged into a brighter day and set off on his walk.

His sandals scuffed through a field of stubble as he made his way to his favorite place: a small wood that overlooked the grounds. Here the morning birdsong was a treat to behold. Badgers also played in the wood, especially at dawn or dusk, and sometimes he would catch a fleeting glimpse of the old dog fox that patrolled the area.

As he approached the wood, he judged the direction of the breeze and decided to walk around the edge of the field. This would leave him upwind from the badgers. Maybe he would then have the chance to watch them a while.

He entered the wood, treading quietly, and was astonished to see, not badgers, but three children. Unaware of his presence, the children lay on their stomachs on a banking overlooking the monastery grounds.

Rodric was unsure, at first, what to do. He didn't want to frighten them. By the look of their torn rags and generally unkempt and filthy disposition, they would run like frightened rabbits if he did that. Yet he couldn't leave them. How could he? Wasn't Jesus supposed to care for his flock? …and wasn't he a disciple of the Lord? Wasn't he supposed to do as Jesus would?

His concern grew as he neared them and got a closer look at their condition. As he recalled the scriptures, he found himself becoming angry. What did the bible say about any man who would hurt a child? *It would be better for him if a millstone was hung around his neck and he was cast into the sea.*

He made his decision and spoke to them. 'Do not run, I will not hurt you. I am a friend,' he said in Celtic, keeping his tone as calm and unthreatening as he could.

Maewyn was on his feet at once, his face shocked and fearful as he quickly assessed Rodric. Before him stood a man who wore the long habit of a monk, tied at the waist with a rope. A Celtic cross rested at his breast, suspended from a cord around his neck. In comparison to the brutes they had met with recently, this man looked benign and genteel. His silver hair was fine and shaved from ear to ear in a Celtic tonsure, allowing long silver strands to flow down the back of his head to his shoulders. His features were fine-boned and handsome. Elowen and Mule now stood beside Maewyn, both of them as gawking and as indecisive as he.

'My name is Rodric,' continued the monk. 'My lord is Jesus Christ and he instructs that I can do naught but well to fellow man. Therefore, you need not fear me. I am here to help you.'

Elowen started to weep, and in total abandon born from extreme weariness, she walked over to Rodric. Too tired to ponder further over the matter, she sobbed: 'We have been through so much … please help us … we have no one now in this world.'

Rodric took Elowen in his arms. Mule joined them and Rodric embraced them both.

Maewyn, weeping himself now, fell to his knees. Finally he could rest.

CHAPTER EIGHT

'We need to ride on till first light, then find a spot to hide in during the day!' shouted Dominic as he rode his horse at speed down the Roman road.

Augustus shouted back as he held on to the girl before him. 'That won't be long; dawn already touches the sky to the east!'

Flint rode behind, reassuring the boy who rode with him. 'Hold tight lad,' he said. 'You'll come to no harm if you just hold tight.'

Murdoc, who rode with the remaining boy, similarly reassured him as he clung to his horse's mane.

'We'll chance the road until the sun rises,' Dominic said. 'Then we take cover and talk about what to do next.'

But Dominic was *already* working on a plan. Finding the wrong children had changed things considerably, but leaving them at the mercy of the slave traders had been unthinkable to them all. After finding them, a hurried, conversation had taken place in the wagon, and they had decided to leave at once *with* them.

Withred, who rode at the rear of the group, cast an anxious glance behind him, aware that riders on fresh horses would catch them before long. He had no way of knowing what advantage they had over their pursuers in terms of distance, but knew their own horses had to be close to exhaustion now. 'I think we should go to cover,' he shouted to Dominic. 'The horses need to be rested and we have put a goodly distance between us and the town.'

'Two more miles,' insisted Dominic as they passed a milestone in the road. He pulled the rein of his horse slowing it to a trot, allowing Withred to ride alongside him. 'There's not enough cover here,' he said breathlessly, 'but if I recall correctly, trees meet the track just a couple of miles further on.'

As they continued at a lesser pace, allowing the horses to regain their stamina, the trees started to encroach towards the road. At a point where a stony path led from the road, Dominic halted.

'This is the best place to leave,' he explained. 'The horses' hoof prints won't be seen by any tracker if we guide the mounts over the stones.' He pointed to the rough scrubland that ran to the horizon. 'The land here looks broken and complicated. Unfarmed and unpeopled too, I guess. There should be plenty of dips and hollows to hide in.'

They left the road over the stone path as Dominic had instructed. Once through to the rougher ground beyond, Dominic dismounted and returned to the stony path. Although unlikely that men riding at speed would notice any disturbance in the stones, he knew that a skilled tracker could read the signs if attentive enough. After replacing a few stones and satisfying himself he had covered their tracks as best he could, he returned to the others.

One hour later, after Dominic had led them on a winding and intricate path through the scrubland, they found a water meadow where grass and reeds grew to shoulder height. Here, they settled on a dry bump in the ground, allowing the ponies to walk in the water, where they drank and grazed from the lush grasses.

While the others explored the land beside the meadow to ensure its safety, the children settled down together. Murdoc stayed back to sit beside them. It was the first time he had been able to study them properly in the light, and he saw that many days of hardship and fatigue had taken its toll upon them. Their faces were stark and pale as they looked at him.

He smiled, wishing to put them at ease. 'What are your names?' he asked. 'We've hardly had time to talk since we fled from the town.'

The girl spoke first, self-consciously pulling the swirl of filthy matted hair from her pretty face, as she looked shyly at Murdoc.

'My name's Cathryn but people call me Cate,' she said in a small voice. 'The boys are my brothers. Art and Ula are their names. Art is the fair haired one.'

He smiled at the brothers, who were scrawny but of a similar size. *Twins, but not identical*, he thought. The boys sat huddled together, still nervous, and reluctant yet to accept Murdoc, who turned his attention back to Cate.

'I think there's a very pretty girl under all that dirt,' he said, as he took Cate's hand. 'My own girl, Ceola, is just a little younger than you, and I know you would get on well with her.' As Cate blushed at the attention, Murdoc noticed that the fair-haired boy was staring at his bow, which still hung from his shoulders.

Murdoc smiled and removed the bow. Crafted by Dominic, it was recurved and powerful, and capable of delivering arrows at high velocity.

He handed the bow to the boy. 'Feel how light it is, lad,' he said. 'One day you may carry a bow such as this.'

Art took the bow and twanged the string. His brother Ula now placed his hand on the bow, feeling its smooth tactile lines.

'They used spears to kill father and mother,' said Ula.

'And an ax to kill grandfather,' said Art.

Cate had moved close to them and there they all sat, arms entwined, as they looked at Murdoc, their eyes blank.

Was no one spared from your village?' asked Murdoc, moved by the horrible simplicity of the boys' statement.

'We didn't live in a village,' said Cate. 'We lived in a hut, all together, beside the great forest. Just our family. Mother, father, we children, and grandfather—just the six of us. We kept a few pigs and an ox and grew grain in a field.'

Murdoc did not know what to say. He was reluctant to ask Cate or the boys for more details; details that would make them live their ordeal again. He could guess enough for now. No doubt, Griff's scout had spotted the children and identified them as ripe for Hibernia. The adults were expendable of course—more so if they had put up a fight. Murdoc looked at the children and instinctively knew the parents and grandparent *must* have fought to protect the dear children that sat before him now.

Changing the subject from the killing, Murdoc asked. 'Did you live on the eastward side of the great forest?'

'If that's the side nearest to the sea, then yes we did,' said Cate, who seemed most at ease with Murdoc.

Murdoc laughed, delighted. 'I also lived beside the great forest, nearest to the shore. And Dominic—the man who led us from the town—he actually lived *inside* the forest for ten years'

Art and Ula looked at each other in wonderment upon hearing this. Ula in particular seemed awestruck. 'How was he not eaten alive?' he asked.

'Because he owns a bow like mine, and by God he can use it,' beamed Murdoc, encouraged by the gathering curiosity and confidence of the children. 'Here he comes now. He can tell you about his life himself.' He stood up as Dominic and the others returned.

Murdoc told Dominic's group the little he knew about the children. After hearing the account, Dominic slumped wearily to the ground, followed by Augustus and Flint. 'Food for thought,' he said, as he winked at the children, 'but now is the time for sleep. All of us need to rest now in readiness for the toil of the night to come.'

'I'll take first watch, then,' said Withred. 'I'm nowhere near to sleep just yet.'

Seven hours later, one hour before dusk, all had slept— some fitfully, some deeply—but all now were awake and attentive to Dominic. 'There is much to discuss,' he said. Now he addressed Murdoc directly. 'This morning when you were talking to the children the rest of us made sure this place was secure and we discussed where we go from here. I'll explain now.'

With a twig, he drew a map on the dusty ground. He had seen maps of Britannia when scouting for the Romans decades earlier and carried the image in his head. He traced a rough outline of southeast Britannia and drew an X upon it.

'By my guess we are here, just over a day's travel from Norwic.' He drew a large circle to the southwest of the X. 'And here, lies the great forest—my home for ten years.'

He drew a line a distance away from the east coast, running parallel to it. He stabbed at it. 'That's the road we travelled upon on our outward journey. It would undoubtedly be the quickest route back to Brythonfort, but this morning set me thinking. We need to avoid the road, even at night.   Therefore, it makes sense to go through the forest. Use it as a shortcut. It's rough ground, though, and although a more direct route, it will add to our journey time. That's why we used the road on our outward journey when speed was essential.'

Reminded of the reason for their journey, Murdoc looked at Flint, who had remained quiet since leaving Norwic. How he was coping with not rescuing his family, he could only guess.

Dominic continued. 'As you all know, I'm familiar with most of the forest and can lead us through it via the old Roman track that penetrates it. On the other side lies the town of Aebbeduna and there we can meet up with Flint's merchant friend and renew our supplies.

'After Aebbeduna, we can get back onto the old Roman road that runs nearby. It will take us westward to Brythonfort and the end of the journey for some.' He paused and looked at Flint. 'But not for all,' he added.

Flint now spoke for the first time about the failure of the mission. 'Though I'm heartened to have saved these children,' he began, as he nodded towards Cate, Art and Ula who sat attentive and looking at Dominic's dusty map, 'I'm devastated not to have got my brothers and niece back. No more boats were to sail to Hibernia from Norwic after the one that was in port, Griff himself told us that. My brothers and niece must have been on the boat that sailed two days before we got to Norwic.'

'And that leaves us with the thorny problem of how to get to Hibernia,' commented Augustus delicately. 'Because this is not over with, is it Flint?'

Flint shook his head defiantly. 'This will never be over until I see them again.'

'So how do we get to Hibernia?' asked Augustus. 'I say *we* because I intend to go with you, even if I have to swim.'

Flint looked fondly at Augustus. 'I know you would, my friend, but hopefully there'll be no need for that. No … I've been thinking about it; we can sail to Hibernia from the western shore, and the man who can help us is a Hibernian.'

'I take it you speak of Guertepir,' Dominic said. 'In the kingdom of Dyfed on the western peninsula.'

'You also know of him then?' asked Flint, surprised.

'Better than that, I've met him. When scouting for Rome, I had occasion to go to Dyfed. Guertepir was friends with Rome. They left him alone as long as he kept the region quiet. His great grandfather, a man named Eochiad, had been the first to come from Hibernia, some seventy years gone. For a quieter life maybe, or at the invitation of the Romans, I'm not sure of the reason. Anyway, his tribe—the Desi—are long settled and live in a ring fort beside a river close to the sea.'

Flint was encouraged by Dominic's revelation. 'That's so useful,' he enthused. 'If you know the man it should make our job of procuring a boat and information from him much easier. He's had contact with Arthur in the past and that was to be my touchstone to him, but this is much better.'

'The man can be a tetchy, awkward bastard,' Dominic said. 'But I'll help you with him—even travel to Hibernia with you.' He turned his attention back to the ground map. 'But first we must get back to Brythonfort to resupply, and by my guess that will take another eleven days. The forest offers a shortcut, but our travel through it will be much slower than the road.'

'Twelve days in total, then, from Norwic,' said Flint, frowning. 'Then eight days from Brythonfort to Dyfed and our meeting with Guertepir.'

'Yes, and that's if all goes well,' Dominic said, 'but now we must prepare to leave. We can chance one more night on the road and that should bring us to the forest.'

They left the water meadows and made their way back to the road, but when only fifty paces away, the sound of approaching riders came to them.

Dominic was onto it at once. 'Into that hollow,' he snapped, pointing to a deep depression a short distance away.

Quickly, they dropped into the shrubby depression, out of sight of the road. Looking at his companions as his pony stamped beneath him, Dominic pointed behind, his expression advising, *Get ready to run for it.* Augustus, nodded his understanding, then gave a shushing gesture to Cate who sat with him on his pony.

Withred, though, had dismounted and was watching the road, careful to remain hidden. 'Twelve of them, at a guess … looks like…' He tensed and his hand went to his sword. His tone now whispered and urgent. 'Nobody move, don't even breath, they've stopped near the track.'

He watched as the leading rider, probably the tracker, dismounted and examined the stony path looking for signs of passage. The man looked towards them, thoughtfully tossing a stone from hand to hand.

Withred had begun to shake as his adrenalin surged. 'Get ready to fight,' he said as he withdrew his sword. 'Dom … help the children down and take them beyond this hollow. The place will be a bloodbath soon.'

Withred continued to watch the Saxon group as Dominic led the children away. Back at the stony path, the tracker still looked unsure. He spoke to the nearest man mounted, probably the leader of the group. After a brief discussion, the tracker threw the stone back onto the path, then after taking one last look into the wilderness beyond the road, he mounted his pony and rode away, followed by the other nine riders.

When Dominic returned, Withred had sheathed his sword. 'That, friend, was too close for comfort,' he said. 'Now we need to let them get further up the track before we set off. They'll camp soon, now the light's failing.'

In the glow of the moon, they made good progress, until one hour into their journey they spotted the glow of a campfire ahead. Following Dominic, they flanked the encampment, before rejoining the road one mile beyond it. For the rest of that night, the woods encroached ever thicker around them as they made steady progress away from the Saxon camp. One hour before dawn, Dominic noticed a flat bed of sandstone abutting the road.

He turned to Withred. 'This looks like a good place to leave. We'll leave no prints here, and once in the forest we'll be gone from them.'

The group stopped. Dominic addressed them all. 'Some of you know the forest,' he said, 'so I've no need to tell you that the going gets tougher from here on. As long as you always follow me and listen to what I have to say, all should be well.'

He turned and rode into the shadow of the trees. Murdoc, who rode at the back, took one last look up the road. He sighed and entered the forest, ready for five days of hard slog.

As he picked his way through a tangle of brambles, Dominic turned to Augustus who now rode with the boy, Ula. 'We need to travel in the daytime from here onwards,' he said. 'Night travel is not possible in the forest as you well know.'

'I reckon the chasing group will be rousing by now, and getting ready to continue the hunt,' said Augustus. 'I know we're all tired, but don't you think it would be better if we continued for the rest of the day and kept our distance ahead of them?'

'Undoubtedly,' agreed Dominic. 'A day's travel will get me to forest I'm more familiar with. From then on we'll have the advantage over them.'

'Tonight we'll sleep well then,' said Withred, who was in earshot, riding behind. 'A night followed by a day in the saddle is enough to put any man into a dead sleep.'

It took them all of the morning to get through the great banks of bramble and nettle on the edge of the forest. The demanding passage hampered their progress, and it was past noon before the going became easier for them, having reached a colony of beech with little undergrowth.

Here they stopped and ate a sparing meal, whilst the horses grazed nearby. When satisfied the horses had recovered some of their stamina, the company resumed their journey and continued through the afternoon.

Two hours before dusk, they came upon a great tangle of bracken that grew profusely in a part of the forest that undulated and dipped, but was relatively free of tree cover.

Dominic led them into one of the deep troughs of bracken. 'Enough is enough,' he said, as he wearily dismounted to stand knee-high in the vegetation. 'Here's as good a place as any to rest up for the night. We're unsighted here and there's water nearby, so we may as well stop.'

'It's unlikely we're being followed now, anyway,' said Withred. 'We made no prints when we left the road.'

Augustus stood beside his horse and lifted Ula down. Cate and Art followed as he took them from Murdoc and Flint's mount. He smiled at the twins as they stood by the bracken. Fondly, he crouched down and touched Cate's cheek. He nodded towards a bracken couch nearby. 'A nice springy bed for three little ducklings,' he chuckled.

As her brothers joined her, Cate put her arms around them and fell backwards into the bracken. She smiled up at Augustus and loved what she saw in the man. Enormous and jovial, he made her feel safe. The other men seemed kind enough, but their stern bearing and single-mindedness still frightened her somewhat.

Augustus, though, always had an amused twinkle in his eye and looked anything but strict to her. She had heard him teasing the other men, heard him laugh his big booming laugh, and could not help but like him. So she was glad when he sat beside her and her brothers in the bracken and began to laugh and joke with *them*.

Murdoc had already dismounted and was pulling the day's accumulated vegetation from his horse's girdle and harness. He still wore the fine tunic he had donned two days earlier when posing as a merchant in Norwic. 'Fine dandies we all make,' he said as he pulled off his tunic and routed through his saddle pack for a shirt better suited to the woods. 'Not sure it's right for four more days riding through this undergrowth though.'

Flint stood beside him. Having stripped his own horse of its harness, reins and girdle, he wiped its withers down with a cloth wetted from the nearby stream. The horse shook—shivering with pleasure as the cool water ran down its withers.

'I could do with a bit of this myself,' Flint said. 'It must feel good to the horses to get the heavy tack off them. Guilt bronze tack is as bad for *them* as embroidered tunics are for *us* in this forest.'

Murdoc unbuckled the harness from his horse. 'Pity we didn't have time to get this fancy stuff off them before we left Norwic.' He paused and examined the harness, frowning. 'Although it seems my horse has already shook one of its cheek ornaments off its bridle.' He held the bridle up. One of the guilt bronzes had gone.

Dominic stopped sorting through his kit and looked at the harness. *Please let it have dropped into the bracken,* he thought.

CHAPTER NINE

One day earlier, just before dawn, Griff had blistered with rage. His hut on the edge of town was small but well equipped. Having no wish to rub shoulders with the scum in his brothel, he used the hut for his overnight stays in Norwic. Now he smashed through it, upturning a table and raging at the cowering man who had brought him the news of the theft of his slaves.

He filled a goblet with wine and shakily lifted it to his lips. 'Fucking imbeciles!' he said, as his wrath exploded again. He threw the goblet at the wall and grabbed the man before him. 'They could have a full night's lead on us. Why do you bring me this news now? Was no one checking on them?'

Bryce, a sailor from the boat, silently cursed the captain for sending him to break the bad news to Griff. Nothing he had to say could assuage Griff's anger. He nervously eyed the glowering dogs that stood behind Griff. 'Someone killed the man sent to check on them,' he sputtered. 'Broke his neck they did. Must have been a giant of a man.'

Griff shook his head in incredulity. 'And so he was left lying dead all night. Did no one notice he was missing?' Before Bryce could reply, Griff raged on, jabbing his finger at his own head as if a great truth had just dawned on him. 'No, no … of course … nobody would notice he was missing because you'd all be fucking drunk as usual. Last night in port and you all get shitfaced. How could I forget that!'

Bryce shifted uncomfortably and looked at the floor. He looked up, now eager to please, as his one bit of good news occurred to him. 'The old women were caught though,' he said. 'They had hardly got out of town when they were recaptured by Ranulf's group returning to the town from the north.'

Griff looked at Bryce, his searing gaze forcing the man to look down at his shoes again. This time Griff positively hissed at him. 'So I lose the children, lose the gold of their worth, and you try to bolster me with news that you have found me a pile of fucking dog meat?'

Unnerved by Griff's sibilance, Bryce gave him a frightened little nod of affirmation, liking his new tone even less than his earlier ranting.

Griff pushed him to the door, his tone now determined and businesslike. 'Right ... fuck off ... get out, and tell your captain I'll see *him* later. You say that Ranulf has returned. Get him to me now.'

'Gone?' said Ranulf, as Griff told him the news a little time later. They stood outside Griff's brothel as the sky began to lighten. Ranulf held a tankard of strong ale. 'This was to be my nightcap, or should I say daycap,' he grumbled. 'The men will not be happy. They've got their minds set on whoring, then sleeping through the day. It was bad enough I asked them to ride through the night, but a day of leisure here today appealed to them. Now I have to tell them to get back on their ponies and set off on a chase.'

'It's a pity your night ride didn't come up from the south,' grumbled Griff. 'You'd have come upon the thieving cunts who took the children, but at least that tells us they took the southern road towards Camulodunum.' He weighed a purse of gold coin in his hand. 'This is for you and the men. It should make it easier for you to drag them from their flopsies. It's a quarter the worth of the children. Another quarter awaits you if you return with them.'

Ranulf took the coin. 'Have you any idea who took them? How many men can we expect to engage?'

'Just five of them, but don't be fooled, I spoke to them yesterday. Said they were buyers for slaves, but I should've known. They looked rugged and vicious. Their features shaped more by combat than trade. Be complacent at your peril, Ranulf, they've already killed in Norwic.'

Irvin, Ranulf's British tracker, joined them. Griff told him the news. 'Ten men, including Ranulf and me, should be enough,' he advised. 'That gives us sufficient advantage in numbers and rapid mobility.'

'Get volunteers,' said Ranulf as he looked towards the brothel. 'The gold-hungry ones will soon drag themselves from their whores.'

One hour later, Ranulf, Irvin and eight other men, all lightly provisioned, bade their leave of Griff.

'We may be half a day behind from what Griff told us,' said Irvin as he rode at the front with Ranulf. 'I can't see them travelling through the day, though. This road runs through Camulodunum all the way to Londinium. It's too dangerous for them, so we must look for signs where they left the road. That's how we'll catch them. If they lie up today, we should be near to them by the time we rest up tonight.'

They witnessed neither sign nor sight of the fugitives that day, until one hour before dusk when Irvine's finely tuned eye spotted a disturbance on a stony track that led from the road.

He held up his hand to stop the men, then dismounted and stooped to examine the track.

Ranulf looked hopefully at him. 'Found something?'

Irvine picked up a stone from the track, a contemplative frown creasing his forehead. 'Maybe,' he mused, as he stood to look at the wild land beyond the road. After a moment assessing the probabilities, he threw the stone back onto the track. 'Probably a deer kicked over a few stones,' he said as he mounted his pony. 'A group of riders would have disturbed the ground more.'

Ranulf pony continued to stamp and snort as Irvine made to continue up the road. 'We need to stop soon,' he said. 'This pony has had enough. It needs to rest and graze. The trouble is they travel when we sleep, and we travel when they sleep.'

'I guess that'll change as soon as they leave the track,' said Irvine. 'They'll have no need to hide during the day if they travel through the forest, and it's my guess that's their intention. Where they head for, I've no idea, but the forest will conceal them, whether they head directly through it or follow its edge.'

'They'll reach the forest some time tonight, we'll reach it tomorrow,' said Ranulf. 'We have to be up at first light and find their entry point. I reckon they'll continue to travel through the day to keep well ahead of us. That'll tire and slow them. Tomorrow should see us gain ground.'

Irvine took the lead the next morning and carefully scanned the scrub on the forest side of the road looking for signs of disturbance. Sometimes he would dismount and walk a good distance from the path. Then he would stoop and scrutinize any vegetation that grew a distance away from the road looking for any signs of passage.

Ranulf and the other eight men followed Irvine's lead, but scanned the trail *beside* the road. 'What happens if we don't find their tracks between here and Camulodunum?' asked Ranulf. 'Does that mean they're sticking to the road?'

Irvine was certain that was not the case. 'No, that would be madness,' he said, as the sound of riders had them looking up the road. He nodded towards the approaching riders, '… and *that's* why,' he added.

A returning raiding party of thirty men clattered past them. Irvine and Ranulf briefly acknowledged them as they passed by.

'That's what they'd have to contend with if they kept to the road,' said Irvine

Ranulf looked anxiously into the brushwood beside the road. 'What if we've missed their trail?' he asked.

Irvine's tone was matter of fact, 'In that case we will be well and truly fucked, Ranulf. It's a big forest. We can't just go in there and hope we'll find them, because we won't. That's why we need to make sure we *don't* miss their trail.'

By midafternoon, Ranulf was beginning to think the quarter purse Griff had given them would have to do. The forest had been beside them for six hours without any visible signs of entry.

Ranulf pondered the possibilities. They could well have ridden past and missed the telltale tracks. If that were so, then every step they now took was a wasted step. They would continue to Camulodunum. The fugitives *had* to enter the forest between Norwic and Camulodunum. They would turn back and scan the roadside again if they had not seen sign of them by Camulodunum.

He was about to tell Irvine of his strategy when his scout suddenly dismounted ahead of him. Kneeling, Irvine picked something up from the ground.

When Ranulf reached him, Irvine was holding a piece of guilt bronze. 'Didn't Griff say the Britons were finely dressed?' he asked.

'Yes, their horses, too, had fine adornments, according to him,' confirmed Ranulf, as he slid from his mount. He took the guilt bronze from Irvine. 'This is the cheek piece from a harness. It's got to have fallen off one of their horses.'

'And the good thing is I found it away from the road, upon the natural sandstone slab that leads into the forest. We may have had a lucky break. I'll look beyond the slab where the undergrowth leads from it.' He walked to a bank of brambles that loomed some sixty paces from the road. When he returned he was smiling. 'Come, we have enough daylight left to start into the forest. They've left a track like an army.'

With the trail easy to read, Ranulf's group made quick progress through the brambles, and reached the beech colony long before dark. Here, Irvine examined the ground again. He dusted his hands onto his tunic as he stood up to face Ranulf. 'Their tracks are fainter but still clear here,' he said. 'By my guess we're not that far behind them now. The bramble and nettles have slowed them down. They did us a favour flattening it for us.'

'Then we must press our advantage and continue till dark,' said Ranulf. 'It seems they travelled both night and day, so they'll be exhausted by now. It would be good to meet them in that condition.'

They reached the bracken outcrop one hour before dusk. Ranulf signalled for his men to halt here. He stood in his saddle and looked out over the green expanse. Irvine did likewise beside him. 'I have to admit that I struggled to see their tracks in the woods,' said Ranulf, 'but even I can see where they've gone through the ferns here.'

'And they're close,' said Irvine. 'I can feel it. They're probably confident that we failed to spot their exit from the road … after all, they chose the perfect place to leave it, so who can blame them. Were it not for the bronze harness piece they would have escaped, but they're close now and we need to be vigilant.'

'After the open woods, this bracken's a good place for them to spend the night,' said Ranulf. 'They'll be nestled in it, that's for sure,' He turned to the men who waited behind him and barked out his orders. 'You two—Hwita, Tidgar, get down off your mounts. Scout ahead a thousand paces. Keep low and hidden, then one of you get back here and report what you find.'

The two men, Geoguths, low in the pecking order and eager to prove their worth to Ranulf, ran on ahead through the bracken. After travelling their one thousand paces, they found nothing other than trampled tracks.

'I'll go back to Ranulf and tell him it's safe to advance,' said Tidgar, a wiry, acne-infested youth of nineteen.

Hwita, the older of the two, had assumed the position of leader of the two-man patrol. He nodded authoritatively. 'Yes do it quickly, so we may get on with this.'

A little time later, Ranulf and the others joined Hwita, after receiving Tidgar's report.

'Same again,' ordered Ranulf, as the ponies stood knee-deep in the bracken. 'Another thousand paces ahead then report back.'

As the two Geoguths left, Ranulf turned to Irvine. 'It's better we catch the Briton's by surprise,' he explained. 'We don't want them waiting for us do we?'

'Or worse still set get caught up in an ambush,' smiled Irvine knowingly. 'Better they ambush two, rather than the entire group, eh?'

'As long as Tidgar reports back we know we're safe,' said Ranulf. 'If he or Hwita don't return, then that will tell its own story.'

Ahead of Ranulf and Irvine, Hwita, who had taken the lead, stopped suddenly. 'Hush! Someone is ahead—a child by the look of it.'

Tidgar joined him and crammed for a look. 'It's a girl,' he said. 'By Woden, she's taking a piss.'

'Grab her,' said Hwita urgently. 'We have to be close to their camp. Grab her and take her back to Ranulf. She's worth much gold on her own, I guess.'

Just as Cate stood up, Tidgar grabbed her. Twisting in his grip, her eyes wide with fear, she recoiled from him. He immediately clamped his hand over her mouth and lifted her with his other arm. Her cries stifled and muted, Cate struggled and kicked as Tidgar carried her past Hwita. 'Stay here and watch, man,' panted Tidgar. 'I'll take her back to Ranulf.'

Irvine, who stood waiting with Ranulf, was the first to see Tidgar returning. He grabbed Ranulf's arm and looked smugly ahead. 'Looks like Tidgar's caught us a wriggly little fish.'

Tidgar's look was triumphant as he approached Ranulf. 'She was squatting, away from her companions, relieving herself. I grabbed her before she had time to think. Hwita is watching up the trail to see what happens next.'

'What happens next is we rush them before they have time to act,' barked Ranulf as he dismounted and took the girl from Tidgar. 'On your pony man—get back there now!' He looked to his other six riders who waited behind him. 'What are you lot waiting for! Follow Tidgar and ride through their camp. Spare none but the two boys!'

Irvine watched as the riders urgently heeled their ponies through the bracken. 'Eight of them should be able to manage the task,' he said confidently. 'There are some bruising fighters amongst them.'

'*Your* job's done though,' said Ranulf. 'Now you need to get back to Norwic with the girl … get her out of the way, in case things get complicated here. Who knows? Griff might give even more gold for her speedy return. I'll catch you up as soon as the men get back with the others.'

Earlier, Augustus had felt sorry for Cate, as she squirmed and sat cross-legged beside him. Knowing the cause of her discomfort, he had tactfully suggested that she find a spot away from the camp to be alone.

Dominic smiled when Augustus joined him and explained where Cate had gone. 'I wondered why Murdoc had come away from his lookout position,' he said. 'No harm done, though, for the time it'll take her. I can't see anyone being near us anyway.'

'You think we've lost the chasers then?' asked Augustus.

'It doesn't do to get too confident,' Dominic said, '…but, really, I can't see how they could have picked up our trail or followed us. I was careful when we left the road. If the roles were reversed I wouldn't have picked up the trail, and I consider myself pretty useful at tracking.'

'By *pretty useful* I take it you mean the best tracker *I've* ever seen,' said Augustus.

'Maybe you haven't seen enough trackers, my friend,' Dominic said modestly. Alert as ever, he now turned to Murdoc who sat awaiting the return of Cate. 'Taking her time isn't she,' he said. 'Maybe we should send one of her brothers to check on her.'

'Give her a while longer, man,' laughed Augustus, intervening. 'She can't just stand there and get on with it like you do, you know. She has to—'

'Cate's not there, she's gone.' It was Art, her brother, and his tone was urgent. 'I needed to go as well. I expected to see Cate but she's gone, and there's a man watching us.'

Withred, ever the warrior, pulled Flint, who had been resting near to him, to his feet. 'Get the boys away from here,' he said urgently. 'Back beyond that rise in the bracken and away from the fight … and Flint … stay with them.'

He mounted his horse as Flint led the boys away. Dominic, Augustus and Murdoc also quickly mounted and joined him.

As their horses grunted and shifted under them, Withred took over. 'I know how they fight,' he said urgently. 'They'll follow our trail and ride straight in here. If we meet them before they get here we may catch them off guard.'

He heeled his horse forward and removed his seax from his pack—the short sword being easier to wield from the saddle than his larger broadsword.

As Withred and the others burst through the bracken, an astounded Hwita jumped to his feet, but fell immediately to Dominic's arrow.

The noise of approaching riders now came to them.

'Dominic with me!' shouted Withred, as he wheeled to the right, away from the trampled track. 'Murdoc, Augustus, go the other way, we must let them through!'

Fully expecting to take Dominic and the others by surprise, Tidgar, eager to build upon his recently enhanced reputation, had decided to front the charge himself. Expecting to participate in a quick and easy engagement, he howled his undying allegiance to Woden as his pony thrashed through the bracken.

But his screaming, open, mouth served only to stop the sideways swipe from Withred's seax, as the Angle met him at speed from his left flank—the crunching cut sending his lower jaw, tongue and all, tumbling to the ground amidst a shower of broken teeth.

'There's six of them!' shouted Withred, as he watched Tidgar's mount crash through the bracken with the incapacitated, grunting, and soon-to-be-dead Tidgar slumped backwards in the saddle.

'Five now!' shouted Dominic as one of his arrows pierced the throat of another Saxon.

The five remaining Saxons checked their ponies' stride and wheeled around in mutual protection, surrounded on one side by Withred and Dominic, on the other by Murdoc and Augustus.

Murdoc hurled his spear at the nearest man, knocking him from his mount—the spearhead and one yard of shaft going cleanly through his side.

With a 'whumf 'the Saxon landed heavily. Murdoc removed his dagger and made to dismount, but Dominic quickly put an arrow into the man, and so finished him. 'Stay mounted Mur!' he shouted. 'Do not give them advantage!'

Evenly matched now, four upon four, each man faced an adversary. Augustus was impatient to finish with the conflict—his rapid thoughts straying to Cate who he knew must be with others further up the track. Better that he get this done with so he could get after her ... get her back.

Back at Brythonfort, he lived a life of contentment with his wife. A life without children, though. Apart from a brief moment, fifteen years past, when their infant son had entered the world but failed to survive, Augustus and his wife had never known the joys or pains of parenthood. Knowing that Cate and the boys had lost their own parents, Augustus had immediately felt deep warmth towards them.

Maybe they could live with him and his wife back at Brythonfort, thought Augustus, as he turned his horse to face his combatant. God, how they would look after them. Teach them to be good people. The children would fill the gap in their lives, and they would fill the gap in theirs. First, though, he would have to deal with the bastard that came at him now with a seax.

His own preferred weapon was the ax. Single bladed and long in shaft, it gave him the advantage of superior reach over the shorter sword of his opponent. His first swipe was lofty and ill aimed, and the Saxon was easily able to duck under it. Distracted, as his peripheral vision caught sight of Murdoc falling from his mount, Augustus was unable to avoid the slashing counterstrike. The seax ripped through his sleeve and cut deeply into his bicep.

'Wrong arm!' shouted Augustus, not feeling the wound in the heat of combat. 'No fucking wonder you fight against children and women. You're all fucking useless.'

Again, he swiped his ax in a horizontal arc, and this time it hit the mark, knocking of the helm off his opponent, to reveal a young looking, mustachioed man with blazing eyes. Augustus' mount shifted so that horse and pony came together. With no room now to wield his ax, he slap-grabbed the chest of the other man, pulling him by his tunic towards him—his great strength easily overcoming the Saxon's counter movement. Quickly, he removed his butcher's knife from his belt and thrust it into the innards of his assailant, twisting it to entangle the man's viscera. He removed the knife and pushed the man away from him.

A bloody Murdoc just managed to roll to one side as the man landed dead, next to him. Having fallen from his mount after having his nose broken by his opponent's shield boss, Murdoc was now at the mercy of the man who stood over him. Eager to follow his advantage, the Saxon raised his ax to finish Murdoc where he lay.

Augustus, still mounted, grabbed the ax causing the man to face him. Still holding his knife, Augustus thrust it into the man's open mouth. 'Get to your feet and get back on your horse, Mur!' he shouted to Murdoc, as he wormed the knife towards the man's jugular.

Murdoc picked himself up from the floor as Augustus kicked his skewered man away from him and onto the floor. He turned to help Withred and Dominic, but found that the pair had already dispatched their opponents — Dominic at range with an arrow, and Withred skillfully at close quarters with his seax.

Withred still throbbed with battle fever. 'Anybody wounded?' he shouted, as he wheeled his horse around looking at the others, alert for any follow up attack.

'One cut arm, one bloody nose,' said Augustus. 'Me the arm, Murdoc the nose.'

Dominic took a quick look at Augustus' arm. 'Quite a deep cut,' he frowned. 'Lucky your arms are the thickness of most men's legs, or it would be hanging off.'

'Forget my arm, it'll be fine, I've got to get Cate back!' said Augustus.

As he made to leave, Withred stopped him. 'Careful,' he warned. 'We don't know how many are left, and there are only four of us here with Flint minding the boys.'

'Then it'd be better if you stay here and go to Flint, said Augustus. 'I'll take a look up the trail. We've no time to lose. Something must be done.'

Withred relented. 'Go, but be careful. If we can get Cate back without endangering her, we will. And don't forget that you carry an injury that needs attention.'

'I'll be fine. It's Cate we need to worry about,' said Augustus over his shoulder as he heeled his horse into action.

Ranulf's concern grew as he waited for his riders. He knew they were adept warriors, so should have returned with the slave boys by now. They had been gone too long and this worried him. Doubt crept into his mind. Perhaps it had been bad judgment by him to remain back and allow the young Tidgar to lead the sortie. He should have led the raid himself, as he always did. It was the only way. As the leader *he* should have led. His doubts and self-recriminations intensified as his agitation grew, until unable to wait any longer, he set off down the trail, alert to any sounds or disturbances.

He had not ridden far when he met Augustus. The Briton was riding as fast as he could over the trampled bracken, eager to find signs of Cate's captors. His arm still bled from his wound, and his head had become woozy as the exhilaration of combat had faded and the deep pulsating ache in his arm had intensified. With his vision blurred, he was barely aware of Ranulf when they came together, and so was unprepared.

Having spotted Augustus early, Ranulf was able to deal with him quickly. He delivered a heavy ax blow across his chest, knocking him backwards and out of his saddle.

He dwelt briefly, on whether to dismount and make sure the man was dead. He could finish him with his ax if he still lived. Time, though, was short. He had to find out what had happened to his men. The man on the ground *had* to be dead after the blow he had just received. Dead or not he wasn't going anywhere soon.

He continued down the track leaving Augustus where he lay. Soon he came to the bodies of his riders—all dead before him, their blood seeping into the ground. Again his mind raced. There was no sign of the Britons. They must be alive. He knew they must still live or their bodies would lie below him. The injuries sustained by his men told a tale of vicious assailants—assailants who must still lurk nearby.

He quickly made his decision. He would return to Norwic and get out of this place. Catch up with Irvine and deliver the girl to Griff. The chase was not a success, but not a total failure either. He turned his pony and sped back up the track, callously trampling over Augustus in his retreat.

CHAPTER TEN

Govan and Nila held each other as they looked at the scorched remains of their village. Two weeks had passed since Ranulf's war band had burned it to the ground.

'Everything's gone,' wept Nila, her hands to her mouth as she took in the scene of slaughter. 'Not even the fence remains.' She looked beyond the village towards the eastward hills. 'My boys … my dear boys and your sweet daughter … they're out there somewhere … alone in that wild, awful land.'

Grim and pale, Govan viewed the devastation before him. He shook his head disbelievingly—his expression as fraught as his tone. 'We can only hope Dominic and the others have found them,' he said heavily.

Forlorn, Nila turned to Govan. 'Fourteen days they've been gone … fourteen days since they left to find them. Any day now they should be back, but I fear their return, Govan … I fear it in case they haven't found them.'

'Better not to think of the outcome, then,' said Govan, having heard Nila echo his own inner fears

A clattering from behind had them turn. Two men from a nearby homestead stood on an ox cart and threw long planks on to the ground. Other men took the planks and stacked them at intervals around the periphery of the ruined village.

'The new fence will be higher than the last one,' said Govan. 'All the better for a bigger blaze next time.'

'Here come Robert and Simon,' said Nila, unsettled by Govan's defeated tone. She wiped her salty face dry with the sleeve of her dress. 'It looks like they've brought the wattle for the walls of the buildings.'

Robert and Simon sat on a cart pulled by an old pony. Piled onto the cart was a high, springy bunch of thin hazel strips.

It was the first time that either man had seen the devastation wreaked by Ranulf. Simon's mind went immediately to the day, more than a year gone, when callous raiders had sacked his own village.

An evil man named Egbert had led the raid that day. Simon had survived the attack having risen early to attend a job in a field away from the village. He had been near enough to witness the raid, though, and the images of what the raiders had done to his friends and family frequently plagued his thoughts and dreams. They would never go away ... he knew that.

For as long as he lived the images would be with him.

That day he had rescued Martha, and they had fled into the forest, only to be recaptured by Egbert. Dominic had then been able to rescue them, and thus his destiny had led him to Brythonfort with the others.

'It's no wonder no one survived this,' said Robert, bringing Simon out of his ponderings.

'A complete new building job, from start to finish by the look of it,' said Simon. 'My old bones will do some creaking before this job's over.'

Robert smiled. He knew of Simon's past hardships and was amazed at the old man's indomitable spirit and energy. Simon was now seventy years old and as such was left to his own devises and not expected to undertake laborious jobs. However, when Simon had arrived at Brythonfort, he had offered his labour to Robert and his team of workers whenever they needed a helping hand, or whenever Simon felt like filling his days with an interesting task.

As it turned out, Simon had proven to be a skillful and effective artisan in his own right, and his recent intricate work in restoring the shrine to the war God, Mars, back at Brythonfort, had seriously impressed Robert. Whether the work was intricate or arduous, though, Robert knew that Simon was up to it.

Robert turned and patted the pile of hazel strips that swayed and lurched behind them as the cart bumped over a grassy tussock. 'No need for your bones to creak on this job Si. You've got the job of weaving these fellows into wall panels.'

'Another *interesting* job for the old man, eh,' said Simon rolling his eyes in mock desperation. 'Meanwhile, you lot have fun clearing out the ditches, up to your knees in shit.'

Robert laughed. 'I can arrange it so you join us, you know. I don't mind exchanging jobs with you. A bit of boredom is a great antidote to wading through shit.'

Simon looked at Robert, a grim cast replacing the humour in his eyes. 'Thanks anyway, but I'll stick to the weaving. The mud in that ditch no doubt covers many bodies, children amongst them.'

The men fell into a contemplative silence as their wagon rolled up to Govan and Nila.

Respectfully, Govan extended his arm to Simon to help him down from the cart. 'I expected to see Will and Merlin with you,' he said as Simon jumped down beside him.

'You'll see them soon,' said Simon, 'they're scouting the surrounding fields and woods, making sure there are no nasty surprises, or should I say nasty *men* lurking around.'

Govan raised a quizzical eyebrow. 'No military presence here then?' he asked.

'Not for now,' said Simon, 'but Will and Tomas—or *Merlin* as you prefer to call him—have been out for over a week, reading the signs and making sure the area is clear. They left just after Dominic and the others set out. One of them rides back to Brythonfort every couple of days to report to Arthur. The high lord still sends out patrols, usually led by Gherwan or Erec, but they can only be in one place at a time, though I guess we'll see them within the next couple of days. Arthur's aware that we're vulnerable here at the edge of the protectorate, and wants to see this rebuilding completed as soon as possible. It's important to him … that we all know.'

'Yes, I hope all this work's worth it,' said Govan, as another cartload of labourers arrived.

Tomas stalked the roe deer, staying downwind from it, his multi-patterned green and russet tunic blending seamlessly into the bracken behind him. As he came within killing distance, he knelt, then locked his breath. The deer, ears twitching and eyes alert, looked around, nervy and vigilant, as it chewed upon the lush grasses of the glade.

As he pulled back on his composite bow, crafted for him by Dominic a year earlier, he remembered the straw deer-dummy he had practiced upon. Repeatedly, he had practiced upon it until perfecting his technique. He knew, though, that a live animal was something else.

He concentrated on keeping the shake out of his shoulder as he pulled the hide string fully back against his nose. His brown eyes never blinked, his gaze intense, as he finally settled his aim upon the kill zone just below the deer's shoulder. The string sang as he released—the time between release and penetration a mere fraction of a second, such was the power of the weapon.

'Good kill Merlin lad!' Tomas turned as Will walked over to him. He was grateful that Will had allowed him the kill, and smiled, not for the first time, at Will's address to him. Will had given him the name after hearing of his craftiness at the *battle at the oxcarts*. He had compared Tomas' guile to that of the small hunting hawk—the merlin. His old friends still called him Tomas, his new friends Merlin, and sometimes this lead to confusion, but Tomas didn't mind; the new name flattered him, and he was happy to answer to it.

The deer lay dead, instantly killed, pierced quickly and cleanly through the heart. Will clapped Tomas on the shoulder as they walked through the ankle-high grass towards it.

'Now you can butcher it and show me what you've learnt,' he said. 'Quarter it and we'll make our way back to the builders at the village. The meat will cheer them tonight.'

'The land is clear of raiding bands around here at the moment,' said Tomas, as he stooped to prepare the deer. 'So we can have at least one night in the company of others.'

As Tomas gutted the deer, Will crouched beside him. He watched as Tomas figured out the best places to insert his knife to butcher the beast. 'That's it, just where I told you,' he encouraged. He let Tomas figure out himself how to dismember the deer, occasionally offering his advice. 'Good lad. Slide the blade along the bone. Twist the limb so it comes away from the body.'

When Tomas had done, Will helped him to bundle the deer into two sacks. Tomas wiped his hands, greasy now with blood, onto the grass before him. Will stood up and slung one of the sacks over his shoulder. 'Quite a bit of weight in this,' he grunted. 'Lucky you killed the deer so close to the village.'

Tomas, after feeling the weight of his own sack, had to agree with Will. As he glanced at Will, Tomas could not help but liken him to Dominic. Both were wiry, quick men, and both had learnt their craft scouting for Rome. He had worked closely with them since arriving at Brythonfort, and realised how lucky he was to have two similar but unique-in-their-own-way, woodsmen teaching him his craft.

Dressed from head to foot in buckskin, his face adorned with a thick beard, Will looked every inch the hunter and trapper as he strode through the low shrubbery ahead of Tomas.

Tomas increased his stride to walk abreast of Will. 'What do you think of Arthur's plan … think you're up to it?' asked Will, who looked ahead and chewed thoughtfully on a stalk of grass.

Tomas grabbed at the head of a tall grass stalk as he passed; pulling it from its node, half way up the stem. He placed the juicy part into his mouth emulating Will. 'Sounds good in theory,' he said, nibbling on the grass. 'We need to get it just right, though. It's a finely planned ruse, that's for sure.'

Will took the piece of grass from his mouth, and blew out a pithy, well-chewed clump. He replaced the stalk and continued to chew. 'We can only trust in Arthur's judgment and hope he's got it right,' he said. 'He has a knack for making the right decisions.'

Simon had started weaving his second wattle panel when Arthur arrived with Gherwan and a company of knights. For many, it was the first time they had seen Arthur. Indeed, many of the men and woman who laboured in the ditch or toiled in the blackened compound, had never even left the boundaries of their own villages, such was the insular nature of their lives.

Arthur was dressed simply; as were his knights, but such was his aura that many could only stand and gawk at him as he approached Robert, who laboured in the ditch with a team of younger men.

'It's heartening to see my most skillful artisan is not afraid to get his hands dirty,' laughed Arthur as he dismounted his chestnut mare.

Robert crouched in the ditch, stripped almost naked, his body adorned in mud. Some of it he wore wet and black, and some of it dusty and grey where it had dried upon his skin. He pulled out a glop from the ditch and slapped it onto the banking, adding it to his impressive heap.

'Unfortunately there's no fine work to do here just yet,' said Robert as he brushed stray locks of hair from his forehead, thus adding another smear of mud to his face. 'And as well as dredging the ditch we're also providing daubing for the walls of the huts.'

'Good economy as ever, Rob,' said Arthur as he cast an admiring eye along the ditch where several other men were scooping out mud. 'Killing two birds with one stone …'

His voice trailed away as he noticed a shape covered by a pair of sacks lying against the ditch— a small shape; the shape of a child.

Robert followed Arthur's gaze. 'It's the first body we found in the ditch, but we know it won't be the last,' he explained. 'Govan knew the child ... a young boy ... knew him from his clothing. Apart from his clothes there was not much left of the lad.' He glanced over to Govan, who still stood with his arm around Nila. 'Poor man has enough to contend with without having to identify the people he shared his life with.'

'They *will* pay for this,' said Arthur, his voice cold and resolute. 'I vow that the men responsible for such wickedness will have their reckoning in this life as well as the next.'

'And I for one would be glad to witness it,' said Robert as he climbed out of the ditch.

Gherwan the knight stood beside Arthur—his mouth set in a tight, grim line as he looked at the sad bundle beside the ditch. He noticed Simon nearby, weaving the willow panels. He looked back to Robert, then at the other workers. 'Good men still exist, though, and I thank Mars for that,' he said reflectively.

'And it's the good men *and* women who labour here that I have come to thank,' said Arthur, his tone now lifted and enthused. 'Gather round, fine folk,' he shouted, 'so I may speak to you.'

Thirty-five men and women, along with twelve children, drew now towards Arthur—all of them in awe of a man who radiated an amalgam of power, charisma and charm.

He began. 'We rebuild this village in defiance to the callous men who ride through our blessed land thinking they can take whatever they wish and kill whoever they wish.' He pointed towards the dead child beside the ditch, his face trembling with emotion. 'We cannot allow ourselves to believe that whoever did that is the representation of humanity.' He took out his knife and held it to his wrist, before continuing. 'I for one would open my own veins with this blade if I though such a thing. No ... today before me, I see the *true* spirit of Britannia; the true *treasure* of Britannia. I am talking about its *good* people. I am talking about all of you. You have left your own villages and come here to rebuild, and in doing so, you restore not just a settlement, but the faith I have in the human condition.'

As Arthur's words cut through the air with clarity and conviction, Simon's hair stood erect on all parts of his body. He now realised why men would follow the man anywhere—through any wilderness and into any danger—without the slightest hesitation. His glance at the captivated, mesmerized crowd convinced him they would do anything, absolutely *anything* that Arthur asked of them.

'Oh, that I had twenty thousand men at Brythonfort to protect all villages at all times,' continued Arthur, with passion. He looked around at the devastation before him, his eyes now stinging with tears. He swept his arm before him, across the scene. 'This would not have happened, if I had unlimited numbers to call upon. That child, and all the blackened corpses removed from the compound, would still be living and breathing. Would still be laughing and loving.'

He paused as he allowed the gravitas of his remarks to sink in, using the moment to regain a measure of his own self-control. Deeply moved by Arthur's words and reaction, women wept and men pinched their eyes to stem the flow of tears.

Arthur continued. 'I will protect you as you labour here. Protect you until this village is rebuilt. Gherwan and the men I've brought here today will stay after I leave, and the larders of Brythonfort will provide to the villages and homesteads you have left behind. Your kind act will be repaid with food for as long as it takes to complete this necessity.'

Arthur looked towards the fields beyond the village as a movement caught his eye. He smiled when recognizing Will and Tomas. The crowd turned to see the reason for Arthur's pause and smile.

'Look!' he shouted, 'how can we doubt our safety when such fine rangers scout the lands around Brythonfort! Better still, they've brought fresh meat for you—a deer I'd guess. Tonight your labours will be rewarded by the smell of venison as it roasts to perfection on the spit.'

The appearance of Tomas and Will served to relax the atmosphere of the meeting. His oration completed, Arthur picked up one of the children and mingled with the workers, chatting with them in his easy manner. The murmur of conversation picked up and began to flow, and ripples of laughter sounded at the delightful prospect of roast meat that night. For now, all was well with the people at the village. For now, they had their lord at hand.

CHAPTER ELEVEN

Fighting to contain his rage, Fincath mac Garrchu paced the floor of the huge roundhouse. His scout had delivered news to him that was both good and bad.

The scout, Latchna, had arrived the previous night during the feast, bloodied and exhausted. The bad news he had delivered was the escape of Fincath's slaves—a girl and two boys. The good news was the slaying of two more of the Uí Dúnlainge brothers, namely Saeran and Beccan.

Latchna had recounted how he had come across the Uí Dúnlainge camp after dark as he travelled from the docks with supplies for Fincath's trading post. The smell of blood was everywhere around the camp, and he soon ascertained that a surprise attack had taken place. The brothers and five other of the Uí Dúnlainge clan had ambushed a cart that was destined for the trading post. Knowing that a boat had arrived from Britannia that very morning, he had guessed that the brothers now held Fincath's much-awaited slaves.

Latchna had gone at once to the trading post where six of Fincath's men had spent the day awaiting the arrival of the British slaves. Latchna had told them of events down the trail, and the men, Latchna included, had decided to act at once, even though darkness was almost upon them. Reasoning that the Uí Dúnlainge brothers would be gone at first light, they decided to strike at night, aware of the risk of combat in the dark, but unwilling to leave it until dawn.

Silently, they had slipped into the camp, but one of the brothers, Beccan Uí Dúnlainge, had heard them and roused the others. The fight had been brutal and clumsy in the moonlight as both parties slowly lost their combatants to death and grave injury, until only Latchna and Saeran Uí Dúnlainge stood opposed.

Luckily, for Latchna, the formidable Saeran had earlier taken a bad injury to his thigh, greatly affecting his mobility, and Latchna was able to slay him after kicking him to the ground. Even so, Saeran had come close to killing Latchna, and had succeeded in stabbing him in his side. When Saeran fell, Latchna stood alone clutching his wound.

On inspecting the carts, he found the slaves fled. Not knowing how long they had been gone, he took up a brief and painful search of the immediate area, but found nothing but tracks leading into the woods. Knowing the futility of embarking upon a chase alone and injured, he had returned to the trading post where he had dressed his wound and spent the rest of the night in a fitful sleep. The next day he had thrown himself over his pony and begun a painful journey towards Fincath's ringfort. All day he had bumped along on the pony's back, arriving at the ringfort long after dark. Here, he had delivered his news to Fincath.

Fincath now looked to his sons, Fróech and Colman. The victory feast had finished in the early hours, and the three of them had continued the debate throughout the night and into the new day.

'We have to get them back,' Fincath raged as he continued to pace the hall. 'Do you have any idea how much gold I sent to Griff for the girl? I could have traded her on if it fitted my purpose. Fifty cows! Fifty fucking cows I could have asked for her!' The King of Cúige Chonnacht would have given such numbers without quibble. He looked at Fróech, who had fixed him with a questioning stare. 'Oh, yes, I know, I know,' spluttered Fincath. 'Maybe her blond hair and blue eyes would have put fire in your belly, and you would have taken her for a wife, but if she was not … if she was not to your liking, I could have traded her for cows for fuck's sake! Cows worth four times the gold I sent to Griff.'

Colman gave his brother a knowing look as Fincath paced away from them. A look that said, *Leave him to exhaust his rage and allow him to lament the loss of his precious cows.*

'So we set out and head south-east to find them,' said Fróech simply, his calm tone a counterbalance to his father's outburst. 'Latchna says they left a trail in the woods near to the docks. Fresh horses are being readied as we debate this. We should reach the woods where the ambush occurred by nightfall, and tomorrow will see us reach their trail. I can see no reason why we shouldn't find them. If they move on foot, their progress will be slow. So cheer yourself father. In two days I'll have the slaves in my captivity.'

'Take twenty men with you, then,' said Fincath, calmer now. 'We've bloodied the noses of the Uí Dúnlainge rabble, and for now they're weak, but we can't take any chances. Take well-armed men and be careful of counter attack. Above all, bring me back what is mine—what I have paid for.'

Colman and Fróech made to leave the hall, but as they walked towards the low door, Fincath stopped them with his last instruction. 'And do not forget that the girl must remain pure,' he said. 'Take away her purity and she's worthless.'

Fróech turned and nodded his agreement to Fincath, before continuing his stride to the door with Colman. He rolled his eyes in supplication as Colman gave him an exasperated look. 'Fucking cows,' he said, when out of earshot of his father. 'That's all he thinks about.'

Maewyn, Elowen and Mule had slept like the dead. A month had passed since the destruction of their village, since when they had only slept in fitful spells, usually in cold and discomfort. The monastery guesthouse was simple and clean and they were its only guests. Springy matting in many layers made up their simple beds, and thick, woolen blankets served to keep them warm.

Maewyn was the first to wake and it took him several seconds to establish just where he was. He remembered the kind monk, whose name eluded him at present, who had found them in the woods and led them to this place. It had been morning then (that he could remember) and by midday the monk had made sure their bellies had been filled with a thick and tasty fish stew. Then, they had given in to their exhaustion, Mule actually falling asleep where he sat, leaning forward with his head resting on the table. Elowen, too, had started to sway as she fought against her extreme fatigue. Maewyn remembered that his own head had also started to nod.

The kindly monk had then enlisted the help of a younger, cheerful-looking fellow, and together, with much puffing and panting, they had carried the comatose Mule to the guesthouse. Maewyn and Elowen, barely awake themselves, had followed in a daze and fallen into the welcoming beds. Here, Maewyn now lay, with no recollection of the last twenty hours.

He sat up and looked to Mule, who had started to stir near to him. Elowen still slept soundly, her small shape hunched and hidden under her blanket.

As Mule's eyes fluttered open, Maewyn gave him a gentle nudge. 'I think we slept through half of yesterday and all of last night,' he said sleepily.

Mule shut his eyes again, but Maewyn did not intend to be the only one awake. He nudged him again. 'Wake up you lazy sod,' he said. 'You fell asleep at the table as soon as you had filled your belly, yesterday. What must the monks think of us?'

'I'm hungry again,' mumbled Mule, keeping his eyes shut in defiance. 'Do you think the monks will give us breakfast?'

'I doubt they'll let us starve, you ninny,' said Maewyn, now distracted as he noticed the filth covering his tunic. He peered closely at the garment pulling it away from him. 'It must be a month past since we were taken from our village and this is the first time I've noticed how dirty I am.'

'It's little wonder you're filthy,' said a voice from the doorway. 'You were too busy with the business of keeping alive before you got here.'

Maewyn looked to the door to see a freckled, ginger haired youth, garbed in a habit, and not much older than Maewyn himself. The youth's eyes sparkled with fun, and his small features and upturned nose reminded Maewyn of a rather startled squirrel. He noticed the monk holding a bundle of simple but clean clothes.

'Glad to see you all slept well,' said the young monk as he laid a bundle of clothes next to each of them. 'We met briefly yesterday but you were all so tired I doubt if you remember much. My name's Ingomer and I have the job

157

of looking after you. Some of the other monks call me Ingle, and you can call me the same if it pleases you.'

Maewyn looked at his new, clean clothes, and nodded his appreciation to Ingomer. 'Thanks Ingobble ... er ... I mean Ingle.'

Ingomer's laugh was shrill and infectious, causing Maewyn to blush and Elowen to stir and sit up suddenly. 'Sorry girl,' he chuckled, 'but your cousin just invented a silly new name for me.'

Elowen rubbed her eyes and yawned haplessly as she looked blankly around at the interior of the dormitory. 'Oh yes, I remember now,' she said. 'We are with the monks in Hibernia.'

Maewyn who still fidgeted with his dirty clothes, pulled the neck of his tunic away from him, and sniffed to assess his odour. He nodded, satisfied at the result.

Ingomer shuffled uncomfortably. 'I was several days unwashed myself before coming here to take my vows. And you know what; I thought I, too, smelt quite good considering. Trouble was my nose had got used to the stink, unlike the noses of the monks who welcomed me into the monastery.' Ingomer cleared his throat. 'Er, if you don't mind me saying, I think that your nose has also got used to the stink, if you get my meaning.'

Maewyn looked at Mule who had also listened attentively to Ingomer's proclamation. They gaped and exchanged frowns as they figured out what the young monk could be hinting at.

Maewyn, as ever, was the first to twig. 'Ah,' he said, his smile breaking out as it dawned upon him. 'You mean we all stink like polecats and don't know it.'

Mule, still open-mouthed, now chanced a sniff under his armpits. Slowly he nodded his understanding to Ingomer.

'I wouldn't have put it quite like that,' said Ingomer, 'but there's a well just outside this dormitory, and I've left some soap and buckets of water there. Perhaps you might all like to have a good wash before dinner. Cleanliness is next to Godliness, so the Bishop keeps telling us, and we've continued the Roman tradition of washing, here.'

At the mention of dinner, Mule finally sat up and stretched. 'Can't we eat first and wash later,' he asked.

Bishop Tassach sat with his most trusted advisors: Rodric, and the scribe, Donard. What to do with the children, was the topic of their meeting.

Tassach was a short, stern man with a ruddy wine-induced complexion, and a reputation for not suffering fools gladly. 'First thing is to stop them smelling like cattle,' said Tassach. 'Then we must make sure they're fed and watered as the good Lord instructs us to do.' He paused, lost in thought, as he considered the bigger picture. 'And that, my good friends, is the easy bit.' He looked at Rodric, then at Donard, his eyebrows raised, inviting a response. 'Well?' he asked. 'Any ideas what to do with them?'

'The way I see it, we have few options,' said Rodric in his matter of fact way. 'From my conversation with the boy, Maewyn, I've learned they were taken from their British village one month ago. To return them to Britannia must be our aim, although how we can do that before next year eludes me.'

'And why so?' asked Tassach.

'The problem is finding a trustworthy boat, Your Excellency,' explained Rodric. 'Most of the merchant boats, whether British or Hibernian, have the roughest and most ungodly specimens of men on board. Quite simply, we cannot trust to send them unaccompanied.'

'And why would this be a lesser problem next year?'

'Because we have charted a small boat in the springtime next year for the transportation of nine of our order to travel to Northern Britannia,' explained Rodric. 'As you may recall, we are to establish an outpost from where we can deliver our ministry to the pagan hordes.'

'Of course … the mission,' remembered Tassach. 'Four months then … we would have to look after the children for four months. Have you considered the consequences of this?'

Rodric looked at Donard the scribe for help. Both had been expecting the question and privately they had pondered over the difficulties of protecting the children. Donard was Rodric's closest friend who spent all of his days copying Latin script in the scriptorium. Aware that the precious Latin manuscripts, including much holy teaching, could be lost forever, the task of duplication and translation had fallen to all of the monasteries in Hibernia, each of which contained a scriptorium and monks skilled in the arts of letter writing and translation.

Donard, himself, was a clever man, and was able to interpret, not only Latin script, but also the look that Rodric now shot his way. It was an invitation for him to take over.

'Yes we are aware of the difficulties,' said Donard. 'But we have few alternatives—the children were to be handed over as slaves to one of the tribes.'

Tassach, now slightly alarmed, looked to Rodric who nodded in agreement. 'Probably the mac Findchado clan,' confirmed Rodric. 'They are known to do much trade in this field with a merchant in Britannia.'

Tassach's face twisted in disgust at the mention of the mac Findchado name. 'Pah!' he spat, 'unwashed pagan rabble, the lot of them. It would serve our cause better if we preached to *them*, converted *them* before going to Britannia. But they'll have none of it. That we know too well.'

Tassach was referring to the time he had sent two of his monks to the mac Findchado ringfort with instructions to introduce the clan to the teachings of Christ. The two had returned stripped naked, tied backwards in their saddles, their heads shaven and painted blue.

Tassach sighed as the image came to him. He paused and drummed his fingers on the scrubbed wooden table before him, nodding slowly as he pondered the possibilities.

'They *will* come and look for them,' he said eventually. 'They are skilled trackers and will find the trail left by the children.' He looked tellingly at Rodric and Donard. 'And the trail will lead them here, and pagans do not accept the idea of sanctuary. Have you thought about the consequences of that?'

Rodric and Donard had certainly thought about all the consequences of having the children in the monastery. So much so, that they had discussed the possibilities late into the night.

Rodric spoke now. 'Yes they will certainly find the trail and come here,' he said. 'In fact, we expected them to arrive yesterday hot on the heels of the children. When they didn't, I sent a man down the track to find out why. It seems a fight took place, and all were dead at the scene. More will undoubtedly follow, as soon as the mac Findchado's figure things out. They, too, cannot fail to find the bodies, and we expect them to follow the trail from there. When they arrive at the monastery, as we're sure they will, we need to convince them the children passed us by. If they believe us, they might just leave us alone. After all, we're useful to them in many ways. Look how they've developed a taste for our bread, our honey, our ale, to name but a few examples of what we provide for them, so it wouldn't suit their purpose to ruffle our feathers too much.'

Tassach frowned and looked unconvinced. 'And how do we persuade them the children passed us by,' he said. 'If the trail leads them here they'll turn the monastery upside down until they find them. Whether we're useful to them of not, they won't stop looking until they find the children, thus proving we lied to them. And I needn't tell you the consequences of that, regardless of their taste for our bread, honey, and ale.'

'But the trail *won't* stop here,' said Rodric. 'The trail will be seen to bypass the monastery and lead to the bogs, three miles distant. There it will disappear into the water.'

'So you intend to walk the children to the bogs and back,' said Tassach, still frowning, still unconvinced.

'Yes, and if we walk back over the same track and create a beaten trail it will be hard for them to separate the outgoing tracks from the returning ones.'

'And can we guess the direction the mac Findchado people will come from?' asked Tassach.

Rodric nodded. 'If they find and follow the trail from the docks, as I'm sure they will, they'll approach us from the woods that overlook the grounds, just as the children did.'

'And we'll know when they arrive,' interjected Donard, 'because we'll keep watch over the woods until they get here.'

'And the children?' asked Tassach.

'They'll be hidden in the grain cellar behind the cow sheds,' said Donard. 'We'll cover them with grain if needs be, until the search party leaves.'

Tassach pushed his chair away from the table, a sign the meeting we over. He frowned at Rodric and Donard as he stood. 'I hope you know what you're doing,' he cautioned, 'because if this goes wrong they'll destroy us.' He walked to the door and turned to them before leaving. 'But what options do we have apart from this one. We cannot give them to the mac Findchados. Our souls would surely be damned if we did that.'

After they had washed and changed into clean clothes, the children felt almost reborn. All wore similar plain white cotton tunics fastened at the waist by a length of cord.

'Sweet Jesus Saviour, we have three angels from above before us,' said Ingomer in mock awe, as he arrived at the well after finishing his morning chores in the bakery.

Maewyn self-consciously hitched his tunic off his shoulder, trying to give it anything but an angelic look.

'Mmm, first time I've been dressed the same as my cousin,' he muttered as he looked towards Elowen, and fidgeted with his tunic again.

Ingomer gave a mischievous smile. 'I wouldn't worry about it, no one will comment on your dress here at this monastery.' He paused; hand on chin, as he smilingly appraised Maewyn.

Unable to contain himself any longer, his shoulders slowly began to shake as his laughter finally erupted. 'Maybe we could stand you on the table at evening prayers, though,' he chortled. 'It would certainly give us inspiration to see such a seraphim in our midst.'

Maewyn gave a rueful smile and looked down at his tunic again, while Elowen could not help but echo Ingomer's laughter. Mule, meanwhile, merely looked puzzled as he tried to figure out Ingomer's joke.

'All right, Ingle,' allowed Maewyn, 'you've had your bloody laugh. Anyway we're washed and changed now and we're all starving.'

Mule immediately nodded in agreement, his eyes awash with anticipation.

Ingle, still chuckling, led them to the refectory, his arm around Mule. 'You have the pleasure of eating alone … and noisily,' he said as he pushed the door open to reveal a room with a long table. 'We monks eat here later … in complete silence.'

Twelve simple stools stood on each side of the table. At the table's head, an ornate wooden chair had pride of place. Ingle swept his arm towards the four nearest chairs. 'Make yourselves comfortable,' he invited, 'I'll get you something to fill your bellies.'

He took a tray from a table at the back of the room and set it down before them. Upon it were two fresh, crusty loaves, a pot of honey, and a hunk of cheese. 'The bread is delicious, I baked it myself this morning,' he said proudly. 'The honey comes from our own hives, and the cheese is the product of our own cows.'

Elowen by now had carved three thick slices from the loaf and piled them with cheese. Mule and Maewyn began to feed hungrily upon them, too busy filling their bellies to respond to Ingle for the time being.

Ingle walked up to the top of the table and sat on the ornate chair. His mischievous face took on a dutiful expression as he raised his hand before him, index and forefinger pointing to the heavens as he blessed them with the sign of the cross. *'In Nomine Patris, et Filii, et Spiritus Sancti. Amen,'* he intoned. 'May the good lord bless—'

Ingomer removed himself quickly from the Bishop's chair as the door to the refectory opened. So quick was his reaction that he fell to the floor, leaving the chair rocking.

Maewyn's laugh at the sight was sudden and explosive, sending a shower of crumbs over the hapless Mule, who merely brushed them from him while continuing to chew. Maewyn turned to the door, red in the face and spluttering, as Rodric and Donard walked in.

'It appears we have just missed Ingle's latest Tomfoolery,' said Rodric to Donard. 'It's just as well the Bishop didn't walk in, or any monks of a *sterner* disposition.'

Donard took a seat beside Elowen, as Ingle dragged a more legitimate stool from the table and sat sheepishly upon it. 'I was just saying grace,' offered Ingle,' just as the Bishop—'

'Leave it at that, brother,' interrupted Rodric, 'lest you dig an ever deeper pit for yourself. There's business to discuss now and it involves all in this room.' He waved the back of his fingers at the children and continued. 'But eat away children, please. I'll enlighten you further as you fill your bellies.'

Rodric then told them of the conversation they'd had with Bishop Tassach—of the likelihood of pursuit by the mac Findchado clan, and the importance of leading them away from the monastery on a false trail. 'So after this meal,' he concluded, 'I would like you all to go with Ingomer to the bog to set the trail.'

In contrast to Maewyn and Mule's hungry feeding, Elowen had nibbled delicately on a piece of bread and honey as she listened to Rodric. 'If we manage to elude them, what then?' she asked, as Ingle filled her goblet with small beer. 'How are we to get back to our land?'

Rodric explained the necessity of them staying at the monastery until the sailing of the missionary boat the following year.

Maewyn looked with dismay, first to Elowen and then to Mule, who was now preoccupied with his second wedge of bread. 'But our mother … and Elowan's father if he survived, will think us dead if we don't go back soon. They'll give us up as lost forever.' He looked despairingly at Rodric, then Donard. 'Is there no chance we can get back to Britannia before next year?'

'None unfortunately,' said Donard. 'As Rodric explained, the only boats that sail will be manned by the roughest of people. Would you have us set you sail with such people?'

'I for one never want to go on a boat again, even if it means staying here forever,' said Mule, remembering his seasickness and Osgar's brutality.

'Don't be silly,' said Maewyn tetchily. 'We cannot remain here. What about mother and uncle Govan? Don't you want to see them again?'

Rodric' glance at Maewyn indicated that he would explain things further to his brother. His tone was gentle and patient as he addressed Mule directly.

'There's no need for you to remain here lad,' said Rodric. 'In the springtime you'll feel much better about crossing the sea, and our voyage will be much shorter—straight across to Britannia, rather than all around it like before.'

He looked uneasily towards the door as his thought strayed to the business in hand. 'First things first though,' he continued. 'First, we must shake the mac Findchado clan off your trail, and hide you well before they come. Otherwise, there'll be nobody crossing the Hibernian Sea next year.'

Fróech, Colman and Latchna grimly surveyed the scene of the fight. Fróech stood over the body of Saeran Uí Dúnlainge. His corpse was on its belly, its cheek resting against the cold earth. Jays had pecked most of the skin and much of the tissue from the cadaver's face, but there was still enough flesh remaining to leave no doubt that Saeran Uí Dúnlainge would never walk the earth again. Fróech spat on the corpse.

Latchna, still incapacitated from his injury, limped to the edge of the clearing and nodded in satisfaction. 'Their trail is clear and leads through this coppice and into the rough scrubland.' He looked to Fróech, to Colman, to the twenty grim men that sat, mounted, behind them. 'It leads towards the monks abode if continuing in its direction,' he added.

Fróech heeled his pony forward as Latchna walked on ahead, examining the trail. 'The monks have them,' he said determinedly to Colman. 'I'd wager a bull's balls that the monks have them.'

'And if they do?' asked Colman.

'If they do, we'll thank them for looking after them and be on our way,' said Fróech. 'Like I said to father; we'll be back *with* them at the ringfort in two days.'

'You think they'll just give them up, then?' Colman snapped his fingers in the air, dismissively. 'Give them up, just like that?'

Fróech shrugged indifferently. 'Maybe … but probably not. They follow the creed of Jesus; the freak who walked on water and raised the dead; the one they tried to tell us about and make us as deranged as them. They are destined to do only good things—kind things—so they'll probably try to protect the slaves.' He shrugged again. 'It's of little matter, though, we'll take them anyway.'

'And teach the monks to do as they're told while we're at it,' said Colman.

'Yes, but only after we've sampled their ale and raided their copious larders,' added Fróech.

By mid-afternoon, they had reached the point overlooking the monastery—the same place that Maewyn, Elowen and Mule had stood upon four days earlier.

Rodric and Donard had expected Fróech's party and now observed them from the valley below, as they slowly made their way down towards the monastery. Bishop Tassach joined Rodric. The remaining monks stood in a huddle beside the refectory.

Tassach tensed as he watched the riders approach. 'You're sure the children are safe?' he asked Rodric.

Rodric chanced a glance at the barn. 'Yes they're in the grain pit, behind the barn, as snug as feasting mice. Ingomer's with them, and will receive a signal and shut the door to the pit if the barbarians decide to search.'

Tassach nodded nervously, but his expression changed to that of the genial, welcoming host as Fróech approached. 'Welcome … it's always good to see our neighbors, whatever the time of day, or whatever the reason,' said Tassach as Fróech dismounted his pony to stand before him. 'We noticed your arrival and have prepared food and ale for you in the refectory.'

Fróech sternly watched as a monk led away his pony to a nearby hitching rail.

On seeing their leader dismount, the other riders did the same, allowing other monks to attend to their ponies.

Tassach, his smile nervous and strained, extended his arm towards the refectory, inviting Fróech and his company of men to enter.

Fróech, still taciturn, looked towards the door, then to his brother. Colman frowned as if considering whether to act upon Tassach invitation. Eventually he nodded, and walked with Fróech towards the refectory.

Tassach fussed around Fróech and his men as they entered. Monks pulled chairs away from tables, and slowly the gathering became seated. Tassach took his seat at the head of the table, Rodric and Donard on either side of him. Tankards of ale were put before them.

Unnerved that none of the mac Findchado clan had yet spoken, Tassach anxiously cleared his throat. 'I hope the ale is too your liking, Lord,' he uttered.' Your favorite bread and honey is on its way, fresh from our ovens and hives.'

Fróech looked disdainfully at Tassach (a look mirrored by his brother Colman), then belched up his first quaff of ale. Tassach squirmed under the brothers' withering stares, wishing he could slump inside his habit and disappear. Rodric, who was surprised at the lack of dialogue coming from the mac Findchado brothers, looked enquiringly over to Donard. The scribe merely raised his eyebrows as if to say, *We can do naught but wait and let it unfold.*

Unfold it did, as Fróech spoke for the first time, the suddenness catching Tassach by surprise. 'First of all,' he said, eying Tassach coldly, 'why do you sit at the head of this assembly? Why, indeed, do you have a better chair than everyone else?' Tassach had no answer ready, so merely shrugged and shifted uncomfortably in his seat.

Fróech allowed the silence to hang a moment, his head tipped quizzically to one side as he appraised the mute Tassach.

After the pause he continued. 'No answer, eh? Just as I though. So let me help you. The fools you sent to convert us last year told us your God created all men equal; an absurd notion and one that forced me to shave off their mad hair and paint their heads blue so they'd resemble the dolts they are. So when I ask you why you sit at the head of the table when your religion instructs that no one should do so, you cannot answer me because it makes no sense.'

Fróech cradled his chin between his thumb and forefinger, his face affecting a look of confusion as he studied the tabletop. Raising his head to look directly at Tassach, he jabbed his finger at him.

'You see, my good priest from hell,' he shouted, 'what makes no sense to *me* is that you sit at the head of a table in a land bequeathed to you by my father, when the successor to this land—to this *tuath*—namely I, Fróech mac Findchado, is left to sit as a servant who waits to gather crumbs from his master's table!'

Tassach, aware now of his slight to Fróech, immediately shot to his feet, and signalled Rodric and Donard to do the same. 'No ... no, I meant you no insult,' he spluttered. 'It's just the way we do—'

Fróech sprung up, grabbed Tassach by the cloth of his habit, and pushed him away from the table abruptly ending his excuses. 'No ... no fucking more, just get down the table and know your fucking place,' he shouted, as he helped Tassach along with a hefty kick at his buttocks. Rodric and Donard followed Tassach and took seats half way down the table.

Once seated at the head of the table, Fróech, with Colman on his right and Latchna on his left, brusquely signalled for a monk to refill his flagon with ale. He studied his fingernails, apparently absorbed with them— his rage switched off for now.

Calmer, he continued. 'You know why we're here, so go and get the slaves for our perusal.' Again, there was silence, so Fróech turned his attention from his fingernails and looked penetratingly at the three monks. 'Well?' he asked, as he held out his hands as if waiting to accept a gift.

Tassach, Rodric and Donard merely looked bemusedly back at him; the room deathly quiet; the tension high.

'Slaves you say?' said Rodric, who could stand the icy silence no longer. 'I'm sorry my lord but I have no idea what you can mean.'

171

Fróech looked at Rodric, then at his brother, Colman, who exchanged a look of exasperation with him. 'Look, we know they're here. We followed their trail. So go and get the slaves,' repeated Fróech with strained patience, each sentence emphasized with a nod of his head.

'If they came as far as this monastery, they did not present themselves to the Bishop, and *that* I swear to God the almighty,' said Rodric.

Tassach's eyes flickered under his knitted brow upon hearing Rodric's oath. *Another one of my monks to roast in hell*, he thought.

'So you're going to make us search this place from roof to cellar,' said Fróech. 'I need not tell you what will happen if I find you are lying to us on this matter.'

'Please feel free to search,' said Tassach, as his composure partly returned. 'We wouldn't lie to you. If we held any slaves, I know you would look after them if they were so highly prized. Believe me; we would hand them to you if we had them.'

Fróech gave another exasperated shake of his head. Now, his tone was impatient as he addressed his men. 'Search as I described,' he barked. 'Leave nothing. Miss nothing.' He turned to Latchna who sat at his left side. 'Use your tracking skills and look for signs around the edges of this place.'

A scraping of chairs on the stone floor of the refectory heralded the start of the search as Fróech's men got to their feet and left the building.

Fróech remained with Colman—the long table now empty apart from Tassach, Rodric and Donard; the other monks having left to observe the search.

'So you have just sworn to your God that the slaves are not hidden here,' said Fróech to Rodric. 'That means if we find them, you will, according to your strange doctrine, roast in the fires of hell.' Fróech's smile was thin as he continued. 'Twice then, you'll suffer; firstly, back at the ringfort at the hands of the mac Findchado clan, where we have a man skilled in the art of slowly boiling our enemies in a cauldron for three days to prolong their agonized deaths, and secondly you'll burn for eternity in the inferno of your own Christian hell.'

Rodric did not reply, but merely attempted to hold Fróech's probing stare, his heart hammering as he fought to keep his gaze unblinking and true.

Fróech drummed his fingers on the table as the deadlock and silence continued. The mac Findchado brothers stared from monk to monk, the atmosphere strained and menacing. This continued until a shadow darkened the door. It was Latchna with news. Swiftly, he approached Fróech and whispered in his ear.

When he had finished Fróech looked at the monks—at Rodric in particular. 'My scout has found the trail of three travellers leading from the side of the hill, near to where we first found the trail of the slaves. It leads away from this place. Your soul and skin may just have been saved my good monk.'

Elowen, along with Maewyn and Mule, squatted in a muted world. After spotting Fróech and his men, Ingle had assisted them into the sunken bell chamber, which was full almost to the brim with grain. Maewyn, Elowen and Mule had then wriggled into a sitting position in the chamber, until only their heads protruded. Stalks and grasses, mixed in with the barley grains, caused them to endure a great deal of prickling and itching. Ingle had given each of them a hollow straw from which to suck air if the situation necessitated them burying their heads under the barley.

He sat by the open, wooden door to the chamber, having emphasised again their need to bury their heads and breathe through the straws if he had reason to shut the trap door. *'This will be the signal that a search has begun,'* he had told them. Then they were then to remain covered until he told them to surface from the grain. On no account, he had stressed, must they resurface unless he, I*ngle*, told them to do so.

For what had seemed an age now, the children had been breathing through the straws. Ingle had left them after receiving a signal that the search had started.

Elowen grasped his hand tightly to keep him calm. Claustrophobic and hot, he had started to wriggle and fidget, and Elowen could sense he was close to panic. Unable to communicate in any way other than touch, she rubbed his hand between hers, hoping to transmit her reassurance to him.

As for Maewyn ... although uncomfortable and hot himself, he had become stoic and resolved. He just wanted the thing to be over and end well. He thought about Ingle and the monastery, his head now swimming with images, as time became suspended to him in the sensory depredation of the barley pit.

He saw Ingle. Saw Rodric. He imagined the serenity of the valley and the monastery. At first, the people had seemed strange to him with their odd clothing and tonsured hair. He had never seen monks before. His village had not practiced Christianity—had not practiced anything really, other than a vague respect towards the natural order of the world. They had been superstitious, of course. Sometimes he would find a way to avoid crossing a stream in case he evoked the wrath of a water God. As for Christ, he had never taken Him seriously, until now.

As he shifted slightly in the pit and spat out a barley grain that had encroached into his mouth, Maewyn realised that the belief in Christ had shaped the lives of the men who resided at the monastery. Maybe they were not perfect people—indeed, Ingle had told him that God made man imperfect—but at least they *strived* to be good, and that was what set them apart from the monsters they had met since their capture.

Maybe he too could become a better person if he listened to what the monks preached. He knew he was capable of love. His bond with Elowen and his brother, for example, had grown stronger than ever. He would die for them now … that he knew.

And maybe he would have more patience with Mule— not scold him so readily—if he could live his life more like the monks. Ingle had promised to show him how to read if he so desired. He might just do that if they got out of this scrape. His ponderings ended abruptly as Mule's foot pushed against him.

Inevitably, Mule's head, searching for air, was the first to shoot out of the grain. As it did, the trap door opened, and Maewyn realised that things had changed yet again.

CHAPTER TWELVE

With Withred and Flint beside him, Dominic now rode tentatively over the trodden bracken looking for Augustus.

It did not take them long to find Augustus' body, lying bloodied and trampled by the track. Dominic was quickly off his horse, while Flint and Withred, ever the vigilant warriors, rode past Augustus to watch for any attack or possible ambush from up the trail.

Content that no such danger loomed immediately ahead, Withred returned to Dominic, leaving Flint to continue his reconnaissance. He dismounted and joined Dominic beside Augustus.

As Dominic took Augustus' head in his arms, his tears were not far away. He glanced hopelessly at Withred. 'It looks like he took an ax blow to his chest,' he said. 'Add that to the deep cut on his arm, and the trampling he took from the horse, and it was just too much for the man.'

Withred was devastated. He had fought alongside Augustus, laughed along with him, and seen him to be a true and solid man. He looked with a sad fondness at him now, seemingly at peace and sleeping.

Dominic gently laid Augustus' head upon the fronded ground, then stood to look up the track for sign of Flint.

Withred remained crouching beside Augustus, and, so, was the first to witness the slight flicker of his eyes. He grabbed Dominic's leg, forcing him to turn, his tone triumphant. 'The injuries may have been too much for a man … yes. But we forget that Augustus is a bull, not a man.'

Dominic watched in astonishment, as Augustus' slowly blinked his eyes, then opened them in a squint against the daylight. Confused, he looked at Dominic. 'Why do I lie here looking at your ugly face?' he asked weakly. 'Is this death? Is this hell?'

Dominic grinned at Augustus. 'No, my friend, it is neither. *You* are alive and *we* are astounded. We found you here after you left us to find Cate.'

At the mention of Cate, Augustus stirred and attempted to rise. Enduring much pain, he managed to sit up, but knew he could get no further. 'I've got to get her back,' he pleaded, close to panic. 'Time runs out for us the longer we wait here. Help me to a horse, I have to find her.'

Dominic had started checking Augustus' injuries. He quickly glanced at Withred, his shake of the head conveying, *This man is going nowhere.*

He turned his attention back to Augustus. 'I'm sorry Gus,' he said gently but firmly, 'but the chase must end here for now. The ax blow came close to opening your veins, but luckily stopped short thanks to the thickness of both your jerkin and your chest. Several of your ribs are broken and your head took a heavy knock when you were trampled.'

He tied a strip of torn cloth around Augustus' arm. 'This injury gives me the most reason to worry, though,' he said as he secured the cloth with a knot. 'Through it, you've lost much blood, though I think I've managed to stem the flow now.'

Augustus looked at his arm as he sat helplessly beside the crouching Dominic. Defeated now, he realised he was too weak to gain his feet. He began to weep. 'But we can't just leave her,' he pleaded. 'She's just a helpless child.'

Troubled, Dominic had few words of comfort for Augustus. 'We may get a chance to get her back … but

177

not now. We have not the time, and you have not the strength. We still have to find Elowen, Maewyn and Aiden, as well as protect Cate's two brothers. To go off on a chase now will only end in more tragedy. We can no longer travel on the road or enter the town of Norwic.'

Flint returned from up the trail. Amazed and delighted upon seeing Augustus alive, he informed Dominic and Withred of the situation as it stood. Ahead was a scene of abandonment and retreat. They had gone—pure and simple. The Saxons had cut their losses and gone.

Withred joined Dominic to assist Augustus to his feet. The big man placed his arms around their shoulders as they knelt beside him. Slowly and with much effort, they were able to stand and pull the flinching Augustus upright.

'It's my ribs that give me the most pain,' he groaned. 'Jesus, I never thought anything could hurt like this.'

Eventually, and after much endeavor, they were able to get Augustus upon a horse. Dominic knew it was the only way to move him. Walking was out of the question. He was too weak … too injured.

Grey in the face, Augustus leaned over in the saddle attempting to ease the pain in his ribs. Dominic rode closely beside him, ready to assist if the need arose, as they made their way back to Murdoc and the boys.

The sun dipped below the flat canopy of grey, radiating a fan of orange light out across the low sky as they struck camp. Night was near, and soon a crackling fire burned in the bracken hollow.

Lifted from his horse by Withred and Flint, Augustus lay surrounded by a great pile of bracken. The boys, Art and Ula, sat beside him, naturally drawn to a man they

178

had already started to regard with great affection. Although weak, he spoke with them awhile before a heavy weariness overcame him and he fell into a deep and snoring sleep.

'It's good that he sleeps,' said Murdoc, his nose caked in dried blood from the blow that had broken it earlier. 'I'll never sleep, though, not with this throbbing in my nose. The bastard broke it with his shield.'

'The bastard who broke it will sleep well,' Dominic said as he attended to Murdoc's nose causing him to jump with pain, '…sleep forever *he* will, thanks to Augustus.'

Dominic twisted Murdoc's nose, causing him to howl. 'Shh! You'll awaken Gus,' Dominic said, trying not to laugh. 'That's one nose straightened. Add that to the broken leg I fixed for you last year and you owe me quite a debt. And Martha will thank me for restoring your handsome face to its full glory.'

Murdoc rubbed his nose and squinted painfully through his blackened eyes at Dominic. He remembered one of Dominic's Roman curses and thought it appropriate. 'Jupiter's cock, that hurt,' he muttered. He continued to rub his nose awhile. 'What's the plan now that Gus is injured?'

Dominic had thought about it. He knew the others were more than happy to trust his judgment. 'We carry on through the forest,' he said as he poked a stick into the fire, promoting a fresh combustion of flames. 'Five days will see us at Aebbeduna. Once there, Flint's merchant friend will help us resupply. Then another five days along another Roman road— a westerly one that should be free from enemies—will see us back at Brythonfort.'

'And then we look to get to Hibernia and find my cousin and brothers,' stated Flint.

Dominic looked over to the snoring and injured Augustus. 'Some of us will go,' he confirmed, 'though I reckon our party will be one man short.'

The next day they threaded their way through rough ground until coming to the route cleared by the Romans—the track that cut through the great forest. This was familiar ground to Dominic, and they were able to make quicker progress upon its stony and straight surface. Augustus bore his hardship and pain without complaint as he sat gaunt with pain and slumped in his saddle, every jolt of his horse causing his injured ribs to grind.

Two days brought them to Dominic's old camp. Here, nothing seemed to have changed since he had left it more than a year gone. Much had happened here the previous year, most of it experienced by all in the party apart from Flint.

Flint had heard many of the tales connected with the camp, and Dominic and the others were more than happy to feed his enthusiasm, as Flint asked about the events that until now he had only heard as stories around the fires at Brythonfort on dark evenings. Now he could put real pictures to his thoughts as Dominic pointed out the collapsed pits where Saxons had perished—victims to the ingenious traps set by Dominic.

For three more days, they travelled until coming to the Augustus' old village. The two old elms still stood at the gateway of the now-abandoned settlement. Here, a year earlier, two ox carts had blocked the way, as a valiant effort had halted the progress of the Saxon warlord, Osric, and his raiding party.

With the aid of Dominic, Murdoc, Withred and Tomas, Augustus and his fellow villagers had defeated Osric and his men, but in doing so, the village had lost most of its men of fighting or farming age—Augustus and two of his brothers being the only three survivors. Seriously depleted of the work force needed to farm the land or further defend it, the decision to leave and move to Brythonfort had followed.

Augustus, who was having one of his better days, sat astride his horse next to Dominic as they sadly surveyed the abandoned and crumbling buildings. 'I expected others to have moved in by now,' he said.

'No … they're a superstitious folk are the Saxons,' Dominic said. 'They attribute great evil to the woods. More so now, I'll bet. The tale of what happened here must have circulated throughout their ale houses.'

With great sadness, they stood by several mounds of stone that marked the graves of those who had died defending the village. Augustus' own brother, Samuel, lay amongst them. That night they took the shelter of an abandoned hut as the sky darkened.

The next morning they awoke to a thin grey drizzle. 'Today should get us to Aebbeduna,' said Augustus, flinching as Withred and Murdoc helped him into his saddle. 'When we had surplus to trade, which wasn't often, it took us a day to get to the market there.'

An uncomfortable day's travel through heavy rain brought them, wet and fatigued, to Aebbeduna. Here, the merchant, Wilfred—a man well known to Flint from his trading links to Brythonfort—took them in and gave them hot food and lodgings. Comfortable that night, they rested well and readied themselves to take to the road early the next day.

Flint was the last to say goodbye and give his thanks to Wilfred. As the others waited on the road, he embraced him. 'Last time we were here you said you expected Aebbeduna to fall to the Saxons,' said Flint, perplexed. 'It's a year ago now and the place still seems prosperous. Why no attack, Wil?'

'*Trade*, my friend,' said Wilfred. 'Provide something they need; something they cannot produce themselves, and they leave you alone. It kills us to do it, but we are not raided so we swallow our pride and trade with them.'

Flint looked up the narrow street of Aebbeduna; at the workshops; at the stacks of pottery and ironware.

He nodded his understanding to Wilfred. 'Long may it continue for you all here,' he said. 'Trade is important to them, that much is true. But they also look at *people* and see a profit … look at your *children* and see gold.' He mounted his horse. 'Goodbye for now. I hope to see you soon in Brythonfort.' He leaned down and grasped Wilfred's arm in one last farewell. 'Remember,' he warned, as he looked intently into Wilfred's eyes, '… be careful who you do business with. Our meeting in these circumstances says it all.'

'I know, and I've listened to what you've said!' shouted Wilfred, his tone rising as Flint rode away. 'And take care of yourself on the road, so we may meet again soon at Brythonfort market!'

For five days the company travelled westwards, mainly along good roads. The organised structure of the few towns they passed had broken down since the Romans had left, and, much like Londinium, impromptu farms had sprung up within town walls, with spare ground utilised for crop and animal rearing. The villages and smallholdings along the route were still untouched by Saxon incursion.

Augustus, grey with pain, remained stoic and uncomplaining. Both of the boys, Art and Ula, rode beside him, always. The bond between the three of them had strengthened and whenever Augustus needed help or support, they were always by his side.

'Our friend seems ever more gaunt and pained,' said Withred to Dominic, as their horses laboured over a pocked and rutted section of the track on the fifth morning since leaving Aebbeduna. 'Brythonfort and a soft bed will not come too soon for him.'

Dominic looked behind to Augustus, who was slumped, as ever, in his saddle. 'You put it well the other day when you named him a bull,' Dominic said. 'Lesser men wouldn't endure the agony caused by broken ribs stabbing through flesh and into innards. I've strapped him tightly, and that must help, but to have to ride a horse in his condition must be torment.'

'Just as well that Brythonfort looms ahead, then,' said Withred, suddenly elated as he grabbed Dominic's arm.

Before them, the land had unfolded and revealed its panorama as they emerged from a hollow in the road. An emerald and brown patchwork of strip fields carpeted the landscape. At intervals, curls of grey smoke percolated languidly into the still air, bearing testimony to the many farmsteads that lay within the hidden folds of land. Seemingly small, such was its distance from them on the very edge of the horizon, stood Brythonfort. Like a distant whale on a swelling sea, it rose proudly and solidly—impressive, even, from five miles distant.

Dominic looked around to Augustus and the others. 'See how the giant smiles,' he said to Withred. 'Long before dark, this day, he'll be able to rest his weary bones upon his bed.'

'He deserves it after what he's endured,' smiled Withred as he regarded Augustus. 'It's a rest for him, but not for us, eh?'

'Not if we're to help Govan and Flint get their loved ones back to these shores.'

'As I thought,' sighed Withred, '*Gods*, I'm weary, but still, I'm ready to go out tomorrow again if needs be … for however long it takes.'

'At least we'll get to rest our arses tonight on a soft surface,' Dominic said as he rubbed and stretched his back. 'Then we continue westwards again to the land of Dyfed and hopefully procure a boat to take us across the Hibernian sea.'

CHAPTER THIRTEEN

Cate had wept and clung to the pony's mane as Irvine put several miles between them and the conflict in the woods. Eventually Irvine decided to rest the pony. Satisfied he had shaken off any possible pursuit, he stopped to make camp for the night.

One hour later, Ranulf rode into the camp, causing Irvine to jump to his feet. Cursing himself for his complacency, he readied himself to fight, thinking the Britons had found him.

'Stay your fucking hand, it's me: Ranulf!' Ranulf snatched his pony to a halt and dismounted.

Irvine lowered his sword. 'Our other men … where are they?' He peered down the trail into the darkening woods.

'All dead. Killed by your fellow Britons,' said Ranulf, as he stabbed his thumb back over his shoulder. 'Some fucking merchants they were!'

Irvine cursed silently and looked at Cate. '*She* will have to do then. Griff loses two of his slaves and we lose eight men.'

Ranulf regarded Cate and immediately considered having his way with her. Grimy but pretty she was, and not worn out like the whores in Norwic or Camulodunum.

'Not a good idea,' said Irvine, reading Ranulf's intent. 'It's bad enough we only return with *her*. Worse still if we compound Griff's anger by giving her back to him soiled.'

'And how will he know that?' murmured Ranulf, distractedly, as he continued to stare lustfully at Cate.

'Oh, he'll know, all right—he'll check for himself. That's what he does. He's a merchant, remember. He checks his goods.'

Ranulf held his stare upon the squirming Cate a while longer. To her relief, he finally turned to Irvine, regarding him with disdain. 'You Britons!' he spat. 'Always thinking of the consequences. That's what makes you so fucking dull.'

Cate stood hunched with trepidation. 'Lie down and get to sleep!' snapped Ranulf, pointing to the ground. '*Fucking* Britons,' he muttered, piqued, as he left to find his own sleeping place.

The next day they arrived back at Norwic. Griff and his dogs met them as they approached his huge alehouse-come-brothel.

'Just three of you?' he frowned enquiringly. 'Please tell me that the others follow behind.'

Irvine and Ranulf exchanged glances. They had readied themselves for the inevitable with Griff. Ranulf knew it could not be dressed up. He might as well get straight to it.

'You were right in assuming that the thieves were not merchants,' he said. 'They saw off eight of my men and got away with the two boys.'

Griff nodded grimly, lips pursed, as if fully empathizing with Ranulf. 'Mmm, ten seasoned and formidable warriors against five of them … that seems fair enough. It must have been hard for you to only outnumber them two to one.'

'Don't get fucking clever!' shouted Ranulf, getting in first. He pointed up the hill towards the dockyard. 'How do you think *I* feel? I've lost eight good men trying to fix the mess created by those fucking salt rats. Don't forget that I could have spent the last two nights sleeping and whoring. Instead, I agreed to try and save your fucking skin so you can continue to trade with Hibernia, so don't get fucking clever with me, Griff!'

Unfazed, Griff shouted back. 'Yes you did chase them for me, but don't *you* forget that you did it for gold! *That's* what motivates you, man, not good intent! As for Hibernia, your fortune is also tied up with it!'

Griff pressed his palms to his temples in frustration. 'FUCK! How could I have trusted that scum on the boat to guard my merchandise?'

He walked to Cate and lifted her braided hair from her face. She shuddered—repelled, then turned away from him. 'She will have to do, I suppose.' He threw her hair away from him and gave Ranulf an icy stare. 'Do I need to check her for purity?' he asked pointedly.

'You'll do it anyway, so what do *you* think?'

'I think you would be very foolish to taint the goods.'

'Set the dogs on me, would you,' said Ranulf, his sneer laced with edginess, as he observed the ever-present mastiffs by Griff's side. Before he could answer, a pale, ethereal youth stepped from the door of the brothel. 'Ah, I see you've brought your lovely wife to town,' mocked Ranulf. He nodded towards Cate. 'At least she won't be tainted by *him*, that's for sure ... or you for that matter.'

Griff ignored him, and instead threw a purse towards Ranulf who snatched it angrily from midair. Griff realised he needed the man and his followers—knew he had pushed him far enough for now. Secretly he had not held out much hope for the return of the slaves. That the girl was here now—the most valuable of the three—was better than he had expected.

'Think yourself lucky that I pay you the full amount,' he said to the glowering Ranulf.

Griff turned to Ciaran. 'Take the girl under your wing; she stays at the villa until the next boat sails to Hibernia.'

CHAPTER FOURTEEN

Fróech mac Findchado had decided to follow the trail to the marshes himself. He watched as his scout, Latchna, crouched to examine the tracks that led from the monastery grounds. 'Do you think they're telling the truth?' he asked Colman, who rode beside him.

Colman shrugged. 'They're not supposed to lie, so maybe they are.' He peered ahead, his eyes following the blatant indentation through the dewy grass. After a pause, he turned to look back towards the monastery. 'It doesn't matter, anyway,' he added. 'The men are searching their buildings as we speak. If they *are* lying to us we'll find them.'

Latchna stood up. 'At least three people passed along here fairly recently,' he said as he flicked a blade of grass from his fingers. 'It's hard to say if anyone accompanied them. The prints blend into each other.'

'Then mount up man, and we'll move on and see where they go,' said Fróech.

For three miles, they followed the tracks until coming to the bogs. Here, three sets of footprints, puddled with brown water, punctured the mud. After ten steps, the footprints disappeared under the water.

Latchna turned to Fróech after examining the prints. 'It looks like someone entered the wetlands here,' he said. 'Any tracks beyond these lie beneath water, so here the trail goes cold.'

'But why would they go through the bogs?' mused Fróech as he surveyed the vast expanse of shallow water. He looked to Latchna. 'Indeed, would they survive if they chose to do so?'

Latchna frowned, perplexed, as he looked over the morass. He nodded. 'At this time of year, especially after the dry weather we've had recently, it could be possible. As long as their luck holds and they avoid any deep mud, they could get across to the other side. Perhaps they chose this route to throw anyone off their trail.'

'You think three children would have the wit for that?' asked a skeptical Colman.

'Who knows how Britons think,' said Latchna. 'Some say they are spawned from demons.'

'Be that as it may,' said Fróech, but the trail ends here for us.' He looked across the bogs again. 'If they, indeed, went this way, we need to pick up their tracks on the other side of the wetlands. How far, Latchna, before we can do that?'

'They are vast,' said Latchna. 'The best we can do is skirt the edges until their trail emerges again. It could take us a day, maybe a day and half to pick it up.'

Fróech chewed on his lip as he considered the possibilities. 'We do nothing until we're certain the slaves don't hide back there.' He tugged the reins of his pony, turning it towards the monastery. He looked at Colman, at Latchna. 'This may be a ruse,' he added. 'If they knew we were coming they may have set this trail to fool us.'

Fedelmid had enjoyed overturning tables and smashing precious glass goblets as he stormed through the monastery buildings looking for the children. He was determined to be the man who found them. As one of Fróech's many cousins, he knew his esteem would rise if he could do just that. Surely, he would get a seat nearer to Fincath in the great hall when the king learned what a shrewd man his nephew was; would get to choose the better women … the prettier women saved for the king's favorites.

He noticed a young monk following him as he emerged from one of the buildings. 'Why do you shadow me, you skirted fuck?' he shouted, looking impatiently around for the next place to search.

Ingle had watched the man as his hunt had meandered ever nearer to the barn. Knowing this would take him near the barley store where the children hid, he had decided to shadow him in the hope he could distract him from any possible search near to them.

'My apologies,' said Ingle. 'My bishop instructs me to ensure that anything valuable is put back in its place if disturbed during the search.' To emphasise this, he picked up a pewter plate, earlier discarded by Fedelmid that lay now on the dusty ground. He blew on it and rubbed it with the sleeve of his habit. He smiled happily at Fedelmid.

'Alright, but just keep out of my fucking way,' growled Fedelmid as he strolled into the barn, scrutinizing it for signs of disturbance.

White, longhorn cows, chewed contentedly—haplessly observing him through their vacant eyes as he climbed the wooden ladders rising to the haylage store above the barn. After a hasty search, and much throwing about of hay bundles, he jumped down. Dusting his hands off upon his tunic, he looked around the barn again. Satisfied that the barn contained no children, he stomped out looking for another place to search.

The skin on Ingle's scalp contracted as he watched Fedelmid walk round the back of the barn. Ingle looked towards the refectory where another monk stood. He signalled to the monk, and then scurried after Fedelmid.

191

'Master, by your leave, refreshments have been renewed in the refectory. The bread is just out of the oven, so if you prefer it crusty and warm then now maybe a good time to eat. Also there are jugs of ale to be had.'

Fedelmid had noticed the trap door that covered the grain pit and strode purposefully towards it. He stopped upon hearing Ingle's words. He turned to look towards the refectory. After a brief consideration, he shook his head and turned back to the trap doors. 'Not got time to eat,' he muttered, '…have to get this done first.'

'I doubt there'll be anything left if you *do*,' said Ingle. 'Others are entering to eat their fill and quench their thirsts as we speak.'

Fedelmid, who had stooped to open the trap door of the pit, now straightened. The bread and ale suddenly seemed enticing to him—more so, now it was destined to line the stomachs of his fellow searchers. He walked away from the pit and pushed Ingle to one side as he passed him. 'It had better be good,' he warned, 'or I'll have you flogged for pestering me.'

Ingle watched Fedelmid until he entered the refectory. The monk standing near the door waited a while, then gave Ingle the thumbs up—the signal indicating that Fedelmid had settled down with his bread and ale. Knowing time was precious; Ingle made straight for the trap door and opened it.

The first thing he saw was Mule's head, panic stricken and gasping for breath. Ingle quickly crossed himself, giving thanks to God for arriving before Fedelmid.

'It's okay, it's me,' he reassured Mule, who had started to cough and blink rapidly as his eyes adjusted to flood of light.

192

At the sound of his voice, Elowen and Maewyn surfaced from the barley, both red faced and coughing just like Mule. Maewyn was the first to stand up, groaning with the effort needed to pull his body free from the grain.

Ingle offered his arm. Maewyn took it and heaved himself completely out of the bell chamber. With Ingle, he then assisted Mule and Elowen out.

Ingle knelt over the pit and smoothed the barley to a flat surface. He quickly shut the trap door.

His tone was urgent. 'Follow me; we've only got a short time before one of them comes back here to finish his search. I managed to get him out of the way just in time, but he'll be back, that's for certain.'

'But surely we'll be found now that we're out in the open,' said Maewyn, as he looked hastily around looking for another place to hide.

'No, we have to get away from here. You need to do as I say,' said Ingle, his tone now near to frantic.

Mule was still trying to blink away his disorientation and this worried Ingle. Thinking quickly, he grasped Elowen's hand and looked into her own bewildered eyes. 'Look at me,' he said, as he slapped Mule's hand into hers. 'Keep hold of him and make sure he keeps up.' Elowen nodded her consent.

'Right; come on … after me,' he ordered, as he took to a trot away from the barn and towards the open, fallow fields.

Maewyn now ran beside him, while Elowen ran behind with Mule. 'We head for that wooded ridge over there,' said Ingle pointing ahead. 'But, for now, we are out in the open.' He cast a hasty look upwards. 'Trust in God that we're not spotted.'

As they ran alongside the stubby edge of the field, Maewyn looked back towards the monastery and realised how exposed they were. Should any of the searchers look their way that would be the end for them. Nothing lay between them and the settlement—neither hedge, nor tree, nor haystack.

'Don't look, just keep moving,' said Ingle, sensing Maewyn's concern. 'There's nothing we can do now but just carry on and hope.'

Maewyn, however, *had* to look again and immediately wished he had not. Men had begun to spill from the refectory after the Monks' ruse of tempting them inside with delicious fare had finally run its course. None, for now, looked towards them as they ran towards the cover of the trees.

A small, shin-high island of wild grass pushed through the brown stubble of the harvested field. Mule's foot found it, causing him to fall flat on his face.

'It had to be you!' scolded Maewyn, as he helped Mule to his feet. He took Mule's hand himself now, dragging him and forcing him to run in a stumbling gait towards the approaching cover.

Ingle got there first and met Maewyn and Mule, guiding them into a shallow ditch beside the shrubbery. Elowen arrived moments later, gasping and panicky. Ingle lifted her down into the ditch. Nestled low, they all blew heavily, their backs against the wall of the ditch.

Ingle allowed them a moment to recover. 'We should be safe here until they leave,' he said breathlessly. 'They approached from the west … and that's the way they'll return … unless they have mind … to trudge through the bogs.'

Fróech, Colman and Latchna arrived from their search of the marshes just as the other men concluded their search of the monastic buildings.

Fedelmid met them with his news. 'They are not here Fróech,' he said. 'We've been everywhere; above ground and below; in hay lofts and grain cellars, and found nothing.

Fróech paused a moment to think things through. If the monks *had* given refuge to the slaves, then they were indeed skilled in the art of deception. On the other hand, the fugitives could have continued past the monastery as the monks insisted.

He made his decision. 'Latchna. You and two men ride round the edges of the marshes and follow any trail that leads from them. I will speak further with the monks.'

Bishop Tassach, Rodric, and Donard met Fróech and Colman as they walked into the refectory. Tassach, careful not to incur Fróech's wrath again, invited them to a seat at the top of the table.

Again, Fróech was brusque, as he signalled to a monk for ale. 'It seems you told us the truth,' he said. He held Tassach in his stare for a moment. 'Either that or you are good at hiding what does not belong to you.'

'All men belong to God,' said Tassach, evenly. '*He* made us and *He* looks over us.'

Impatient, Fróech waved away Tassach's words. 'Phaa! I've no time for that nonsense now. The slaves belong to my father, paid for by him, and owned by him. What concerns me is that you may have seen them … you might even know where they are.' He looked now at Rodric. 'We know how to extract the truth out of a man,' he said as he eyed Rodric from head to foot. 'Know the best parts of a man's body to apply pain to.'

With torture in mind, Fróech glanced at Colman, seeking his endorsement, but Colman, who had now decided that the children had not strayed to the monastery, shook his head.

Fróech turned back to Tassach. 'It seems that your God smiles on you this day … my brother is eager to return.'

He stood, drained his flagon, then pointed a threatening finger—individually at Tassach, Rodric and Donard. 'We *will* be back, though,' he said. 'If I find you have lied to us, you will all shed you skin in the boiling pot.'

CHAPTER FIFTEEN

Upon reaching Brythonfort, Augustus came under the care of the herbs woman, Rozen.

After removing his shirt to reveal his bruise-ridden torso, Rozen gasped and insisted he lay down at once.

Augustus watched as she brought in a ceramic jar. 'A salve made from the common daisy,' said Rozen in response to Augustus' questioning look. 'The daisy heads are infused in olive oil for several days.' She moved to sit beside Augustus. She put her hand into the jar and scooped out a glop of amber syrup. 'This is what's left after the flower heads are removed. It will heal your bruises and also sooth the pain within.'

Augustus fought the impulse to wince as Rozen began to work the salve into his skin. 'It's good you can heal me, Roz,' he said. 'I need to ride tomorrow or the day after. We head to the west coast to find a boat to Hibernia.'

Rozen laughed as if Augustus had just made the most ridiculous statement she had ever heard. 'These injuries will not heal in two days,' she said, '… rather two months or more. You are going nowhere, Gus, for if you do, you will certainly die.'

'And he will be no use to me or these boys if he does,' said Modlen, as she entered the room with Art and Ula.

Modlen, too, gasped as she observed her husband's torso. Glistening now with the salve, the contusions seemed angrier than ever. Augustus raised his arm. She took it and kissed it tenderly, the look in her eyes leaving him in no doubt that he would be remaining at Brythonfort.

After Dominic's group had returned to Brythonfort without the children, Govan and Nila had been devastated. Later, though, Dominic had been able to give them hope when telling them the search would continue in Hibernia.

They had thought long and hard about the best way to get the children back. To take an armed force across the sea was out of the question. Arthur had argued that such an action would be fraught with problems, not the least of which would be the resupply of provisions and weapons. Logistically, he had argued, it would be unfeasible. Eventually, it had been agreed that just four men—Dominic, Flint, Murdoc and Withred—would seek out the captors of the children and approach them directly.

Posing as agents of Griff, they would verify their legitimacy by attempting to procure business for them. They would also ask if the quality of goods had been up to Griff's usual high standards. In this way, they hoped to find out more about the children: their whereabouts; their condition; the opportunity to flee with them back to the port and over the sea. First, though, they had to find out who held them.

Eight further days were to pass, before Dominic and Withred, along with Flint and Murdoc, overlooked the pristine and glistening Hibernian Sea on the western peninsular of Dyfed.

To seek the assistance of the Hibernian exile, Guertepir, was their intent. Below them lay his ringfort— its ramparts towering above the shoreline. A steep track ran downwards and away from them to the ringfort's one entrance.

'I hope these riders are friendly,' Dominic said, as he observed a group of twelve men moving up the track towards them.

'Depends what mood Guertepir's in,' said Flint. 'He's grown into a whimsical bastard by all accounts, prone to sudden changes of temper.'

'He should be used to Britons by now,' said Withred. 'After all, he himself is second generation. It could be argued he's British himself.'

'Don't you be saying that to him,' Dominic said with mild alarm. 'He's proud of his Hibernian linage—his great grandfather, Eochiad, was a great king, who came here in exile—so don't you ever suggest to him he's anything other than Hibernian.'

And what of Saxons … or Angles in my case?' What are his feelings towards the Germanic people?'

'He used to kill them for Rome,' Dominic said, 'so it would be better if you leave the talking to me.'

The riders reached them. 'What is your business with the Desi folk?' asked the lead rider.

'To speak with your chief a while,' Dominic said. 'It concerns business over the water. Tell him that Dominic, the Roman scout, has returned to speak with him.'

The rider, Diarmait, looked them over and concluded that the men before him, just four in number, could be no possible threat.

'Very well,' he said. 'Follow me, and surrender your weapons at the gate.' He wheeled his horse around and trotted back down the hill. Dominic looked at Withred, then shrugged and followed Diarmait down the hill.

Guertepir sat in his hall beside his woman. Thick, steel-grey hair hung to his shoulders, a centre parting ensuring that it fell to either side of his face. Curiously, his wife's hair matched his own in colour and length, so that from a distance they resembled gender-opposite twins.

Up close, though, their difference was obvious. Guertepir's face was blotched with drink; his enlarged, porous nose riddled with rosacea. Thick, self-indulgent lips were lavender in colour, hinting at an inner disease.

Almaith, his wife, also possessed a red face; in her case resulting from the powdery rouge she applied liberally to cover her pitted, grey skin. Her eyes were bovine and dull.

'Bring them in,' said Guertepir to Diarmait. 'Dominic visits you say. Let me see the wild fucker with my own eyes.'

Soon, Dominic, Flint, Murdoc and Withred stood before him. Guertepir took a quaff from his ever-present cup of wine, seemingly more interested in it then the men before him. 'Best thing the Romans did for this isle, leaving us with this,' he said, as he lifted and admired his cup. 'Get mine from Gaul. Finest there is.' He signaled to a nearby retainer to fill four more cups. 'Drink your fill,' said Guertepir, waving his fingers at the cups, 'while I take a look at you.'

Dominic nodded his thanks, then lifted his cup to Guertepir. 'Your health, my lord.'

'You've not changed much, Dom,' said Guertepir, a thin smile playing on his lips as he appraised him. 'Still an ugly bastard.' He looked at Murdoc and Flint. 'Bet you wished you had the looks and youth of these two. Arthur's men are you?'

Flint spoke. 'Yes, we both live at Brythonfort with Arthur.' He looked towards Murdoc. 'My friend here was dispossessed by the Saxons and ended up at Brythonfort as a refugee.'

Guertepir grimaced, seemingly pained with the effort of having to listen to Flint's words. He looked at them and nodded his comprehension, before turning his attention to Withred. Almaith had also noticed him and grabbed Guertepir hand. Guertepir pulled it away at once.

Withred's head was still shaven; his beard now grown to his chest. Craggy and brutal, his face bore the scars of many battles.

'Hell and fuck, what have we here?' said Guertepir, 'A man who actually sends fear into my wife … not an easy feat, *that*, I'll tell you.' Seemingly amazed, he looked at Dominic then back to Withred. 'I never thought any man could outdo Dominic in ugliness. What's your name man?'

'I am Withred of the Angle people.'

'Ah, a man from across the Oceanus Germanicus,' said Guertepir, seemingly unperturbed. 'You ride with Dominic so I take it you are on the side of the Britons?'

'Indeed my lord,' bowed Withred.

Guertepir cackled with laughter and looked at his wife. 'Who would have thought such a beast would possess such a silver tongue and fine manners. Usually beasts only *howl* as my sword enters their bowels.'

Almaith, who seemed to prefer to communicate only with gestures, merely smiled and licked her lips— seemingly attracted now to Withred.

'Well, I've taken a look at you and I like what I see, so to speak,' said Guertepir. He looked directly at Dominic, his tone darkening. 'Now perhaps you can tell me what you are doing riding through my fucking lands. The

Romans are long gone and I no longer kill Saxons for them.' He looked at Withred. 'That's as long as they don't get *too* near.'

'We seek only information and a boat to Hibernia,' Dominic said.

'*Only* information, *only* a boat,' said Guertepir. 'You make it sound as if you're asking merely for another cup of wine.' He regarded Dominic a while. '*Continue* then,' he said with some impatience, his interest now evoked. 'Tell me why I should help you?'

Beginning with the abduction of Elowen, Maewyn and Mule, he told Guertepir of their futile pursuit to Norwic and their discovery that a cattle lord in Hibernia had bought the children. 'Knowing as we do, that you still have contact and knowledge of what goes on in Hibernia, we thought you would be the man to help us move further on this matter,' concluded Dominic.

'*Move further,*' said Guertepir. He took a gulp of wine then looked at Dominic, his expression one of contempt. 'I have a mind to *move* you to my dungeons for having the impertinence to march into my hall and demand my help.'

'A request my lord, not a demand,' Dominic said, aware that he could not afford to upset Guertepir.

Guertepir took another quaff of wine and signaled for his retainer to refill the cups of Dominic and his men. He frowned … sighed … frowned again. Finally, he said, 'mac Findchado bastards.'

Dominic looked perplexed and asked, 'I'm sorry?'

'Fincath mac Findchado,' said Guertepir irritably. 'He probably has your children—the posturing bastard loves his slaves. He's an enemy of our clan, the Desi, and because of that you're in luck; I *will* give you my council on this matter.'

Dominic sighed, inwardly relieved. 'I thank you for that, Guertepir,' he said.

'No need to thank me, you'll die over there … know that. As for providing you with a boat, that is another matter; do you think I can just conjure a boat from the sky?'

'First we would appreciate your advice on how to find this Fincath,' Dominic said, aware that he must not rush the man. 'Any talk of a boat can come later if needs be.'

The hall was draughty and Dominic noticed Almaith rub the chill out of her arms. The opportunity was not lost on him. 'But forgive me; we would be ill-mannered guests, indeed, if we did not bring gifts for our hosts.' He looked to Flint. 'If you would allow my friend to leave the hall for a moment, perhaps we can address this lapse of ingratitude.'

Guertepir readily nodded his assent, eager to see his gift from Arthur.

Flint returned with two bundles of fur. He unfurled them upon the great table before Guertepir. Almaith gasped at the shimmering red cloaks that lay before her. Stitched from scores of squirrel skins, the cloaks were voluminous and opulent. Clasps of gold, engraved with intricate Celtic knots, ensured the cloaks would sit securely over the shoulders of the wearer.

'Oh my, they're so beautiful,' said Almaith, her hand going to her mouth, her tears near.

Inscrutable as ever, Guertepir ran his hands through the silky fur. 'You've moved my wife to words … even to tears, and I commend you for that. These are fine garments and I give you my thanks for them.'

'They are the result of many kills and much needlework,' Dominic said. 'Months in the making, they were destined for the backs of Arthur and his woman. We thought they would look just as good on the backs of Guertepir and his lovely wife.'

Flattered by Dominic's words, Guertepir continued to stroke the cloak. Eventually, he turned his attention to Dominic. 'And so we come to the subject of Fincath mac Findchado,' he said. 'His fort is only one day's travel from the main port. Even a dullard could find his way there, but if you decide to approach him directly you'll need a good story.'

He paused and looked at the four men in turn, his eyes finally returning to Dominic as he pondered their chances. He knew Dominic; knew that any scheme put together by him would be thorough.

With this in mind, he said: 'I suppose you've already worked out what you're going to do, so I'll tell you about Hibernia.'

For the next two hours, Guertepir told them everything they would need to know about Hibernia — of how to approach Fincath, and what to avoid saying if, indeed, Fincath felt inclined to let them hold breath.

Never once did he mention a boat, always maneuvering away from the subject of travel. Eventually, tired and ready for more wine before he took to his bed, Guertepir dismissed them, granting them quarters for the night in an outlying hut away from the ringfort.

'Lucky we got him on a *good* day,' Dominic said with some irony, as they walked towards their quarters. 'Now we have the information we need.'

'But no boat yet,' said Withred. 'Without a boat the information is useless.'

'Tomorrow we meet with him again,' Dominic said, '… and tomorrow we need to leave and get this thing done. We can only hope he grants us the means to get across the sea.'

The next day, Guertepir's man, Diarmait, roused them. 'My master would have you meet him at the shore below the fort,' he said. 'Follow me. It's a steep but short climb down to where he waits.'

Murdoc walked beside Dominic as they tailed the long-striding Diarmait down the hill. 'Sounds promising,' he said. 'If we are to meet him by the sea, maybe he has a boat for us.'

'And maybe he plans to throw us to the fishes, knowing the tetchy bastard as I do. We'll know soon, whatever. There he is, see, beside the wharf.'

Guertepir stood, legs apart and hands on hips, waiting for them. Resplendent in his new cloak, he seemed untroubled by the thin November breeze that blew in from the sea. Tied to a capstan beside him bobbed a smallish, one sailed skiff, the word PELAGUS painted on its prow.

Before they could speak, he pointed to the vessel. 'This boat comes with a condition,' he said. 'It also comes with a pilot.'

He looked towards a small shack along the wharf. He beckoned a man from it. The man—wiry, tough looking, and weathered—walked towards them.

'Meet Druce,' said Guertepir. 'I own the boat, he sails it for me and earns his living by supplying my tables with cod.' Dominic's party reciprocated Druce's nod of greeting. 'He's also sailed across to Hibernia for me on several occasions. No need then for you to worry about currents or direction, Druce will get you across the sea in one day if the wind is favorable.'

'And the condition you mentioned?' Dominic said, warily. 'You said the boat comes with a condition.'

'Ah yes … the condition,' said Guertepir. 'Fincath's sons killed one of my wife's cousins last year—a dispute over cattle ownership as usual. The man was dear to her and she seeks retribution for his death. Last night, after you left to take your rest, it occurred to my wife that the opportunity for revenge had neatly presented itself with your arrival. She requests, therefore, that you bring back the head of one of the sons of Fincath mac Garrchu.'

Guertepir said the last sentence as if he were requesting that Dominic merely bring them back a piece of driftwood. The nuance of Guertepir's tone was not lost on Dominic.

Dominic's own tone was one of incredulity. 'That's all you want? Just a head, eh? You want us to bring back a man's head, and that's the price for using your boat?' He looked towards the bemused Withred, Murdoc and Flint. Withred shook his head.

'That's it,' said Guertepir, matter-of-factly, 'Take it or leave it.' As he looked at their reaction to his statement, something suddenly occurred to him. 'Oh … don't worry about the killing,' he said in an attempt to reassure them. 'Whichever head you bring back will belong to a man who has done many wicked deeds himself—a man who has killed and beheaded many others for next to naught wrongdoing.'

Dominic was having none of it, and had decided the conversation could have no possible conclusion. 'I do not kill a man unless *I* know he has done evil,' he said. 'We will find another boat. Thanks for the information you gave us last night. I wish you good day.'

As he turned to leave, followed by Withred, Murdoc and Flint, Guertepir looked up the hill and signaled to Diarmait who waited there. Followed by a group of thirty armed foot soldiers, Diarmait walked quickly back down the hill towards them.

Instinctively, Withred reached for his sword, cursing as he realised he had been forced to surrender it the day before.

'You disappoint me, Dominic,' said Guertepir, as the body of armed men arrived to surround them. 'I thought you would exact justice for me where justice is due. Now you have forced my hand.'

Dominic realised the futility of the situation, as did the others. Any action by them would be pointless and inevitably end with their deaths. He thought of the children again, and realized this was their only chance of getting to Hibernia. He made a quick decision. He would give his assurance to Guertepir, and worry about the requested severed head later. He was furious with Guertepir, but outwardly, he was calmness itself.

'All right, stay your hand; we will do as you ask. We hardly have a choice, do we?' he said.

'None … other than to die here and now,' said Guertepir.

'And you would risk war with Arthur for the sake of a severed head?' Dominic said.

'Better that, than war with my wife.' Guertepir was only half joking. He looked to his man, Diarmait, then at Murdoc. 'Take *him* back to the fort, he stays here.'

Expecting a reaction, ten of Guertepir's men quickly surrounded Dominic, Withred and Flint.

Guertepir turned to them, his tone one of mock reassurance. 'Don't worry; he'll be looked after until you return with your precious children … and the head. Then he will be free to return with you to Arthur.'

Glaring now, Dominic wrested his arms away from the men who restrained him. His full attention was on Guertepir. 'Harm him and the might of Arthur will be brought down upon you. Believe me when I tell you this. I thought you an honorable man, Guertepir, awkward and skittish, yes, but honorable nonetheless.'

'And so I am,' said Guertepir, trying to sound reasonable. 'The trouble is you underestimate the importance we Hibernians place upon repaying like for like, blood for blood, heads for heads. I will *honour* our bargain as soon as you return with the *head*. Oh … and one more thing; not any old head will do. The head will have an indelible mark on the brow: the mark of the snake. Only Fincath and his sons wear the sign. It marks them as high born. No other head will do.'

He looked up the track to Murdoc and his accompaniment of guards as they walked towards the ringfort. 'Bring me the wrong head,' he said pointing towards Murdoc, 'and I will give you *his* handsome head in return.'

Again, the guards restrained Dominic as he moved towards Guertepir. 'Do that and you will answer to me,' Dominic said. 'You will regret the day—'

'I've no time for this,' said Guertepir, impatient now. 'That's the second time you've threatened me. Do it a third time and I'll have you and your companions thrown into the sea.' He turned to address Druce who stood nearby looking less than comfortable. 'You told me earlier that a favorable tide is with us?'

'As we speak, my lord,' said Druce.

'And you are ready to sail now? Have you provisions on board?'

'All is stowed, my Lord.'

'Their weapons too?'

'Everything, my Lord.'

Guertepir held out his hands, shoulder high, palms up, as a conciliatory gesture to Dominic. 'See … I give you back your weapons. I send you to Hibernia armed to the teeth. Not such a bad man am I?'

'It would be hard to behead a man with the ledge of my hand,' Dominic said, 'so maybe your action has method behind it.'

Guertepir had had enough of talk. 'Put them on the boat,' he said to the guards surrounding them. 'Watch from the promontory and make sure the craft has passed from sight before you return to me. Leave two men to continue the watch until nightfall.'

Pushed towards the boat, the three men followed Druce. Once aboard, Druce skillfully adjusted the boom to catch the wind, and soon the skiff was skipping over the sea.

Druce sat at the rear of the Pelagus, his hand on the steering oar as he watched the horizon. 'I am but a sailor,' he said to Flint who was the nearest to him, '… a Briton like yourself. I do as Guertepir bids. I have no choice in the matter, otherwise my family starves and so do I. Neither do I have interest or knowledge of your business in Hibernia, other than your intention to visit Fincath mac Garrchu.'

Flint regarded Druce. He seemed honest enough. He certainly knew how to make the boat respond to his every command. 'Yes, I know,' said Flint. 'Guertepir has a blade held at your throat as well. I already knew you were obeying a man who can make you hungry if he so wishes.' Flint leaned forward and Druce took his proffered hand. 'We hold no grudge towards you,' said Flint. 'Just get us to Hibernia safely so we can get this done with.'

'And more importantly, get us back safely,' said Withred who had gingerly crawled along the boat to sit beside Flint. 'I have no love of the sea and don't wish to drink from it.'

Druce laughed. 'Don't worry, if this wind keeps snapping at the sail we'll reach Hibernia by nightfall. Once there you can drink ale my friend, and leave the brine to the fishes.'

Withred, who feared the oceans, was thankful when Druce's prediction proved accurate. A fresh, following breeze ensured the boat travelled at a steady seven knots and they sighted the Hibernian port ten hours after leaving Dyfed, and sixteen days after Maewyn, Elowen and Mule had arrived at the same port.

The dock master, Guairá, was a friend to Druce, and embraced him as he stepped onto the quayside. Druce told him the reason for his voyage. Told him he had brought three Britons to meet with Fincath at his ringfort.

Guairá greeted Dominic and the others. 'I can offer you basic but clean lodgings for the night,' he said. 'And for a reasonable fee, I have ponies that will take you to Fincath. A day's travel mounted will see you there.'

Unwilling to travel the night over unknown ground, they decided to accept Guairá's offer. They spent the night in a small cabin beside the docks.

A quiet day greeted them at first light. Druce, who was to stay behind, had agreed to wait at the docks for as long as it took Dominic, Flint and Withred to conclude their business with Fincath. He readied himself to work for his food and lodgings by assisting Guairá and his stevedores.

Guairá led them to the stables and picked out four well-used but sturdy looking ponies. 'Remember, take the road from the docks and climb up towards the trading post,' he told them. 'There you'll find Fincath's men. He leaves two of them there always to handle trade from the port. When learning of your intent to visit Fincath I wouldn't be surprised if one of them decides to take you to him.'

They gave their thanks to Guairá, bade their farewell to Druce, and set off upon their journey to meet Fincath mac Garrchu.

'We can only hope the flaw in our plan doesn't rear its ugly head,' said Withred as they made their way up the stony track from the docks.'

Dominic had squinted ahead, seemingly lost in thought. Withred's words brought him back to the here and now. 'It's on my mind too,' he said. 'In fact, was on my mind just before you said it.'

'What's the likelihood of this Fincath knowing *all* of Griff's men, *all* of his agents and seeing us as fakes, then?' asked Withred.

'Unlikely,' Dominic said, 'or we wouldn't be risking this. It's a long way to Norwic from here, so contact must be rare. But you're right; it *is* a possible flaw in the plan.'

Flint had been listening to the exchange. 'What if Griff's agent is already here,' he said. We're *seriously* in trouble if he is.'

'Maybe we're about to get advance warning of that,' Dominic said as the trading post came into view. 'The men in that building are the first to meet visitors to Fincath.'

As they approached the trading post, a man came out to meet them, bleary-eyed and worse for wear.

'Looks like they keep a little wine back for themselves before dispatching it to their master,' said Withred. 'Another one sleeps inside, by the sound of the snoring coming from that hut.'

Daman was the senior man at the trading post. His companion for the last two weeks—the man now unconscious from drink in the hut—was an out-of-favour retainer from Fincath's hall, named Odhran. Fond of drink, he had pestered Daman to pilfer wine and ale from supplies destined for Fincath. It had not taken Daman long to give in, and had soon shared Faelan's habit of excessive and regular consumption.

Life at the trading post meant long days spent doing nothing at all, and Daman had discovered the tedium to be bearable when his head swam with drink. Last night they had really gone at it, and it was with reluctance, that morning, that Daman had dragged himself off the floor when hearing the approach of riders. After casting a watery glance at his wrecked companion, he left the hut.

He stood at a slant, one arm stuck stiffly out against the hut as he steadied himself. His voice held a hint of a slur as he addressed Dominic: 'What's your business here, traveller?' he said.

Dominic got straight to the point. 'We are Britons from Norwic and representatives of Griff. Having travelled a long way to get here, we now wish to meet with Fincath, your lord.'

Faelan fixed his fuddled, red-rimmed eyes on Dominic, a hint of suspicion now flickering beneath their rheumy outflow.

'*New* men are you? he asked. 'Normally he sends the fiend with the black skin. Ugly as a whore's cunt he is. Ambriscus … Ambrosicum …Ambrosius, yes Ambrosius, is his name … I think. Gives himself a Roman name and has ideas above his worth.'

'Ambrosius has other things to do,' Dominic said, committing the name to memory. He was relieved that Flint's earlier fear that an agent of Griff's might already be visiting Hibernia was unfounded. 'We have been sent here instead, and are to negotiate further business with Fincath on behalf of Griff.'

Faelan looked up the track where it curved over a low hill and disappeared from view. Something niggled him, but his befuddled brain refused to unearth it. Eager to get back inside and sleep off last night's wine, and too tired to challenge further the stranger before him, he pointed up the track.

'That's the way to Fincath. Follow it, do not deviate from it, ignore any lesser track that runs from it, and you shall reach the mighty ringfort before the light fades.'

'Then we'll get on our way,' Dominic said. 'My thanks to you, fellow.'

Faelan scratched his head, his legs wobbly, as he watched Dominic's group ride over the hill and out of sight. Finally, it came to him. 'The slaves … they escaped.' His mutterings continued as he entered the hut, eager to seek his bed again. 'Fincath will have their innards … the slaves … run away, they did.'

Thirteen days after Fróech and Colman's search of the monastery, they sat with Fincath in his hall. Before them stood several jugs of ale, many now empty.

'Fucking monks,' said Fincath. 'If I find out they lied to us I'll burn their buildings to a char. This time next year, no one will know they ever walked this fucking island.'

'Maybe we should go back and catch them unawares … send Latchna back maybe,' said Fróech.

Fincath poured himself another flagon of ale from the jug. 'He found no tracks coming from the marshes, you say?'

'None,' said Fróech, as Fincath slid the jug over to him. 'He reckons they perished in the marshes; their bodies sucked out of sight. There the lie, under the mist and mud, he says.'

'More than likely they lie under the monastery blankets,' said Fincath. He looked to his other son. 'What say you Colman? Has the ale weighted your tongue tonight?'

'Yours is loose enough for ten of me father,' said Colman, 'and it's monks' ale that loosens it.'

Fincath rubbed his belly and belched loudly. 'It's good stuff, that's for sure. That's why they still live untroubled in this tuath—that and their bread and honey.' He studied his flagon, considering his options. He peered quizically from under his brow line at Fróech. 'You think we should send Latchna back then?'

'It'll do no harm,' said Fróech. 'Many days have passed since we left the monastery. If Latchna observes the monastery for a couple of days, he's bound to see them if they're there.'

'And then we can get them back and destroy the monks along with their bread, ale and honey,' said Colman.

The irony of Colman's tone was not lost on Fincath, but before he could respond, Fróech interjected.

'What we do to the monks can be discussed at another time,' he said. 'Merely making an example of their Bishop may be best.' He waved away the immediacy of the problem. 'But, we can deal with that when and *if* we find the slaves. What's important now is Griff being aware of our anger towards him. He'll have replacements sent as soon as he finds out. He knows he can't afford to lose our trade, and more importantly to him: our gold.'

'His boat's captain should be back at Norwic by now, so Griff *will* be aware what happened here,' said Colman.

'After I finished beating him around the dock and screaming my displeasure at him, he took the first tide and left,' said Fróech. 'The fat bastard should have got back to the British shore two days ago with the news.'

The solitary door to the hall opened, causing the flames on the lighted brands to dance and sputter as a chill breeze entered and whispered around the room. A retainer stood at the door, looking back towards the road that led from the hall.

'You'd better have a good excuse for allowing that draught to freeze my balls, lad,' said Fincath, as he stood and shook his flagon at the retainer.

'Three riders approach from Britannia, my lord,' said the retainer quickly. 'They are Griff's men. Come to check on business with you.'

Fincath and Colman looked at Fróech. 'It can't be,' said Fróech. It's impossible for these men to have been sent by

Griff … not so soon.' They stood together, their swords brandished, as Dominic, Withred and Flint walked in.

Fincath approached them and saw they were without weapons. His retainers knew better than to allow strangers into his hall armed. The last man who had been careless in the matter had had his eyes gouged out—the orbs thrown to the hounds. Fincath, himself had done it.

'Where's the black man,' said Fincath as he pushed Dominic chest, causing him to stumble back three steps. Any thoughts that Flint and Withred had of responding, vanished, as twenty of Fincath's guards stomped in through the door. The rattle of metal upon armour sounded about them as Dominic faced up to Fincath.

Dominic had anticipated this reaction from Fincath and had his story ready. He was to be the spokesman. 'Ambrosius is indisposed,' he said as he recalled the name from his meeting with Faelan at the trading post. 'He was wounded as he strove to protect Griff in a scuffle at Norwic docks. We are here to check you are satisfied with the goods sent, and also to hear of anything else you may desire from our island.'

Fincath felt the restraining hand of Fróech upon his arm. He looked at the hand, and then at Fróech, whose expression advised *not so hasty, hear what he has to say.* Fincath jerked his arm away. He turned his attention back to Dominic.

'It's lucky for you, that my son seeks to quell the ire of an old man,' he said. He swept his arm around him, inviting Dominic to look around the vast hall. 'You're here to check we are *satisfied with the goods* are you. Do you see any goods!'

Dominic, along with Flint and Withred, floated his gaze around the hall. Long lines of empty tables filled the floor space. Lighted brands and oil lamps provided the main source of light, yet many puddles of dark shadow infested the hall, making the place seem poorly lit and gloomy. A clutter of plates and several jugs of ale beside three disturbed chairs, told Dominic that Fincath and his sons had been the rooms only occupants until moments previously.

After looking around, Dominic took a closer look at Fincath and the two younger men who stood beside him. Like Fincath, they were stocky, strong looking men. All three had a snake symbol inscribed upon their foreheads. He remembered Guertepir's words when describing the highborn of the tuath: '*The head will have an indelible mark on the forehead: the mark of the snake.*' The men had to be Fincath's sons. Dominic groaned inwardly as he recalled Guertepir's price for releasing Murdoc when they returned. Another problem they could do without.

'Well? What do you see?' said Fincath.

Dominic shook his head. 'Nothing, my lord. Nothing but tables and chairs.'

Fincath nodded; his bottom lip pushed up like an arch; his smile upside down and grim. '*Nothing but tables and chairs,*' he nodded. 'That's because your slaves didn't even arrive here. Stolen, they were, even before they reached my trading station. What do you say to that, good envoy of Griff?'

Dominic looked to Withred, looked to Flint. None of them had to pretend to be astounded at the news, but Dominic now had to think quickly and respond. The children were either captured or dead. Now things had changed.

Astonished, he replied. 'We had no idea they had escaped. The man at your trading post told us nothing.'

He thought quickly. 'It's just as well we're here now, then. Now, we can try to deal with your problem.'

'And you *will* deal with this problem, believe me,' said Fincath. He looked at the captain of the armed men surrounding Dominic, Withred and Flint. 'Just you and six men remain here. Dismiss the others,' he told the captain as he sheathed his own sword.

Dominic chanced a quick glance at Withred. A brief and telling flicker of Withred's eyes told him he was happy that Fincath had sent away most of his men—told him that Fincath now believed they were Griff's men.

Still, Fincath wanted to be sure. 'How did you get here,' he asked. 'Why did you not sail with the others who came?'

'We sailed from the western shore,' Dominic said. 'We had business to attend to in the west for Griff, and it took us nearer the western shore. From there it is a shorter sail than from Norwic.'

At the mention of the west, Fincath's eyes narrowed. 'You sailed from the west you say. That must have taken you to that bastard, Guertepir.'

Dominic decided it would be better to verify Fincath's assumption, realizing that any attempt to wriggle around it would evoke Fincath's suspicion again.

'Yes we did go to Guertepir,' Dominic said, 'but trade is trade, and if Griff stopped doing business with everyone who was at conflict, he would soon be in rags.'

Fincath spat on the dusty floor. 'But Guertepir, for fuck's sake! That spawn of a poxed harlot would never have been born if my great grandfather had managed to remove the head of Eochiad, his ancestor. Cattle thieves the lot of them; and you tell me that Griff now does business with them.'

218

He looked at Fróech and Colman, who shook their heads in disgust, but Fincath's resigned sigh hinted that he was nonetheless ready to talk business.

He waved Dominic and the others to the table. 'Sit,' he said. 'We will discuss what Griff can do to make this right.'

A lengthy discussion ensued as Fincath negotiated replacements for the escaped children. Dominic played the part of the hard-nosed agent well and quibbled with Fincath, before reluctantly agreeing a much-reduced price for the next shipment of 'goods.'

'And it will be gold on delivery this time,' said Fincath. 'Make sure Griff is aware of that. Take it or leave it, tell him. If he decides to leave it, he can say goodbye to any future trade with me. No more gold goes to him until I see the next slaves with my own eyes.'

As Dominic continued to play the part, Flint squirmed inwardly. Although aware that Dominic had to go through the motions, he, nevertheless, could not help being alarmed at the thought that Maewyn, Elowen and Mule were abroad and possibly alone in this strange land. The thought filled him with the utmost compulsion to run out of the hall and start his search for them immediately.

His discomfort was not lost on Dominic who made to wrap up his business with Fincath.' So you want a girl-child and two youths to replace the slaves who escaped. Also twenty barrels of iron ingots, as well as finished goods: hauberks, helmets, spears, cloth. I'll take gold now for everything but the slaves. Griff, himself, has to give payment up front for finished goods—the slaves he will have to chance from his own pocket for now.'

Withred's eyebrows shot up on hearing Dominic's request for gold from Fincath. *Clever bastard*, he thought. Gold would come in handy for bribes. Better still, it would provide recompense for the disposed villagers back home in Britannia. The Hibernian was partly responsible after all. Without him providing a market for slaves, the raids would not happen.

Fincath eyed Dominic coldly. 'Your master taught you well it seems. His fist is as tight as a runt's ring-piece.'

He turned to Colman and whispered to him. Colman left the hall. Fincath now turned his attention to Flint and Withred.

'Silent ones you are,' he said. He studied Flint, blatantly looking him up and down. 'Looks like you're more used to war than trade, fellow.' Before Flint could respond, Fincath turned his attention to Withred, giving him the same appraisal. 'As for you man; it would be better if I keep the children away from you lest you keep them awake at night with your fearful visage.'

Withred scratched the stubble on his head as a flicker of a smile played upon his lips. 'Maybe I'm not fair to look at,' he said, 'but I'm certainly fair in trade, and that's all that counts here.'

'Nevertheless, trading is a recent occupation by the look of you,' said Fincath as he re-examined Withred. 'And by the sound of you, you're Saxon.' He looked at Withred's scalp, then grabbed and scrutinized his hands. 'Head covered in scars, hands full of callouses. Hardly the hands of a man who stacks rolls of linen and silk, are they?'

'I am of the Anglii tribe, not Saxon,' corrected Withred, without animosity. 'And you're right; my hands are formed by the stroke of cold, hard iron, rather than the

220

caress of soft cloth.' He nodded towards Flint. 'But like my friend here, my role is to protect Griff's men.'

'You'll certainly need your skills if you hang around Hibernia too long,' said Fincath. 'There's always someone here to part travellers from their gold.'

Colman re-entered the hall carrying a bulging purse. He threw it on the table next to his father. Fincath picked it up assessing its heaviness in his hand. 'Speaking of gold, here's the amount as agreed earlier,' he threw the purse to Dominic, '…less the gold for the replacement slaves—that will be paid when I see them with my own eyes.'

As Dominic caught the purse, he noticed that darkness had fallen outside. Briefly, he considered making his excuses and leaving to travel through the night to look for clues to the children's whereabouts.

Then it occurred to him that scrambling around in a dark and strange land, only to greet the morning exhausted and unfulfilled did not seem such a sensible idea. No … it would be better to stay the night with Fincath and glean information from him about the theft of the children.

'You think the children may be dead?' he asked, with this in mind.

Fróech answered for his father; the first time he had spoken. 'Dead … no. Their trail carried to the monastery, a good day's ride from here. Then it disappeared into the marshes beyond. Latchna, our scout, skirted the bogs but found no trails leading from them. He guesses they perished under the mud, but I am not so sure.'

Dominic, along with Flint and Withred, realised that they needed to get to the monastery at the first opportunity and pick up the trail. Unwilling to arouse

Fincath's suspicion further, Dominic considered it unwise to ask the whereabouts of the place, so he gave Flint and Withred a quick warning glance not to ask any more questions.

Fincath, now tired and ready for his bed, stood and made to leave. 'You are our guests for as long as you wish to stay,' he said. 'Although I make no apologies for admitting I'll be glad to see you return quickly to Britannia. The quicker you get news back to Griff, the quicker I get my slaves.'

'In that case,' Dominic said,' you'll be glad to learn that we thank you for your offer of a bed but will stay one night only. Our business in Hibernia is now over, and we purpose to travel back to Britannia on a favorable tide tomorrow if possible. The year draws on and the sea doesn't suffer fools in winter.'

'I'll send in women and bed rolls to warm you then,' said Fincath, as he walked to the door, flanked by his son. 'The tables in here will have to do to sleep upon and rut upon.'

'By your leave, we need only bed rolls,' Dominic said.

'Boys then?' asked Fincath perplexed and unable to understand why any man would refuse a strumpet for the night. 'Perhaps you prefer boys?'

'No boys either,' Dominic said. 'We wish to start at first light, so sleep is important to us. Carnal pleasure can wait until we get back to Britannia.'

Fincath shrugged. 'As you wish … just bed rolls then,' he said, as he left the hall.

Fincath ushered Fróech and Colman towards his dwelling near to the outer wall of the ring fort. Once inside, he sat at his table and accepted three cups of wine from his wife.

With a nod, he dismissed his woman from the room and looked questioningly at Fróech and Colman. 'Well? What do you think? Did Griff send them?' he asked.

Fróech shrugged. 'Who knows? We've only their word for it, but why would they come to us if they're not from him?'

'I know one thing,' said Colman. 'They have our gold in their purse and they leave with it tomorrow.'

'It suits our purpose if they *are* who they say they are,' said Fincath. 'And they knew the name of Ambrosius, so they must have been near Griff at the very least. One thing's for sure; they couldn't have come at a better time as far as our loss is concerned.'

'Still, it would make sense to watch them and find out if they have any other reason for being here,' said Fróech.

Fincath nodded in agreement. 'Latchna is the man for *that* task. They should go straight back to the docks in the morning if they are telling the truth.'

'Then let Latchna tail them at dawn and make sure they sail back to Griff,' said Fróech. 'If they deviate from their plan in any way, then that makes them liars, and I'll have their heads on poles before the next night falls.'

During the night, Dominic, Withred and Flint had had much to discuss, and much to plan. In view of the startling news of the escape of Maewyn, Elowen and Mule, Flint had to be persuaded not to leave in the dark and start the search at once. Dominic had explained the folly of such an action, and finally Flint had settled down somewhat, but still he continued to pace the hall restlessly as he enthused over the next day's actions.

One thing they all agreed on was the pressing need to find the monastery and the marshland behind it.

Withred had reasoned that the monks would have given the children sanctuary according to the tenets of their Christian faith. The monks may then have persuaded Fincath's men that the children had passed them by and got lost in the bogs.

Withred's theory had bolstered Flint but not helped him settle. More than ever, he had paced the room and stressed the importance of getting an early start, so they could get on with the business of finding the children.

Eventually, though, his tiredness had overcome him and he had taken his bedroll. Exhausted, physically and mentally, he had quickly fallen asleep alongside Withred and Dominic.

As the medley of three snoring men came to him, the man left his hiding place in a shadowy corner of the hall and made for the door. He had heard much … he had heard enough. Now he could use the information to his gain. The dawn would be interesting. The dawn would restore his fortunes.

CHAPTER SIXTEEN

As the days had rolled by, Maewyn, Elowen and Mule had settled into a quiet routine at the monastery. At night, they slept in the loft above the cattle barn, away from the main cluster of monastery buildings. Rodric had considered it the safest place, as it would allow them to slip away unnoticed if the need arose.

Ingle spent as much time with the children as his schedule would allow. Maewyn, in particular, would frequently accompany him as he went about his everyday life, often helping him with his chores.

Always they talked. Incessantly they talked: about their lives before they met; about their families; and often about Ingle's vocation.

One day as they herded the cows back to the barn, Maewyn (who had absorbed much of what Ingle had told him about the life of Christ) had asked Ingle, 'How can you be so sure that Jesus walked the earth as a man? How can you believe he is the son of God?'

'It is spoken of in the bible', said Ingle. 'And the bible records events from the past, just as the Romans recorded events from *their* past. That is how we know things: through the written word.'

Maewyn was not fully convinced. 'Ah yes, my father once told me that a great scribe named Tacitus was responsible for writing much that is known about Rome. What he wrote we know now to be true, but some of the things the bible claims to have happened makes me scratch my head at times.'

'Faith—that's what you need,' said Ingle as he tapped his stick against the rump of a wandering cow. 'Back in line, you silly lump,' he grumbled at the stray, before turning his attention back to Maewyn. 'Sometimes it doesn't pay to think too much about what Jesus told us. Just believe in it, Maewyn. It's far simpler if you just believe.'

But, much of what he told us I *do* believe in,' said Maewyn. 'That all men and women are of the same importance in this world. That all of us have a place in it...' He paused, his head awash with recent memories. 'But why must some men be bad? Why must they kill? Why must they take what is not theirs to own? Why did God allow evil men to kill my father?'

'But God does not direct the actions of men,' enthused Ingle. 'That's the whole point. He tells us how to live and we get on with it as best we can. The men who killed your father can never have heard the teachings of Christ or his followers. How could they? Matthew told us: *Thou shalt love thy fellow man as much as thyself.* That is the message we monks seek to give to anyone who strays into our enclosed world. *That* is why we are here, not just to grow vegetables, milk cows, brew ale, and pray. Every bad man we can convince to be good is one less bastard walking this earth.'

Maewyn could not help but smile at Ingle's colourful tone. 'And that's one less bastard in heaven,' he said, as he opened the barn door to allow the cows in. At his words, Ingle quickly crossed himself, hoping to cancel out out his indiscretion. As the animals ambled past him ruminating and flicking their tails, Maewyn laughed aloud at Ingle ... the clown.

'What?' asked Ingle, smiling himself now.

'It's you,' said Maewyn. 'You just can't help yourself can you? I've seen Rodric and the others killing themselves not to smile at some of the ungodly things you say, and the rapid crossing that follows.'

Ingle pointed to the sky. 'I'll just have to hope *He* has a sense of humour then, won't I?'

Maewyn slapped the rump of the last cow to enter the barn. 'If He hasn't, then I don't think I want to be in his company,' he said as he clattered the timber doors shut.

As October blended seamlessly into November, Maewyn spent many similar days, laughing and talking with Ingle. Sometimes Mule and Elowen would accompany them, but mostly Maewyn and Ingle went about their business as a pair.

Mule, for his part, had taken a liking to the fishponds. The monks had excavated the ponds years before for the purpose of breeding fish for the table. Donard, the scribe, had fashioned a rough rod and line for Mule, and the youth spent many of his days fishing for the bream, eels and lamprey that teemed within the murky water.

Unsurprisingly, Mule had fallen into the pond one day after struggling to grab an eel. Elowen had watched as the monks had pulled him out, and from that day onwards, she had fished alongside him, fearful he would surely drown if left to his own devices.

In the evenings, Rodric, Ingle and Donard would sit with the children in the refectory, with quills and ink and scraps of discarded vellum from Donard's scriptorium.

On the wall, Donard had tacked a piece of calfskin. Written upon it were all the letters of the alphabet. Each night he pointed to the letters and the children would write them down upon the vellum. Soon, Elowen and Maewyn were able to recite the entire alphabet and write the letters down when asked to do so by the monks.

For Mule, it was a task beyond his ability, but he was happy just to scratch incoherently upon his piece of vellum whilst mouthing the names of letters that bore no similarity to the scrawling before him.

As the nights passed in front of the tables, Elowen proved to be an able pupil, but Maewyn in particular demonstrated a sharp and acute intellect that was far above anything that Rodric and Donard had previously witnessed. Within a week, Maewyn had learned to write sentences in Latin, and in doing so, he learned to read short passages from the Bible.

One night after the children had left them, Rodric remarked to Donard, 'He's a clever one is Maewyn. Never have I seen anyone learn their letters at such a speed.'

Donard nodded sagely. 'Yes, and we have had many boys pass through here, some of them extremely astute in their own right, but none like him, that's for sure.'

Rodric smiled as he remembered the day he found the children as they hid at the rise overlooking the monastery. 'He got them away from capture and to safety here, and for a lad of his years that was something. His spirit is resolute, that I've always known, but the speed of his mouth surely demonstrates his intellect. It's impossible to best him verbally; his riposte is as sharp as your quills, Donard.'

Donard laughed. 'Yes I know, I've noticed he always has to have the last word with Ingle, and that fellow is no oaf himself.'

'The children suffered at the hands of a man on their sea voyage,' said Rodric, as he considered Maewyn's indiscriminate use of his mouth. 'Ingle told me the tale. A bad fellow he was, intent on revenge and murder. Even then, Ingle tells me, Maewyn could not help but backchat the man; was unable to remain silent as the monster spat his venom at Maewyn and the other two. Maewyn told Ingle much more as well about their hardships since they were taken; has spoken at length with him about his disillusionment with the nature of man.'

Donard picked up the vellum before him, the piece that Maewyn had practiced on before leaving for the barn. It read: *The book of the generation of Jesus Christ, the son of David, the son of Abraham.*

'Ingle tells me that Maewyn had no faith in anything before he came here,' said Donard absently, as he held up and studied Maewyn's neat handwriting. 'Saw Christians as deluded fools to be laughed at and teased. Now, Ingle says that Maewyn is ravenous in his quest for knowledge.'

'Maybe he's just trying to make sense of the world,' said Rodric with a shrug, '…trying to find a reason why some men will die for you, yet some will happily torture and kill you.' He looked tellingly at Donard. 'You think he may be considering following the path of Christ?'

'Stranger things have happened,' said Donard, as he placed the parchment back on the table and looked at Rodric. 'One thing's for sure though; Maewyn will come to his own conclusion. He's not one to be preached at. Ingle is quite positive on the matter.'

Maewyn *had* come to his own conclusion; he had concluded that the teachings of the bible, as conveyed by Ingle, were at least worth further consideration. Since he had started to write the beautiful script, form together the words, and assimilate the language of Latin, his hunger to find out what further insights the strange book had to reveal had become insatiable.

First, though, he had to learn to read whole sentences and understand what they meant. The books at the monastery were artifacts beyond any price, and he knew the monks would never allow him to practice on them unsupervised. For now, he had to rely on Ingle reciting passages of scripture to him.

After a morning of helping Ingle, Maewyn found himself at a loose end when the young monk left him at midday to attend sext: the fourth of seven prayer sessions required of him every day. He was aware that Mule and Elowen would be at the ponds so decided to join them there.

He found his brother lying on his belly, chin propped in hand, watching his fishing line for movement. Beside him, Elowen sat, chewing on a stalk of grass and staring absent-mindedly into the water.

Mule rolled over on his back as Maewyn plonked down beside him. 'Two today up to now,' he said proudly. 'One lamprey and one bream.'

Maewyn looked up and down the water line, frowning when he saw that no fish were in evidence. 'Well … what happened to them?' he asked.

'The bishop says we have to put the tiddlers back,' said Elowen, replying for Mule, '… that way they'll grow big enough for the table and feed six men instead of two.'

'Seems a bit pointless to me,' said Maewyn. 'Waiting here all day to catch fish, then throwing the things back in the water when you finally manage it.'

'Not all the fish go back in the water,' corrected Mule. 'The big ones we take to the kitchens …'

The man was careful as he parted the bushes to get a better view of the children. Seventy paces below him beside the fishpond, they indulged in their idle chatter. Typical of children, they were lost in the moment— oblivious to anything else around them in the world.

The man had carefully flanked the monk whose job it was to watch the main trail into the monastery from the woods. Flanked him then made his way to a place where he could look out over the grounds. Poaching had been his purpose. Maybe steal a cow while the monks prayed; he knew they prayed at noon.

However, this was far better. Knowledge was power, and he had found the missing slaves. The slaves who had been the talk of the tuath.

CHAPTER SEVENTEEN

Govan helped Simon and four other men drop the large wooden gate into the hinge-pegs that were set into the edge of the upright beam. Already positioned, the other gate rested securely on its hinges.

'There ... the gates are in place,' said Simon as he stood back with Govan and the others to study the completed job.

Before them, the stockade curved away from them and out of sight. Both gates rested in an open position, allowing them to see the completed huts within the village compound.

'Four weeks to build it from a ruin ... an incredible effort,' said Govan. He frowned and kicked at the dirt beneath his feet. 'And two weeks since Dominic and the others left for the west coast and Hibernia.' Squinting through one eye as the sun slid from behind a cloud, he looked at Simon. 'Do you think they'll be there by now, Si?'

Simon silently mouthed his count as he pondered the question, his head bobbing in unison as he added up the probable days required for the journey to Hibernia. 'Should have arrived three or four days ago by my reckoning,' he said. 'They should be well into their search by now.'

Govan looked along the dredged ditch beside the stockade. Now cleared of bodies and debris, green water filled it to within a hand's width of the rim. He remembered the day of the raid when he had floundered in its depths; the day they had stolen his beloved Elowen; the day they had slaughtered, Bran—his truest friend and brother. He thought of Mule and Maewyn, now alone somewhere in the world with Elowen.

Noting his distracted stare and aware of his anxiety and worry, Simon placed his hand on Govan's arm. 'They'll get them back, don't ever doubt it,' he said. 'We couldn't have four better men searching for them. If they are there to be found, Dominic will find their trail.'

'Where else *could* they be?' asked an alarmed Govan, as Simon immediately regretted the tactlessness of his last words. 'What if they were *not* taken to Hibernia? What if Dominic and the others have crossed the sea for no purpose?'

'I've no doubt they *are* there,' said Simon, eager to put this particular worry from Govan's mind. 'I was not thinking clearly … they could be nowhere else. They sailed from Norwic to Hibernia—that we know.'

Govan, still troubled, looked through the doors of the compound towards the huts within. 'This was a place of death, forty-six days ago,' he said.

Simon looked surprised at the exactitude of Govan's recollection; a look not lost on Govan. 'Yes … I've counted every single day that's passed since my girl was taken from me,' explained Govan, 'and I'll count the days until she comes back, or until the day I die if she does not.'

'And I will count with you.'

Both men turned to see Nila who had come to see the completed village.

'I will also count out every day until my boys come home, as I know they will.' She looked at the compound, at the ditch, at the huts. 'A place of death then, and a place of death now,' she said.

Shivering, she walked towards the gates. Govan joined her and took her hand. Together they walked through the portal and reluctantly entered the new village.

For several days, Tomas and Will had watched Ranulf's raiding party slowly move towards the lands protected by Arthur's militia. Having travelled several miles from Brythonfort, the two rangers had gone beyond the boundary of the protectorate, intent on giving early warning of Saxon incursion into the land beyond Aebbeduna.

'Be careful of their scout, I know him from old,' said Will, as he lay on his belly beside Tomas on a hill overlooking the Saxon camp. 'Traitorous bastard by the name of Irvin. Worked for Rome, but went over to the Saxon cause. Sold out for gold, can you believe that?'

Tomas squinted as he strained to see into the camp two hundred strides distant. 'He has no love of his own folk then?'

'None at all. I worked with him a spell, and spoke with him on a few occasions. Of the Cantiaci tribe in the southeast, he is. Bitter and hateful against the Catuvellauni people to the north of him. Doesn't care if they're fellow Britons or not. Just hates them because of some blood feud that's been going on forever.'

'I'm Catuvellauni, but I would never fight against my own people,' said Tomas. 'I know of the conflict you speak of, but most sensible folk have put it behind them long ago, along with all the tribal disputes— at least we can thank Rome for that.'

'Bastards like him never do put it behind them, though,' said Will, holding his hand up as a visor against the dipping sunlight. Shifting his position to get a better view of the camp, he continued. 'It was a small progression for him to go from hating the Catuvellauni to hating the rest of the native people here. Like I said, money moves him, that's what he loves above all else. Fuck the lives of our people as far as he's concerned.'

Tomas tried to spot Irvin from the group below. Most of the men wore similar garb: knee length tunics gathered at the waist by leather belts; woolen britches and leather shoes. A few wore chainmail hauberks that covered their heads and shoulders only.

Only one man stood out, and Tomas had a good idea who he was. His imposing manner and confident air, and the way the men suddenly changed their bearing as he went to them, told Tomas he had to be Ranulf. His armour, too, was different. Unlike the other men, his hauberk covered his entire body, reaching down to his knees.

A horse and rider entered the camp, causing Will to snatch at Tomas' arm. 'That's him … that's Irvin,' said Will. 'I'd recognize his riding style from a field away.'

'No doubt he's been looking for easy pickings,' said Tomas.

'He'll find nothing but small farmsteads round here, but by the size of that party below they're after a bigger prize: a large settlement and all the people in it.'

'That will take them back to our lands, then. They need to move ever westwards if they are to find untouched villages…' Tomas voice drifted to silence as Ranulf and Irvin walked to the edge of their camp. 'See,' he whispered. 'Irvin seems keen over something. He's pointing to the west. Maybe he's found something to interest Ranulf. Maybe they're ready to move on.'

'It will fit with Arthur's plan if they do, but they'll not move today. I know Irvin; he likes a full day ahead of him when on the trail and it will be dark soon.' Will turned to look at Tomas. 'Talking of Arthur's plan, do you have confidence in it?'

Tomas nervously loosened his neckerchief a touch and looked at Will. 'Confidence in the plan … yes, but that doesn't mean it doesn't frighten me shitless.'

Will smiled as he assessed Tomas. *Scared shitless you may be*, he thought, *but you still have the balls to do it.* Eventually he gave a little laugh. 'Scared, you and me both,' he said. 'So it's just as well that men like us will run through fires for for Arthur.

CHAPTER EIGHTEEN

The emerging dawn was visible as a thin grey line on the eastern horizon as Dominic's group thanked Fincath for his hospitality.

'Do not forget that I want my replacement slaves as soon as possible,' said Fincath, who was dressed in a linen nightshirt that reached to his ankles. 'And I will not pay until I look into their eyes and touch their skin.'

Dominic grunted as he heaved himself onto his pony. 'Worry not about the slaves being stolen this time,' he said. 'Armed men of standing will guard the next shipment,' he nodded to Flint and Withred, '… maybe even these two bruisers.'

Fincath rubbed the chill out of his shoulders as he stood hunched beside Dominic. 'As long as I get my slaves, I care not who guards them,' he said. He slapped the rump of Dominic's pony sending it into a slow walk away from him. 'Just get you down to the docks and catch the tide,'

Dominic now put his pony into a trot followed by Flint and Withred.

Fincath watched as they rode through the gates of the ringfort and down the hill and out of sight. Two retainers pushed the heavy gates shut with a woody clatter and secured a thick oak beam into the hasps fitted to the gates.

Fróech joined his father and placed a fur stole around his shoulders. 'Latchna's on his way,' he said. He's provisioned for one day only … one day is all it should take for the Britons and Angle to get to the docks. If they go elsewhere they have lied to us and Latchna will return with news of their treachery.'

'If that proves true then we need to be ready to ride out tomorrow,' said Fincath. 'The one named Dominic has my gold in his purse and I will take both his head and the gold from him if he has another reason for being on this island. If they have not been truthful they will all pay dearly.'

Fróech looked over towards a huge, carbonized iron cauldron that hung over a stone fire ring. 'If they *have* been lying to us then they deserve a death befitting cheats. Remember … we once made a man's death last five days as we boiled him in that. We could do them one at a time while the others watch and anticipate their own torment.'

Fincath hugged the fur stole around him and smiled as dwelt on the past execution. 'The agonized screams of dying bastards are melody to my ears,' he said. 'It's been too long since we've heard the prolonged tune of death within these walls. I suppose it's less effort to remove our enemies from their heads—too fucking quick for some of them though.' He walked over to the cauldron, smiling as he placed his hand upon its crusty rim. 'It would almost be worth them lying to us, just to get this going again.'

Their nostalgia was interrupted as Latchna arrived leading his pony. 'I am ready to go, my lord,' he said.

'Do not on any account let them see you,' said Fincath, turning his attention from the cauldron. 'As soon as you see them leave on their boat, return back here. Collect Daman from the trading post, and leave him at the docks overnight in case they attempt to fool us and return to the shore.'

'And if they don't go to the docks?'

'Then return to me at once. Establish which direction they head for and get back here without hesitation. Travel through the night, do not rest … do you hear me?'

'Clearly, my lord' said Latchna, as he mounted his pony and rode towards the gates.

Flint looked concerned as they rode down the track in the direction of the docks. 'We'll get to the docks by nightfall,' he said, 'but that doesn't help our cause. We need to find the monastery, and we have no idea which way to go.' He turned in his saddle, looking back up the hill. 'For all we know we may be riding away from it.'

'We have no option but to ask someone where it lies,' said Withred, 'but the people in these parts are loyal to Fincath. Unless we want to bring his wrath down upon the monks, we need to be careful who we ask.'

'You reckon if he finds out we went to the monastery and rescued the children he would kill the monks?' asked Dominic.

'Undoubtedly,' said Withred. 'He's no Christian himself, that's for sure. The monks provide him with comforts, and that's why he leaves them alone, but he's not a man to upset, that I'll warrant. If he finds out—'

'Ahead!' interrupted Dominic.

Looking furtive and afraid, a man waited for them fifty paces down the track.

After surviving the trial-by-neck, Kael had stumbled into the pitch-black Hibernian night seeking shelter. Already disowned by his family for his cold-blooded murder of a young herdsman in a quarrel over a game of dice, he was at a loss of where to go.

On that first night, he had slept shivering at the edge of the track that led to the docks. Swollen and constricted after his ordeal, his throat continued to bleed, causing him to hawk out great globules of bloody mucus throughout the night.

The next day, exhausted and near to collapse, he had walked like a drunken man down the track towards the trading station. Daman, the man who worked there, had once been his friend. He was Kael's last hope.

Daman was well aware of Kael's past indiscretions, and knew he had been destined to endure the trial-by-neck. He was astounded, therefore, when Kael had appeared alive at his door.

Looking up and down the road to ensure no one witnessed his assistance to Kael, Daman had ushered him into the hut — his curiosity, as much as anything else, driving his actions.

After hearing Kael's tale, and subsequent pleas for help, Daman had given Kael water. Food was out of the question for Kael, who found it impossible to swallow anything solid.

Knowing he would be branded as a sympathizer to a callous murder if it was known he had helped Kael (and therefore would undoubtedly be expelled from his much coveted position in the trading post); Daman had told Kael he could give him shelter for one night only.

Subsequently, Kael had left the next morning, provisioned with enough food and water to last him several days.

Two further miserable weeks went by for him, during which time he took to scavenging and stealing food whenever the opportunity arose. For two days, he had a brief respite when the dock master, Guairá, employed him to help unload a large shipment of grain from southern Gaul. During this time, Guairá permitted him to sleep in the warehouse alongside the rats, and so gave him temporary respite from the cold and miserable nights.

The job ended along with the shelter it provided, and after leaving the docks, Kael made up his mind to seek out the monastery and the monks. Desperate, he had decided to steal from them. Their cows were highly prized and he could barter much for one. Enough, maybe, to set him up away from the isle; get him a passage away over the sea to Britannia where no one knew of his crime. There he could start a new life.

When he saw the children — the children who had to be the missing slaves that Daman at the trading post had told him about — he realised there might be an easier way to get himself on a boat to Britannia … an easier way than having to steal, then sell, a cow.

However, as far as passing on the information for profit, Fincath was out of the question. He knew Fincath; knew he was furious that he had survived the trial-by-neck; knew he would accept the information from him and then expel him from the tuath as before — perhaps even kill him.

Unsure of how he could profit from what he knew, Daman returned to the docks to seek work. Guairá had nothing to offer him this time, but whilst at the docks Kael had noticed a British boat berthed at the wharf — the boat which had carried Dominic, Flint and Withred.

Guairá had given Kael a brief explanation of the Britons' business, telling him they were agents for a slave trader in Britannia; told him they had left that morning to meet with Fincath.

The significance was not lost on Kael. They were slave traders, he knew of missing slaves; surely, they would thank him generously for such news. The information had to be advantageous to them. He looked at the British boat and fancied himself sailing back to Britannia on it.

He learned that almost half a day had passed since the Britons had left the docks, so he decided to follow them to Fincath's ringfort, intent to keep their trail fresh.

He arrived after midnight and decided he would learn more. Knowing of a tight squeeze-through under the palisade, he *swam the ditch and entered the ringfort. A similar breach in the roundhouse afforded him entry, and he crawled into one of the many shadowy corners just as Fincath and his sons had left, leaving the Britons alone.*

He had moved even closer to the Britons, and been able to listen to most of their conversation. Although strange in accent, he understood most of what they said. What he heard astounded and excited him. They had actually made the trip to find the children.

Unwilling to risk any commotion—any chance at all that Fincath would discover him inside the ringfort—Kael (who knew of the Briton' intention to leave the next morning) left the compound. Tomorrow he would meet them on the open trail away from the ringfort.

He slept alone and exposed for the rest of that night—the last time he intended to do so. Now he had news that would undoubtedly take him to Britannia. Better still, it was news that would command a payment of gold.

Dominic rode up to Kael, followed by Withred and Flint. 'What's the story, fellow?' he asked as he looked down on the care-worn Hibernian who waited on the track for them.

'One you'll be interested to hear,' said Kael, '… but it comes with a price.'

Dominic raised a quizzical eyebrow. 'A price you say. For something to be worth a price it needs to be a commodity desired by the buyer.' He looked Kael up and down, his gaze stopping upon the angry welt on his neck. 'You look to me like you've been through a battle, man. What can you possibly have to sell?'

Kael's smile was sly, flickering only briefly, and barely lifting the corners of his mouth—the kind of smile, thought Dominic, that would get a fellow his teeth knocked out in a tavern.

'Before I sell, I need to name my price,' said Kael. 'Information about stolen slaves does not come cheaply.' He paused and nodded mysteriously at Dominic and the others.

Flint was off his mount at once and pinned Kael by his biceps. 'What do you know about them,' he demanded as he pushed Kael into the shrubbery beside the track. 'Where have you seen them? Fuck any payment—I'll pay you with cold iron unless you spit out what you know.' Kael cowered, his eyes wide and terrified, as Flint withdrew his dagger from his belt.

Withred dismounted and walked over to the pair. He restrained Flint's arm. 'Maybe we need to talk further before we spill any blood,' he said. 'I'm sure we can come to an agreement that's acceptable to us all.'

Flint, pushed Kael away, but continued to glare at him. 'They are alive then,' he said, as his tone slowly changed from anger to hope. 'You have seen them alive, man … where?'

Looking hard-done-to, Kael adjusted his ruffled tunic. His tone was sullen. 'I have news that's to your advantage and you make to kill me. I *will* give you the information you need, but please just let me name my terms, that's all I ask.'

'Name them then … and quickly before I ignore my friend's advice,' said Flint.

Kael came straight to the point. 'I want passage to Britannia when you set sail, and the means to set myself up when we get there.' As he said his last words, Kael's eyes darted to the purse tied to Dominic's belt.

Dominic still mounted, looked to Flint and Withred. Flint shook his head, Withred looked unsure.

Dominic spoke. 'By "*means to set myself up*" I presume you want gold from me. A passage to Britannia *and* gold. May I ask why you wish to leave Hibernia?'

'Does it matter,' said Kael, now frustrated and impatient. 'I just have the desire to leave this wet clod of an island ... there's no more to it than that.' Kael couldn't believe he had to explain himself. He had expected things to go much smoother than this; had expected the Britons to be more reasonable and readily accept his offer. But ... no ... they stared at him, even now. Three stern, menacing men, not satisfied with his explanation.

'All right, all right,' said Kael, tetchily, unable to endure Dominic's questioning stare a moment longer. He knew he had no option but to invent an excuse for leaving. 'I had a disagreement with a favourite shitlicker of Fincath's.' He flapped his hands dismissively before him. 'It was just a disagreement over some cattle, but the man took it straight to Fincath. Now my name's not worth shit in this tuath; now I need to get out.'

Dominic studied the man. He knew he was lying. Regardless, he decided to press him about Maewyn, Mule and Elowen.

'Tell me what you know about the children,' he said. 'I will give you a handful of gold, but only after we have the children on the boat and are a safe distance away from these shores ... and, yes, you *can* sail with us if you deliver the children. Now tell us your tale.'

Kael recounted his story; of how hardship had come upon him after his quarrel with Fincath. He finished by explaining how desperation had forced him towards the monastery, where he had seen three children—two boys and a girl—fishing by a pond. Flint got Kael to describe the children.

'It's them … no doubt,' said Flint, excited now. 'How long to the monastery from here?' he asked Kael.

'A day and half mounted.'

'We'll be there by mid-day tomorrow then,' said Flint as he climbed upon his pony. He offered his arm to Kael, who took it and swung onto the back of his mount.

Flint led the way, their passage easy and uninterrupted down the good track that passed by the trading post. No man stirred there. *No doubt sleeping off more of Fincath's wine,* thought Dominic who (ever the tracker and scout) rode at the rear of the group, alert to any movement or potential danger.

As late afternoon passed over into evening, little light remained in the sky. Withred wheeled his pony back down the track towards Dominic. 'There's good grass and water ahead for the ponies and a level space for a camp,' Withred told him. 'Unless you intend to press on through darkness it looks to be a good place to stop until morning.'

'Stop we will then,' Dominic said. 'I don't fancy trying to follow the trail over rough ground. Kael said the monastery lies on the other side of a wood.' He looked behind him, then at Withred. 'We've been followed since we set out', he said. He paused as a startled Withred searchingly eyed the track behind them.

'Fincath must have put a man on our tail,' continued Dominic. 'He's kept well back but I've seen him a couple of times when I withdrew into the cover beside the track.'

Withred sighed. 'This complicates things but it doesn't surprise me,' he said. 'I would have done the same if three strangers had turned up on my threshold then left the day after with a purse of my gold. What should we do now?'

'Like you say, it complicates things,' Dominic said. 'As soon as we turn from the track, it confirms we were lying about going straight back to the docks. He'll be back to Fincath at once, then we *will* be in trouble.'

'We have to stop him then,' said Withred.

'Undoubtedly; there's nothing else we can do.'

'What do we do with him?'

'Keep him quiet.'

'Kill him, you mean?'

Dominic looked troubled. 'I find it hard to kill anyone who's done me no harm. For all we know the man might have been forced by Fincath to follow us.'

'My thoughts too,' said Withred. 'I've never killed a man unless he deserved it, or attacked me.' He rubbed his forehead, frustrated at the complication. 'It was never going to be easy. Already we have the problem of getting Murdoc out of Guertepir's grasp when we return to Dyfed—we won't be taking a severed head back with us, that's for sure— and now this. What do we do?'

'First, we ride to the front with Flint and Kael. Then I'll try to deal with it.'

All day, Latchna had been careful to ride out of sight behind the trackside shrubbery. When the criminal, Kael, had joined up with the three Britons, he had considered returning at once to Fincath, but had eventually decided to follow them, reasoning it would take only another few hours to establish whether the Britons intended to take a boat to their homeland. If they did, it would mean their meeting with Kael was of no significance; if not, he would return at speed to Fincath with news of British *and* Hibernian treachery.

For the rest of the day he kept out of sight—in the shrubbery just off the track—as he shadowed his quarry. Frequently, though, he stepped back onto the track to confirm the position of the distant group of riders.

One man, obviously a tracker himself, had ridden at the back of the group, and it had taken Latchna much of his skill and guile to remain hidden from him.

Now, as the riders stopped ahead of him, Latchna concealed himself behind a grassy mound. Five hundred paces distant, the tracker and another man spoke.

Latchna watched as they turned to head towards Kael and the other Briton who waited for them. As the sun dipped under the low hills westwards, he saw the four riders leave the track.

He considered the significance of this. As the docks were still five miles distant, they had either pulled into cover to camp for the night, or changed their route significantly. He had to be sure before he returned to Fincath.

If they camped, he would have to wait the night out to ensure they continued to the docks the following day. If not, and they continued in a direction away from the docks, he would need to return to Fincath news of British subterfuge.

Careful now, he tethered his pony and stealthily made his way on foot through the trackside brush, making for the point where the riders had left the main route.

Clever bastard was his immediate thought as Dominic grabbed him from behind and slammed him to the ground. *Not one twig snapped, not one branch rustled.*

Dominic jammed his forearm across Latchna's throat; his knife—a trophy from the Saxon, Bealdwine, who he had killed in a British forest—held to Latchna's face.

'Just keep still and don't even think about fighting me,' warned Dominic.

Aware he was out of his depth Latchna became compliant.

Dominic continued. 'Good man, you've obviously got no wish to die. Now turn on your belly and give me your arms.'

Again Latchna complied, allowing Dominic to bind his arms from behind.

Dominic pulled him to his feet, then pushed him forward. 'Don't talk, just walk … ahead, until I tell you to stop.'

'It's you! Latchna!' said Kael as Dominic placed his hand on top of Latchna's head and pushed him down upon his rear, next to Withred's recently-made fire.

Sitting cross-legged, his arms tightly bound behind him, Latchna eyed Kael disdainfully. 'Yes it's me, he said. 'The man you owe your life to. If I hadn't arrived with news of the slaves' escape when you were playing tug of war with the cow, your eyes would have popped out of your detached head.'

Kael flicked a sly glance towards Dominic and the others. All had turned to look at him.

He turned away from them and back to Latchna. 'Sounds to me that you're still licking Fincath's arse,' he sneered. 'Still a liar, too, by the sound of it.'' Pointing to Latchna, he turned to Dominic. 'This man's killed many people who deserved to live. He is a known liar and will say anything to save his own skin. Kill him now, is my advice, unless you want to chance him getting news of your plans to Fincath.'

Dominic had not shifted his gaze from Kael since Latchna had spoken. 'I do not kill any man on the say so of another,' he said, coldly. He turned to Latchna. 'Until you spoke, I reckoned we had only one problem … now maybe we have two. Why was he subject to torture? What disagreement with Fincath was so bad that he put that welt upon his neck?'

Latchna eyed Kael with disdain, his smile sardonic. 'Told you he had a disagreement with Fincath did he?' Latchna gave a dry little laugh. 'No … he had a *disagreement* with a lad over a game of dice; disagreed with him so strongly that he cut his throat and allowed him to bleed out like a butchered swine. Then he robbed the—'

'Do not believe the lying lackey!' Kael stood over Latchna jabbing his finger in accusation. 'I've told you; he will say anything to save his own—'

Dominic now intervened, grabbing Kael, who looked ready to attack Latchna. He threw him back to Flint. 'This is getting us nowhere. It's one man's word against the other, and we still have a job to do.'

He looked both men over and could not help thinking that Latchna seemed the more worthy man. Something in the way he had responded to the shiftless Kael rang true with him. Maybe Latchna was just a scout like himself, doing his job for Fincath. Anyway, why would he lie about Kael?

Turning to Withred, Dominic made his decision quickly. 'We'll leave this man here with you, Withred. Guard him until we get back with the children. Then we'll leave him bound and make for the docks.' He looked at Latchna whose relief was palpable. 'Don't worry, we *will* leave word of your location here, and as soon as we are at sea someone will release you.'

Latchna looked relieved. 'Being bound for a couple of days is but a small worry to me … I expected you to kill me.'

'Give me reason too and I will,' said Dominic. 'Scouting for Fincath, however, is not reason enough.'

Withred, who shared Dominic's perception of Latchna and Kael, spoke to Flint who still restrained Kael.

'Did he tell you how to get to the children as you rode with him today?'

'Yes he did,' said Flint. 'The way seems straightforward … over some rough ground, but straightforward it seems.'

Withred's look to Dominic was telling. *Now we know the way to go, do we really need a murderer in our company.*

Dominic read Withred's look immediately. He looked to Kael. 'I will not take a killer to Britannia—will not expose the children to your presence. You lied to us, of that I have no doubt. Somehow, you escaped execution and I will leave it at that. You, too, will remain here with Withred, and be released—'

Kael's rising fury suddenly exploded as he grabbed Flint's knife from its belt loop, jerked free of him, and lurched forward. Latchna had no chance to defend himself as Kael thrust the dagger through his heart, killing him instantly.

Flint hit Kael from the back, knocking him to the ground. Still wielding Flint's dagger, Kael was able to wrest himself from Flint's grasp and stumble to his knees. As he made to attack Flint, Dominic's arrow entered his eye. Feebly, he pawed at the arrow before falling dead to the floor.

Dominic attended to Latchna. He looked to the others, the shake of his head confirming what they already knew.

Flint was furious with himself. 'I let him take my knife and an innocent man was killed. UNFORGIVABLE!' He snatched the arrow from Kael's skull and tossed it back to Dominic. Then he pulled his dagger from Kael's dead grip.

Withred could not help but smile at the young man's frustration. He put his hands on Flint's shoulders and looked him in the eyes. '*Every … fuck-up's… a.… lesson … learned*,' he said slowly, stressing every word. 'You'll never fall for that move again, so take comfort from it.'

But Flint was far from comforted. 'My line of work means I cannot afford to make fuck ups. Fuck ups lead to the grave for people like me.'

As Withred and Flint had spoken, Dominic had begun the task of removing Kael from sight. Grunting as he dragged him towards a clump of thick shrubbery, he said, 'This man fucked up, that's for sure. Always thought he'd be a problem … seemed a shifty bastard from the beginning.'

Dominic placed Kael out of sight and went to Latchna. The man lay dead on his side, his arms still tightly bound behind his back. 'This man may or may not have deserved to die—who knows what his past deeds were—but no man should die as he did.' He looked to Withred and Flint who were gazing thoughtfully at Latchna. 'Your turn,' he said as he pointed to him. 'Drag him next to Kael. My old back's done enough.'

The next day, at first light, they took to the track.

Flint pointed to a colony of trees in the distance. 'According to what Kael told me, half a day's ride through those woods should see us to our destination. If we keep beside a faint path that runs near a stream, we'll come to the monastery.'

Looking pensive, Dominic tapped at his teeth as he thought things through. After a brief assessment, he said, 'We need to get the children and be back at the docks by evening. Fincath will send his sons out today, be sure of that, so time will be tight for us.'

To Withred, he said, 'I think it would be better if you continued down the track to the docks. Druce will need to ready the boat for the journey back home, so you need to alert him. It's crucial the boat is ready to sail and we're on it as soon as we reach the docks.'

'That leaves just two of you,' said Withred, concerned. 'What if things go wrong again?'

'They'll come after us in numbers, I'm sure, so it doesn't make any difference how many *we* are … we'll die anyway if we can't avoid them. Speed is the thing now. We need to get this done and get on the boat.'

Withred mounted his pony. 'I'll see you at the docks, then,' he said, aware that Dominic's shrewdness had not failed them up to now. 'Get there by this evening, though, or I'll be frantic.'

Kael's description of the route proved true, and by midday, Dominic and Flint viewed the monastery grounds from the same outlook used by the children seventeen days earlier.

Dominic spotted a young monk coming up the path from the fields below—a lad, no doubt, sent to watch for intruders.

'We need to avoid him,' he whispered to Flint, as he pulled him into a pile of bracken before them. 'We need to view the grounds for ourselves first. The monk will deny the children are here, he has no choice, he doesn't know who we are.'

They lay still as the monk passed by. When satisfied he out of earshot, Dominic and Flint parted the green wall before them to give them a view of the grounds below. They watched, as below them, Mule walked over to the pond, hand in hand with Elowen. Maewyn was not with them. Flint looked to Dominic his face both elated and trembling with emotion.

'We've done it Dominic,' he whispered, his eyes welling. 'We have crossed the sea and found my brother and niece, and hopefully Maewyn is nearby.'

Dominic hugged him then, as the strain and tension of the last few weeks—the worry that his brothers and niece could be dead— finally voided from Flint. Now he sobbed, unable to contain himself, such was the flood of relief and emotion that engulfed him.

'Go to them. Let them know you have travelled the earth to get them back,' Dominic said, smiling through his own tears.

Flint stood and waded through the bracken until he was clear of its snagging grasp. The slope ran down before him to the pond. He looked to Dominic, his face now radiant. Unable to speak, such was his euphoria; he turned and began to run down the slope. 'Aiden! … Elowen!' His tears came again as Mule and Elowen looked up towards him. 'I've come for you!' he shouted. 'We are going home!'

Fincath gnawed on his nails as he peered from the ringfort's gates. A day and night had passed since he had dispatched Latchna to follow the Britons. To determine their route was Latchna's mission; to confirm whether the Britons had been true to their word. Either way, Latchna should have been back by now. After all, hadn't he ordered him to spend just one day on the task. He would personally whip the man to the bone if he had tarried needlessly.

He turned, as Fróech and Colman (both mounted) approached him. Behind them, ten other men sat astride ponies, ready for the chase.

'Don't run the horses into the ground,' fussed Fincath, as he held onto the noseband of Fróech's pony, keeping its head still. He peered up at his son. 'You have all day … and this evening should see you at the docks.' Fróech looked to Colman and rolled his eyes, the look saying, *'The old bastard's telling us how to do our jobs again.'*

Fincath pointed to the man directly behind Colman, as he continued to address Fróech. 'Eion's almost as good a scout as that lingering bastard, Latchna. Have him watch for any deviation from the trail. If so, send five men with Colman to investigate. *You* continue to the docks. It must be determined whether the Britons have left as they said they would.'

Fróech heeled his pony into a walk through the gates. Fincath walked beside him, still holding the pony's noseband as he peered up at Fróech.

'Their heads … I want their heads,' he hissed. 'If they are still on this island, whatever the fucking reason, you are to bring me back their heads.'

Fróech patted the blade at his side. 'Sharpened this morning to a very keen edge … sharpened for that very reason.'

Finally, Fincath let go of Fróech's pony, allowing him to jab it into a canter down the hill.

'And if you see Latchna!' shouted Fincath, 'tell him to get himself back to me at once. *He* has some explaining to do!'

The twelve men continued down the track until they approached the trading post at mid-afternoon.

Colman rode at the head of the assembly with Fróech. 'We'll look in on Daman and hear his news,' he said. 'Maybe he's seen the Britons pass by.'

'Daman's got a helper now,' said Fróech. 'Remember that drunken shit, Odhran, who spilled a goblet of wine on father … you *know* … the one who's lucky to be alive still.'

'Ah yes,' said Fróech as it dawned on him. 'Father punched him around the hall. Knocked his teeth out and broke his nose; kicked him that hard he probably ruined his manhood too.'

'Well,' said Fróech as he dismounted, 'we're about to be reacquainted with him.' He pushed through the door into the dim room. 'Daman,' he shouted. 'Daman, have you seen …'

He voice faded as an awareness hit him. As his eyes had become used to the low light, he had noticed that a comatose Daman and Odhran lay before him. Both were now snoring loudly under the storage shelves. Beside them lay two upturned and empty flagons of Fincath's prized Gaul wine.

Fróech's face was a picture of astonishment as he took in the scene.

Daman, a cord of elastic spittle hanging from his lower lip, had stirred and opened one blurry eye to look at Fróech. He frowned as the gravity of his situation slowly penetrated his brain. He sat up, banging his head on the storage shelf. *It was Fróech! … Oh fuck! … Oh shit! … It was Fróech standing over him!* Fróech grabbed him and pulled him to his feet. Hardly able to stand, Daman wobbled before him.

'F-F-Fróech,' he attempted, but Fróech, who was having none of it, dragged him to the door, and threw him outside.

Fróech followed him, cold and furious. He threw him to Colman, 'Hold him there, till I come back,' he said with cold fury.

Back inside, hands on hips, he towered over the still-snoring Odhran. 'Too pissed to even hear me,' he said, icily, as he removed his knife.

Outside, Colman had dismounted and grabbed Daman who swayed before him, looking cowed and wretched. Colman's face was a picture of disgust to rival Fróech's as he appraised Daman. Daman could only look to the floor in shame.

Colman was about to give Daman a lambasting when Fróech walked from the hut. In his left hand, he held Odhran's head by its hair … in his right hand he held his own bloody knife. He tossed the head away and watched it roll across the crusty ground.

'He'll fucking sleep forever now,' said Fróech, as he wiped his knife across a clump of grass, leaving it a mixture of green and streaked crimson. He looked at Daman who continued to look at the ground. 'Now before I do the same to you, what have you to say?' He walked to Daman and grabbed his hair, forcing him to look him in the eyes.

'N-n-nothing,' my lord,' spluttered Daman. 'Except that he ...' shoulders hunched, he pointed to Odhran's head, '... except that he pestered me day and night to break into the wine.'

'And have you no mind of your own, man?' asked Fróech, his voice laced with disgust.

'No ... I was weak my lord,' admitted Daman, looking down to his feet again as soon as Fróech let go of his hair.

Fróech pushed Daman towards Colman, then jabbed a thumb behind him towards the hut. 'Kick him back in there, brother.'

He looked to a rider mounted nearby. 'Ennis ... you stay here with the drunkard, and make sure he tidies the place and himself up before we get back. We need him here ... he can live for now, but I'll let father have the last say on that one.'

Colman returned after kicking Daman back into the hut. He looked down the roadway. 'Some use that was,' he said, 'now we have no idea whether they passed here or not.'

'Probably did,' said Fróech. 'Eion has been looking for signs all day, and they've not left the main track, he reckons.'

'Onwards and downwards then,' said Colman as he heaved himself onto his pony.

When half way to the docks from the trading post, Eion spotted a disturbance in the ground.

He reported to Fróech. 'Ponies left the track here, my lord ... could be carrying the men we look for. It's a well-

257

used side track and there are a lot of prints but at least three ponies have left fresh prints.'

'How fresh?'

'Today or yesterday without doubt.'

Fróech yearned for Latchna's guidance, unaware that the scout lay dead alongside Kael fifty paces away. Fróech knew that Latchna would have been more precise—would have known *to the time of day* when the Britons had passed.

'Looks like we part company here, then,' Fróech said to Colman. 'Father said you and five men are to follow any deviating trail we come upon.'

'A familiar trail too,' said Colman. 'Remember when we went to look for the escaped slaves?' He nodded towards the narrow path that led into the trees. 'Well that's the way we went ... leads to the monastery eventually.'

Fróech remembered now. Frowning, he asked Colman, 'You think *they* may be looking for the slaves? But *why*? And why would they travel to the monastery?'

Colman shrugged. 'Who knows? Perhaps they gained information from somebody on the way down to the docks. It's still possible the fugitives could be at the monastery; haven't we always suspected the monks of hiding them?'

'But why would the Britons seek them?' asked Fróech.

'Makes sense really, doesn't it? They'll save their employer, Griff, a lot of gold if they can find them and return them to father. No doubt Griff would repay such an action generously.'

'If that's the case, then they should arrive here soon by my reckoning.'

Fróech now seriously considered going with Colman. He looked at Eion, aware that he was still not fully confident in the man's abilities. *What if he was wrong? What if the Britons had gone to the docks and took sail already?* If so, he could get back to the comforts of the ringfort by tomorrow night and put this thing behind him. Yes, he would go to the docks with the remaining four men and send Colman to follow the trail to the monastery.

Mule's mouth hung open as Flint ran down the hill to him. It looked like his brother, but how could that be. Here he was in a strange land across the sea, and Flint lived on the other side of the sea. Elowen confirmed that it was indeed Flint when she ran towards him. 'Flint,' she screamed, 'I knew you would come for us.'

Flint met her and took her into his arms, twirling her round and round as he hugged her.

'I never would have stopped looking as long as I held breath in my body,' wept Flint. 'How could I have done that?'

He stopped twirling as Mule clamped him in his strong grip. Hugging Flint and Elowen at the same time, Mule laid his head against Flint's shoulder. 'Our da is dead,' said Mule. 'Now you must be our da.'

Flint hugged Mule back, flooded with love for him. 'Lad … I'll be whatever you want me to be.' Now he looked towards the monastery as Maewyn's absence again dawned upon him.

Elowen, who continued to beam up at him, put his mind at rest. 'Come, we'll go to Maewyn,' she said. 'He's working in the scriptorium with Donard.'

'He's learning his letters,' added Mule, 'and he's real good at it.'

Flint laughed. 'You lot are impossible. I've worried myself sick over you all, and when I get here, you two are having the time of your life, fishing; and Maewyn's becoming a scholar. Whatever am I going— '

Ingles cry of alarm, had them turn to observe the young monk running down the hill towards them. Between them and Ingle strolled Dominic, seemingly unperturbed as Ingle closed upon him. Ingle held his habit hitched to his knees to aid his movement, his white legs pumping frantically below him.

Dominic held up his hands, palms outwards, as Ingle rushed up to him. 'Whoa! young fellow,' he said. 'We are friends.' He pointed to Flint just as Ingle skidded to a halt before him, his hands bunched into bony fists. 'Does that man look like he's trying to hurt them?'

Ingle peered downwards towards Flint, squinting and scrunching up his small, freckly nose as he took in the scene below. Reluctantly he shook his head. 'It doesn't appear so,' he conceded.

'That's because he's the boy's brother and the girl's cousin,' said Murdoc.

'He's … Flint?' said Ingle, who knew the name well from the many stories the children had told of him.

'The very man,' nodded Dominic. 'All the way from Britannia with me and another fellow. All the way from Britannia to find them, we've come.'

Ingle relaxed and unbunched his fists. 'Come, I'll take you to the bishop,' he said. 'He'll be amazed to hear this.'

Flint's reunion with Maewyn held all the emotion and surprise of his earlier meeting with Mule and Elowen. Maewyn had wept upon seeing Flint as a great surge of relief and joy engulfed him. The burden of being the one to ensure the safety of Mule and Elowen had gone. Now he had his brother—the man they all idolized—with them. No one could hurt them now. Now, they were safe.

Later, the four of them walked with arms over shoulders into the refectory where Bishop Tassach awaited them. Beside him sat Rodric and Donard. A little way down the table sat Ingle and Dominic.

Tassach smiled as the happy group entered. Spreading his hands, he invited them to sit down.

He tipped his head towards Dominic. 'Our friend, Dominic, counsels a speedy departure so this meeting must be brief.' His brow became knitted, and his expression took on a graver cast, as he continued. 'Speedy it must be because, in all likelihood, according to Dominic, Fincath or his sons have already started their chase.'

He looked towards the door as the sound of grunting ponies filtered into the room. 'Such is the urgency to get to the docks by nightfall that your mounts are ready and provisioned as I speak.'

Flint looked at the four monks in the room and realised what danger they had risked (still risked) in taking in the children. 'But won't our visit cause you problems with Fincath?' he asked, concerned.

Rodric, who had previously spoken at length with Dominic about the matter, shook his head, dismissively.

'No doubt we will have a visit from the mac Garrchu people before long but we have our story ready for when they arrive. We'll say you came looking for the children but to no avail. Then we'll tell them you left to search the bogland. That should keep them off your tails until you get to your boat.'

Dominic stood, restless and eager to leave. 'Yes, and we really must get going,' he said. 'Withred and Druce await us—hopefully with a ready boat and a helpful tide. It's vital we set sail tonight.' He looked out of the narrow slit window of the refectory. 'We still have half a day of good light if we leave now.'

Flint and the children stood to say their goodbyes to the monks.

Tassach and Donard talked briefly with Dominic, as Rodric embraced Mule and Elowen.

Maewyn spoke to Ingle. 'You made me laugh all day and every day and I thank you for that. Above all, you helped me realise that not all the men in this world are evil. For many days after we were taken, we met only awful people and I was beginning to think that the world had gone bad forever.'

'Never think that,' said Ingle. 'Remember that the Lord above will repay both good and evil when the day of reckoning comes.'

Maewyn laughed. 'Well, if he needs a court jester then you've got it made.' Unable to hold back any longer, he hugged Ingle, then. 'Thank you, thank you,' he said as his eyes moistened. 'I listened to everything you told me about the Lord *and* everything else, and although sometimes I turned it into a joke I really did listen.' They hugged for a while longer before Ingle left to say his goodbyes to Elowen and Mule.

Donard approached Maewyn and looked at him fondly. 'I enjoyed my time in the scriptorium with you,' said the scribe. 'Never have I had a more apt pupil than you. Another ten weeks and you would have been reading the Latin script without hesitation.'

Maewyn blushed at the praise. 'It was not me, but the way you explained it so clearly,' he said modestly. 'And the stories you translated were truly awe inspiring. It's easy when the payment for reading the script is the unfolding of such wondrous stories.'

Donard took a step back and raised one enigmatic eyebrow at Maewyn. 'Maybe we could make a monk of you yet,' he mused. Then his serious look melted away, 'But it's no good preaching at you; you will come to your own conclusion—that we all know.'

'You know me well then,' smiled Maewyn.

'And we may still meet,' enthused Donard. 'Remember, we sail to the north of your country—to Deva—four months from now. Perhaps we could meet you there; I'm sure you'd like to see Ingle again.'

Maewyn looked surprised. 'Ingle sails with you?'

Donard looked furtively over to Ingle who was now saying goodbye to Dominic. 'Yes, but don't tell *him*,' he whispered. 'The bishop has decided his tendency towards irreverence could do with a bit of hard travel to blunt its edge.'

Maewyn's smile was skeptical. '*That*, it will never do,' he said.

Three hours later, Dominic, Flint and the children, having ridden through the woods, approached the track leading to the docks. Dominic rode ahead this time, aware that the chase would be well under way by now, and would come from the direction of the main track.

Flint knew something was afoot when Dominic returned from up the trail filled with a sense of urgency. 'Get off the track now, six riders head towards us.'

Flint, who carried Elowen on his pony, was quickly into the cover of the broom outcrop beside the track. Mule and Maewyn, sharing the same pony, followed. Dominic was the last to enter. He dismounted and turned to repair the parted shrubbery as best he could.

'They're still a fair distance up the track,' Dominic said as he led his pony into the broom. 'We have a little time now to get deeper into the cover.'

The ponies pushed further into the scrub until an unyielding entanglement of shrubbery completely halted their progress fifty paces in.

'Stay here and be silent,' whispered Dominic to the children. 'Flint, come with me.'

They silently returned to the edge of the track. Kneeling in the cover of the broom, they watched as Colman and his five riders made their way towards them. Ready to fight, should things go wrong, Flint's sword swayed in his grasp. Dominic nocked an arrow into his bowstring. 'Move back with me, out of sight but within earshot,' he whispered to Flint.

Despite his hurried attempt at repair, Dominic knew that a visible trail lead from the track. A good scout would not fail to see it … he would see it, even in the dark. With heart bounding, he drew his bow to its full tension and prepared to engage the Hibernians.

Colman looked quizzically at Eion as he reached him. 'Why do you stop?'

'Some activity on the trail here, my lord. It looks like they might have halted here.'

'Well they've not passed us, so it must've been on the way to the monastery. Maybe they stopped here to rest.'

Eion looked thoughtfully into the undergrowth, unaware that Dominic and Flint stood only ten paces from him. He studied the broom, looking for disturbance, but none was apparent to his eye, so he looked at the ground beneath his feet. Here, the spoor was obvious, leading both up and down the track.

Frowning, he pondered a while longer. Finally, he turned to Colman who waited impatiently behind him. 'We keep to the track, my lord. Their marks are strongest straight ahead towards the monastery.'

Dominic and Flint slowly and silently exhaled their relief as the group moved away. After waiting a while, they ventured to the side of the track again.

'Kael killed their best scout when he saw Latchna off,' Dominic said, as he looked up the track. He looked down to the disturbance in the ground. 'How could he not see *that*? I was ready to fight them; we have been fortunate Flint.'

'Then, let's hope our luck lasts until we're safely on board the boat,' said Flint.

Ingle saw Colman's entourage coming and reported to Tassach at once. When he arrived at the monastery, Colman dismounted and walked over to the waiting Tassach. 'Where are they,' he demanded.

'Been and gone,' replied Tassach as he fussily rearranged his habit. 'Gone to the marshes to look for the slaves.'

'Why would they come here first?' asked Colman, unconvinced. 'And how did they know to go to the bogs?'

'They were told by a traveler they met. He told them of the rumour that slaves had escaped and fled to the marshes. 'The route to the marshes passes us here at the monastery and that is why they stopped a while.'

Colman eyed Tassach. 'Always you have a good story for us when we come to you, and maybe that is just what this is: a good story.'

As he held Tassach in his stare, Rodric, who could see that his bishop was beginning to wilt, stepped in.

'It is not a story, my lord, it is the truth. They stopped here only a little while, then left for the wetlands. They were seeking the children: their intent to return them to your father, thus saving their master, Griff, his losses.'

It confirmed what he, Colman, had worked out for himself earlier. The concurrence of Rodric's explanation, now suggested he might have been right in his assumption. He looked towards the trail that led to the marshes. 'How long since they left?' he asked.

'Half a morning, my Lord, their trail is still fresh to see.' answered Rodric. 'They held hope they could find the children.'

'They will not find them, they are already dead,' said Colman impatiently.

'Well in that case they will be near the sea by now. We told them of a shortcut that leads from the marshes to the docks should their search prove fruitless.'

'Then that's the way *we* will go,' said Colman as he beckoned tetchily to the monk who held his pony.

To follow the trail to its conclusion and meet up with Fróech at the docks was now Colman's intention. Without ceremony, he mounted and rode from the monastery.

Blowing softly in relief, Rodric turned to Tassach who mirrored his response. *Just as well, we sent three monks to lay a trail again,* he thought. *Now they have something to follow.*

Three hours after leaving Dominic and Flint, Withred had arrived at the docks at midday. Druce, who was eager to get back to his life in Britannia, was more than glad to see him. Together, they readied Druce's boat, Pelagus, for the return journey. By late afternoon, the boat was provisioned and ready to sail.

Withred looked up the hill that led from the docks. 'This is going to be tight,' he frowned. 'Dominic and Flint should be here soon, if everything went smoothly for them.'

'The tide couldn't be better so I hope they *do* arrive soon,' said Druce.

The top of the boat's sail was just visible beside the wharf. The low tide had the boat bobbing fifteen feet below them, accessible by a hemp ladder. A further fifteen feet of deep water lay beneath the boat.

Guairá, the harbourmaster, looked down at the boat. 'Tricky beggar to get into, that'll be,' he said. 'Hope your friends, when they arrive, don't have anything bulky to load.'

Withred considered the situation as it stood. He knew the time had come to tell Guairá and Druce the reason for visiting Hibernia. If things had gone well, Dominic and Flint would be well on their way to the dock by now. When they arrived, he could not risk a spontaneous bad reaction from the two men before him. It would be better if he dealt with any problems *now*, rather than have complications later. Druce would be no problem, he was quietly confident about that, but Guairá was an unknown quantity. Where his loyalty lay was anybody's guess. The man seemed affable enough, but for all he knew he could be Fincath's cousin. If Guairá reacted badly then he would have to take care of him.

'The load is not bulky, Guairá,' said Withred. 'In fact it will load itself, or should I say *they* will load *themselves*.'

Guairá's head shot back in surprise. 'You're telling me you are taking people back to Britannia?'

Withred nodded and looked at Druce, whose face rivaled Guairá's in astonishment. He told them the tale of the children's capture and the reason they had set off to find them; told them that Flint was a brother to the boys and a cousin to the girl. When he finished, he looked from Druce to Guairá. Transfixed, both men had listened to the tale without interrupting him.

Druce was the first to speak. 'I have children,' he said, 'and I would have done the same. In fact I would sail around the known world to find them.'

Withred sighed, relieved that he would not have to deal with his sailor. That would be a problem in itself. He looked at Guairá, trying to read the man, but he remained inscrutable. Withred subtly dropped his hand to the hilt of his sword.

Guairá saw the movement, but only smiled sadly. 'There's no need for that, man,' he said. 'Unlike Druce here, I have no children … my wife is barren, you see.' He swept his arm around the docks. 'This here is my child, and here I live with my woman.'

He noticed that Withred still gripped his sword. 'You fear I will tell Fincath, but I will not, and I will tell you why.' He pointed up the track, towards the woods that were visible at the top of the hill. 'Your friends come from the monastery beyond the woods, and they come with the children. Have you any idea what Fincath will do to the monks if he suspects they were involved in this?'

Withred nodded and was about to answer but Guairá continued. 'I told you I have no children, but I do have a

268

nephew who I love more than life. Ingle is his name, and he is a novice at the monastery. If Fincath suspects that the monks surrendered the children to your friends, my nephew will die. Need I say more? So stay your hand, Withred; you have no need to worry about me.'

Withred, who still looked up towards the woods, was about to respond when Fróech and four men crested the hill some four hundred paces distant.

Guairá followed Withred's gaze and was on to it at once. 'They've not seen you yet, so get to the warehouse and don't move,' he said to Withred. 'Let me and Druce deal with this as best we can.'

Withred hesitated a moment. By his reckoning, Dominic could not be far behind Fróech's group and that meant trouble. Should he fight or should he hide? Realising the probable conclusion of the former option, he heeded Guairá advice and ran, crouched, over to the warehouse.

Guairá quickly took charge. 'Get down to your boat and busy yourself,' he said to Druce. 'You need to keep out of the way. They'll know your boat is British—her Latin name gives it away. You won't see Latin displayed on any boat from *these* shores.'

'What will you tell them?'

'The Gods know,' said Guairá. 'I've not had time to think. Just get yourself down to your boat.'

Druce swung onto the hemp ladder and clambered down its fifteen frayed rungs to his boat.

Fróech and his entourage soon reached the docks. Guairá was a long-term acquaintance of his clan, and approached him as a friend. 'Guairá, you old bull … it's good to see that you still breathe,' said Fróech as he clasped the dock master's hand.

Guairá affected a delighted laugh. 'And you, Fróech,' he reciprocated. 'At my age, I'm grateful each morning when the situation is so.'

Fróech smiled, then looked around him, now eager to get on with the purpose of his visit. Frowning, he walked to the edge of the wharf. He returned to Guairá. 'I'm here to make sure that three Britons who carry my father's gold have sailed, as they said they would, back to Britannia.'

'And so they have; they left just after midday,' Guairá said without hesitation. He had rapidly cobbled together his story as Fróech had walked to the wharf.

He could only hope the Britons would see Fróech's party when they crested the hill above the docks, which could be any time now from what Withred said. If they had any sense, they would wait and hide until Fróech left. After that, they would be free to sail away.

Fróech's expression edged on the side of skepticism. 'You're sure they were the people I seek?' He pointed behind him towards the wharf. 'A British boat lies moored below. What is *its* purpose?'

'It brought grain this morning … grain bound for the south,' said Guairá. 'It arrived just as the Britons—three useful looking men—left with their pilot.'

Fróech nodded, lips pursed, looking satisfied with the answer—a look that said, *Yes, you have just described the men we seek.* Fróech looked up the hill, possibly anticipating his pending departure. Guairá now dared to hope he had fooled Fróech.

On the contrary, Fróech was becoming uneasy as he further dwelled upon Guairá's statement. How could they have made it to the docks so quickly if they had diverted to the monastery, as his scout had suggested?

Moreover, it was just too neat a story from Guairá. What about the British boat now docked? The boat might well belong to the Britons who carried his father's gold.

'The man in the boat … I would speak with him,' said Fróech, determined to examine the matter further.

Taken aback by Fróech's sudden demand, Guairá, nonetheless, readily agreed to call for Druce, knowing it would arouse Fróech's distrust if he did not.

He shouted down to Druce who sat as if busy unraveling a twist of rope. 'Druce, fellow!' shouted Guairá. 'My friend, the cattle lord would speak to you.' He turned, smiled, then winked knowingly at Fróech. He shouted back down to Druce. 'Maybe you'll get a job from him … fetch his father some grain from the warehouses in Gaul.'

Fróech's looked to his man, Cillian, who stood beside him. The look said, *He's just told him what to say.* Understanding the look, Cillian nodded.

Druce was soon up the ladder, standing uneasily before Fróech. Fróech asked him about his journey, and Druce, much to Guairá's relief, concocted a story of his voyage from Gaul with a hull crammed with grain.

'Small boat for grain?' observed Fróech.

'The price for grain is high so late in the year,' said Druce. 'A larger shipment would cost far more than my buyer could afford.'

Guairá' tensed as Fróech asked Druce: 'And your buyer is …?'

Fróech had looked at Guairá as he had asked Druce the question; his look telling Guairá to, *Let the man answer this for himself.*

'A man in the west, named Renan,' invented Druce. 'A settler … new to the island.'

Fróech was not fully convinced. Guairá had said the grain headed south. The trader said it had gone westwards. Maybe an understandable mistake, but still, he could not take the chance. He would take the man back to his father. If he was with the Britons, he was undoubtedly their sailor. Without him, they were going nowhere. If they had already left, then so be it. He would leave Cillian at the docks to hole the boat as an added assurance.

'It would please me if you would come with me to speak with my father about trade with Gaul,' said Fróech to Druce. 'It will be worth your while, believe me.'

Druce looked uneasily to Guairá. The dock master shrugged as if to say, *There's no way out of this … you must go for now.*

Fróech clicked his fingers and Cillian brought his pony over to Druce. Smiling, Fróech invited Druce to mount.

After avoiding Colman's party, Dominic's group soon came to the dock road. Upon reaching it, Dominic dismounted and examined the ground looking for clues. Flint crouched beside him. Dominic was thoughtful as he rubbed the trail dirt through his fingers and looked down the track.

'Problems?' asked Flint.

'Mmm,' murmured Dominic, frowning now as he considered their predicament. After a moment, he came out of himself and looked to Flint. 'Five riders recently split from Colman's group. They went down towards the docks.'

'Probably his brother, Fróech,' said Flint. 'I hope Withred has the wits not to show himself to him.'

'No need to worry about Withred,' Dominic said. 'The problem now is: how do we deal with this?'

'We'll do what Withred has no doubt decided to do: hide until they've gone.'

'And hope Colman doesn't turn up to complicate things further,' Dominic said.

Flint looked at the children who watched and waited from the elevation of their mounts. Elowen and Mule shared the same pony now. Maewyn sat on the pony he had shared with Flint. Dominic told them of the developments at the docks. Mindful of the importance of lying low if they sighted the Hibernians, the group now continued down the track.

But they encountered no one, and Dominic was the first to reach the rise that overlooked the docks. Below, he saw Fróech and his men. He dismounted and led his pony back ten strides, out of sight of the men below.

A stockyard full of steers abutted the track next to where he stood. Dominic tied his pony to the rough fence that encircled the stockyard, flinching as one of the steers crashed against the fence. The commotion increased as the beasts within jostled for position. Trying to ignore the noise, Dominic looked down to the docks again. His concern leaped when he saw Fróech talking to Druce.

Dominic walked back, out of sight of the docks and halted Flint and the children. Quickly, he updated them on the developments in the dockyard.

'Can we take them?' asked Flint, unable now to see any other way around the problem.

'Four of them—three of us with Withred—maybe, said Dominic. We've had worse odds.' Still uncertain, Dominic sighed, then nodded towards the children. 'But they make things tricky to say the least. However this plays out, they must be protected.'

Flint agreed, and was about to suggest they wait and watch a while, when one of the steers in the compound again hefted its bulk against the nearby fence. Dominic just managed to grab the reins of the nearest two ponies as the din spooked them. Flint attempted to do the same with Mule and Elowen's pony, but the pony reared and eluded his grasp. He watched, aghast, as the beast ran down towards the docks with Mule and Elowen upon it.

Withred looked through the dusty, slatted wall of the warehouse. Frustrated and feeling impotent, he had watched as all the developments on the docks had unfolded before him. Earlier, his instinct had almost driven him to intervene and engage the men who had forced Druce to mount the pony.

Having managed to control his urge to act, his plan now was to stay hidden and follow the Hibernians when they left with Druce. Somehow, he would get him away from them. He had no choice—the man was their mariner.

He tensed when he saw an astonished Fróech suddenly look up towards the dock road and order three of his men up the track. One of his men remained and stood with him beside the wharf.

Withred's plans changed again when the pony carrying Mule and Elowen appeared, heading towards the wharf. The pony—wild-eyed and panic stricken—managed to come to an abrupt halt before reaching the deep drop into the water. Mule and Elowen fell heavily to the ground. The pony, head tossing and tail swishing, then rattled away along the wharf.

Fróech quickly grabbed Elowen, who had rolled forward towards him. Mule lay motionless, apparently stunned.

'Guairá, you lying bastard, I'll have you flayed,' muttered Fróech, looking around for the dock master. Holding Elowen tight, he looked up the hill as his men ran to meet Dominic and Flint. He looked towards Cillian. 'Get down the ladder and hole their boat!' he shouted, as it dawned on him that he could use the girl to his advantage.

Then, Withred burst out of the warehouse.

Fróech's eyes shot wide with surprise, but his gaze never left Withred as he shouted to Cillian.

'See how big the warehouse rats grow, Cill. One has escaped to have its shit-eating life ended.'

Cillian stayed put by the wharf side as he watched Withred moved carefully towards Fróech.

'At least I don't hide behind the skirts of a girl,' shouted Withred. He gave Elowen a reassuring look— *Don't worry, I can get you out of this*—as she trembled in Froech's grasp.

He continued to chide Fróech. Laughing at him now, he shouted, 'If I'd known that the best that Hibernia can offer uses a child as a shield, then I wouldn't have endangered myself raiding the worthy men of Britannia for all those years. Instead, I would have come to Hibernia to fight its cowards.'

Cillian, eager to boost his standing with Fróech, drew his sword. 'I'll finish the upstart for you, my lord. His clever tongue, I will soon feed to the fishes.'

Withred looked at Cillian. Obviously high ranking, the man, like Fróech, wore a full-length chainmail hauberk, probably imported from Britannia. *Good protection against the slash of the sword but not the stab*, thought Withred, who was singularly unimpressed by the man.

As Withred readied himself for combat, Cillian's eyes widened with a mixture of surprise and apprehension as he observed the practiced and confident way Withred wielded his broadsword—the weapon swaying in his practiced and expert grip. His anticipation of a tough fight proved unfounded, however, when Fróech—his pride dented by Withred's words—shoved Elowen to him.

'No need for you to finish him, just keep hold of the girl' said Fróech, coldly eying Withred as he drew his own sword.

Cillian lifted his knife to Elowen's neck and looked to Druce who sat mounted and unsure of what to do, nearby. 'Don't you even think about helping him,' said Cillian to Druce.

Just as Withred and Fróech came together in combat, Dominic shot his first arrow towards the group of three men who rushed up the hill to engage them.

The arrow found its mark, hitting the leading man in the hollow below his throat. The man fell dead, but the two remaining Hibernians were quickly upon Dominic and Flint before any more arrows could fly.

The ensuing melee saw Hibernian axes pitted against British swords. Amidst much grunting and clanging, Dominic and Flint weathered a brutal torrent of frenzied ax swings. Wild and enraged, the Hibernians were nevertheless accomplished combatants.

Flint had spent many hours in Brythonfort academy under the tutorage of Erec—a hardened warrior and weapons instructor. Trained relentlessly to defend and counter-attack against every type of weapon, including the ax, he now found himself fighting on pure instinct.

Erec's words came to Flint—*Allow an aggressive assailant to tire himself, then strike when his muscles scream for mercy*—just as his opponent paused after delivering a combination of relentless ax swings—all of which Flint had deftly avoided.

The Hibernian's arms, which had become leaden, dropped for just a moment, but it was enough for Flint. A powerful and swift horizontal swipe cut cleanly through the flesh of the man's ax arm, leaving the limb articulated and useless. Quickly, Flint strode close and thrust his sword through the man's chest, finishing him.

As his man dropped, Flint's side vision revealed the other Hibernian fighting with Dominic behind him. Without pause, he spun and delivered another powerful sideways slash, which served to cut through the man's clothing and spine. Paralysed, the man dropped to the ground.

Dominic quickly dropped to one knee beside the stricken man and slicked his knife blade across his throat.

He pushed himself up off the dead man and stood up. 'Tough bastard, that,' he panted to Flint, 'lucky you were here.'

He noticed Flint signaling to Maewyn to hold still. The boy sat astride his mount further up the hill looking as if he was about to ride down to aid Elowen and Mule.

Dominic stood and looked towards Maewyn. 'Keep your position,' he shouted. 'We'll deal with this.'

As Maewyn reluctantly nodded his head, they turned to witness the conclusion of the fight between Withred and Fróech.

'NO!' screamed Flint as he set off to run down the hill. Aghast, Dominic followed him.

Earlier, as Dominic and Flint had taken on their three assailants, Withred had watched Fróech closely as he shuffled towards him. Crouched and wielding a broadsword similar to his own, Fróech jabbed and feinted, looking for an opening in Withred's defense.

Unblinking and intense, Withred bounced lightly on the balls of his feet, ready to let Fróech show his hand first. He would assess the man's fighting ability by defending his first strikes.

A sharp intake of Froech's breath signaled that Fróech was coming for him. Grateful Fróech had given him the subtle warning; Withred was nonetheless surprised at the speed with which Fróech delivered his first attack. It was an overhead swipe, delivered rapidly and skillfully towards Withred's carotid.

Withred barely parried the powerful hack, its force knocking him backwards. Fróech followed it with a backhand slash aimed at Withred's midriff.

The double maneuver was standard fare. Withred—who was almost balletic, such was the grace of his movement—instinctively swept his sword upright, elbows uppermost, to meet a blow he fully expected.
Fróech repeated the two strikes (neck then midriff) and again Withred met steel with steel.

Like Cillian, Fróech was wearing a knee length hauberk, and Withred knew that a slashing blow would not breach it. However, such a blow *would* knock the stuffing out of Fróech. A momentary opening was all he needed, and he was able to land a heavy sword strike past Froech's defenses and into his ribs.

Fróech exhaled a huge 'whoeff' as the blade crunched into his side—his chainmail managing to halt the progress of the blade. Staggering backwards, his ribs now broken, Fróech fought the desire to scream his agony at Withred.

Withred's eyes widened with surprise as, unexpectedly, Fróech came at him again. Processing his thoughts rapidly, Withred decided to take a risk. Quickly, he dropped his broadsword and removed his short, slender stabbing sword from his belt, just as Fróech, who seemed to have limitless reserves of stamina, swung another powerful swipe at his neck.

Withred fell to his right knee to avoid the whistling steel, at the same time lunging forward with the seax. With his full weight behind it it, the blade pierced Fróech's hauberk a hands width above his navel. Only the cross guard halted its progress as it pierced the chainmail—the blade emerging slick and bloody behind Fróech.

Fróech's mouth dropped open in surprise as he looked down at the handle of the seax sticking from him. Never had he fought anyone like the man before him. Phantom-like, the man had avoided or blocked his best moves, then in the blink of an eye, run him through with a subtle combination of grace and power.

Standing back, as Fróech dropped his sword and fell to his knees before him, Withred quickly retrieved his discarded broad sword. Now he looked at Cillian, who stood, mortified, after seeing the defeat of his lord—a man whom he had deemed immortal. Cillian backed towards the wharf, still holding Elowen.

Withred kicked Fróech's broadsword over to Cillian. 'Let her go and defend your master or I will remove his head here and now,' said Withred.'

Cillian hesitated a moment, knowing as sure as night followed day and day followed night, that he would die if he took on the man before him. The alternative was to plead for his life like a coward and that was *worse* than death. After a moments further hesitation he chose to fight. He let go of Elowen.

Mule dreamt that Maewyn clashed two pans above his head to wake him as he slept in his warm bed back at the monastery. He opened his eyes in a series of blinks as his blurry vision cleared. He discovered that the clashing was not pans but swords, then winced as he felt the bump on his head and realised what had happened.

Not far from him, two men fought—neither of whom he recognized. Another man stood a distance away holding Elowen, his knife at her throat. This had him on his knees in an instant. He turned as one of the men who fought gasped and fell to his knees. Then he turned back to look at the man who held Elowen and saw him let her go.

Mule knew the man could yet harm Elowen, and acted without further thought. Gaining his feet, he rushed at Cillian and hit him full on. He grasped Cillian as they fell a full second through the air before hitting cold, brown water.

Cillian gasped and instinctively grabbed on to Mule as the weight of his hauberk dragged him under. His lungs filled with water as he spiraled—with Mule in his cold embrace—down to the seabed fifteen feet below. His last air escaped him in a procession of gurgling bubbles as he lay on top of Mule on the rocky floor of the harbor.

Mule, kept his mouth clamped shut in an effort to keep the water out (and his breath in) as he tried to heave Cillian's dead weight from him. A shadow from above interrupted the diffused watery light, causing Mule to look to the surface just as it exploded with the entry of another man.

After his fight on the road, Flint had watched as Mule had run at the man on the quayside. His only thought when he saw his brother tumble out of sight was to save him. Knowing that Mule could not swim, Flint sprinted down the road and crossed the plank decking of the dockside.

Briefly aware that Withred stood over a kneeling man near to the edge of the wharf, he leapt from the decking, his legs still running as he dropped through the air. The air left his lungs as he hit the water, reducing his buoyancy and causing him to sink. Panic hit him then as he realised that, like Mule, he could not swim.

Disorientated, he spiraled downwards through the water, not knowing up from down, until he saw Mule trapped under another man. A single, wide bubble came from Mules mouth as their eyes briefly met. Flint turned and kicked his way back to the surface. He knew he would swallow water if he did not. Gasping, he broke the surface, took in a lungful of air, then started to sink again.

Mule had mouthed the word 'Flint' *as he had watched him sink to within an arms distance from him. He had noticed Flint's eyes wide with terror as tiny bubbles escaped from the corners of his mouth. Then he had watched as Flint twisted round and returned to the surface through the effervescent water. Unable to free himself from the dead weight of Cillian, Mule had died then—his last image; his brother and hero: Flint.*

Druce just managed to grab Flint by his hair as he exploded to the surface.

Having watched as events unfolded, Druce had jumped from the Hibernian pony that Fróech had earlier insisted he sat upon, and quickly climbed down the hemp ladder to his boat. He had jumped onto its oak decking just as Flint surfaced nearby, and so was able to prevent the Briton from sinking back into the depths and drowning.

With both hands grasping the back of Flint's tunic, he now dragged him over the gunwale of the Pelagus.

Flint flopped like a landed herring on the decking of the boat. He gained one knee and looked desperately to Druce. Coughing and exhausted, he said, 'He's still down there, I have to … I have to go back in … and get him.'

Druce was having none of it, and knelt between Flint and the open water, just as a series of bubbles broke the surface. 'It's no use, Flint,' he said weightily. 'The lad has just released his last air.'

Some of Flint's energy returned to him then, giving strength to his screams as he gripped the edge of the gunwale next to Druce. 'I cannot leave him in there. I CANNOT ABANDON HIM!' His voice rose in intensity as he looked over the edge of the boat, and peered desperately into the depths.

Druce gripped Flint's dripping arm, squeezing it in consolation *and* restraint.

He looked up, the world now seeming muted, surreal, and slow moving to him, as Withred and Dominic reached the edge of the wharf. Druce shook his head to them—*the lad has drowned*—and Elowen, who held Withred's hand, let out her own piercing scream of despair.

Dominic, who stood behind Maewyn, had the wits to restrain him before he could emulate his brother and jump into the water. The boy kicked and shrieked as Dominic pulled him away from the edge of the wharf.

Two hours later, a grim-looking Druce and Withred sat with Flint, Maewyn and Elowen in the warehouse beside the wharf. They had deemed it sensible to remove them from the quayside and the temptation to plunge into the water to get to Mule.

At first, Flint had paced the warehouse, wailing and confused, unable seemingly to stick within his own skin; such was the intensity of his grief. Maewyn and Elowen had wept intermittently between bouts of babbled conversation. Now, like Flint, Maewyn merely leaned forward, elbows on knees, fists against his temples, as he looked blankly down at the floor. Elowen, who sat beside them, had started to weep again.

Outside, Dominic spoke to Guairá as they stood on the edge of the wharf looking into the water. Twenty feet below them, glinting from the bottom of the seabed, Cillian's chainmail resembled the scales of a dead fish swept in by the tide. Mule was barely visible as a hazy shadow beneath him.

'You must leave on the ebb tide before Colman arrives, and that means this evening,' Guairá said, turning to observe the low sun. 'I will recover the lad as soon as the water has dropped enough.'

'What will you tell Colman,' asked Dominic.

'That you arrived without the children and had an argument with Fróech and his men.' Guairá looked at Fróech's body, which lay face down nearby. 'I'll tell him the argument got out of hand; that you fought and were responsible for the death of his brother.'

'What about you? ... What will he do to you?'

'What can he do? My trade is cargo not conflict. I'll play the devastated Hibernian who could do nothing but watch in horror.'

Dominic looked towards a group of stevedores who laboured nearby. 'How loyal are they?' he asked. 'One loose tongue could lead to your head being removed.'

Guairá pointed to the open sea. 'See that cold water ... they would swim to the horizon for me *all of them* if I asked them to. They are all outcasts from Fincath and they hate him. I was their last hope. In employing them I effectively saved their lives.'

'And your nephew, Ingle, and the rest of the monks?' asked Dominic 'Will they be left alone?'

Sadly, Guairá looked down into the water ... looked at the shadow of Mule. 'As long as I can get that lad out and hidden before Colman arrives, then the monks should be fine,' he said. 'If Colman has no reason to believe you found the children, he has no need to punish the monks.

Dominic had also been looking at Mule's pitiful form as Guairá spoke. 'What will you do with the lad?' he asked.

'Give him to the monks as soon as it's safe to do so,' said Guairá. 'They will respect him and lay him softly into the ground.'

Dominic nodded, sighed, then gripped Guairá's hand in gratitude. 'Oh, that this could have ended happier.' He cast a brief glance towards the warehouse. 'Thank you my friend, now I must tell Aiden's family that we are about to leave without him.'

CHAPTER NINETEEN

Murdoc had no way of knowing how long he would be under house arrest in Dyfed, and the uncertainty was driving him to despair.

Four days had passed since his companions had left for Hibernia with Druce. Allowed to roam freely within the walls of the ringfort, Murdoc had spent his days pacing the grounds like a caged animal. He had no thoughts of escaping, fearing the act would merely inflame Guertepir. Undoubtedly, the man would then exact his ire upon Dominic's group when they returned. Besides, Guertepir always had two men guarding the ringfort's one gate.

Apart from an occasional brief word with the guards, Murdoc had spoken little to anyone during his incarceration. Having rarely glimpsed Guertepir, each of Murdoc's days had seemed to last a lifetime.

A simple hut set against the walls of the fort provided him with shelter, as well as a hard bed of straw. When the light of the day faded in the early evening, Murdoc would take to his bed, hopeful that sleep would relieve him from the tedium of his existence. Meanwhile, Guertepir and his lackeys would feast nightly in the great hall.

Consequently, Murdoc would spend several hours awake in the darkness of the hut, while the sound of laughing and revelry came from nearby. Unknown to Murdoc, Guertepir's strange wife, Almaith, would come to the hut in the early hours and gaze at him as he finally slept. She carried a small, tallow candle, and by its low light, she would gaze at Murdoc's athletic form and handsome, candle-lit face, whilst pleasuring herself where she stood.

On the fifth morning, as a thoroughly morose and dejected Murdoc embarked upon his eighth lap of the ringfort, Guertepir's man, Diarmait, burst through the gates and strode with purpose to the great hall where Guertepir was holding counsel.

Moments later, Guertepir emerged, draping himself within his squirrel cloak as he walked quickly to the gate. He chose to ignore Murdoc and passed from sight through the gate, quickly followed by Diarmait.

'You're sure it's them?' asked Guertepir, as they hurried down the hill towards the landing bay, now followed by twenty of Guertepir's guards.

'It's still half a mile out, but close enough for me to recognize the sail,' said Diarmait.

'How many are in the boat?'

'Again, hard to tell, but it looks like at least five. Possibly even six.'

As they waited by the dockside, Guertepir nodded and gave a satisfied smile as the boat neared them. 'Yes it's them,' he said, 'and they have two children with them.'

Diarmait looked surprised. 'Then they've only been partly successful. They set out to find three.'

Guertepir was untroubled, his tone indifferent. 'As long as they've got what *I* want, I don't care.'

Druce skillfully tacked the boat shoreward until he was able to set it into a graceful curve towards the landing. Five men who waited on the wooden jetty caught the ropes thrown to them by Druce and Withred, then skillfully entwined the ropes around wooden capstans.

Now secured, the boat offered a stable platform from which to disembark.

Grey with fatigue, Dominic was the first off the boat. Flint followed, with Elowen and Maewyn, while Withred hung back on the boat with Druce.

'Five days. You have done well,' said Guertepir as he played the genial host and spread his arms in welcome. Dominic stood back, ignoring the embrace.

Unperturbed, Guertepir nodded; once to Elowen and once to Maewyn, as if doing a count in his head. 'Two? … just two?' he asked.

Dominic was reticent, not wanting to go into detail with Guertepir. 'One lad died. That's all you need to know,' he said abruptly.

'Oh,' breathed Guertepir, as if empathic. 'But, please … take the children up to the fort; they will be well looked after until you choose to leave.'

As Flint pushed past Guertepir with Elowen and Maewyn, his look to Dominic was telling. *Be careful of the old bastard, he's got more on his mind than the children.*

Guertepir watched them as they walked away, his face affecting a look of pious concern, but when he regarded Dominic again, the look had gone. 'Why are they still in the boat?' he said, frowning and pointing towards Withred and Druce.

Dominic turned to the boat and signaled to Withred, then turned his disdainful attention to Guertepir as Withred strode towards them carrying a sack. 'He held back, because he knew what *really* concerned you,' Dominic said.

'Here,' said Withred, as he tossed the sack to the ground at Guertepir's feet. 'It was all I could do to hide it from the children.'

Guertepir looked impassively at the sack, then nodded to Diarmait who stood nearby. Diarmait came over, stooped, lifted the sack, then pulled Fróech's head from it. He held it out for Guertepir to examine.

Guertepir's look was inscrutable as he studied the head. He cleared the matted hair from the forehead to reveal the snake symbol. He gulped, cleared his throat, then smiled at Dominic. 'Justice seems to have been done,' he said. 'Now you can take your man, Murdoc, and go back to Arthur's dung heap.'

CHAPTER TWENTY

Rozen, the herbs-woman, had tended Augustus' wounds daily until he had been able to leave his bed. Then gradually he had built up his stamina until he was able to walk (though still with considerable discomfort) further each day as his vitality returned.

On a quiet November day, he strolled with Modlen around the walls of Brythonfort with Ula and Art. After their rescue by Dominic's group, three weeks earlier, the boys had taken up residence in Brythonfort. Here, the childless Augustus and Modlen had accepted them as their own.

Augustus now walked with his arm around Art's shoulders, while Modlen held Ula's hand. They climbed the stone steps to the paved sentry path that ran alongside the curtain wall. After reaching its heights, they looked eastwards from the wall.

As a thin breeze ruffled Ula's blond hair, he asked Modlen, not for the first time, 'Will anyone ever go to the eastern coast again and look for Cate?'

Modlen glanced at Augustus. His face had taken on a troubled look upon hearing Ula's words. She was well aware that Augustus constantly wrestled with an inner guilt since he had left Cate behind in the forest. Rationalize though she may with him about the inevitability of the decision, she could, nevertheless, get him to accept it. Cate's abduction was a constant torment to Augustus—an itch that would not go away. It was insatiable irritation.

Modlen now looked into Ula's enquiring eyes and cupped his small face in her hands. 'Yes, of course someone will look for your sister. As soon as Dominic returns and Augustus regains his strength, we will talk with Arthur about it.'

Augustus sighed at Modlen's words. 'It's two week since Dominic left for Hibernia. Who knows when he *will* return? Soon winter will be here, and any journey back to Norwic to find Cate will then be difficult to say the least. Now should be the time to set out to find her, why can't Arthur see that?'

Modlen had been through this before with Augustus, but she remained patient, knowing as she did, how the subject plagued him. She placed her hand on his thick arm and looked tenderly into his bleak eyes.

'Arthur is expecting trouble before the winter sets in,' she said. 'He expects the raiding parties to come again before the weather keeps them at bay. He needs all his men at hand. The scouts are out looking for Ranulf, or any other warlord who decides to chance his hand. If Tomas or Will return with news of invaders then all the men of the protectorate will be needed to repel them.'

'I will go and look for Cate then,' said Art suddenly. 'I think I can remember how to get back to Norwic. If I'm sneaky I will be able to steal her from the bad men.'

'And I will come with you,' said Ula. 'Together we'll be able to carry her back here if she's hurt.'

Augustus and Modlen turned their attention to the twins as they thrust their spare frames forward in defiance.

Augustus smiled and knelt before them. Taking Ula's small hand and enclosing it gently within his meaty fists, he looked sadly at him.

'How brave you lads are,' he said, glancing at Art, also. 'But the wilderness of Britannia is no place for twelve-year-old boys to walk alone.'

His heart ached now as he looked at them. Having witnessed the bloody slaughter of their parents and much-loved grandfather, the boys had had to deal with their own inner demons. It was apparent during the day when they would mutter and fidget apparently for no reason, and at night when their sleep echoed with desperate little screams and murmurings. Augustus and Modlen often exchanged sorry looks when hearing the boys' torment.

Already, though, their love for Augustus and Modlen was growing. Often, they spoke about their new guardians when lying in their beds. Modlen was kindness, itself; always ensuring they had clean clothes to wear and comforting food to eat.

As for Augustus, they knew he had taken great injury for them. Although seemingly kind and good, the other men he had travelled with seemed stern to them, such was their determination to pursue a greater mission. They knew that Augustus, too, had tried to go with the others when they had left for the west, but his injuries had prevented him, and for that, they were grateful. From that day, they were relieved that his recovery had gone well, and when finally able to walk they had all their time with him.

Strong yet gentle, he had walked with them through the woods that lay near to Brythonfort. He had found them good trees to climb and helped them clamber onto the first branches if they were too high for them to reach. Then, Modlen had scolded him when the boys had returned home with tales of their tree climbing adventures. Augustus had only laughed, saying, *'Lads should be lads, and, anyway, the climbing will make them agile and tough.'*

As Augustus now watched Modlen with the boys, he thought of Cate. Thought of how she would love Modlen; how Modlen would love her; how different Cate's life would now be if he had prevented Ranulf from stealing her. His torment would not go away. He knew it never would.

CHAPTER TWENTY-ONE

Tomas and Will had spent the entire day shadowing Ranulf's group as they moved ever westwards towards Arthur's protectorate. They had watched as the group of seventy men had passed by small farmsteads, ignoring the people who dwelt within them.

'They are too few to attack Brythonfort, but enough to sack a large village,' observed Will as they rested up, hidden from Ranulf and his men who had halted for the day.

'That's why they leave the farms alone,' said Tomas. 'They want slaves in numbers *and quickly* so they can get themselves out of dangerous country as soon as they complete their raid.'

'I think the time may have come,' said Will. 'Time we split up. You're on your own from here on, Tom.'

He parted the bushes before him. Two hundred paces away, Ranulf and his tracker, Irvine, sat together having a discussion beside a lively campfire. Satisfied that now was a good time to leave, Will went to retrieve his pony.

All that day, Tomas had expected Will to make the decision. He knew, the closer they got to Brythonfort and its villages, the more important it had become to warn Arthur of the approaching threat. From now on, he would be scouting alone. Will was about to leave for Brythonfort.

He embraced Will, as he returned with his pony and made ready to leave, knowing their goodbye would have to be brief and discreet.

'Two days should get you back to Arthur,' said Tomas quietly. 'So hopefully we'll meet up within four days if all goes well.'

Will looked edgy as he mounted his pony and lifted its reins to send it in a slow walk away from the lookout. 'All *will* go well, you have to believe that,' said Will as he left Tomas to his own devises.

Ranulf warmed his hands on the fire and continued to stare into it as he spoke to Irvine. 'The men are getting impatient. Twenty days in the saddle and still nothing to show for their hardship.'

'It doesn't do to rush these things' said Irvine, himself staring as if entranced into the fire. 'All the villages are already plundered up to here, and the population is sparse.'

Ranulf looked from the fire and nodded to the woods ahead. 'We're getting perilously close to Arthur's lands. From now on we need to be extra careful.'

'That's why you employ *me,*' said Irvine pointing into the fire. 'I stop you getting your arse scorched.'

'The route ahead is new land for us,' said Ranulf, ignoring Irvine's observation. 'Maybe tomorrow will dawn upon a juicy British village to sack.'

Irvine stood and stretched the stiffness out of his back, groaning as he spoke. 'Maybe … but any untouched villages from now on could well be within half a day or less of Arthur's roaming militia.' His stretching done, he peered through the falling light towards the surrounding shrub growth. 'I'm uneasy and I don't know why,' he frowned. 'I think I may take a look around after dark.'

'As you will,' said Ranulf. 'Just be sure you're alert at first light to resume your duties.'

Two hours after dark, the camp had settled to a familiar routine. Six guards had taken first watch around its periphery and these sat beside small fires. Others sprawled on the ground as they played dice by the firelight in the main camp. Some, who would be on guard duty later, had chosen to steal a few hours sleep.

Irvine strolled around the camp edge having brief words with the guards. Then, happy the camp was under no immediate threat, he decided to take advantage of the dim light provided by a full moon and clear sky. Quietly, he walked to the nearest bunch of shrubbery, sixty paces distant.

Here, he observed the hoof prints of Will's pony. Stooping to get a closer look, he could see the prints were fresh and led away from the camp. *It's not where you're going, but where you came from,* he thought, as he strained to see beyond the moon-shadow cast by the shrubs. He could see enough to follow the tracks backwards as they encircled, then led away from the camp.

He tensed as he noticed the tracks led to a group of bushes that provided a good overlook of the camp. *They've been watching us!* The thought made his skin tingle and heart race. He patted his waist checking on the position of his knife. Not sure if anyone still lingered behind the bushes, he decided to investigate.

After taking a looping rout to bring him to the back of the bushes, he paused and listened. Yes, it was unmistakable; he could hear breathing … slow laboured breathing. He removed his knife and, crouching and silent, made his way to the base of the shrub. There, illuminated by moon glow, slept a youth. A recurved, laminate bow was on the ground beside him; a full quiver of well-crafted arrows propped up against the bushes.

Tomas opened his eyes just as Irvine stooped over him.

CHAPTER TWENTY-TWO

Eight uneventful but arduous days passed before Dominic and his five companions once again feasted their eyes on distant Brythonfort.

'I'll never get sick of looking at it,' said Murdoc to Withred, as he held his hand to his eyes against the low sun.

Three miles distant, the great earthwork buttress (from which the stone walls of the fort seemed to be a natural rocky continuation) rose imposingly from the surrounding flat countryside.

Murdoc turned in his saddle to witness Maewyn and Elowen's first ever sight of Brythonfort. He turned back to Withred. 'That's the first time since we set out from Guertepir's fort that I've seen them look anything other than devastated.

Withred looked back to observe the children briefly. 'That's the magic of Brythonfort for you,' he said, smiling at Murdoc. 'It makes you forget yourself—pushes your troubles away with its great bulk.'

'It will take them a long time to get over the death of that dear lad,' Murdoc said, looking now towards Flint who rode ahead with Dominic. 'Flint blames himself for not catching the pony when it bolted down the hill.'

'I know—and try and tell him otherwise and he just won't have it,' said Withred. 'He's an angry man just now. Nerthus help any Saxon *he* comes across.'

Arthur's right-hand-man, Gherwan, and a group of riders approached them when a mile from Brythonfort. Dominic met him.

'Twenty-one days since you left us, Dom,' shouted Gherwan. 'Hibernia and back in twenty-one days. It's no wonder you're becoming a legend in these parts.'

'A legend would have come back with everything he went for,' said Dominic, heavily. 'The older boy, Aiden—the one they called Mule—drowned in a Hibernian harbor protecting his cousin.'

Gherwan now noticed that just two children rode with the group. He looked to his friend Flint, Mules brother, who rode beside Maewyn and Elowen. He waited until Flint reached him—his look to Flint and the children rendering words unnecessary.

Flint's face was as stark and pale as the toneless November day. 'The men who caused this must die,' he said simply, as he passed by Gherwan and began the climb up to Brythonfort's one gate.

A sad, reflective group of people sat with Arthur in the great hall later that afternoon. Will had also arrived that morning to report the situation from the countryside to Arthur.

A long discussion had ensued and Dominic, Withred and Murdoc had listened with fascination, and a great deal of trepidation, to Arthur's consequent plan to deal with Ranulf.

Flint sat with Elowen and Maewyn, awaiting the arrival of Nila and Govan. Flint fidgeted, nervous of their arrival.

An air of solemnity permeated the hall, causing its occupants to fall to silence now that Dominic and Will had delivered their briefings. All now dreaded the arrival of Nila and Govan.

Arthur nervously tapped the table, looking out from under his brow at the door. As he briefly shifted his glance to Dominic, Murdoc and Withred, he thanked the Gods of fortune for bringing men of their caliber to Brythonfort. With them, he knew he had a real chance of dealing with the inevitable flood of raids that would continue to come his way.

His thoughts evaporated when the door opened. Nila and Govan walked in, their faces a mixture of expectation and dread as they looked to the table. *They don't know,* thought Arthur … *they have no idea who made it back.*

Elowen was up at once and ran to Govan, who received her in his arms with a choking cry of relief. As the sound of their reunion filled the hall with its amalgam of joy and tears, Nila looked blankly around the room, her panic slowly rising as Flint and Maewyn approached her, their faces bleak and crestfallen.

Their look, as much as Mule's absence, told Nila what she needed to know.

Arthur, Dominic and Withred closed their eyes in unison, their own faces twisted in pain, as Nila suddenly screamed her maternal loss at the room. Repeatedly, her screams seared through the great hall, as Flint and Maewyn stood embracing and rocking her, as if the rocking would exorcise her desolation and send it to another place.

Dominic and Withred, both weeping themselves now, left the hall, unable to cope with the intensity of Nila's grief.

Outside, Modlen awaited them. The boys, Ula and Art played nearby. Her brown eyes were moist and troubled as she heard the sound of Nila's distress from within the hall. As Withred brushed his tears away with the heel of his hand, Modlen went to him and held him in her embrace.

'Ranulf killed the son and effectively the mother by raiding their village,' said Withred brokenly. 'And now he approaches this land again.'

Dominic now embraced Modlen as she came to him. 'It's so good to see you, Mod,' he said. He looked at the boys who leapt about in their play nearby. 'And the boys are looking well-nourished and lively.' He attempted to lighten the mood somewhat. 'But why would that surprise me? You've had a lifetime of cooking for that great bull of a husband of yours.'

Modlen's eyes dropped at Dominic's reference to Augustus. Dominic, aware of her sudden anxiety, gently touched her arm, prompting her to look him in the eyes.

'He's gone, Dom,' she said desperately. 'Three days ago I woke to find him gone. He's gone to Norwic for Cate … I knew he would … it was driving him mad.'

CHAPTER TWENTY-THREE

Tomas shuddered and thought of Egbert as he looked into Ranulf's cold eyes.

Egbert had been his tormentor for two years after the raid on his village—a raid that had resulted in the death of his parents and sister. The man had been a monster, pure and simple; a monster who had regularly beaten and humiliated him during his tenure as his slave.

Eventually Tomas had been able to escape from the clutches of Egbert. Then he had met Dominic and his life had changed completely.

Now as he looked at Ranulf, he saw Egbert ... saw Egbert's detached and emotionless eyes. *Dead eyes. The eyes of a doll,* thought Tomas.

'Tell us what you know and I might just consent to kill you quickly,' rumbled Ranulf as Irvine pushed Tomas towards him.

'I have been following you for over a week,' said Tomas, shakily, knowing it would be a great folly to lie to the man.

'And the purpose of your scrutiny?' asked Ranulf.

'To keep an eye on you and warn Arthur of your intent regarding his lands.'

'Seemingly a warning that has already begun,' Ranulf said as he glanced towards Irvine. 'My scout has read the tracks and tells me that you had a companion ... a companion who is already scampering back to Arthur as we speak.'

Again, Tomas could see no sense in refuting this. Two years under Saxon bondage had taught him it was better not to risk their ire by denying what was patently obvious to them. He knew his life was uncertain now, so he had to think quickly. Had to buy himself time.

'Yes, I had a companion; a man named Will,' said Tomas. 'He is to bring Arthur's men down upon you within two days.'

Irvine had become alert upon hearing Will's name. 'I know the man,' he said. 'Our paths crossed briefly when we scouted for Rome. A good tracker he is; a man who will have no trouble leading Arthur to us.'

Cursing, Ranulf left Tomas and walked towards the fire as he weighed his options. He stopped at the fire, took his dagger from his belt, and then turned his attention back to Tomas. 'I promised you a quick death and I will keep to my word, but first I must consider if you are of any further use to me.' He walked to Tomas, grabbed him by the chest, and placed the blade of the dagger across his throat. 'So before I slide this steel across your gullet and bleed you out, tell me … *are* you any use to me?'

Before Tomas could answer, Irvine spoke. 'The boy knows the land and no doubt knows which way Arthur's men will come. Maybe he could lead us away from him … lead us to a village.'

'Or we could fight Arthur and get this done with once and for all,' said Ranulf. He stared at Tomas, his knife still pressing against his neck. 'What say *you* boy?'

Tomas, wide-eyed and hardly daring to breathe as he looked into Ranulf's rabid eyes, gave a barely perceptible shake of his head. 'No, it would be your end if you took on Arthur,' he mumbled. 'H-he outnumbers you by one hundred men and his knights fight the Roman way. You would have no chance against them.'

'Do you know which way they will come then?'

Tomas knew Ranulf would swipe the knife across his throat the instant he gave an answer that did not suit him. He had to buy time … that or die. He thought quickly. 'I know the way they will come, yes,' he said. 'I can also lead you into the western lands, away from them, if you wish to continue your campaign.'

Ranulf considered this. He had just concluded that his only option was to withdraw from the west; admit defeat; return to Griff empty handed. What the boy had said about the might of Arthur's force made it almost inevitable. Now, though, there might be another way. If the boy could lead them away from Arthur—lead them to a village to plunder as Irvine had earlier implied, then perhaps they could get something out of this.

He looked to Irvine—his trapper's shrug saying, *Might as well hear what he has to say.*

Ranulf took the knife from Tomas's neck and pushed him an arm's length away. 'You *do* know that there is no guarantee for you in this. Do as you say and I might, just *might*, let you live. Let me down—and that means lead us anywhere near to Arthur's knights—and I will kill you as soon as I see them. That will be the first thing I do upon seeing any mounted men come against us. To kill you will be my immediate priority if I see but one rider.'

Tomas' mouth was grit-dry as he considered Ranulf's words. His life teetered on the edge of an abyss; he knew that only too well. He also knew what he must do now, and what the likely consequences of his actions would be.

He answered Ranulf. 'I will not give you reason to kill me, why would I? I will lead you to a place where Arthur expects you not to go.'

Ranulf studied Tomas, his head cocked to one side as he tried to figure the boy out. 'And you would do this thing? To save your own skin you would lead me to your own folk?'

Tomas looked tellingly at Irvine then back to Ranulf. 'Do not be surprised,' he said. 'I would not be the first Briton to ride against his own kin.'

The next morning, allowed to ride at the front of the group alongside Irvine, Tomas led the group northwards.

The change in direction was not lost upon Irvine. 'I take it that this is a temporary change of course, designed to take us away from Arthur?'

'Yes, Brythonfort lies directly westwards from here. Arthur will have set out as soon as the sun rose. He can be no more than a day's ride from us now.'

'And as soon as he sees our present tracks he will be on our tails ... a day behind, granted, but after us just the same.'

'That's why I chose this route,' said Tomas. 'Several wide, shallow rivers cross the land ahead. Their shale and gravel beds will hide our tracks. Arthur will be left with nothing to follow.'

Irvine gave a half smile, and now curious of Tomas' motivation, regarded him. 'You really think Ranulf will let you live after this?' he asked.

Tomas shrugged. 'Who knows? One thing's for sure though; I'm alive now and that didn't seem likely yesterday.'

Irvine smiled to himself then, knowing that whatever the outcome, Ranulf would either kill or enslave Tomas.

Later that morning, true to Tomas' assurance, they crossed three wide, shallow rivers. The third river ran westwards and they continued along it stony bottom for two miles, the ponies fetlock deep as they splashed through the water. At a point where the river narrowed and began to descend, Tomas and the Saxon group took to the riverbank.

Irvine watched as the calm, green, swirling water changed to an agitated milky-white as it descended and tumbled down the rocky incline before them. Now standing in his saddle, Irvine peered up the track that led from the river.

'I've been here before,' he said to Tomas, as Ranulf joined them. 'We came down this track. I remember now. We reached this river and decided to turn around and find another way.'

Ranulf slowly nodded as the surroundings rang a bell with him also. 'Yes … yes, you're right. We did come this way.' He looked at Tomas, less than happy. 'Why, then, have you brought us to land we have already cleared?'

'Quite simple,' said Tomas. 'Arthur doesn't expect to see you here, so he rarely sends men out to this region. His patrols visit land and villages still untouched—the land you were heading to before you found me.'

Ranulf rode over and pushed his face close up to Tomas—so close that Tomas could have counted the pores on Ranulf's nose, had he the mind to do so.

With simmering incredulity, Ranulf asked, 'And why do you think I would be interested in following you now into land where there is no plunder?' He pointed to himself by placing the fingertips of both hands upon his chest. His voice was low and unpleasant as he jutted his chin out towards Tomas and said, 'Do I *look* like I need the fucking exercise?'

Uncomfortable at being nose-to-nose with Ranulf, Tomas shifted awkwardly in his saddle. 'But there *is* plunder ahead,' he said. His attempt at a reassuring smile came across as a nervous and jittery grimace. 'A newly rebuilt village lays just one day's ride from here.'

Ranulf, frowning, looked to Irvine for confirmation. Irvine nodded. Ranulf turned his attention back to Tomas. 'You're telling me the village I burnt to cinders three moons ago, now stands again?'

'Not only does it stand, it is full of new people,' said Tomas, nodding in emphasis. He explained further. 'Arthur was full of remorse for not protecting the people you burnt to death. That's why he made it his mission to rebuild the village. Then he found needy people—people who had come upon hard times—and moved them in.'

Ranulf pulled at his lower lip as he thought over what Tomas had just told him. 'Ah … so you have just told me where I need to go … I see it now,' he said as he slowly ramped up the severity of his tone. 'And what happens after that? Let me guess … it goes like this: I free you now, then I journey with my men to the village to find that it is still a burnt-out fucking shell. Then just as I scratch my balls because I have nothing better to do, as well as swear to Woden that I will seek, find and kill you if it takes me the rest of my life, Arthur and his army appear and proceed to practice their sword skills upon us. Have I got that just about right, boy?'

'Except that you *won't* let me go, you are not that foolish,' said Tomas, knowing that his life was very expendable at that moment. 'I know that only too well, that is why I have told you the truth.'

'But your problem now is this,' said Ranulf in the same unpleasant tone, 'whether you speak the truth or not, I don't need you anymore.' He impatiently beckoned to a nearby man to donate him his short ax.

Tomas had his answer ready. 'You do need me …
that's the point,' he said earnestly. 'Do you think I would
have put my life at risk by telling you about the village if
I didn't have good reason to?'

'And your reason is?' asked Ranulf with a skeptical
half-smile, as he accepted the ax from his subordinate.

'I can get you inside,' said Tomas. 'Otherwise they will
see you coming and bar the gates again. Then you will
either have to lay siege—a risky plan within Arthur's
lands—or burn it to the ground again and end up with
nothing but charred corpses.'

'So, I let you go inside and *you* bar the gates anyway,'
said Ranulf as he studied the ax in his hand as if ready to
use it at any moment.

'And then get burnt to death with the rest of them, I
hardly think so.'

Ranulf sighed. 'This is getting us nowhere.' He turned
to Irvine. 'What do *you* suggest we do?'

'Hear the boy's plan in greater detail and then either
kill him or go with it,' said Irvine.

Ranulf curled his lip, nodding slowly as he pondered
upon Irvine's words. He looked at Tomas. 'Speak then,'
he said.

'We approach at dark when the gates are shut,' said
Tomas. 'That way, no one sees us coming. Then you press
your men against the palisade near to the gate while I
shout for entry. Before they open the gates, they need to
hear my voice—no other voice will do—followed by this
noise "*Ki-Ki-Ki*" the sound of the merlin. As soon as the
gates open you can enter with the men and I go my own
way.'

Ranulf was not convinced. Something was not right.
Unable to believe that Tomas could so callously betray

his own people he again looked to Irvine for guidance. 'Well you heard him … *do* I kill him now?' he asked.

Irvine knew that in slaying Tomas, they would have to abandon the mission and travel back to Norwic empty handed. As a greedy man, this did not lie easy with him. After a brief consideration, he spoke.

'I can guess why you feel the need to kill him, but maybe there *is* another way. Like me, no doubt, you fear the lad is buying time, or, less likely, he has set up a trap—maybe the village is full of Arthur's men. Fanciful but possible I suppose.'

'*Exactly* what I was thinking,' said Ranulf nodding his agreement. He looked disdainfully at Tomas, then turned back to Irvine 'What is your other way?'

'Quite simply, I do what you hire me for,' said Irvine. 'I ride on ahead through the night and try to reach the village by mid-morning tomorrow. That gives me a day to watch the place,' he looked searchingly at Tomas, '… *if* it still exists.' Tomas squirmed slightly and attempted to give Irvine his sincerest look. 'That gives me nearly a full day to watch the comings and goings and see if anything suspicious is happening. Who knows … I could possibly find and excuse to actually take a look inside. I *am* British, after all.'

Ranulf mulled Irvine's idea over. *He also* hated the thought of returning to Norwic bereft of slaves. Reluctantly, he accepted the compromise. He tossed the ax back to the man who had given it to him.

To Irvine, he said, 'Leave, then …tomorrow we can decide what to do after your surveillance.' He turned to Tomas. 'As for tomorrow, it could be your last day. If I have even the slightest doubt about you, I will send you to your bestial ancestors.'

Unusual for him, Irvine travelled throughout the night. Once he had turned westwards again, he found the track he had used three months earlier with Ranulf. After riding over its undulating surface, and passing many small farmsteads that appeared only as darker shadows against the dim backdrop of small, wooded hills, the track straightened and headed towards the village.

The sunrise was tardy and begrudging as the village finally came into Irvine's view. Relieved that no militia guarded the village, Irvine resolved to get closer. A small copse lay some distance from the village and Irvine decided he would settle there for a while and merely watch.

Before he did this, he took time to ride around the periphery of the stockade, examining the ground for signs of recent troop movement. Finding none, he returned to the copse.

The village looked newly finished—the wooden palisade rearing to the height of two men; its timber looking raw and freshly sawn. Irvine concentrated his attention on two strong-looking gates, yet unopened. Beyond the gates, within the compound, grey smoke from several domestic fires curled languidly into the windless atmosphere above the settlement.

Chilled by the late autumn air, Irvine pulled his woollen cloak around his shoulders and hunkered down beside a holly bush. He prepared himself for a long wait. Beside him, his pony nodded and stamped, snorting out billows of foggy air.

Two hours passed without event or movement from the village. Irvine fought the compulsion to sleep, such was his weariness. Inevitably, though, he began to nod.

A rattle from the gates awakened him, making him tense and alert. Two men had opened the gates and now pushed them back against the palisade fence. Both men stood at the gates looking outwards for any sign of movement. The men, both tall and loose limbed, dangled digging tools over their shoulders.

Irvine could hear their murmurings as they left the gates and walked away from him, heading for the fields that lay around the back of the compound. Soon, a mixture of men, women and small children followed. Irvine was now satisfied that most of the workforce had left to work in the fields.

As he thought about Tomas' plan he could see the sense in it. To get inside the compound when it still contained the entire population of the village made more sense than the messy alternative of chasing people around the fields.

Inside, there was still movement, though. Probably women with small children, and men too old to work, thought Irvine. He considered approaching the village … even entering it. He had to be sure that no nasty surprises awaited Ranulf when he stormed the place that night. With this in mind, he began to think of an excuse that would enable him to get beyond the palisade fence.

Days earlier, Govan had left the great hall of Brythonfort with mixed feelings. His joy at seeing Elowen safe had been shattered when Nila had started to emit her awful screams of grief. As he became aware of the reason for her anguish—the death of Mule—he had hugged Elowen even tighter as their joy transposed into deep sadness. The blend of intense, conflicting emotions had left him drained, and for two days after he had felt dazed and detached from the world.

On the third day, Govan had returned to the newly built village, leaving Elowen, Nila and Maewyn behind, for now, to stay at Brythonfort.

On his second morning in the village, he had stayed behind as the others left for the fields—his work that day to attend to snags and jobs that still needed doing around the newly built-compound.

At first, he didn't notice the stranger who approached him as he worked to improve one of the iron hinges on the gate. A shadow fell across him. He looked up, squinting against the low sun that had just found a narrow, clear gap between horizon and slab of cloud. The man before him looked weathered and weary, but seemed friendly enough.

'How can I help you, stranger?' asked Govan.

Irvine, unaware he had shouted ultimatums over the wall to Govan three months earlier, measured the man before him and reckoned he could easily dupe him.

'I look for work, sir,' said Irvine, adopting the broad lilt of his native Cantiaci people. 'Came upon hard times after raiders put my village to the torch … was lucky to get out alive, I was.'

Govan gave out an apologetic sigh and shook his head. 'So late in the year, there's not much we can offer you,' he said. 'The fields are fallow and the grain ruined after this place was burnt to ashes in the autumn.'

Irvine affected a look of astonishment. 'What … you're telling me that this has been rebuilt since then? That this place is new?'

Govan stood up to face Irvin. 'Smell up, my friend,' he said proudly. 'Newly cut timber, the smell of renewal and hope.'

Irvine played up to Govan, moving his head around whilst sniffing loudly. 'Yes … yes … you're right now you come to mention it … this place *does* smell new.' Again, for Govan's benefit, Irvine adopted an expression of admiration and wonderment. He looked into the compound, leaning forward to get a better look—the very image of the respectful stranger who will not take a step inside without invitation.

Govan took the hint. 'Please come and look inside if it interests you. I'll show you around if you like.'

Irvine's look of gratitude engulfed Govan. 'You're most kind, sir,' he said. 'Of course I'd love to look inside, if it's not too much trouble.'

'No trouble at all.' said Govan genially. 'Please follow me.'

Irvine could not believe his luck. Not only had he managed to delude the man, he was now going to get a conducted tour. He nodded appropriately, showing the right amount of interest as Govan showed him around every nook and cranny of the village.

Here and there, children skipped and shouted, lost in their games. Irvine had guessed right when thinking that only the old and young had been left behind when the others had gone to the fields. Politely, he nodded his greeting to the scattering of elderly villagers who went about their business within the compound.

Having finished their walkabout, Irvine and Govan walked back to the gate. 'Well … I'll be on my way,' said Irvine. 'Maybe I'll try the smaller farmstead … who knows, they might need a man handy with ax and mattock.'

Govan wished him luck and said goodbye, watching as Irvine walked down the track towards the grove.

As soon as he reached the trees, Irvine checked that Govan had resumed his work on the gate. Satisfied he was no longer the object of his attention, he resumed his position, lying low by the holly bush. For the rest of that day he watched the village until the field workers returned just before dusk.

The last two men to arrive were the two men who had opened the gates earlier in the day. *First out last in … hard-working fellows,* thought Irvine as the two men pulled the gates shut behind them. A clattering from within, told Irvine that the men had placed stout beams into hasps to secure the gates.

Now all he could do was wait for Ranulf and the boy to arrive with the rest of the men.

He did not wait long before he saw Tomas riding up the track towards him. Two other men rode beside him.

'How far behind are the others,' asked Irvine, as Tomas slid from his pony to stand before him.

'Not far. Ranulf told me to ride ahead and report to him if anyone lingered in the darkness. If not then I'm to stay here and wait.'

'Then stay you shall, because everyone from the village is now inside the palisade.' Irvine nodded at Tomas, the nearest he would ever come to praising him. 'It seems you were telling us the truth. The village is newly rebuilt and full of profit for Ranulf.'

Tomas gave Irvine an indifferent shrug, as if to say, *That's what I told you … why did you doubt me?*

Irvine looked at the two mounted men, Sigward and Alfwald—the same two who had captured and trussed Maewyn and Mule two months earlier. 'I see that Ranulf sent you along to keep your eyes on the captive,' Irvine said.

'Aye … didn't trust the little bastard not to run off,' said Sigward. 'Still doesn't trust him.'

Irvine looked up the track as the gloaming closed around them. 'We need to get this done with as soon as Ranulf arrives,' he said. 'The sky will be moonless tonight under this cloud, and we can't use brands until this is done.'

Twilight was turning into a heavy gloom before the main body of men, led by Ranulf, arrived.

Ranulf looked sternly and questioningly at Irvine. 'Well?' he asked.

'As the boy told you,' said Irvine, pointing back towards the dark shadow of the village. 'All are now within its walls—forty souls by my reckoning. Unguarded by Arthur's men, too, just as the boy said.'

'Any fighting men amongst the occupants?' asked Ranulf.

Irvine shook his head. 'None that I could see. A couple of hefty bastards opened and shut the gates, but apart from them, mainly peasant types and women.'

'How old were the women?'

'Child bearing mainly, though I did see some younger ones who would appeal to the right buyers and bring a good price.'

'It will have to do,' said Ranulf gruffly. 'Yesterday, I thought I'd be returning to Norwic holding nothing but my cock, now at least we'll get *something* from this journey.' He looked at Tomas. 'Listen to me,' he

314

threatened, as he grabbed Tomas by his jerkin and pulled him close. 'Do not stray from your task for one moment or I will kill you, do you understand me?'

As Tomas nodded emphatically, Ranulf glared at him through the dim light. The Saxon was still uncomfortable at how things had gone. Everything seemed 'too' perfect. But Irvine, who was the best tracker he had ever ridden with, was certain the village was undefended, and that would do for him. His only concern now was the boy. It just didn't sit right with Ranulf that the whelp would so readily betray his own people.

But then again, he, Ranulf, *did* have the power of life or death over him, and he knew the fear of death made people act out of character. So maybe the boy was just trying to save his own skin, and, anyway, he had already decided what to do with him after the raid. The lad spoke the Saxon tongue and thus was sale-worthy. He would sell him to Griff for a decent price. Why kill a profit?

'Right,' continued Ranulf, as he shoved Tomas away from him. 'Get to the palisade now and deliver what you promised.'

'Follow me, then,' said Tomas. 'Remember, you must keep out of sight while I get them to open the gate.'

Tomas waited by the gate while Ranulf and his men quietly made their way to the adjacent fence. Two abreast, they lingered in its darker shadow while Tomas walked to the joint between the two tall gates.

With the edge of his fist, he gave three bangs on the gates. 'Open up,' he shouted. 'It's Tomas—or Merlin if you like—from Brythonfort, and I seek shelter for the night.'

A movement from behind him made Tomas turn. There, Ranulf stood, war ax in hand, ready to bludgeon through and enter as soon as there was the slightest crack in the gate. No sound came from within the compound, so Ranulf silently and urgently pressed Tomas to call again.

This time Tomas's call got a response. Tomas recognized the voice. 'Tomas you say. It *does* sound like you, lad, but I must hear more.'

Tomas cupped his hands to his mouth and gave out a shrill *'Ki-Ki-Ki.'*

Now there was only silence; silence that shredded the nerves of the men who waited. Ranulf fidgeted as more of his men piled up behind him ready to enter—the smell of their nervous sweat, strong and cloying in the chill air. Ranulf was about to urge Tomas to call out again when the hollow *clunking* noise of timber against timber sounded, as someone lifted the horizontal beam from its securing hasps on the inner gate.

The gates slackened (almost seemed to inhale), and that was enough for Ranulf. Pushing Tomas to one side and forgetting about him in that moment, he shoved the gate back to reveal the dark interior of the compound. Followed by his men, who briefly backlogged at the gate such were their numbers, he ran into the village. Utter darkness met him, and no man stood before him.

A dim glow from a nearby hut slowly became apparent. Desperate for light, Ranulf dispatched two men to grab the brand that was burning within They emerged moments later, their faces lit yellow by the firelight. Ranulf took the brand from the man who held it.

'The hut was empty,' said the man, unnerved at the silence within the compound.

Ranulf pointed to several murky shadows that had slowly become visible as his eyes got used to the darkness. 'Get into the huts now!' he shouted, pointing at the shadows, his face angry and devilish in the brandlight. 'We've not come here to dance in the dark like a group of fucking druids! Round up slaves! Kill any who resist!'

Before the men could move, the same hollow, *clunking* noise came from the direction of the gate. All seventy men turned towards the sound.

Ranulf then noticed the straw beneath his feet, just as the first of the fire arrows screamed into the compound.

Months earlier, when Arthur had first come up with his plan, it had initially raised a few eyebrows from the few men who were aware of it. Wracked with guilt at his failure to protect the village, he had called a meeting with the artisan, Robert, and his group of workers. Simon had also been present, as well as Gherwan. Will and Tomas had also attended.

On their way to the great hall, and unsure of what to expect, Robert and Simon had speculated the reason for the meeting.

'It's a honour indeed to be summoned to the lord's hall to offer our counsel,' Robert had said.

'Aye he's been troubled since the tragedy at the village,' said Simon. 'This will have something to do with that, mark my words.'

As they entered the hall with the rest of Robert's workers, Arthur and Gherwan, as well as Tomas and Will, already awaited them. Once seated, and without preamble, Arthur put forward his plan to rebuild the village.

Simon looked at Robert and nodded sagely, as if to say, I told you it was about the village, now we're going to be busy.

'Nothing of what I've just told you will have come as a surprise,' said Arthur, after he had allowed them a brief period

to absorb his news. 'What I am about to say now, however, will.'

All were attentive as Arthur gave quick glances at Gherwan, Will and Tomas, who were already aware of Arthur's intentions. Gherwan, stern and taciturn, gave Arthur a hardly perceptible nod of encouragement to continue. 'The rebuild is to be superficial—the thinnest of timber used to construct the palisade fence, and the village structures themselves left empty of furnishings,' said Arthur.

Frowning, Robert and Simon looked at each other, baffled as to why Arthur would want them to build in such a way.

'A thin fence would offer scant protection and soon fall foul of the elements, my lord,' said Robert. 'Would it not make sense to build something that would last a lifetime, rather than a few years at most?'

'It need not last a lifetime,' replied Arthur, '…merely a few weeks, for I intend to burn the village down.'

For the first time in his life, Robert thought Arthur, his lord, might have allowed past events to affect him, even unhinged him, but before he could speculate further, Arthur continued. 'The Saxon, Ranulf, and his band of murderers, will come back, we can be sure of that, and when they do I have no intention of chasing them around the fields until they scatter and return alive to Norwic as is their want when outnumbered.'

Arthur banged the table in emphasis. 'No! … I want them in one place, and that place is the village you will build for me. There they will die the death they saw befitting for my people. There they will burn, and in doing so the Gods will be appeased. Better still, I will not lose a single man to them in conflict.'

A moments silence ensued before Robert felt compelled to respond. He felt slightly ashamed for doubting Arthur, but could see a flaw in the plan. 'If I may …,' he started. 'The idea is a good one, but the problem I can see is how to get Ranulf and his men into the compound, and once inside how do we keep them there?'

Arthur's nod suggested he had been expecting the question. 'First, we'll lure him inside the village, then we'll stop him from getting out,' he explained. 'Yes,' he emphasised, as Robert's expression turned from puzzlement to dawning awareness, 'you will build gates that can be secured from the outside also.'

'And how will you get him to enter the village?' asked Simon, himself utterly intrigued by Arthur's scheme.

Arthur looked over to Will, inviting his input.

Will said, 'I leave with Tomas after this meeting, and we'll seek out Ranulf, or any other invaders, for that matter. Then we'll follow them and track their progress. Once they are near enough to our lands and we feel they are ready to raid, I'll return and inform Arthur.'

'And Tomas?' asked Simon.

Arthur took over now. 'If I may, Will,' he apologized. He looked intently at Simon, knowing he and Tomas had gone through much hardship together before they had come to Brythonfort. 'Tomas will allow himself to be captured, and then lead them to the village.'

Simon was not happy. 'And what if the fiend decides to kill him? How can you know how Ranulf will react when he finds out he has been under scrutiny from Tomas?'

'We do not know,' said Arthur,' but Tomas assures me, he knows how to handle Saxon despots, having had much practice in the art.'

Simon looked at Tomas. 'And are you happy with this, lad?'

'Happy enough,' said Tomas, not wanting to distress Simon further. 'It was my idea. I put myself forward for this. If I can survive two years under Egbert, I'm sure I can last long *enough to get this done. I'll make myself more useful to them alive than dead. That's how you survive with these people.'*

'And what did Dominic say of this,' asked Simon, knowing as he did, the close bond between Tomas and Dominic.

'He was only at Brythonfort for two days before he continued to the west in his quest for the children, so luckily for me he didn't have more time to persuade me not to do it. Before he left, though, he gave me his advice as usual.' Thomas smiled. 'Told me he had confidence in me, but to take great care.'

'And so you should,' said Simon, deeply worried, as the meeting drew to its conclusion.

Two days before Ranulf's entrapment in the compound, Will had gone to Arthur with his briefing, leaving Tomas to play his part with Ranulf. After delivering the news, Will immediately left and returned to watch Ranulf's group again.

Arthur had camped just two miles from the village, and with him were Flint and forty other handpicked men. Dressed as peasants, their aim was to present an image of a rural community to Ranulf and his plunderers. All the men were archers, the women and children volunteers.

Knowing they had only a day at the most to prepare— Arthurs group, which included Govan, moved into the village, the many huts within the compound having already been stuffed with tinder-dry straw.

Robert, the artisan, had practiced at Brythonfort until he had found the optimum density at which to pack the straw. Too loose and it burned out to quickly … too dense and it would not ignite.

Before dawn the next day, Will returned. Having shadowed Irvine throughout the night, he knew the man had reached the village and hidden in the copse. Will had then entered the village through the small, disguised gate at the back of the compound. Once inside he imparted his information to Arthur.

The next morning, knowing that Irvine was watching the village, Arthur and Flint, who were dressed convincingly as peasants, opened the gates of the compound. Shortly after, they left for the fields with the rest of the village occupants, leaving Govan behind as a safeguard.

Govan, who knew that Irvine was watching the village, had had to think quickly when Irvine had actually approached him, acting the dispossessed peasant. He guessed the reason for the man's audacity and decided to show him around the village, keeping him away from the windowless, straw-stuffed huts.

After giving him his tour, Govan had furtively watched as Irvine had left him and returned to the copse to continue his observation.

Just before dusk, Arthur and the others had arrived back from the fields, secured the gates behind them, and waited for Ranulf's approach. When the first knock on the gates had come from Tomas, everyone inside the compound had left by the back gate— everyone except Arthur and Flint. After wisely ignoring Tomas' first request for entry, they had acted upon hearing the second summons and opened the gates.

Alongside Flint, Arthur had sprinted across the compound and had gained half the distance to the hidden, back gate before Ranulf had pushed the main gates open. Whilst Ranulf and his men were still getting their bearings within the village, Arthur and Gherwan stood outside having gone through and locked the small back gate.

Now, as he lay beside the main gates, Tomas was unceremoniously grabbed, then hoisted to his feet. Thankfully, the shadows before him were familiar. 'Dominic, Withred,' he whispered joyously. 'What a sight you are after these past two days.'

Suddenly he remembered he had to shut the gates. Luckily, Withred was on to it and quickly dragged them together. Dominic picked up one end of the heavy securing beam. 'Get the other end, Tom,' he urged, 'or else they'll be back out.'

Together they lifted the beam and dropped it into the securing hasps. Dominic gave Tomas a brief hug and patted his back. 'Good to see you, lad, and what a hero you are after what I've heard.' He looked to the compound and pointed above it. 'Now you can watch the sky light up for your reward.'

'You two are not supposed to be *here*,' said Tomas, as he embraced Withred who had come to him.

'No. We finished our little trip to Hibernia, and then we were supposed to rest, according to Arthur,' said Withred. 'But how could miss *this*.'

Tomas was about to ask Withred about Hibernia when the first of the fire arrows began to fly from behind the back of the compound.

The brazier burned with a bright yellow fire fifty strides from the palisade. A pile of fire arrows, half the height of a man, their points wrapped in fat-soaked hemp, lay near to the brazier. Arthur and his archers lined up and waited their turn to light their arrows from the flame.

Arthur allowed Flint and Govan to the front. They were to send over the first arrows. With faces twitching

322

with resentment, they pulled back and released. 'From Bran and Mule,' they muttered as the arrows flew in an incandescent arc over the palisade.

Ranulf's face was a mixture of rage and panic as more fire arrows soared over the palisade. 'How could I have trusted that little British FUCK!' he raged, as Tomas' treachery dawned upon him.

Instinctively, he looked towards the gates just as an arrow found the thatched roof of a nearby hut. Loosely thatched, the roof immediately ignited and fell into the straw-packed room below.

Ranulf and Irvine held up their arms against the heat as they ran past the burning hut. Upon reaching the gates, they pulled back on the empty hasps that had previously housed the securing beam. The gates gave slightly but solidly resisted their pull.

As he looked despairingly at the gates, Irvine's back felt as if he walked shirtless on the hottest of summer days. He turned to look at the inner compound—his eyes shot with both incredulity and sheer terror, as more of the huts caught fire before him. Ranulf, meanwhile, resorted to futilely kicking the gates.

His men ran, panic-stricken, between the igniting huts, desperate to escape the climbing temperature but having nowhere to go.

Outside, Arthur had instructed his men to avoid lighting the fence itself, but many huts stood twenty paces from it, and these now blazed keeping the men away from the perimeter.

As the first awful scream sounded, Ranulf, terror-stricken, looked wildly around. Running towards him—his arms batting wildly against his body—ran Seward.

Ranulf moved to one side as his man crashed into the gates, then fell to the floor where he wriggled and twisted as if a soul damned to eternal suffering. Irvine looked with disbelief at him. He looked at Ranulf, his haunted stare asking, *Why doesn't he die?*

Ranulf looked absently at his tunic sleeve. It had had started to steam, such was the intensity of the heat now radiating within the compound. He looked back to Irvine and saw that he too was steaming. He watched with horrid fascination as Irvine's hair began to frizzle and contract into his scalp.

Stifling a desperate, mad giggle, Ranulf opened his mouth to inform Irvine of his ruined hair. As he inhaled he sucked scorching air into his lungs. Gagging and coughing now, he clutched his throat, just as one of the huts went up with a great 'whoomp.'

As Irvine fell to his knees, now shrieking and alight, Ranulf took off in a desperate, pointless run, a shower of orange sparks drifting down around him. Thick grey smoke now swirled around the compound, agitated by the convection currents created by the blazing fires. Seeking relief from the heat that engulfed his body, he cast aside his helmet—too hot, now, to even touch.

The stench of scorching meat caused Ranulf to gag, just as the tunic that underlay his chainmail hauberk ignited. He noticed, with an almost morbid fascination, how the fabric burned beneath the chainmail … almost like a fire behind a grate.

As the tunic burned itself out, Ranulf could feel the skin on his torso begin to tighten and split. His ensuing howls and screams sucked yet more blistering hot air into his lungs, further compounding his torment. He slumped to his knees as his own hair began to combust, and like

Seward, he fell to the ground; his body going into an orgasm of agony.

He was not the first to die, nor was he the last. Later, as the fires finally began to abate and die down, all seventy of his force lay charred and dead on the seared floor of the compound.

As the blaze had taken hold, Arthur and his men (the women and children having returned to Brythonfort in the ox carts long before the arrows had started to fly) retreated away from the heat. Here they waited — their need to add to the flames no longer necessary.

As they sat in a stubbly field, their arms resting lightly on their splayed knees as if they were awaiting the sunrise, Dominic, Withred and Tomas sauntered towards them.

His shadow backlit by the burning compound, Dominic sat on his haunches before Arthur. 'That cannot have gone better,' he said.

'It should send a warning to any future raiders.'

'*What* are you two doing here?' asked Arthur, slightly exasperated, yet glad, as ever, to see Dominic and Withred.

'Thought we'd look out for Tom,' said Dominic, jerking his thumb back over his shoulder to where the lad stood with Withred. 'At least we left Murdoc back at Brythonfort as you wished.'

Arthur shook his head resignedly, not in the least surprised by Dominic and Withred's appearance. 'No doubt his good lady, Martha, had something to do with that. It would be better if you two had women to keep you at Brythonfort — that way you would get nagged to take rest when you need it.'

'To smell bastards burning is worth a whole month of rest,' said Withred, his stark profile burnished gold by the blaze from the compound as he turned towards it.

Arthur stood and went to Tomas … embraced him. 'Well done lad,' he said. 'I never doubted you'd come through this. I'll have the minstrel write a song praising your deeds—it will tell of the boy who helped to remove a prickly thorn from the tender arse of Brythonfort.'

As Tomas smiled sheepishly, Dominic laughed along with the others—happy for now, but knowing it would be weeks before he could finally rest.

CHAPTER TWENTY-FOUR

It was the heart-rending sound of Ula, as he cried out for Cate in his troubled sleep, which had finally moved Augustus to leave Brythonfort. He had risen early that day, knowing that Modlen would have been appalled at his intention to leave alone and travel to the east coast. Worse still, he knew she would prevent him from leaving, because Augustus, who feared no man, always listened to his wife.

His twin brothers, William and John, who looked upon him more of a father than brother, had seen him off that crisp, November morning. Later that day, they would tell Modlen the reason for Augustus' absence and consequently endure her ire for letting him go.

The dark night was speckled with silver and still held no hint of dawn as Augustus set off towards the Roman road. A day's ride would see him to the road—a road he had travelled on months earlier when riding to Norwic with Dominic.

He intended to take the same route and pass through Londinium. If stopped and questioned, he would be a merchant travelling to Norwic to do business. His saddle pannier contained a selection of miscellaneous items to back up his story.

Dawn came, and his first day went without event as he managed to reach the Roman road by evening. Stiff from his first day in the saddle, and still feeling the soreness of his past injuries, he camped that night beside the road.

The next morning, he again left at first light, knowing that seven more days lay before him before he would come to Londinium.

The villages he passed on his way were, at first, British; but this changed the nearer he got to Londinium. Here, Saxon incursion had led to the displacement of the British peasant by the Germanic. Barefoot, blond children, fascinated by his size, would watch in awe as the British giant passed by their homesteads.

No one challenged him on his first days, the occasional groups he met on the road having no dealings with war or raiding, and by the midmorning of the seventh day of his journey, he sighted Londinium.

Here, he had a side mission, and after clattering over the one bridge that spanned the river named *Tamesa*, he entered the tumbledown town.

Months earlier, when visiting the town with Dominic and the others, he had been moved by the plight of a brave little family who were struggling to survive by scavenging on the shores of the river. That they were Saxon mattered not to Augustus. He saw them merely as good people trying to make their way in an unforgiving world.

This day the riverside was empty but for one man who squatted and jabbed his bark-stripped stick into the shingle shore. A wicker basket was beside him. Augustus decided to approach him.

'Good morning to you, fellow,' boomed Augustus. 'My name is Gus and I seek a man named Godwine … a man spare of build who has been known to work these shores.'

The man, still squatting, held up his hand to shield the sun from his eyes as he squinted up at Augustus. 'A Saxon he is, and I know him well,' said the man. 'Even tempered and agreeable fellow, lives against the wall in the town.'

Augustus was in luck; the man was British and spoke his tongue. 'Yes … that's him,' said Augustus. 'Just wanted to make sure he was still around. Thank-you for your help.'

He was about to leave and continue into the town when it occurred to him that Godwine did not speak Celtic, nor he Germanic. He turned back to the man. 'Tell me, do you speak the Saxon tongue?' he asked.

The man stood up now. 'Enough to get me by,' he said as he picked up his basket of finds. He shook the basket towards Augustus, its hollow rattle suggesting the man had not had a good morning. 'The man who buys this off me is Saxon—so are most of the people in this town for that matter—so it helps me get a better deal if I can actually talk to them.'

Augustus rummaged in his belt purse and took out a silver coin. Holding it between thumb and forefinger, he displayed it to the man. 'This is yours if you would do me the favour of coming with me to see Godwine ... talk between us so we can understand each other.'

Looking at the silver bit, the man realised it bettered anything that lay in his basket. 'Of course I'll come,' he said. Augustus tossed him the coin. 'My name is Hueil and it will be good to take the strain from my knees for a while.'

Godwine recognized Augustus at once. *'Once seen, never forgotten,'* Murdoc had once said of Augustus—an insight that now sprang immediately to his mind. Godwine's wife, Hild, and daughter, Udela, joined Godwine as Augustus gave him a great bear hug in greeting—a hug that left Godwine's feet dangling. After kissing Hild on the cheek, he held out his arms for Udela, who after a moment's hesitation, consented to be lifted and hugged (*gently*) by Augustus.

He looked at the child and noted her face was not as full as he remembered. Hilde and Godwine also looked undernourished and unwell. Hueil assumed his role as interpreter as Augustus began to chatter with them.

He learned that the pickings on the shoreline had been sparse, and food hard to come by. Two days had passed since the family had eaten anything other than kelp carried from the sea by the river.

After listening to their tale, Augustus thanked the Gods he had decided to visit them on his way to Norwic. 'I suppose you wonder why I came,' he said, after giving Udela back to Hilde. He walked to his pony and routed through its pannier. 'Apart from wishing to see you all again, it was to give you this.'

He pulled out the fishing net and folded it across his arms to show it to Godwine. Found in a dusty basement in Brythonfort, the net's origin was uncertain. Augustus had come across it during his convalescence, and upon finding it, had immediately thought of Godwine and his family. He had promised himself, then, that he would take the net to Londinium one day. Circumstances had now provided him with the opportunity.

Godwine looked stunned as he viewed the pristine and unused net. He stroked the weave, as if entranced, as Augustus held it forward for his inspection.

After a while, he looked up to Augustus with brimming eyes. 'Thank you,' he said, his voice emotional and barely above a whisper. 'You do not know what this means to us.'

Hilde, now holding Udela, came over to Augustus, her tears coursing freely down her face. Together with Godwine, she hugged Augustus.

That night, the family—along with the interpreter, Hueil—had their first cooked meal for three days; the food donated by Augustus. Together, they ate a hearty supper around a crackling fire, and spoke long into the night.

The next morning, Augustus said an emotional goodbye to Godwine and his family, promising he would return when the opportunity arose.

Five further days were to pass before he got his first sight of Norwic. Although arduous (Augustus was still not fully recovered from his injuries), his journey from Londinium had been uneventful. The campaigning season was now over and the road held no threat. Only casual travellers and merchants journeyed upon it, and they merely nodded their greeting to him as he passed them by.

He still had to find Cate and could only hope she was still in Britannia. What Griff had said, led him to hope she was. The first time Augustus had met him (inside his whorehouse along with Dominic, Withred, Murdoc and Flint), Griff had told them that no more boats were to sail to Hibernia from Norwic that year. Consequently, he now approached the town with a cautious optimism.

As Murdoc's words came to him again—'*Once seen never forgotten*'—he knew he had to be careful. With this in mind, he covered his head with the hood of his tunic and rode into the town's open square.

Like before, the market was in full sway, and, once again, the Icini pork seller stood behind his rough, wooden stall. Augustus knew from their previous meeting that he hated the Saxons. He also knew that the man didn't miss a trick.

As Augustus approached him, the pork seller anticipated a sale. 'Ah ... a traveler by the look of you and, by-your-leave, a great big fellow to boot.' He had already begun to slice of a huge hunk of meat from the haunch that lay before him. Augustus fished in his purse and took out a silver coin. He threw it on the table where it spun a moment before settling with a woody rattle.

The pork seller nodded his appreciation before scooping it off the table and popping it into his apron pocket. 'Thank you it will make a lovely ornament which I will—'

'—have made into an amulet for the price of half a pig, then sell on the finished item for a full pig,' finished Augustus for the pork seller.

The pork sellers head shot back as he smiled his curiosity at Augustus. 'Do I know you?' he asked.

Briefly, Augustus removed his hood.

The pork seller recognized him at once. 'Whoa, you're a brave fellow to come back here,' he said. 'Lucky for you that Griff is out of town after what you and your friends did that night.'

Augustus put his hood back up and took hold of the huge piece of pork before him. He took a bite, ravenous after his day on the trail.

'It's *Griff* I want to find,' he said, through a mouthful of pork. 'I think he may have something he shouldn't have.'

The pork seller nodded knowingly. 'I'll not ask you your business ... sometimes it's best if you don't know too much in this town ...' The man paused a moment, before sighing resignedly and continuing. 'Look … I don't know why I'm telling you this and your business is your own, but here I go anyway.' After a quick look around to ensure nobody was in earshot, he gave Augustus a serious look. 'I know what you and your companions did the last time you were here. I also know that one of the children—a girl—was recaptured and brought back to the town.' Now enthralled, Augustus stopped chewing as he listened to the little man before him. 'So if you want to find her you're right to look for Griff—she'll probably be with him at his villa.'

'No more boat's sailed, then,' said Augustus. 'I feared she may have been taken over the sea somehow, even though Griff told us that no more trading boats were to sail this year.'

'Only fishing vessels have left this port in the last three months,' said the fish seller.

'How can you be sure that Griff has her at his villa?'

'Because he needs to protect her purity and so her worth … and he can best do that back in the security of his villa.'

And Griff himself? Would *he* not be tempted to defile the girl?

The fish seller smiled sardonically and looked at Augustus as if to say, *You've met Griff and you don't know?*

'Tempted to defile a boy, yes, but not a girl, if you get my meaning,' said the vendor with a little laugh. 'Even his bodyguard's had his balls chopped off, so you've no need to worry on that score either. Listen … if you want to find Griff, then that's easy—he'll be at his villa, ten miles along yonder road.' As he said this, he furtively jabbed his crooked finger towards a track that ran northwards from the town, '… lives there with his slaves

... and his dogs.' He emphasised the mentioning of the dogs with a meaningful look and little nod of the head.

Augustus had already briefly met the mastiffs on his previous visit and was aware of their ferocity, but had not really thought too much about them until now. Now, he realised he may have to deal with them should he go to the villa. *Would* have to deal with them *when* he went to the villa, he reminded himself.

The pork seller offered Augustus a cloth. After wiping his hands and mouth with it, he thanked the man for his information and took the northern track.

CHAPTER TWENTY-FIVE

Twelve days after Augustus had left Brythonfort, his brothers, William and John, had approached Dominic for help. Having witnessed Modlen's anguish over Augustus' disappearance they had made the decision to set out to find him. This, they realised, would be easier if they had Dominic with them. They knew he could get them rapidly eastwards through the forest.

Unknown to them, though, Dominic had already made the decision to look for Augustus. He had always intended to wait until the Ranulf problem was resolved before he set out, so when William and John met him they were surprised to find he was already preparing to go.

After a brief discussion, they agreed to leave together, and two days after Ranulf and his raiders had become corpses they readied themselves to leave.

'If all has gone well for him,' said Dominic, as he stood beside his pony equipping it for the journey, 'he should have reached Norwic by now. Possibly even be on his way back.'

'He will if he's found the girl and somehow managed to rescue her,' said William, who was a younger version of Augustus himself.

In fact, as Dominic looked at the identical twins before him, he saw *two* young Augustus' and this filled him with confidence for the upcoming journey.

'We can only guess at how it's gone for him,' said Dominic. 'If we assume he he's had a smooth run of it, he'll travel by night and hide by day. He'll also return through the forest, if I know your brother. He's not stupid; he knows that's the best way to shake off any chasers.'

'Is that the way we'll go then?' asked William as he hauled his brawny bulk up onto his pony.

'Yes certainly,' said Dominic. 'Five days will get us to Aebbeduna on the edge of the forest and near to your old village. With any luck, Gus will be well into the forest by then. If he keeps to the main track, we should meet him in there. Then we can help get him back … raise his spirits and take the burden from him.'

'And fix him if he's taken injury,' said John, concerned. 'He was still not right after being hurt before. Only a man of his strength could set off on such a journey alone when still recovering from such pain.'

'That's Gus for you,' said Dominic as he swung onto his own pony. 'A heart as big as the forest, and fists as big as turnips.'

Modlen came to them then, with Art and Ula by her side. William and John bent forward in their saddles and hugged their farewells to her. William then offered his arm to Art, John did the same to Ula. Effortlessly, they pulled both boys up to them and sat them on their ponies. Beaming, the lads looked down to Modlen and over to Dominic, more than happy in the company of their new uncles.

Modlen went over to Dominic and fondly put her hand on his arm. 'Thank you for doing this,' she said. 'I have hardly slept since he left.'

'It's no burden to try and help a man I love dearly,' said Dominic. He nodded towards the boys. 'Look at that,' he smiled. 'Two sets of twins … one pair missing a brother, the other pair missing a sister.'

336

'Then Godspeed so that all may be united soon,' said Modlen.

CHAPTER TWENTY-SIX

The small hill provided Augustus with a good view of the old villa. Set out as a perfect square with a central courtyard, the villa had but one entrance. Tegula tiles made from local clay covered the pitched roofs—the nearby abundant clay deposits having also provided the material for the brick walls of the buildings. The structures were pristine, and overlooked a fountain-adorned courtyard. An inner veranda attached to the inner walls of the buildings provided a covered walkway around the perimeter of the courtyard.

The November day was cool and muted, somewhat diminishing the sparkle of the villa. Even so, Augustus had never seen such a magnificent structure. In comparison to the villa below him, he now realised he had unwittingly spent his entire life inhabiting a primitive hovel.

He considered what to do next. Because the villa had only one entrance (no doubt an adaptation introduced by Griff for his security), this was a problem. Yet, to enter the villa was unavoidable. If Cate was inside, as he hoped she would be, then he had to find a way in and rescue her.

To simply walk down and go through the gates, then have a casual look around, was not an option. For now, he could do no more than sit, watch, and wait.

One hour passed as Augustus awaited developments. During this time, he had seen two figures and two dogs take air in the courtyard. He guessed one of the figures to be Griff—the other, larger figure, was a black man.

It was the first time in his life that Augustus had set eyes upon a Negro, and the sight of the man made him gasp. Everything from the man's black skin and tight hair, to the fluidity of his movements, which although graceful, hinted at bridled strength, was alien to Augustus. *Another problem to deal with and me still not back to my best*, he thought, as he shifted his weight onto his elbow to ease the pain in his torso. He was at a loss now. He could not think what to do next.

A further hour passed before his simmering frustration changed to attentiveness as a covered wagon rolled down the road below him and up to the gates of the villa. Inside the villa's perimeter, two women emerged from their quarters and scurried across the courtyard to open the gates. The wagon entered and continued to the opposite side of the square.

As Augustus watched, Griff and the Negro summoned the women to fetch horses. The wagon's driver, meanwhile, entered the building, and emerged pushing two bound figures towards the wagon's open back door. Both were adult; both seemed aged.

The gates to the villa were still open as the wagon driver mounted his cart and lifted his reins to send the hefty dray across the courtyard and through the gates. Augustus tensed with anticipation as Griff and the Negro, with the dogs bounding around them, mounted their horses and followed the wagon. He realised the opportunity to get inside the villa had just unfolded before him.

He watched as the entourage passed below, before taking a side trail that wound beyond a grassy knoll. Looking back at the villa, Augustus could see the gates were still open. *An oversight or normal practice? ...* he didn't care. *Now was the time to move!*

Grimacing from the pain in his ribs, he got to his feet and made his way down the hill. He glanced around nervously as he walked across the open expanse of ground in front of the building. When reaching the outer wall of the villa, he stopped by its open gate. He chanced a look inside and saw the courtyard empty. The two women had gone.

Nerves jangling, he slipped through the opening and entered, then made for the wall adjacent to the gates. As he reached the veranda, he welcomed its concealing shadow and crouched to make himself small. The veranda continued to the next corner, then turned a right-angle to run alongside the next wall of the villa until reaching another corner, and so on, continuing as a square to join the gates again.

Augustus could smell wine. He noticed a row of large, sealed, clay jugs near to him, and realised he must be next to the wine store. Now he decided to make his way around the inner walls of the villa, keeping under the veranda. If Cate was here, he must surely come to her if he continued around the square. *Surely, she must be in one of the rooms.*

He quickly moved behind the cover of the wine jugs as the two women again ran across the floor of the courtyard. Their urgency and anxiety unsettled Augustus, but he was unseen by them as they passed him by, ten paces away.

They ran to the gates, which they immediately shut. Their relief was palpable—the women had forgotten to shut the gates and had feared a lashing from Griff for their lapse. Augustus realised how lucky he had been to enter the villa The women, now at ease, walked back across the courtyard, giggling with relief and nervous energy. Augustus allowed them to enter a room at the far end of the courtyard before he emerged from behind the wine jugs and moved on.

He reached the first inner corner of the villa and started to follow the next wall. An intricate mosaic floor lay under his feet. He was careful to tread lightly so as not to produce footfall upon it.

He came to his first door and listened carefully outside before giving it an exploratory push. Crouching, he opened it enough to peek into its gloomy space. The smell of stone and water, and the sound of hollow dripping, told him he had found the bathhouse. Seeing it empty, he moved on.

The next rooms (also empty) were austere but well-furnished, and Augustus guessed they were probably the quarters of a high-ranking servant—possibly the black man he had seen earlier.

He cast a nervous glance across the courtyard towards the gates as the Negro again entered his thoughts. *He had to get this done. Had to get Cate, and get out.*

He reached the second corner and started to move along the side of the third wall—the one that faced the gates. He passed another apartment. His careful look through its window opening confirmed that it was lavish and opulent. *Griff's fun palace, no doubt,* he thought. The next door, which was twenty strides away and open, led into the room where the women had entered.

Augustus pressed his huge bulk into the shadows as the women again walked out onto the courtyard. This time, chattering amongst themselves and lost in their tittle-tattle, they strolled past Augustus, merely yards from him. They walked towards the wine store and entered it.

He waited until they were out of sight before moving silently to the nearby open door. Voices came from within the room—one a girl's, the other an adolescent boy's.

Augustus patted his belt and found his knife. Happy it was there should he need it, and knowing that time was running on, he slid into the room and shut the door behind him.

Before him, seemingly relaxed and well cared for, sat Cate, chatting with Griff's boy, Ciaran.

Both, now startled, looked at Augustus as he entered the room. Augustus hushed his lips, then held up his palms—the gesture telling them to keep calm and quiet. Ciaran immediately shrank back against the wall ... away from Augustus' intimidating bulk.

Cate, for her part, blinked disbelievingly at Augustus, as he stood before her, larger than life. After a brief moment of disorientation, during which time Augustus had started to think she might not remember him, Cate ran to him.

Only too well, did she recall how the man had made her feel safe. She thought of her brothers and realised she may yet see them again.

'We have to go *now!*' urged Augustus, knowing there was no time to talk. He let go of Cate and glanced at Ciaran, who still cowered by the back wall.

Augustus' glance was not lost on Cate. 'His name's Ciaran and Griff treats him terribly,' she said. 'He's been my friend here. Please, can we take him with us?'

Augustus could see no problem with it. He did not have the time to argue the matter, anyway. He looked at the youth. 'Come on lad,' he said. 'You're about to take a long trip through the forest, do you think you can manage that.'

Ciaran, still wide eyed with astonishment, gave a quick look towards Cate, who nodded her encouragement. Ciaran reciprocated Cate's nod, turning it to Augustus. 'Y-yes … I think I can manage it,' he said.

'Follow me then and keep close,' said Augustus as he turned and left the room.

In the brief time Augustus was in the room with the children, the two women, having concluded their business in the wine store, had investigated a summoning knock coming from the villa's gates. After peering through an observation slit, they lifted down the beam securing the gate and allowed Griff, Ambrosius, and the covered wagon, back into the compound, just as Augustus emerged with Cate and Ciaran.

Griff immediately recognised Augustus, who stood immobile and shocked beside the children. Meanwhile, Ambrosius, who held the dogs, made to move against him, but Griff now realised that an opportunity had presented itself, and quickly stayed s' arm.

Ambrosius signaled for the wagon to pass them by and continue towards Augustus. The dogs, meanwhile, pulled against their leads, eager to do their grisly work upon him.

Griff, though, realised the animals would be indiscriminate in their maiming, and so risk injuring and possibly killing Cate and Ciaran if set free. With this in mind, he grabbed the dogs from Ambrosius and continued to restrain them.

Augustus still stood at the far end of the compound, his body now shielding Cate and Ciaran, whom he had shoved behind him.

Griff advanced ten paces with the dogs and stopped. He knew he had the upper hand. His man, Ambrosius was lethal with a sword, having been a knight with the legions before being caught and castrated by the Gauls— the mutilation being the uppermost consideration when Griff had employed him.

Even so, the big Briton opposite seemed formidable to Griff. Although gaunter in the face since their last meeting, the giant exuded a massive corporeal presence. Griff glanced at Ambrosius, who quivered with the strain of his suppressed inactivity, awaiting his instruction. It would be his sword against the Briton's knife. Ambrosius locked his stare upon Augustus, awaiting Griff's command.

Griff, though, had already decided that no Gladiatorial combat would occur within his compound that day. He would not risk his best man to injury, no matter what his weaponry advantage. No ... he had already formulated a far better plan than that.

As the horse and cart stopped ten paces from Augustus, its rider remained seated—a high, safe distance from him.

The restrained dogs gave low throaty growls as Griff shouted to Augustus. 'You have been caught in the act, Colossus, and now you have nowhere to run!' Augustus looked around on hearing this. He instinctively backed up towards the building. 'It's no use heading for the villa,' continued Griff. 'There is no opening large enough to allow your bulk through.' Augustus now stopped his backward progress, but still stared defiantly at Griff.

Griff walked a further five paces across the dusty floor of the compound with Ambrosius beside him. Again, he gave Augustus his ultimatum. 'Do as I tell you and the girl will live. Try to move against me and I will release the dogs.'

Augustus tensed as he looked at the two animals. Before him were beasts that had no respect for his size or power—beast that would not only attack him if released, but also attack Cate and the youth. He knew he was in a quandary; knew there were few ways to get out of this. Desperate, he attempted to reason with Griff.

'Why not just send your man to fight me?' asked Augustus. 'Surely you must have confidence in him— after all it would be his sword against my butcher's knife. If I win, I take the girl,' he nodded towards Ciaran, '… and the lad as well, if he wishes to leave.'

'What … and just leave me with my two servant wenches?' laughed Griff dismissively as he pointed to the women who now watched events from the veranda near the wine store. 'No, my giant, there will be no fight here today … I'll not have my courtyard despoiled with your blood … but don't worry, you *shall* have your fight, but not here … not now. And, yes … I accept your terms. Win the fight and you can leave with the girl.'

Augustus nodded his assent, having little other choice. 'What would you have me do then?' he asked.

'Get in the wagon,' said Griff, simply. 'It will take you to a place where you can have your battle, away from the fragility of my beautiful villa. That's your choice … throw down your knife and get into the wagon or I *will* release the dogs.'

Cate grabbed hold of Augustus upon hearing this. She looked beseechingly at him. 'Don't do it … please don't do it,' she pleaded. 'I know what they do to people who leave in the wagon.' Augustus looked at Ciaran. The youth gave him a barely perceptible shake of the head, his expression advising, *Listen to her … do not get into the wagon.*

Yet Augustus *had* to get into the wagon. He knew that. He had no choice. He would be hard pushed to protect *himself* from the dogs, should Griff let them go, let alone protect the others.

Pained at what he had to do—what he must tell Cate— he whispered to her.

'I *have* to do it. I have to get in the wagon or the dogs will be set free. Maybe something good will come of this … just wait and hope … that's all I ask.'

Cate, sniveling and shaking her head, continued to cling on to Augustus. Gently, he removed her arms from him and pulled her away.

He turned to face Griff. 'As you command, I'll get into your wagon!' he shouted. 'Let's get this done with, so I may return to my home with this child!' He threw down his knife and nodded to the driver who had climbed down from his seat.

Anticipating the forthcoming show, the driver, who loved his work for Griff, opened the back door of the wagon and impatiently beckoned Augustus to get in.

CHAPTER TWENTY-SEVEN

The day after the massacre of Ranulf's force, the cleanup began. Built to ignite quickly, the huts had been mere facades packed with straw. After the burn, nothing remained standing apart from the palisade fence.

Arthur assessed the damage along with Robert, his chief artisan. They also surveyed the scene of slaughter. Scattered around the inner space lay seventy corpses; all were soot-black; all were crisp and charred.

As they walked to the centre of the compound, six, high-sided, ox-drawn carts, entered. In each cart sat two men.

'Is the pit ready for the bodies?' Arthur asked Robert, as the men jumped from the carts and started to sling the cadavers onto the plank floors of the wains.

'Yes … by the woodland away from the fields,' said Robert. 'More than the evil bastards deserve, I reckon.'

Arthur nodded his partial agreement. 'Yes, I too would have let them decay, but we have the children to consider. I don't want them looking at the rotting bodies. If left in the open, the buzzards and kites would soon dismember them and scatter their bones across the fields. It's better we get them out of sight and out of mind as quickly as possible.'

'They don't walk this earth anymore, that's the main thing,' conceded Robert as he walked to the inner wall of the wooden palisade and slapped his hand on its surface.

Arthur also rubbed his hand over the seared timber. 'Will the fence be sound enough for purpose after the new structures are built?' he asked.

'Probably better than if it had *not* been scorched,' answered Robert. 'The fire brought the oils to the surface of the wood and that'll protect it from the weather.'

'It's good that the heavy work we did in clearing the ditch and building the fence was not in vain,' said Arthur, '…good that the fire did little damage to either.'

'Yes, now we can start to build the huts again—this time to shelter *people* rather than straw.'

As the first of the loaded carts rumbled past them bound for the mass grave, Arthur had the cart driver stop. He beckoned Robert to join him at the back of the wagon. Eight bodies lay there. Some had already started to bloat, causing putrid, pink cracks to break through the black, crispy outer skins of the cadavers.

Robert shot his head back in disgust at the sight, as Arthur rolled one of the husks onto its back. The head was seared to the bone and unrecognisable, and apart from an intricately crafted hauberk, the body was naked.

Arthur fingered the hauberk. 'Say hello to Ranulf, the cause of our heartbreak. This chainmail tells me it's him.'

Robert winced at the sight of the very dead Saxon plunderer. 'D'you think we've seen the last of them, now *he's* gone?'

'For now, but not for ever,' said Arthur. 'I've no doubt more of his kind will chance their hand, but at least we've avenged the people *he* wronged.'

With this in mind, Robert asked, 'How's Nila, Flint and Maewyn taking the loss of Mule?'

'Not good,' Arthur sighed as he slapped the back of the wagon, signaling the driver to continue on his way. He pointed to Ranulf's corpse as it bumped about on the floor of the departing wain. 'Nila lost a husband *and* a son because of that man, but the loss of a son to any mother is

348

the deepest cut of all. She has her other sons close to her at all times … seems terrified that, they too, will be taken from her. Flint seems to be coping the best … talks of getting back on patrol as soon as his mother can let him go.'

'And Maewyn?' asked Robert.

'Troubled and intense, he is … not like him at all. He's taken to visiting the Christian shrine at Brythonfort … seems to give him comfort. His meeting with monks in Hibernia appears to have had a profound effect upon him.'

'Well at least the two lads have something to take their minds off their loss,' said Robert. 'I can only hope the new village we're about to build here brings Nila out of herself.'

As he walked with Robert to the open gates of the compound, the mention of Nila led Arthur to think of her friend—Augustus' wife, Modlen. He pointed eastwards beyond the fields. 'Somewhere out there Dominic rides. Modlen told me this morning that he's set out to look for Augustus … rides eastwards towards the great forest with William and John.'

Robert smiled and shook his head in amazement. 'Where that man gets his energy from beats me. It seems his mission in life is to find lost people.'

It had taken Dominic five days to get to Aebbeduna at the edge of the forest, and the town had changed little since his last visit, months earlier.

He looked for Wilfred—the merchant friend of Flint— and found him beside a workshop passing the time of day with a smith. The smith had been working on a sword, his constant reheating and reworking having produced a beautiful patternation throughout the steel blade.

Wilfred met Dominic with delight, hugging him as Dominic introduced William and John.

'Aye, I can tell they're Augustus' brothers,' said Wilfred, as he stood back and smilingly appraised them. 'He's not with you then?'

Dominic, who had hoped Augustus might have reached Aebbeduna by now, told Wilfred the reason for his journey—told him of his concerns over Augustus' state of health; of the peril Augustus had put himself in by setting out alone.

Wilfred shared Dominic's concern as he left the smith to his work. Having no time to hang about the three travellers made to leave at once. Wilfred walked to the edge of town with them. Before them, two miles distant, they could see the edge of the forest.

Wilfred wished them luck as they mounted.

'A day's travel into the woods will see us at our former village,' said William.

'Yes, and hopefully we'll have met Gus by then,' said John, frowning with concern as he heeled his pony towards the brooding forest.

Wilfred shouted to Dominic as he followed William and John down the trail. 'Farewell and seek me on your return for a warm bed and good ale.'

Dominic waved his thanks to Wilfred. He turned to his beloved forest.

CHAPTER TWENTY-EIGHT

Augustus sat against the back wall of the wagon, elbows on knees, his fisted hands pressed against his temples as he looked down at the dusty floor.

He knew the biggest trial of his life was about to begin. All he had was his strength. Whatever Griff was about to throw at him he had nothing but his great strength to meet it with.

The wagon's jolting ceased, yet the wagon still moved forward. *A smooth surface below*, though Augustus, *this is where it will happen.*

The wagon stopped and Augustus looked to the door.

Moments passed and he sat in silence. A slight movement of the wagon told him the driver had detached the pony. *Probably taking it out of harm's way,* thought Augustus. The silence continued as snatches of past conversations filtered into his head. Something that Murdoc had said came to him. *'Sweet Jesus Saviour; he feeds the old ones to his dogs.'*

He jumped as the driver released the securing twine from the door.

Light flooded in, causing Augustus to hold up his hand as a barrier against it as it needled into his eyes. The driver, his shadow framed in the outline of the door, beckoned him out.

An undercurrent of nervous excitement quavered in the driver's voice. 'You … get your fat arse out here!' he rasped.

Augustus moved to the door and dismissively pushed the driver aside with the back of his hand.

He stepped out.

After giving the driver a look of utter contempt, he looked around. He stood in a disused amphitheater; he didn't need to be a Roman to know that.

His eye caught the shifting figure of the driver as the man jumped inside the wagon. As he watched, he threaded the twine through the door and tied it from the inside. Augustus could just about make out his eager eyes—just about hear his panting breath—as he peered through the wicker door waiting for the spectacle to begin.

He walked to the door and gave it an exploratory pull. It did not shift. The driver had tied it well. Again, he shot the driver a disdainful look—*pathetic little bastard*—before walking to the side of the wagon.

He turned from the wagon and shifted his gaze to the decaying terrace that ran down to the arena floor. The floor looked disturbed, as if a contest had taken place recently. Then he noticed the blood and remembered the two people who had earlier been loaded into the cart at the villa. *'Sweet Jesus Saviour; he feeds the old ones to his dogs.'*

Twenty steps up the terracing stood Griff, with the dogs and Ambrosius.

As Griff looked at Augustus, he knew he would boast for years to come about how his dogs had brought down and tore apart the giant Briton. As soon as he had seen the man at the villa, his only thought had been to get him to the arena and set the dogs on him. As the dogs now growled and yelped under his restraint, he smiled in anticipation of the forthcoming show.

Studying the Briton who gazed calmly back at him, Griff could see that he was unafraid. The man looked as if he had already made his peace with his Gods and was preparing to die.

Griff hoped he had not given in; hoped he wouldn't go down without a struggle. It was better when they struggled. It made the dogs frenzied—made them inflict even greater damage.

Augustus looked up, impatient now for the thing to start. He lifted his great arms in defiance and bellowed, 'Come on then, you depraved fuck, get on with it!'

That's better, though Griff, *now watch the dogs go to work.*

He set loose the dogs. They hurtled down the steps eager to tear into Augustus, who had not strayed far from the wagon, and as the first of the dogs hit him, he had already climbed up onto the top of the metal-rimmed wheel of the wagon. The dog attempted to get a hold on his shin, but fell back as Augustus kicked out the leg forcing it to release him.

Both dogs now leapt at him as he turned and grabbed the top of the cart, but the broad expanse of his back defeated the efforts of the dogs to bite into anything loose and they fell back to the floor of the arena.

From above Griff exchanged a quick glance with Ambrosius. This was new to him. Usually, his victims' fear froze them into passive inactivity. That or they attempted to fend the dogs off, and that was when it got *really* interesting. Nobody had ever attempted to climb out of harm's way onto the wagon's roof before. Except that it wasn't out of arms way. Not when you had an archer of Ambrosius' skill standing beside you.

'Ready your bow,' Griff said. 'Knock him off the roof but don't kill him, I still want to see the dogs finish him off.'

With a great heave, which drained much of his strength, Augustus pulled himself up to his waist onto the wagon roof, leaving his legs dangling over the edge.

Below, the dogs had erupted into a frenzy of frustration as they threw themselves at Augustus, their jaws closing with hollow snaps as they found only air to eat.

Augustus splayed out his palms, and with a heave and a great deal of grunting, managed to drag the rest of his body onto the wagon's roof.

There he crouched, as if awaiting the start of a sprint race, slack jawed and panting as he took in the arena below him.

The arrow hit him before he saw it … its onrushing *whoosh* heard a fraction before it pierced the meat of his right shoulder. The impact knocked him onto his rear on the very edge of the wagon.

Shooting his arms behind him to arrest the momentum of his fall, he found only an airy void. Frantically, he fanned his arms, as if back paddling in water, and so managed to avoid toppling backwards over the edge of the wagon.

He snapped the arrow by its feathered end, leaving a hand's width of broken shaft to protrude from him and stem his bloodflow.

Aware that another arrow would follow, he remained crouched as he looked over to Ambrosius who had now walked down to the bottom steps of the arena. The dogs had returned to him. Unfulfilled and pulsating with energy, they bounded and yelped at his feet.

As Augustus shuffled across the top of the wagon, he noticed that its rush-work roof gave a little under his weight. He gave the roof an exploratory thump. His hand merely bounced upon it, having no effect. Then he noticed a small rent in the wicker and managed to worm a thick forefinger beneath it. He pulled, and a shard of willow snapped away from the plane of the roof. Now he shoved four of his finger into the resultant breach. Again, he pulled, and this time a fist-sized hole opened up.

His glanced over to Ambrosius—a glance that saved his life. As Griff had joined him, Ambrosius had again let fly an arrow, but this time Augustus was able to throw himself flat onto the roof of the wagon as the arrow parted the air above him. Now he looked through the hole in the roof. Below him, the now-nervous Saxon driver, deprived, for now, of his show, looked up fearfully at Augustus.

Augustus knew what he had to do and took the chance to stand upright. Knowing he had only seconds before his big outline would invite another arrow strike, he jumped and brought his feet down with a great stamp upon the breach in the roof.

Griff watched, with a fascination bordering on admiration, as the big Briton disappeared through the top of his wagon.

Ambrosius immediately made to approach the wagon, but Griff stopped him.

'No need for that,' said Griff. 'The big bastard's going nowhere. He can't stay in there forever. The dogs'll have him when he comes out. You watch … we'll get our show yet. Just watch the dogs—'

The wagon door exploded outwards, muting Griff, as Augustus tumbled onto the floor and crouched to face the onrushing dogs.

When Augustus had dropped through the roof, the driver had made a futile attempt to get out of the wagon. Dismissively, Augustus had thrown him to the back of the cart where he had hit the wall and slid to a sitting position, his mouth agape with surprise. After undoing the twine that secured the door, Augustus had then kicked the door open and left the wagon.

He dealt with the first of the dogs as it leapt at him. Crouching in front of the open wagon door, he was able to divert the flying dog past him and into the wagon, without it taking so much as a bite from him.

Quickly, he secured the door with the twine, just as the second dog leapt onto his back. Now he had only one dog to fight.

He stood upright with the dog still clinging to him as mad screams and frenzied snarling came from inside the wagon. Here, the second dog had already started to inflict its frenzied maul upon the driver.

After shaking his dog free free, Augustus had just enough time to raise his arms to deflect it from his face as it again leapt at him. The weight of it was enough to make even Augustus stumble backwards towards the wagon. Again, the dog jumped, and this time Augustus went down.

Griff and Ambrosius had gone back up the steps to get a better sight of the struggle. When Augustus fell, Griff had exchanged a quick, knowing glance with Ambrosius. *He won't get up from this*, was the consensus of the glance.

Augustus pulled at the dog's ear as it attempted to bite into the flesh of his midriff. Completely oblivious to the tugs, the dog continued to tear at him until it had opened up a flap of skin. Beneath the flap, Augustus' flesh glistened raw and vulnerable. *It's trying to eat me alive,* thought Augustus as he swiped his fist at the dog's head.

The enraged dog—now frothing and snarling—turned its attention to his face. On his back now, Augustus jammed his elbow under the dog's muzzle as its jaws snapped at him a finger's width from his nose.

He was aware that one bite on his face would signal the end for him. He could see no way to gain advantage over the dog, but was not prepared to stop fighting, even though his energy had almost gone and his arms screamed for relief. As the quiver in his arms became a shake, he imagined, with an uncontrollable morbidity, what it would feel like to have the flesh ripped from his face.

Then he remembered the arrow in his shoulder.

With his last reserves, he took the full weight of the dog on his right arm only. Reaching across with his left hand, he snatched the arrow from his shoulder. It emerged bloody and glistening, causing Augustus no conscious pain in its removal, such was the intensity of the struggle.

Just as his right arm collapsed under the sustained weight and pressure of the mastiff, he jammed the leaf shaped arrow point through its eye, deep through its socket, and into its brain. A small, curtailed yelp was all the dog could manage as it immediately flopped dead upon him.

'CHRONOS!' Griff's scream was shrill and girl-like as he witnesses the demise of his bitch, causing Ambrosius to look at him with concern. Now Griff could only stand mute and horrified—his hand pressed to his open mouth.

'Shall I finish him?' asked Ambrosius as he drew his sword.

Griff, eyes wide with shock, hand still to mouth, could only manage a tiny nod. Ambrosius left and trotted down the steps and across the arena floor to Augustus.

Augustus managed to climb to his knees and fill his great lungs with air. Only now did he notice that the screaming from the wagon behind him had stopped. A wet chomping, and occasional crunching, evidenced that the dog inside was now feeding on the driver.

As Ambrosius ran towards him, Augustus knew that his struggle was not about go away any time soon. His thoughts raced madly. He considered getting into the wagon and shutting the door to give him a brief respite, but thought better of it when hearing the dog feed.

Without shield or weapon, and exhausted after his struggle with the mastiff, he knew he had little chance against the fresh, adept man who now ran towards him. As Ambrosius quickly closed on him, Augustus looked at the dead dog on the floor at his feet.

Grabbing the collar of the dog with his right hand, its stumpy tail with his left, he lifted it chest high just as Ambrosius bore down him.

He hoisted the body of the dog above his shoulders to meet the first overhead vertical strike from Ambrosius. The sword crunched through bone and tissue, almost cleaving the dog in half. Ambrosius immediately followed the strike with a waist high horizontal swipe at Augustus' midriff. Augustus just managed to block the cut with the now-articulated body of the dog. The dog fell in half.

Still grasping the collar of the riven dog, Augustus tumbled back towards the wagon. He was done in, he knew it—his next action would be his final one. As Ambrosius shuffled towards him, readying himself to deliver his deathblow, Augustus threw the half-dog at him as a last act of defiance.

Ambrosius' avoidance of the dog carcass caused him to shift his balance as he attacked Augustus with another overhead slashing swipe. This gave Augustus the extra moment he needed to avoid the attack.

Ambrosius' sword rang shrill as it hit the metal rim of the wagon, creating a myriad of orange sparks. The sword flew from his hand; such was the force of the impact.

Augustus, now exhausted, could only fall upon Ambrosius, relying on his great weight to pin him to the side of the wagon beside the wheel.

Ambrosius twisted round in Augustus' grasp, his eyes wild as he looked towards the floor searching for his sword. He attempted to wriggle free, but his strength was no match, even for a much-depleted Augustus, who gripped him bear-like.

Augustus was now able to place his meaty hand on Ambrosius' forehead and slide his fingers through his crinkly hair. He slammed the head back against the metal rim of the wheel. Repeatedly, he slammed the head until it imploded into a ghastly heap of broken skull and brain tissue.

Griff had looked on, aghast, as the fight came to its unlikely conclusion. Unable to take in what he had witnessed in the arena, his only thought now was for his remaining dog.

'Titon,' he wept, as he ran to the wagon, intent on letting the mastiff loose again. He did not fear the huge Briton who knelt exhausted beside the wagon—he knew he had nothing left … all his fight had gone.

However, Griff was wrong. With his last reserves, Augustus—who was aware of Griff's intent—was able to get to his feet just as Griff reached the back door of the wagon and begin fumbling with the tightly knotted twine that secured it. His whimpering matched that of his incarcerated dog beyond the door. Chattering and whining inanely to himself, he cursed Augustus for tying the knot too tightly.

Having just managed to slacken the knot, he was hit by Ambrosius' sword, wielded by Augustus. The blow smashed into the nape of his neck, decapitating him cleanly.

Augustus stepped back to allow Griff's body to flop to the ground beside his head. He dropped the sword, too shattered now even to bear its weight. With his arms hanging limply beside him, he looked, first at Griff's head, the lips of which still twitched as if attempting to spit out one last curse at him, then up to the grey, scudding clouds above.

Now his great body wracked with huge gasping sobs … sobs of relief … desperation … utter exhaustion. He looked around at the carnage he had caused, looked at his wounded stomach, and wondered how he would ever get back to Brythonfort.

With a stumbling, weary gait, he walked out of the arena. Now he could collect Cate and the youth. Now he could take them home.

CHAPTER TWENTY-NINE

One day into the forest, Dominic, William and John came to the abandoned village. Once the home of William and John, the village was the scene of the *battle at the ox carts,* where a Saxon force—led by Osric and Egbert—had been defeated. By a mixture of guile and bravery, and led by Dominic and Withred, the village had managed to stem the tide of Saxon incursion that day, but in doing so most of the men of the village had been lost. The relocation of the survivors was then inevitable, and the remaining population had soon made the journey to Brythonfort.

William and John were somber as they looked at the village for the first time since they had left it, two years earlier. Their youngest brother, Samuel, lay buried—along with all who had died that day—in a grove behind the village. He had fallen victim to a Saxon ax after fighting bravely on the final day of the battle. Now his brothers intended to visit his grave before moving on into the deeper forest.

Dominic followed respectfully behind them as they made their way along the short track that led to the graves. Overgrown, the track proved awkward, and Dominic was immediately alert when his woodsman's eye noticed that recent passage had occurred upon it. When William and John abruptly stopped, Dominic quickly nocked an arrow to his bow.

John, who walked ahead of Dominic, held out his arm telling him to hold fast. Over his shoulder, he hissed, 'Don't make a sound, Dom. Figures linger near the graves … and listen … someone cries out.'

Augustus had found the pony outside the arena. Earlier used to pull the cart, the driver had led it to a grassy area beyond the gates to protect it from possible attack from the dogs. Augustus had been grateful to find the beast, although he had no idea how he was going to mount it; such was his level of exhaustion.

Eventually, he managed to pull himself up onto the pony, and could only let the beast find its own way back to the villa, as he lay slumped against its neck.

Back at the villa, the two slave women opened the gates for him. Shocked and with hands to mouths they blanched when they saw him gore-daubed and dissolute. Augustus was to learn from Ciaran later, that Griff only had a small household, consisting of Ambrosius and the two women.

The women led him to the bathhouse. Here, Cate and Ciaran came to him, and Augustus briefly told them his tale.

Shocked, yet delighted to discover he had accounted for Griff and Ambrosius, they left him to his bath. When he had finished, the two women dressed his wounds as best they could and led him to Griff's opulent room.

Augustus had no idea if Griff had any accomplices who might visit—might be hostile to him. Quite simply, he didn't care now. He knew he had to rest at least one night before making the arduous journey back to Brythonfort. One night's rest could mean the difference between life and death for him, but that night his sleep was plagued with feverish episodes, and the next morning he awoke fatigued and unfulfilled.

After meeting Cate and Ciaran on the square, they prepared to leave. The two slave women hugged Ciaran and Cate and looked with concern at Augustus. Wincing, he hauled himself onto the biggest of the three well-provisioned ponies they had brought from Griff's stable.

After assuring the concerned Ciaran they would be fine—would find other employment or stay at the villa until someone came to investigate— the women gave the travellers one last embrace before saying farewell.

The group rode all that day—Augustus pained and grey as he leaned into his abdominal wound and rode at the front of the group. He had little fear of meeting any large groups of riders now the campaigning season had ended. As for chasers … frankly he had ceased to care. Whatever happened now would happen. He had done all he could.

The next day they entered the forest. Augustus knew now that he would not survive the journey to Brythonfort. The wound inflicted by the dog had begun to throb and weep—the vitreous gunge soaking through his bandage. His arrow-torn shoulder, too, pulsated with every beat of his heart.

Cate and Ciaran, who helped him when they could, were his main worry now, and the reason he had entered the forest, rather than stick to the road. Should he die, he knew they would be unlikely to survive on the road without him. On the open road, they would be victim to any travellers they met harbouring malicious intent—and they were bound to meet a few.

Therefore, he had chosen the forest in the knowledge that Dominic would come that way. Dominic would have set out to help him, of that he had no doubt. He knew the man too well. Once on their trail he would find them—find Cate and Ciaran, at least.

For four days, they struggled through wood and hollow yet saw no one. As Augustus slowly got weaker,

Cate took to bouts of crying as she rode at the back of the group and observed him before her, bent over in his saddle, open mouthed with pain, hardly able to keep himself upon his pony.

Ciaran, once pristine and feminine in his demeanor, now looked every inch the soiled and ragged traveller—his ginger hair dirty, his clothes soiled and unkempt.

Towards the end of the fourth day, Augustus, now feverish, slipped from his pony and lay unmoving. Cate and Ciaran attended him, frantic with worry, thinking that death had finally come to him.

However, Augustus was still alive. The fall had been gentle enough, but his wounds now screamed. Incredibly, Cate and Ciaran watched, as Augustus raised himself to his knees and turned his pained and lined face towards them.

He pointed up the track. 'Not far now,' he mumbled. 'My old village … it's not far…'

He weakly beckoned Ciaran to help him to his feet. Squinting at Cate as if she was a vague acquaintance who eluded his memory, he swayed for a while where he stood.

Blinking away his confusion, he managed to look up the trail again. Then he looked at his pony. Giving a weak little laugh, he shook his head. 'Can't get on that … have to walk … not far now …'

He stumbled forward like a drunken man walking home from the alehouse. Cate followed with the ponies, whilst Ciaran supported him by his elbow.

Soon they came to a grove dotted by piles of stones. 'Sam's here … my brother,' whispered Augustus as he nodded to Ciaran. 'This is where they'll come to find us … here they'll come to see his grave.'

He lurched towards a big pile of stones at the edge of the grove. He slumped down heavily upon them. His face now seemed peaceful to Cate and Ciaran as he looked up to them—a face flooded with relief now that his terrible trial was about to end ... now that he was with his brother.

Lying down on top of the stones, as if settling on his side to go to sleep, his voice was weak and distant. 'Put me with him when I go ... the others will come ... do not worry ...'

Cate could take it no longer.

'NO!' she screamed, as the tension of the days exploded from her. 'No ... do not do this to me. I have lost one father, I will not lose another.' Kneeling beside Augustus now, she pummeled her small, grimy fists into his thick thighs. 'Wake up ... wake up, damn you!' she shrieked.

As Augustus remained unmoving, Ciaran put his hand on Cate's shoulder, uncertain of how to help her through her anguish. He had only known Augustus for seven days (an unwell, dying Augustus true enough), but he had already started to love the man, just as Cate so obviously loved him.

Cate turned desperately towards Ciaran, and her face immediately froze to neutrality. Behind him, three men approached.

Dominic, she recognised, so she knew that all was well for now. Two other men, who had to be Augustus' brothers, such was their likeness to him, walked behind. Dominic quickly ran over to Augustus, followed by William and John.

As Dominic stooped to attend to Augustus, Cate pulled anxiously at her trail-stained dress as she wept behind them. 'He died,' she sobbed. 'You're too late … he just lay down and died.'

Dominic looked up frowning as he pressed two fingers against Augustus neck. 'No … his heart still beats, he is not dead, girl.' He looked to William who stooped beside him. 'We must get him to Aebbeduna and Wilfred. There, he may be comforted, though I fear the journey will kill him.'

CHAPTER THIRTY

Six months were to pass before Maewyn, Flint and Nila stood on the shores of Hibernia.

Two months prior, they had made the journey to the old Roman town of Deva in Britannia to meet the Hibernian monks who had crossed the Oceanus Hibernicus to spread the word of God. Here, a small number of people still lived within the walls of the town, leaving each day to farm the surrounding lands.

After meeting Ingle in the simple lodgings appointed by the monks for their stay, Maewyn and Flint had embraced him warmly, before introduced him to Nila.

Maewyn explained to Ingle their intention—to accompany him after his short stay in Britannia; their purpose to visit Mule's grave.

Ingle told them what had happened on the days following Mule's death.

True to his word, Ingle's uncle, the dock master Guairá, had removed and hidden Mule's body, before Fróech's brother, Colman, had arrived at the docks. (Later, his body would be taken to the monastery and buried near to the ponds that Mule had so loved to fish.)

Guairá had then told Colman of how the Britons had sailed away without the children, believing them all dead, having perished in the marshes. He also told them of their fight with Fróech's force on the dockside.

Colman had been devastated to see the headless corpse of his brother, but had believed Guairá's story. Assuming the children dead, he had taken Fróech's body back to Fincath. For a full month after that, Fincath had held a wake in honour of his son. Like Colman, he now believed that the children had

perished in the marshes. The monks would not be troubled
again.

Eight weeks passed in Deva, before Ingle readied himself to return to Hibernia with Flint, Maewyn and Nila. During that time, Maewyn accompanied Ingle and the other monks as they visited remote communities, introducing the word of God to the peasant folk.

Maewyn himself helped deliver the message on some occasions, having now partly embraced the Christian doctrine. After Mule's death, he had struggled to find any meaning to life; any purpose to the vicious world he inhabited. He had grieved long and hard for his brother, and his thoughts had often gone back to his previous brief stay in Hibernia with the monks.

Here, he had found a peaceful world far removed from the surrounding, menacing, lands. Here, the monks had managed to live an ordered life, and the reason for that order was their worship of Christ. The monks possessed little; wanted nothing material from the world, yet seemed happy and fulfilled.

At Brythonfort, Maewyn knew he needed to go back to Hibernia—now felt that he possibly belonged there—and had finally persuaded his mother to travel with him to Hibernia to visit Mule's grave.

As he stood overlooking the monastery grounds with the others, Maewyn knew he had come to his spiritual home; knew he would never go back to Britannia. Rodric met them and took them to the refectory for food and drink. Here, Flint and Maewyn reacquainted with many of the monks they had met on their previous visit, including Donard the scribe, and the bishop, Tassach.

After refreshments, they went to the pond where a solitary cross bearing the name *'Aiden'* stood. Huddled together in mutual consolation, the family shed their tears beside the grave.

'He loved it here,' said Maewyn, to Flint and Nila, as he stood back to view the cross and the green pond. 'Here, he would lie on his belly, alongside Elowen, and chatter his days away waiting for the fish to bite.'

Flint smiled when remembering the day he and Dominic had found the monastery. 'He was doing just that when I first saw him,' he reminisced. 'The day we left for the docks ... the day he died.'

Many days were to pass at the monastery, until one morning as he walked the nearby woods with his mother, Maewyn expressed his desire to stay with the monks and increase his learning of the Holy Scriptures.

Nila was not surprised. Since Mule had died, Maewyn had changed and become far more introspective. She already felt that she had lost part of him and now wished only for his happiness and peace of mind. Reluctantly, she concluded that it would be best for him to stay, and before they had finished their walk, she had given him her consent.

Bishop Tassach had consulted with Rodric and Donard and all had concluded that Maewyn's vocation was sound. They would accept him into the postulancy, a trial that would last six months, then, if found to be of the right mettle, they would accept him as a novice.

On the day that Nila and Flint left to return to Britannia, a glaring irony occurred to Flint. 'Here you will live under the nose of the very man who would have enslaved you, and he will never know. To him you will just be another monk from the continent.'

Maewyn had embraced Nila then, and many tears fell at their farewell. They would meet again, he knew that, but for now, his place was in Hibernia.

Later, he watched as his mother and Flint sailed away—watched until the boat had gone completely from view.

History would remember Maewyn and his decision to return to the Hibernian monastery. There he would become a novice and be named Patricus. There he would become a great man whose ministry would serve to rid Hibernia, not of its snakes, but of the snake cult of the mac Garrchu people, who would become Christian. There he would be with God, and just as importantly, he would be with Mule.

After Nila arrived home, she took up residence in the new village. Here, with Elowen and Govan close by, she would never feel alone.

Newly built nearby—a small, stockaded fort housed a legion of Arthur's fighting men under the leadership of Flint. Now the men could react quickly to any Saxon incursion.

Employed to cook for the men, Nila was now able see Flint every day, and so life became bearable for her after the loss of Aiden.

Modlen, however, had coped less well than Nila. She had the children, Ula, Art and Cate, now, but missed Augustus terribly. Missed how he could be gentle in the way that big men *could* be gentle; missed his booming laugh; his sense of fun. Above all, she missed how he made her feel safe and protected.

The children also ached with longing when they thought about him, because, like Modlen, they too had felt safe with him—felt that, at last, someone had come into their world, not to punish and hurt them, but to love and protect them. His absence had pained them; it would not go away; they yearned for him.

Modlen's life within Brythonfort's walls was far from easy. Together with Sarah and Anna (two women who were left widows after the *battle of at the oxcarts*), she rose early each morning to toil beside the bakery ovens. Her days ended in the afternoon, and that was the best time for her; the time she felt less like a workhorse and more like a mother, because for the first time in her life she had her two boys and girl to return to.

After a particularly hot day in the bakery, Modlen took the bandana from her head and used it to wipe the beaded sweat from her face. Sarah, similarly inflicted, wafted her own face with her scarf as she watched the last of the loaf-filled trolleys leave the room.

Modlen could not help smiling at Sarah as she comically stuck her tongue out of her wide, open mouth, and panted to emphasise her discomfort with the heat. Modlen was about to say what a particularly warm workday they had endured when Arthur stepped into the doorway.

He beamed at Modlen. 'They're here,' he said. 'The day you've been waiting for. They approach the gates.'

Modlen look said it all. *At last, after six months, the day has come!*

As she ran down to the gates, Dominic was the first to appear. Rozen, the herbs woman, rode beside him.

Riding behind them, framed by the archway of the huge gatehouse, rode Murdoc and Augustus. Cate sat sidesaddle before Augustus on his pony. The boys Ula and Art skipped and gamboled alongside them, unable, seemingly, to contain themselves, such was their joy at seeing Augustus.

Murdoc's own daughter, Ceola, sat with Murdoc upon his mount. As Augustus reached Modlen, he handed Cate down to her, then gingerly dismounted.

Modlen took Augustus' great bearded head in her hands and looked directly into his pale-blue eyes. 'Four months turned into six,' she wept. 'I thought I would never see this day … the wait was like six years.'

Augustus, much reduced in bulk now, pushed the heel of his hand into his eyes to stem the flow of his own tears. Overcome and unable to speak he could only *look* at Modlen; could only love her.

Modlen let him go and stepped back to study him. Her tears flooded again as she saw what he had become. 'Whatever happened to affect you so?' she sobbed.

'Nothing that a few weeks of your cooking won't mend,' said Augustus as he wiped his hand, wet from tears, onto his tunic. A twinkle replaced the tears as he continued, 'And meanwhile you'll have to put up with bedding a slender fellow, eager for love.' Modlen went to Augustus again, hugging him close, her laughter now displacing her tears.

Murdoc embraced Martha, as Ceola went to play with Ula, Cate and Art, who stood with their arms around Augustus and Modlen. Soon Dominic joined Murdoc and Martha, and they walked together up the path to the great hall, leaving Modlen, Augustus, and the children to their reunion.

'I thought he would surely die when we took him to Wilfred,' said Dominic. 'He had barely the strength to breath and his wounds were going putrid.'

'Just as well you sent for Rozen then,' said Murdoc.

'Aye, it was she who got rid of his fever and saved him.'

Martha addressed Murdoc as she glanced back down the hill. 'Modlen had given up hope, you know. As the time dragged on, she thought he would die in Aebbeduna. She was readying herself to travel there. Then twelve days ago you left with Dominic to get him, and she never slept from that day.'

Dominic looked tellingly at Murdoc … at Martha. 'He *told* me what he did back there.' Shaking his head in wonderment, he continued. 'His modesty will prevent him from telling anyone else, but believe me it was a deed that defies the words to describe it.'

Arthur, who had now joined them, had overheard Dominic. 'Nevertheless you must tell me of the deeds when we get to the great hall. For now, though, Augustus has earned the right to rest.' He looked to the walls of Brythonfort, his eyes anxious. 'But now we need to talk. Moves are afoot. I have summoned Withred and I need your counsel.' Dominic read the look in Arthur's eyes and knew that, for him, rest was not something that was going to happen any time soon.

Martha sighed inwardly as Dominic exchanged a knowing look with Murdoc. She wondered why men could not live in peace. Wondered if there would ever be a time when the killing would stop.

She looked up to the December sky—a sky that tumbled with turbulence and unrest. *How apt it is*, she thought. *The perfect canopy for this troubled land.*

The End

The third book in the Dominic Chronicles will be available summer 2014

15396937R00214

Made in the USA
San Bernardino, CA
23 September 2014